QUINTON II

LORD OF DEERAIT

"Hedial! Tell me what that spawn of Darkness and Master of Iniquities has to do with you!" the wizard Ontar demands vehemently from the High Council in Hesion. Within a short time Ontar, Admaria, Quinton and the beautiful Allecenia are in the mysterious Occult Dimension battling against the Demon and his cohorts. The two Ulgruffi are transported to the very centre of Hell where its hierarchy desires to destroy them and gain access to Phentara.

The dissolute Kinerth and Reorgin attack Quinton and the guards on the Hesion road. Reorgin is slain. His demise precipitates the civil war in Deerait. His father, Koreorgin, desires revenge and attacks the important town of Estyork. Quinton, the royal guard and the shock regiments with their Deerait allies are outnumbered almost six to one. They battle ferociously to hold the provincial capital . . .

The Street of Taverns in Hesion is the centre of the most villainous quarter of the Deerait capital. Over a thousand cut-throats hold sway in defiance of law and order until they make the mistake of assailing two innocent Zancericts as Quinton, the King of Rionder, rides along . . .

In this volume you will meet Allecenia, the most beautiful woman ever to be born on Phentara. She becomes Quinton's beloved and sees him for the first time after she and her father are assaulted in Estyork by Kinerth and Reorgin . . .

QUINTON II

LORD OF DEERAIT

*(being Volume 2 of the
Historical Beginnings of the Admarian Empire)*

by

JAMES CRAWFORD

TOAD PUBLICATIONS

To Alice with Love

First published in Great Britain 1991
by Toad Publications Ltd.,
42a Durford Road, Petersfield, Hampshire.

© *James Crawford, 1991*

ISBN 1 872314 01 5
Typeset by Heath Setting, Petersfield
and printed by Cox & Wyman Ltd.,
Cardiff Road, Reading, Berkshire.

Cover Design by Peter Silvester

FOREWORD

A few months after his birth, Quinton was orphaned when the small kingdom of Rionder was attacked by the Baron Enmarkan and his troops from the state of Broechnaar on the continent of Rontmethar. His parents were cruelly slain, but the babe was taken to the wild Mescarg steppes by those who became his guardians. The latter were the renowned wizard and sage Ontar and his beautiful wife Admaria, the last living descendants of the once great Ulgruffi nation, the Riondese warrior Gordan who had saved the child during the final bitter battle for the city, and the four Polingsi tribesmen, Casterandir, Turubin, Sleworivan and Shlasmil.

Quinton grew to early manhood on the vast undulating grasslands, instructed in magic, mysticism, science and the arts by Ontar and Admaria. His martial education was supervised by Gordan and the four Polingsi among the people of the small Nai-Zind tribe. He remained totally oblivious of his heritage and destiny until allies of the Nai-Zind were overwhelmed and enslaved by the warlike Ker-Mantids.

The Ulgruffi's protegé proposed a revolutionary strategy to save the clan among whom he had been reared. On hearing the dynamic suggestions of his ward to help the tribe and their Ouselorn friends, Ontar revealed to the youth not only that he was the heir to the throne of Rionder but also that he was related to the caranxem, or chieftain, of the Nai-Zind through a mutual and famous ancestor, Dinmonad. Consequently Quinton was accepted as paramount ranxem, or supreme leader, by the Nai-Zind who readily followed his direction. An alliance of all the free tribes was accomplished: they defeated the Ker-Mantids and their allies in battle on the Garsbut Plain, thus bringing every single clan in the western steppes under one rule.

The next stage of his military tactics provided for war against the superior numbers of the large Phlorcartid nation of steppe dwellers to the east. From past history it was anticipated that the latter would assail their union on the instigation of the mighty Casman Empire, the greatest power on Rontmethar. However, the Phlorcartids were willing to serve Quinton faithfully because of the reverence in which they held Ontar and Admaria; additionally, they bore a bitter resentment against the Empire, engendered by the evil way in which the latter manipulated their lives.

This union of the entire steppe peoples into a single entity inevitably brought down the wrath of the Casmans upon them. The Empire had the military capability of being able to field one and a half million men, each of its ten provinces supplying an army corps of one hundred and fifty thousand soldiers. For centuries, imperial strategy had always required that its neighbours be weak; a union of steppe peoples, no matter how pacific its intentions, entirely contravened Casman policy.

As a direct result the Jaddair army corps marched into the steppes to destroy the tribal force, which it outnumbered by almost forty thousand troops. The King of Rionder and his guardians had trained their warriors in revolutionary tactics, which enabled them to defeat the Casmans. Because of an archaic military law the warlord, Terfieldst, united his troops with those of Quinton and they were numbered among his most faithful adherents in the war against their own hedonistic nation.

With the absolute knowledge that the Empire would seek the destruction of his forces and enslave his peoples, Quinton and his army withdrew over the Mescarg mountains and down into the Rionder Valley. After an epic march they just managed to escape the fearsome steppe winter, thus obtaining a valuable breathing space before Casman launched further troops against them. The next phase involved either the conquest of Deerait to the south of the Rionder Valley, or, more hopefully, the formation of an alliance with the great maritime nation.

During his final summer on the steppes Quinton had sent Felgorian, one of his Riondese subjects, to ascertain the sentiments of the Deeraits. The young paramount ranxem, who had also been told by Ontar that his destiny was to rule the planet of Phentara, realised that his time was limited to perhaps two years before the Empire marched against him once more. His principal desire for a compact with the southerners was to obtain their fleets, for they were the finest sailors on their world, and to use them to attack Casman. This was the position as Quinton and his Inner Council waited in the forests of the Rionder Valley for the return of their Deerait ambassador.

Introduction to the Second Volume of the
Historical Beginnings of the Admarian Empire

After the defeat of the imperial corps from the province of
Jaddair, Quinton, Ontar, Gordan and the four Polingsi led their
combined steppe and Casman army in an arduous march to
reach the haven of the Rionder Valley lest the treacherous
winter snows catch them on the vast Mescarg plains. They
were wholly successful in this endeavour and their weary
forces were dispersed to quarters already prepared for them in
the forests. Admaria and Likans, the Polingsi wizard, had been
instrumental in organising the camps and in the preparation
of food and shelter for the massive army of nearly a quarter
of a million soldiers who now served under the green linz
standard of Rionder.

When the second volume commences, Felgorian, the
Riondese ambassador to the Deerait nation, is returning to
report on his findings about conditions in the large agricultural
and maritime state and principally on its degeneracy into
anarchy, almost verging on civil war. He is unaware of the
victory on the steppes, but is cognisant that success beyond
the Mescarg mountains is only the first stage in the vast
conflict with the Empire; the second is the annexation of
Deerait, because of the paramount necessity of obtaining the
magnificent fleets of the latter to assault the imperial coastline.

One of the bitterest foes whom Ontar had to encounter
during his long life was the Demon Hedial, Evil Incarnate. The
mighty wizard and his foster son, together with Admaria and
the most beautiful woman ever to be born on Phentara,
Allecenia, battled valiantly in another dimension to eliminate
the threat of the Lord of Iniquities and his minions from our
physical plane. Had Hedial succeeded in leaving the Outer
Circles, the Mother Planet of our Empire would have perished
and probably Evil would have wiped out our Galaxy, or
enslaved its inhabitants as zombies. Quinton and Ontar wrote
the narrative of their occult experiences during a sojourn on
the Sacred Islands in the Chofanrit Ocean, otherwise this
fantastic episode and others would have remained entirely
unknown.

It is also evident that Hanshair, the Nai-Zind commander
of the royal guard, and Perlow the Chofir were told a little of
why they had been advised that they might never see their King
again. In the second excerpt of the Lay of Quinton, Hedial is

9

mentioned. The friendship of Hanshair with the two Ker-Mantids, Adrigal and Onlestic, increases much to the satisfaction of Ontar. Indeed, Hanshair performs most admirably during the siege of Estyork, fully justifying the faith his leaders possess in his abilities. His fellow tribesman Souriin also evinces considerable military aptitude at the same time; this talent eventually leads to his becoming a full general in the imperial service in later years. Among other warriors who distinguish themselves in the conflict are Rahamb and Perlow. The latter devises a stratagem which demoralises their Adiorenji adversaries; he also saves Quinton's life again.

The Deerait races had several colours of skin — brown, black, white and yellow. The most peculiar characteristic was that offspring often did not have the same complexion as their parents. It was not uncommon for a black child to be born to two yellow or white parents or even for both the latter to have several children of differing but not mixed colours. Ontar once stated that this circumstance originated because of chemical combinations in the soil millenia before which have now vanished. One advantage was that a colour bar did not exist in any of the four tribes: no stigma existed if a person wed another with a different skin.

Some readers have commented on the losses sustained by the Casman army corps from Jaddair, sensibly wondering why its casualties were not more severe. The explanation is forthcoming in this volume, when Gordan converses with Terfieldst and Ceanill shortly before his departure for Estyork. The reason for such an apparent lapse on my part was because of a wish to adhere to certain consecutive parts of the History, which I discovered in the Imperial Palace library here on Esgan-Thal and throughout the Empire, especially among the archives of the Sacred Order on Phentara.

Again, I have received many communications from others who have guessed the solution to this point. I do believe my intention to make the readers think and work out problems for themselves is justified, perhaps like our first Emperor and his Inner Council did so long ago. If a point is not clarified immediately the explanation will be disclosed at a later stage.

In this volume Castle Xzlus and the Keollin escarpment are mentioned. Koreorgin, the horbspan of the Relyanese, is aware of the terrible activities of the High Priest, Rhaitall. The walls of the fortress enclose the sacred shrine of the goddess

Caramanj. At this stage, Ontar and his friends have no realisation of the importance of Castle Xzlus to their plans: however their involvement with the supreme deity of the Adiorenji pantheon is not disclosed until the Third Volume of the Historical Beginnings of the Admarian Empire.

Once more, I must express my gratitude to my dearest friends, the Grand Duke Themos Malas and the Grand Duchess Aurelyn for the invaluable assistance freely given in the writing of this History.

Vanber, Prince Consort and Duke of Cander,

Imperial House of Quinton of the Empire of Admaria, Imperial Palace, Esgan-Thal

The Lay of Quinton

(This second extract from the epic poem by Hanshair the Nai-Zind, his Ker-Mantid friends Adrigal and Onlestic and Perlow the Chofir of the Imperial Guard covers briefly the period from Felgorian reporting on his journey to Deerait until the army under Gordan relieves the siege of Estyork and vanquishes the superior Relyanese forces investing the town.)

Felgorian far did travel
And his news to our King did tell
That in Deerait all was not well.
Against Casman he had to stand,
So south rode to an alien land.
In Estyork which was Cottis seat
The Lady Allecenia did meet.

Her beauty so wondrously fair,
A rare delight beyond compare,
Entrancing those who in it share.
Her courage strong did never fail,
When with Quinton, she fought Hedial.
Ontar and Admaria did expel,
With magic, the Demon to Hell.

In dimension, beyond, unseen,
Where seldom mortals ever been,
Was ejected dread evil, obscene,
Else Phentara fell from Light
To dwell in wicked, endless Night,
The quartet unselfishly did go.
They saved our world, as we now know.

On the Hesion road, the guard fought.
Adiorenji revenge was sought;
Their losses rashly bought.
In Hesion's wicked street of inns,
The King's men cleansed it of sins,
When shy Zancericts were assailed,
And robber barons' attacks failed.

High Council nobly did consent
To join with Quinton for good intent.
Ontar's crystal gave war portent.
Then Souriin and Rahamb came
To Sicruci to find great fame.
The King, Ontar command did take
Lest foes into the town did break.

With King Quinton besieged inside
Brave Gordan with host did ride
And saved Estyork from hostile tide.
Yet this valiant victory gain
Was merely first in the campaign
To make our ruler with accord,
Of Deerait, the Supreme Overlord.

Chapter One
The Report of Felgorian

The early morning sun gradually dispelled the mists which hung in wraithlike tendrils over the cultivated fields and pastures in the northernmost sector of the province of Sicruci in the land of Deerait. Its warming rays struck the tall figure of a Riondese urging his linz along a sylvan trail, not far from where the vast forests commenced on the border of the great agricultural and maritime nation on Rontmethar, the smallest continent of the planet Phentara. The experienced rider wore camouflaged clothing of green and brown which blended extremely well with his woodland surroundings. The slight breeze ruffling the leaves blew gently on the long black hair which hung to his shoulders. He was totally immersed in thought, as was evinced by the seriousness of his expression; nevertheless his strong hands automatically guided and controlled the reins of his giant, dark green, shaggy, six legged steed.

The trail which he followed kept him away from the accustomed route travellers had once taken through the vast expanses of the Rionder Valley. He was cognisant of the fact that hardly anyone dared to enter the confines of the forests, since it was known abroad of the bitter conflict which had raged for years between the Riondese and the garrison of Baron Enmarkan in the city of Rionder. Twenty two years had passed since the fateful night when Broechnaar squadrons had launched the treacherous assault, and, in spite of sustaining terrible losses, had seized the town. The King and Queen had perished while their subjects had been compelled to flee into the fastnesses of the forests: the survivors had never forgotten nor forgiven the perfidy of the supposedly amicable visit.

His huge mount galloped effortlessly onwards for long hours, during which the only living creatures to be seen were birds or small animals scurrying through the undergrowth. Even though it was now winter the equable climate of the region was revealed by the fact that most of the trees still bore myriads of leaves, with the beautiful variegated tints of orange and gold indicative of autumn; they thrust their proud branches towards the azure sky in which the warm sun shone. Occasionally streams babbled and gurgled over rocky beds where trout moved idly, feeling the slight seasonal chill which made them listless. The traveller had no time to spend in regarding these wondrous examples of Nature. His mission was urgent: although he was aware of its importance he did not envisage that his whole planet might be affected by his tidings, for those whom he served as ambassador had not yet imparted to him what they hoped to be the summit of their endeavours.

The warrior, for such he was from the weapons he bore, barely paused throughout the day. Even his midday meal was eaten in the saddle; he partook of food from a large hide pouch, quenching his thirst from the water flask fastened securely by a thong to the pommel of his saddle. Time was precious; he desired not to lose a single moment if it could be avoided. His travels had taken him over vast distances during the past months and he hoped that somehow the results of his embassy would prove fruitful.

The sun gradually descended from its zenith. The afternoon passed and, inexorably, the long enveloping shadows of evening began to gather as they had done from time immemorial. Still he pressed resolutely onwards: his tireless steed, apparently sensing the urgency of its master, galloped along the grassy trail, as fresh as if its journey had just commenced. Although he realised that he would eventually have to make camp, the fatigued Riondese determined to utilise every last second of daylight. At length the gloom of evening caused him reluctantly to slow his mount to a trot. He had scarcely done this and begun to glance around for a suitable place to spend the night when suddenly he heard someone hailing him.

"Felgorian! Over here!"

"Yes, Sire! Where are you?" he exclaimed, expressing his astonishment as he recognised the voice.

"Here, my crown bearer!" replied a young man, stepping from behind a giant rektur tree on the left. "Follow me. Our camp's in a hidden dell, about a hundred yards from here. We watched your progress on Ontar's crystal. You have done exceptionally."

The eleven foot high steed, with the shaggy fringe which concealed its two magnificent orange eyes, had made as if to attack but the firm hands of its master held the reins in check and the beast relaxed. The rider guided it after the youth, until

15

finally the weary traveller came through a screen of bushes, on both sides of which vigilant sentinels stood on guard. The encampment was perfectly concealed, the fires of hecul chips emitting no smoke which might be noticed by an enemy. In the glow of the flickering flames, Felgorian was able to see his liege more distinctly.

Quinton was an extremely handsome youth, almost seven feet in height with wondrous grey blue eyes, long black shoulder-length hair and a tremendous personality. After making a magical pass to subdue the huge linz, the young King of Rionder instructed one of his guards to tend his companion's steed. He then beckoned his ambassador to accompany him into a shamianah pitched nearby under a tall tree. Before entering, Felgorian glanced around at the camp, and was very impressed by the efficient manner in which the hide tents had been laid out in lines.

The Riondese followed his monarch, and, once inside, was immediately greeted by the celebrated wizard and mystic Ontar and his wife Admaria. These notables were the last living members of the once mighty Ulgruffi Empire which had dominated Phentara millenia ago before vanishing into legend. The renowned sage and his spouse seemed ageless, a young looking very handsome couple with an aura of grandeur and majesty; so they had always appeared to the forefathers of the Riondese and the Mescarg steppe tribes.

A stalwart, alert Ker-Mantid warrior bearing a long spear stood on guard outside the huge tent, while a woman from the Nai-Zind tribe prepared the table. Felgorian washed himself in a basin of warm water, which Admaria had had ready for him in a side room; he dried himself with a soft cloth and felt slightly refreshed after his arduous journey. When he had completed his toilet and returned to the main room of the shamianah, Quinton bade him be seated at the table which had been laid for four persons. The servitor, whose name was Felthim, left to fetch their evening meal while the two Ulgruffi and the young King conversed with their ambassador to Deerait.

"When would you like to hear my report, Sire?"

"After we've eaten. We watched your progress through Ontar's crystal, whenever we had time during the past few months."

"Have some wine, Felgorian. We three partake of water or

16

milk in case we have to use magic," Admaria said, indicating a large pitcher on the table.

"You'll probably have some questions of your own. We'll be most pleased to answer them," Ontar smiled understandingly.

"Yes, indeed, Great Sage," the traveller replied, pouring some of the sparkling green liquid into a smooth wooden beaker.

"I can guess perhaps what is uppermost in your mind. We did encounter a Casman army corps on the Mescarg steppes. We also defeated them. They've allied themselves to us because of an archaic law of theirs. Then we withdrew across the steppes and through the mountains. We just escaped the snows which came early this year. At present our forces and their dependents are dwelling in the forests to the north of here, entirely unknown to either the Deeraits or the garrison stationed by Enmarkan in the city of Rionder. The organisation and conclusion of this campaign far exceeded our total expectations," the wizard declared with satisfaction in his voice.

"That is marvellous news! It means we should have almost a quarter of a million men under arms. I can't get over the fact that you defeated a Casman army corps! It's unbelievable! Heolanwertin won't be in the least pleased when he hears about your victory. He's bound to know one of his army corps has marched to the steppes," Felgorian pointed out.

"He does. Terfieldst, the provincial governor and warlord of the Casman province of Jaddair, a most pleasant person by the way, did confirm that he'd sent couriers from Mikghiltherid to Choolsay, shortly before he marched west. The Emperor will know that the steppe tribes have formed an alliance, both the western clans and the Phlorcartid nation. However, he won't know yet that his corps has been defeated. The imperium will probably conclude that the Jaddair army has had to winter on the steppes," Admaria stated.

"So, we've gained some time. We can't be certain, but it may be almost two years before the Casmans find out where to send forces against us," Quinton commented.

"Let me think. Yes, this coming summer they may manage to send a corps west if no news is received from the Jaddair warlord. If that second corps has to spend the winter on the steppes before returning home, it will certainly be two years. Oh, what if it comes over the mountains? Silly question! Ontar

17

was going to seal the pass by casting a spell. You told me that on your coronation day," Felgorian nodded, stifling a yawn.

Quinton and his foster parents looked at the Riondese ambassador closely and immediately realised how exhausted he was. The interior of the tent was lit by candles but they perceived the weariness of his long journey, reflected in the dark shadows under his eyes and the lines etched into his face. Admaria leaned over to take his right hand. Felgorian was rather surprised but did not demur when the beautiful woman traced an invisible symbol on his palm. She then spoke several syllables in the language of the Ulgruffi before releasing her gentle grasp.

A few moments passed, then Felgorian felt strength flowing into his limbs, almost as if he had partaken of the elixir of eternal youth, which was often mentioned in children's tales. His weariness departed. He also felt intuitively that the shadows and lines on his face had been erased while his vigour was renewed.

"Thank you, My Lady. I feel as if a terrible burden has been removed from me."

"You are most welcome. We should apologise to you for not having done this sooner. The spell I've just cast has caused you to return to normal. All traces of fatigue, shadows under your eyes, lines and wrinkles prematurely etched have been totally removed. You'll feel rested. Your strength and vitality will have been restored. The state of exhaustion will not return. It is only just that I've done this. You've ridden for long months unselfishly to serve our cause, completely regardless of the effect on your health, to bring us vital information with all speed. What you have done is as important as the battle on the Mescarg steppes," Admaria smiled gently.

"Nevertheless I sincerely thank you again, My Lady." Felgorian expressed his gratitude before turning to his King to say, "I believe I saw the steppe warrior by the name of Hanshair when I was dismounting. Did he bring the crown of Rionder with him?"

"That is his name. No, he didn't bring it with him. I commanded him to give it into Gordan's keeping. He will keep it safe lest any mischance occur. Although we haven't yet heard your report we thought it advisable to ride to meet you. There are three hundred guards in our escort. Oh, here's Felthim," Quinton remarked as the serving woman, assisted by

18

a willing guard, appeared with platters of food.

Before and after the meal they bowed their heads to thank the Great Power for His Beneficence to them. While they ate they chatted pleasantly, temporarily dismissing the problems of the future. However this interlude could not last too long; eventually the table was cleared and Felthim withdrew, leaving the quartet alone. Felgorian had enjoyed his food and expressed his pleasure before enquiring whether he should now commence his report. Quinton concurred and listened intently with his foster parents to the details related by his ambassador about his journey to the principal centres of the Deerait nation.

After departing from the camp of his King in the realms of the Phlorcartids that summer, Felgorian had raced across the immensity of the undulating Mescarg steppes. On his route he had encountered warriors on the grasslands, escorting Phlorcartid wagon trains to safety, away from the region of the anticipated battle against the Casman army corps from the provincial capital, Mikghiltherid. In the mountain pass, he was greeted by Polingsi and Riondese, checking on the state of the highway, which had been cleared in preparation for the great influx of wains and armed forces from the plains.

Once into the Rionder Valley, he had rested at home for one night before hastening southwards, until at last he emerged from the fringe of the forests and entered the land of Deerait. Its sailors were recognised as the finest mariners and navigators on the oceans of Phentara; the peoples were also excellent farmers, who ploughed and raised crops, and were noted for animal husbandry. The nation itself consisted of four tribes; these were the Adiorenji, Dariondi, Vilatmori and the Deeraits, the latter being the most numerous.

For many centuries they had warred continuously amongst themselves, only uniting finally in the face of the awesome threat represented by the young, vigorous Casman Empire, when the latter began to expand throughout Rontmethar. They combined to form the Deerait nation, and their armed forces hastily gathered together to do battle with the invaders. In this endeavour they had the Riondese for allies; although the forest dwellers were relatively few in comparison to the military strength of the new nation, they fought valiantly against the imperial forces which had marched over the steppes through the sole mountain pass and down into the Rionder Valley.

Not only did the six Casman army corps outnumber their

19

adversaries but the soldiers of the Empire were far better disciplined and more experienced in warfare. The Deerait alliance was totally vanquished on land and the whole country was overrun and subjugated. However the entire battle fleet escaped to sea and used the Hayleink island as a base to assail the Casman Empire. The latter did possess a small fleet, but this was annihilated by the Deeraits, with the result that the imperial coastline as well as Deerait itself was raided mercilessly. Against such tactics the Casmans had no response, for they were basically a land people with no desire to sail the oceans. The principal reason for this was the lack of natural harbours along their immense seaboard.

The Emperor finally conceded that this state of affairs could not continue, and negotiations were instigated to arrange peace talks. The Deeraits realised that, although they could never hope to defeat the imperial army corps, they could virtually dictate terms. In the event, a treaty was signed at the Casman port of Matheird: the Empire agreed to withdraw its forces from Deerait while the latter consented to cease all naval raids and live in peace with the great power.

Both parties adhered strictly to the terms of the treaty. The four peoples, led by the Deerait tribe, commenced the long process of reconstructing their devastated homeland. However, with the passage of time, the Casman Empire had started to decline and, as the long centuries went by, Deerait began almost imperceptibly to follow the same course. The four main sections gradually reverted to an insular outlook in spite of the attempts of the High Council to keep their union alive. Although quarrels broke out between the three tribes and the Deeraits, some resulting in violent skirmishes which the leaders generally tended to ignore, open warfare had not yet erupted.

This anarchic state of affairs had been known to Felgorian when he had visited Hesion and other principal cities as ambassador for King Quintar: but, in the years from the fall of Rionder to the present, matters had changed drastically, so he discovered during his journey. He was still well received in the main centres of population, for the courtesy and resolution of the Riondese had always earned them respect in every quarter of the Deerait nation. Additionally, there had been many valuable trading agreements between the two states. The Deeraits supplied merchandise in return for special woods and cultivated herbs. There was also knowledge which the Riondese had in plenty: they had shown the southerners the arts of reading and writing in the Common Speech, which the latter had let lapse, and had demonstrated the basic elements of the science of mathematics and how this could be applied to navigation.

Felgorian learned from some of his former friends and acquaintances that the Adiorenji, Dariondi and Vilatmori had now sunk all their grievances and were almost united against the Deeraits. This meant that a combined population of two and a half millions was in common alliance against one and a half million people. Since their fleets were equally balanced any conflict which arose would have to be settled on land, although naval operations would play an important part in any strategy adopted by the protagonists.

"That is how things stand, Sire. From my own personal observations and those of people I talked to, the Deerait tribe is faced with an almost inevitable civil war with the other three groups composing their nation. My assessment is that the Deeraits will be defeated eventually. Then, given time, the others will fall out. Deerait will return to the squabbling and internal warfare of the era before the Empire attacked long ago. I think it's a great pity. The Deeraits themselves have always been the best administrators and the fairest since the creation of their united nation. They have always shared the government impartially with the other three peoples. Each tribe had representatives at the High Court in Hesion until eight months ago when they all walked out for no apparent reason.

"With regard to any future conflict with Casman, the four Deerait tribes could not care less. Whenever I brought the subject up very little interest was shown. They just could not envisage it happening again nor the wholly unlikely event of the Mescarg steppe tribes crossing from the plains to the Rionder Valley. Those who did ponder it for a few moments said that they would send their own forces to deal with any steppe invaders.

"By the way, I did learn that a Treaty of Neutrality, a non-aggression pact, was agreed between Broechnaar and Deerait not long after Rionder fell. I'm sorry, Sire, but I don't feel as if I managed to accomplish anything. I think my mission has been a waste of time," Felgorian concluded apologetically.

21

"No indeed, my friend. It has given us a definite idea of the sentiments of the Deerait nation. We now know at worst that the Deeraits would attempt to send a force against us. That's provided they aren't hampered by civil war. Consequently we can use this knowledge of impending conflict to assist our purposes. I know you will concur with this, Ontar," the King of Rionder said emphatically, reassuring his ambassador that his journey had been essential.

"Yes. It's our only course of action. The time for guessing and hoping is over. As was mentioned earlier, we have probably two years before the Casmans fully mobilise against us," the sage nodded.

"What are your immediate intentions, Sire, if I may be permitted to enquire?" Felgorian asked with respect.

"You certainly may. You've made great endeavours on our behalf. You've journeyed long distances for many weeks without respite, a most notable and unselfish accomplishment. As Admaria said earlier, your mission was just as important in its own way as our exploits on the steppes this past summer. For several winters past, we have planned what we should do in given circumstances, especially the contingency of the Deeraits squabbling amongst themselves. Admaria will confirm this," the youth remarked, bringing his foster mother into the conversation.

She smiled at Quinton before addressing the Riondese ambassador. Felgorian looked at the beautiful dark haired woman who seemed young and ageless, bubbling over with the vibrant vitality which Ontar and his liege possessed too. This aura had been obtained through the study of mysticism in which the young King was now well versed.

"It was our intention to make a sally into the land of the Deeraits, if your information proved to be as you reported. Since it is, we shall ride through the farmlands of Sicruci to Estyork in particular. The Deeraits have always been a major stabilising factor in the political and economic affairs of their nation. It is a pity the union is disintegrating. Nevertheless it will, or so we hope, be extremely advantageous for our purposes," Admaria explained in the light of the candles illuminating the interior of the large tent.

"I understand, My Lady. Yet, I wonder if three hundred warriors are enough. We may encounter trouble and, unless I'm wrong, you won't want to use magic if it can be avoided.

22

I'm also assuming that I'll be coming too," Felgorian remarked.

"Yes, we would very much like you to do so. Elestia and your family know we would like you to accompany us. However, we decided that the choice is to be yours alone. You can return to your loved ones, or come with us," Admaria said kindly.

"I shall certainly come with you. I served your father, Sire. Much as I love my family, it is my duty to serve you. We have waited many long years for you to return and one day avenge the sack of Rionder, and remove the evil of Enmarkan from Rontmethar. When all that has been accomplished, and we've completed our formidable task, we shall have time enough to enjoy peace with our families," the Riondese ambassador declared in firm tones.

"Thank you, Felgorian," Quinton said with sincerity.

"Now, as you've just stated, our escort of three hundred warriors may be insufficient in view of the dangerous times in Deerait. Nor do we wish to use magic, if avoidable. That would result in unwanted attention being drawn to ourselves. So, we'll depend on the scouts and on scrying. Notwithstanding, Gordan has ten thousand shock troops on stand-by at all times. We'll be ready to contact them in case support is required," Ontar affirmed.

"Good. I'm glad about that. There's far too much dissension and unrest to the south of here. Even Estyork under governor Cottis has its share, and he's a strong, wise ruler. If we do become involved in serious trouble, and I believe there's a good chance we shall, it's reassuring to know that support can be made available," Felgorian nodded his approval.

"We travel south tomorrow morning at dawn, so let's retire," Quinton said, rising to indicate that their discussion had ended.

"Adrigal!" Ontar called to attract the attention of the guard on duty at the door of the tent.

The Ker-Mantid warrior entered in response to the summons of the wizard. The latter instructed him to conduct Felgorian to where comfortable quarters had been prepared for the ambassador in a tent, beneath the mellow beams of the first moon of Phentara, Ilix the Enchantress.

"We'll just have to ride out tomorrow and hope that something will occur to give us an opportunity to advance our strategy against the Empire," Quinton mused thoughtfully, just after the traveller had departed.

"You're concerned, aren't you?" Ontar enquired.

"Mmm. It's just that after a few years of hectic activity, especially after the momentous occurrences of this summer, we seem almost to have stopped."

"Of course, it does seem so at present. Admaria and I have the same feelings. So do Gordan and the Polingsi. Nevertheless, times will change again," Ontar nodded with a smile.

"You're right as always," Quinton agreed. He embraced both his foster parents before retiring to his quarters in the comfortable shamianah.

An hour before dawn the entire encampment was astir. The cooks quickly prepared a hot breakfast in the field kitchens. Once everyone had eaten the guards broke camp swiftly and efficiently. Within twenty minutes Hanshair, the guard commander, reported that all was ready for their departure.

"Excellent. Pass the word to proceed," Quinton ordered from where he sat astride the giant linz, which he had shared with Casterandir. Shortly after their arrival in the Riondese forests the Polingsi had been given a new mount by Beltarik from the common herd.

The column proceeded at a brisk pace, while all around them ranged twelve scouts. These new royal guards were from the invaluable regiment commanded by Forsever, the Nai-Zind warrior who was a cousin of the King of Rionder, and the Ouselorn ranxem, Mirchanrope, neither of whom was with them; it had been decided that both should remain in the depths of the forests to instruct their Casman adherents in steppe methods of surveillance and concealment, so that the latter would have more potential. Gordan, the supreme general, the four Polingsi and their subordinates were also occupied in supervising the training of their imperial allies in the novel methods of warfare which Quinton, Ontar and the others of the Inner Council had devised during the enforced incarceration of the long, bitter steppe winters. These tactics had been put into excellent practice in the battles and actions which they had fought.

The well armed cavalcade rode confidently along the forest trail, up which Felgorian had journeyed the previous day. The pace was brisk in the crisp early morning air. The sun rose to give warmth and shone in slanting, misty fingers between the trees. Birds and animals fled at their approach, which was made with as little noise as possible. The scouts sent back

24

reports precisely on time about the region around them; but, as anticipated, there were no travellers, for the state of war between the Riondese and the Central Plains garrison deterred many from entering the vast forests, even without the fear of demons and evil spirits which were believed to dwell therein.

By evening they had almost covered the distance to the beginning of the Deerait farmlands. Camp was pitched approximately half a mile from where the trees ended. The pack heculs were unloaded as the warriors commenced the task of preparing night quarters. With great efficiency tents were erected, fires were lit, animals were tended and sentries posted, not only around the perimeter of the encampment, but also all the way to the edge of the forest. Such precautions might prove wholly unnecessary, but Quinton, Admaria and Ontar did not wish to take any risks if at all avoidable.

"Felgorian, you mentioned last night that Estyork suffers from trouble between the tribes," Ontar recalled during the conversation after the evening meal.

"Yes, that's so, Great Sage. I saw quite a few petty quarrels and disagreements between the Deerait citizenry and the Adiorenji from the Ebrordin mountain region in Relyan province. That's to the west of Sicruci."

"In that case, I propose that sixty guards accompany us to the town. They can change their dress to Deerait attire. They'll also have to let their hair hang free. Other details can be checked before we leave," Ontar declared.

"If I may suggest, Felgorian and I had better travel on heculs and leave our linz here," Quinton pointed out.

"Two linz will create quite a stir. Mine did when I passed through Estyork, coming and going. The citizens hadn't seen one for years. Oh, new ordinances have been posted in the past month, regarding the bearing of weapons within the walls. Unless one belongs to the military, no shields, bows or arrows are allowed, but swords can be worn. The gates are closed between sunset and sunrise. No one is permitted to enter or leave during the night, unless special authority is obtained directly from the headquarters of the provincial governor," Felgorian said.

"Mmm. Times must be difficult if the governor of Sicruci has to adopt such measures. Estyork used to be such a peaceful, friendly place. Anyone could enter or leave, or bear full arms at any time. I'm saddened to think that Deerait has now fallen

25

so low, even if it does assist our designs," Admaria remarked with regret.

"If the bearing of arms is limited, I think we'd better travel in small groups. Some can enter through each main gate. A large party of strangers might not be permitted entrance, especially when our facial characteristics differ from the average Deerait," Quinton remarked.

"Yes, we have to be careful. Three hundred strangers would certainly be noticed by the town garrison. Sixty, if remaining apart, just might get by. We'll have to keep apart, but contact must be maintained somehow in case an emergency occurs. Perlow can leave his guard section and come with us," Admaria declared firmly.

"I agree. Hanshair says he's the best officer he's ever trained. Look, I'll use my rotar horn to signal assistance. The various section leaders can do the same," Quinton said before rising to pass on the orders for the morning to the Nai-Zind guard commander.

The centre of population, which had been discussed, was the large fortified market town and capital of Sicruci province of the Deerait tribe; it was situated only sixty miles from the Ebrordin region in Relyan, one of the main Adiorenji homelands. Its inhabitants were mainly engaged in the buying and selling of agricultural products brought in from the surrounding district. Estyork handled sales of fruit, vegetables and animals, which were supervised by officials controlled by the provincial governor on behalf of the Deerait nation as a whole. It was the duty of the latter to maintain law and order, especially among the many frequent visitors of the other tribes who passed through the town, since Estyork stood at a commercial and strategic crossroads.

The provincial capital was enclosed by high walls, many feet thick, the stones having been quarried some miles distant. Although sentries were stationed on the battlements, their vigilance had become somewhat lax because of the long years of peace. However, they were able to survey the farms and homesteads scattered between fields and orchards to the west, south and east. Their view to the north gave a shorter, similar aspect, but was against the panorama of the vast forests which stretched for many leagues up the Rionder Valley.

Inside Estyork were cobbled thoroughfares with shops and houses: in front of both the latter were occasional tall, leafy

26

trees. In the middle of each wall was a stout gate from which a boulevard stretched, until it met the other three in a very large central square, on the north side of which the district commander had his garrison fortress. Around the square, and in several minor streets leading from it, were the majority of the hostelries where travellers and visitors spent the nights and had their steeds stabled. The greater part of the taverns bordered the square, where the custom had grown up for stalls to be pitched for the market held every four days.

On the southern side of the town were jetties on the Avidnive which flowed slowly and majestically from the Ebrordin mountains through farming country to reach the Chofanrit Ocean at the large seaport of Hesion. The river broadened rapidly from its source on Mount Idebeginn until it reached such a width that large, flat bottomed vessels with one huge sail could easily berth at Estyork. These huge barges plied to and fro with the produce of the markets, sailing downstream and calling in at other towns on the way until they reached Hesion where the rulers of the Deerait nation held their High Court or Council. From there, the government of the country was conducted as it had been for centuries since the end of the Casman War. Although the High Court represented all four tribes, only the Deeraits met there now because of the drastic deterioration of relations between themselves and the other three peoples who composed their united nation.

Thus it was that Estyork became the place where Quinton first encountered the race of seafarers and farmers, whose fleets and assistance he required in his war with the mighty Casman Empire. Besides being the first town he had ever visited in person, the provincial capital of Sicruci was also to witness another event of supreme importance in the life of the young King of Rionder. He was to become acquainted with two very eminent people, both very dear friends of Ontar and Admaria: one of them was to have an immense personal influence not only on his life, but also on the future of Phentara and the dynasty of the Admarian Empire.

Just before the second moon, Selix the Panther, had set, the guards selected to accompany Quinton, his foster parents and Felgorian were ready to commence the journey to Estyork. Among those chosen were Hanshair, Adrigal, Onlestic and Perlow. Each warrior was dressed in attire which differed

27

considerably from the normal furs and hides worn by the steppe peoples. Depending on the sex of the wearer, the Deeraits clad themselves in tunics and trousers or skirts manufactured from wool obtained through foreign and domestic trade.

Fortunately the Casmans from the province of Jaddair had brought considerable supplies of orange cloth with them, which were intended to repair soldiers' uniforms. There was also a large number of rolls of different coloured material. Gordan had ordered that the Polingsi and Riondese women make tunics and trousers from the latter fabric, once the decision had been made for Quinton's visit to Deerait. The capable seamstresses quickly fashioned sufficient clothing to accommodate the entire force several times over.

Any difference in the pigmentation of their skins was irrelevant since the members of each Deerait tribe varied from black through brown to white and yellow. There would be no language difficulty because the Common Speech was used throughout the Deerait nation, almost replacing the local tribal dialects. The Deeraits had sensibly maintained the Common Speech; they had been quick to perceive how useful it would prove in trading with foreign merchants.

Its origin was now obscure but was believed to have come from the Sacred Islands of Wizards in the Chofanrit Ocean long ago. Indeed, Ontar and Admaria had once confirmed this fact to Quinton: it had been a gift from the mystics to their world in an attempt to bring the warring factions closer together. In this sincere desire for peace the Order of Light had been quite successful at first, for the very savage times had mellowed for many years although, unfortunately, they did return. The introduction of this new language had also helped to extend the knowledge of the various races of Rontmethar and the other five continents about one another in addition to providing a valuable means of communication in territories where very few had the ability to read or write.

Once the contingent of sixty guards and Perlow had been inspected by Ontar, Admaria, Felgorian and Quinton, the journey to Estyork began in the interval between the setting of Selix and the dawn. The young King, his foster parents and ambassador were satisfied with the dress of the warriors, and hoped that their different facial characteristics would not arouse too much interest. The escort split into groups of six before riding swiftly off into the forest under the canopy of the innumerable stars. The luminaries twinkled and gleamed overhead, unaware that they too were destined to come under the sway of the House of Quinton when the Admarian Empire extended dynamically into the infinite vastness of interstellar space.

"There's the town gate in the north wall, Sire," Felgorian indicated in the early morning light.

"Yes, I see. Yonder are farmers bringing in their produce for the market," Quinton replied, noticing carts and wagons drawn by rotars, trundling ahead of them towards Estyork.

"There will indeed be a market today in that case. That will mean more crowds than usual. Perhaps we'll be fortunate. Our numbers and strangeness may not be noticed in the confusion and hubbub," Admaria remarked.

"Look. There's Adrigal and Colmar with four more of our guards. There, about a hundred yards ahead, passing those wains laden with vegetables. I like the way they're keeping in twos, yet only ten yards apart," Ontar nodded, his keen eyes glimpsing the Ker-Mantid warrior and his section.

"The fact that today is a market day will certainly help us. If I remember correctly, it should be for dairy and agricultural produce only. Animal trading usually decreases from this time of year until the spring, because the main calving season commences in a few weeks. There's a difference between here and the steppes in that respect, I should think," Felgorian commented from where he rode behind his monarch and Perlow.

"That's correct. The calving season occurs about three months after the rotars and heculs awake from their hibernation," Ontar confirmed.

As they approached the north gate the bustle of the crowds on the dusty road increased, with wagons coming in from several directions. The Deeraits chatted and shouted greetings to one another for market days were times of enjoyment as well as of business. Several of them remarked the handsome quintet, and the bearing of Quinton and his foster parents gave rise to more than momentary speculation.

Somehow the five travellers managed to keep together in the throng: finally they rode past the stout, massive wooden gates and under the lofty archway into the town of Estyork. Felgorian and the two Ulgruffi were accustomed to towns and cities, but Quinton and Perlow were filled with wonder and intense interest. The King of Rionder had often been shown pictures in books when Ontar and Admaria had been teaching him about his world; again, he had used the crystals of his foster parents to scry the regions and centres of population on Phentara, but actually to arrive inside a town was a new and vivid experience for the youth.

The hectic noise and intense activity absorbed his attention. Teamsters drove massive wagons down the broad boulevard in front of them, guiding their patient rotars to the market square. Small carts bore families from the country to enjoy an outing. Shopkeepers, who had already taken down their shutters and opened for business, were calling for custom while their assistants prepared colourful displays of cloth, furniture, meat or whatever their employers sold.

The small party had proceeded about two hundred yards along the northern boulevard, from which side streets ran off to houses and other buildings, when a hooded man and woman caught sight of them. Meaningful glances passed between the couple who immediately pushed through the throng to follow the quintet ahead of them. Quinton, Ontar and Admaria continued to attract considerable attention, for their beauty and bearing were exceptional and caused much comment among the passers-by.

With Felgorian preceding them they continued along the broad boulevard until they reached the great square where stalls were being erected under the supervision of officials in dark green livery. Although a busy day was anticipated not all the produce brought to Estyork would be sold there. Many of the huge wains turned off to drive along beside the city walls to the wharves, where flat bottomed barges were moored, waiting to transport cargo downstream to Hesion and other towns on the River Avidnive.

"We can fasten our steeds yonder. There's room for them," Felgorian indicated, carefully omitting the title Sire from his speech, but nevertheless evincing high respect for the young King of Rionder.

Around and in front of the inns and shops were hitching rails for the benefit of those attending the market. Everywhere Deeraits were dismounting and fastening the reins of their heculs. The latter animals were hardy, sand coloured tailless creatures with four legs and a head which tapered to a point;

they surveyed their surroundings through three gentle violet eyes which gave an entirely deceptive impression of their true nature: they were vicious brutes with long yellow beaks which had to be kept closed by tying both halves together with strong rope. Although their physical characteristics were similar, those possessed by the Deeraits were not as fierce as their fellows on the Mescarg steppes. Ontar had taken the wise precaution of casting a simple spell on the mounts of the entire expedition to Estyork lest any unnecessary commotion occur. It was doubtful whether any of the Deerait people of the time had ever seen, let alone encountered, a steppe hecul; if he or she had, that individual would have been fully cognisant of its ferocity in comparison to the steeds he or she was accustomed to riding. Nevertheless it was not the wont of the Ulgruffi sage to take inessential chances.

Not far behind the quintet the man and woman, who also wore a veil effectively concealing her face, hastened along the bustling thoroughfare to catch up with Ontar and his companions. They would have succeeded in this endeavour but unfortunately the man bumped by accident into a white skinned Adiorenji warrior who immediately expressed his savage wrath.

"You stupid fool!" he snarled, hurling the man against the wall of a nearby inn, where he began to strike him across the face.

The woman lacked for nothing when it came to courage. She promptly seized the Adiorenji by the hair, which drastic action caused him to yell with pain for her attentions were not in the least gentle. She threw him to the ground but matters did not rest there. One of his several companions, elegantly dressed and with a green jewel on the pommel of his sword, reacted swiftly by grasping the veiled woman's left hand. He then proceeded to twist her arm savagely up her back. She gasped with pain as the first Adiorenji regained his feet and strode angrily over to her. Her black veil caught his attention. He sneered cruelly and raised his hand to tear it from her face, under the hood of the long brown cloak which she wore.

The incident had caused a crowd to gather but the latter merely watched the proceedings. Some of them did entertain thoughts about interfering but the two Adiorenji were well known and had several armed house carls in attendance. Their

32

presence in Sicruci was determined by trade between their homeland in the province of Relyan and merchants in Estyork whom they visited annually to negotiate the renewal of produce contracts. They had only been in the town for four days but had already provoked two minor incidents; each occurrence had involved bringing out patrols from the garrison to quell the disturbance caused. The governor realised that the Adiorenji, who belonged to the hierarchy of their tribe, were in the wrong but, being fully aware of the precarious state of national peace, did not punish the miscreants, much to his own chagrin.

Eight sturdy house carls accompanied their masters and were prepared to support them in their actions. The Relyanese, like the rest of Deerait, were not as tall as the Riondese or the steppe tribesmen, being on average eight inches smaller, but were stoutly built with determined, stolid features. While one of their overlords raised his hand to rip away the veil from the woman's face they watched the crowd for any hostile movements, which they did not anticipate from the Deeraits. However there were others abroad who had decidedly different views, for Quinton and his companions had witnessed the rough handling of the hooded couple just as they prepared to dismount.

When the commotion caught their attention and they saw the two cloaked figures, Admaria and Ontar looked significantly at each other in surprise. A meaningful glance passed between the eminent mystics. They both leaped agilely from their steeds. Admaria called to Quinton and Perlow to follow them, and to Felgorian to tie the reins of their heculs to the hitching rail. The youth did not question the request from his foster mother; he jumped down from his saddle and followed her in the wake of her husband. The mighty sage was already thrusting a passage through the press; like an arrow speeding from a bow Ontar entered the open space and quickly weaved past the surprised carls. He thrust his drawn sword against the back of the Adiorenji warrior at the precise instant the latter was about to touch the veil.

"Remove that facial covering and you perish! And you, let go her arm!" the sage snapped in vehement tones with such power that neither assailant bothered to argue.

Slowly the warrior lowered his hand away from the veil; simultaneously his comrade released her left arm and moved away towards the attendants. While he was doing so Admaria came across through the line of house carls who made no attempt to interfere with her progress, so regal was her bearing. She led the woman to where the man was now rising to his feet and addressed them both kindly in the mellifluous tongue of the Ulgruffi. This astonished Quinton who had arrived on the scene with Perlow just behind his beautiful foster mother. The young King of Rionder was fluent in the ancient language but only had time catch a few brief phrases before he, Ontar and his personal bodyguard became fully occupied with more pressing affairs.

"Take them! Never mind me!" the Relyanese snarled, although the sage still held the point of his sword to the man's back.

His companion and the eight attendants hesitated. Suddenly the warrior threw himself forward to roll away from the wizard. His comrades immediately moved towards Quinton, Ontar and Perlow, unsheathing their swords while their fellow rose to his feet and joined them. The crowd shrank further back to form an unbroken semi-circle with the wall of the inn as diameter, completely hemming in those who had opposed the will of the troublemakers.

Quinton, Ontar and Perlow reacted swiftly to the threat, holding their weapons ready to meet the anticipated onslaught. They took the precaution of spreading out slightly to cover Admaria and her two companions. The young King, the eminent mystic and the Chofir fearlessly awaited the approach of the Adiorenji warriors and their house carls, who were now advancing cautiously towards them. Quinton glanced quickly at Ontar; the latter looked at his foster son and both laughed heartily to the amazement of their opponents who paused.

"You are the King of Rionder and paramount ranxem of the Mescarg steppes," the sage spoke in Ulgruffi.

"Indeed I am. I have almost a quarter of a million men under arms to obey my every command. Here we are engaged in a street fight with only Perlow to help us at the moment," Quinton smiled in response. He replied in the same beautiful tongue, one of the many invaluable accomplishments he had been taught by Ontar and Admaria during the years spent on the rolling Mescarg plains.

The smiles on the faces of two of their adversaries caused the Relyanese to hesitate for a few seconds, during which they looked enquiringly at one another. Nevertheless they resumed their cautious advance over the cobblestones with swords wickedly held before them. Quinton and Ontar both realised that conflict now seemed unavoidable and regretted that they had been prevented from bringing their stout shields with them. They were aware that the Deerait sentinels on duty at the gates would have refused them permission to enter Estyork had they been bearing such articles. Neither desired to attempt magic, for this would bring even greater attention to them.

The stout Adiorenji drew nearer, anticipating an easy victory over the tall, handsome man and his two smaller companions who had resolutely decided to oppose them. Suddenly Felgorian pushed through to the edge of the crowd. The Riondese immediately guessed what had taken place and what was about to occur. He called out in an attempt to stop blood being shed.

"Reorgin! Kinerth! Hold fast!" the ambassador bellowed commandingly.

"What? Felgorian, what do you want? Don't interfere!" the Adiorenji who had mistreated the woman snapped in surprise.

"These three are my friends. I would be grateful if you would not attempt to attack them."

"You may have visited my father recently, but that gives you no right whatsoever to interfere in my personal affairs! Keep out! Be warned or you will pay the penalty too!"

"Reorgin, you are prepared to shed blood?" Felgorian spoke with considerable anger in his voice.

"Yes, I have to defend my honour!" the Adiorenji snarled in reply. He was becoming even more enraged because mutterings of disapproval from the crowd were now being directed vociferously against his party.

"Then it will cost you and your carls your lives. Here are more of my friends. Three here. Four over there." The Riondese gladly indicated where Hanshair, Adrigal, Onlestic and others of the guard had come to the forefront of the semi-circle of onlookers. The steppe tribesmen had been attracted by the huge crowd. When they realised what was about to happen their reaction was spontaneous.

They strode proudly through the Relyanese and their servants to stand with swords unsheathed in front of their ruler and his companions. The tall steppe warriors looked every inch fighting men of the highest calibre. They were the royal guards of their King, the mighty wizard Ontar and the Lady Admaria, to whom they were absolutely devoted, and for whom they would sacrifice their lives without question or hesitation. Their adversaries realised that they were strangers from outside Deerait. The icy fingers of fear clutched at their hearts for these men were obviously highly skilled in the martial arts. A poignant silence fell, lasting for long moments before finally being broken.

"Well, Felgorian, there is always another day!" Reorgin declared angrily, sheathing his sword to signify that the confrontation was over. "I can wait!"

"Of course you can wait! But bear this in mind. You were ten against three before the others and I came. You think that you would have won, fighting against those three alone. Reorgin, remember this! I know both the man and the youth. I also know their small comrade. It would have cost the lives of you and your companions facing him alone. He is valiant and a superb swordsman. He alone would have slaughtered your entire party very easily. My interruption and the arrival of these other gentlemen probably saved your lives!" the Riondese stated emphatically in cold tones, which shook the entire Adiorenji contingent because of their undoubted sincerity. The ambassador had learned details of the mighty battle on the steppes from Hanshair, Adrigal and Onlestic. The trio had heaped praise on Perlow.

"Good for Felgorian. Yet our desire for anonymity in Estyork has been completely shattered. Here comes a contingent from the town guards," Quinton indicated to Ontar.

"It can't be helped. If that veil had been removed things would have turned out far worse. We shall have to see what happens," the wizard smiled, replacing his sword in its scabbard.

The young King of Rionder had no time to ponder on the significance of his foster father's words, or on the strange fact that the woman and her companion were regarding him with obvious interest, before Admaria called in her native tongue, "Both of those we rescued are fine!".

"Excellent!" her husband acknowledged with obvious pleasure.

Quinton had no opportunity to speak to either of them, other than to think his growing assumption that the hooded couple were known to the two Ulgruffi was apparently correct, before the squad of twenty guards in the dark green uniform of the

36

Estyork military forces arrived. Each soldier had a long sword in a dark blue scabbard strapped to a belt on his left side and wore a close fitting black skull cap; each bore a strong square dark blue shield in his left hand while his right held a long wooden spear with a large metal tip. The patrol wore highly polished leather shoes and evinced a high standard of military competence.

"They're from Cottis' personal guard. That's signified by the dark blue on their shields and scabbards. On market days they have the responsibility of policing the square and streets in this area. The average garrison soldier is nowhere as efficient," Felgorian spoke to Quinton in Riondese.

"They certainly do look well trained," the youth concurred admiringly in his native language which Ontar, Admaria and Gordan had taught him during the terrible steppe winters.

"Greetings, Reorgin, Kinerth. It does appear that you have once again been engaged in some slight public disturbance. You do seem to attract trouble. Anyway, I do believe this incident is now over. Perhaps you and your house carls should go about your business," the officer in command of the troop suggested wryly.

"Alright, we shall do so, Unyamed!" Reorgin snapped very discourteously before leading his companions away through the crowd who opened quickly to permit their passage.

"Strangers, I suppose that you won't have any objections to accompanying me to garrison headquarters," the officer remarked, striding over to Quinton and his entourage.

"We would very much like to know why we should. We did not start this trouble, as you may or may not have seen," Ontar declared in his thrilling voice.

The officer, abashed by the mystic's tones, vital personality and gray eyes which seemed to penetrate to his very soul, changed his attitude and said very respectfully, "Sir, I did not see. However, it isn't for that reason I wish you to accompany me. Reorgin, Kinerth and their house carls will be departing from Estyork tomorrow. Governor Cottis has no desire to accommodate them in any way whatsoever.

"From what I was able to gather briefly from the shouts of the crowd, you and your companions humiliated them. They certainly would deserve it but the Relyanese will wish revenge for what you've done. Blood could be shed in the streets of Estyork between now and their departure. It is my duty to avoid this possibility. That's why I must ask you to come with me. Most certainly not for the purpose of imprisoning or punishing you and your friends."

"In that case we shall be pleased to comply with your request. May my young companion here blow his horn to summon others of our company? Quite a number have entered your beautiful town to see its sights today," Ontar requested with a kindly smile of amusement.

"Please do so," the officer nodded. Unyamed was very relieved for, besides the overwhelming bearing of some of the strangers, the thought had just forcibly struck him of the total competence of their personal bodyguard. He felt that his own superior numbers would prove of little avail against those already present.

Quinton untied the magnificent black rotar horn from his belt and raised it to his lips. He blew three loud blasts, two long and one short, which resounded throughout the square and nearby streets. A flock of purple pigeons, or eyecords, which had been peacefully roosting and cooing softly on the rooftops, flew with an agitated whirring of wings up into the blue sky where a few fluffy clouds were being ushered gently southwards by the slight breeze.

The sentinels on the battlements and their fellows throughout the city wondered what the sounds meant as they momentarily paused before continuing with their duties. Cottis, too, heard the summons from where he sat in the judgment hall of his fortress, and delegated a trooper to ascertain its cause. The signal reached the ears of all Quinton's bodyguard. They hastened rapidly along the thoroughfares to where their King awaited their presence. Ignoring the suprise in the eyes of the Deerait officer and his squad, the youth commanded his soldiers to bring their heculs. They all accomplished this duty within a few minutes. At the same time Perlow and Felgorian left to fetch the steeds which Quinton and his four companions had ridden into Estyork.

"Now we're ready to follow you. We'll walk our heculs. Please lead the way," the young King of Rionder commanded.

"Yes, Sir," the white Deerait officer murmured with respect, feeling no desire to question who should be in charge. He snapped orders for his troop to disperse the crowd; the latter had already retired some distance because of the greater area required for the heculs and their owners standing in a column of fours.

"Admaria, please bring along those we rescued. The Adiorenji must not be given the opportunity to assault them again," Ontar advised his wife.

She nodded her acquiescence and the hooded couple walked beside them as they proceeded for the short distance to the end of the busy thoroughfare. The large party turned across the cobbled square and passed through the lines of market stalls. Their progress was watched curiously by the citizenry and visitors to the town who were present. They finally entered the fortress where their arrival was expected by the district commander of Estyork and the governor of the Deerait province of Sicruci. Cottis had already been informed by the runner, whom he had sent to ascertain the reason for the blowing of the rotar horn, that approximately sixty strangers were being conducted to his headquarters as a precaution against the bloodshed which the Relyanese would exact, if at all possible.

The provincial governor awaited them in the great hall where he administered justice each market day to those who presented petitions. Believing the arrival of so many strangers to be an extraordinary circumstance, he delegated his administrative duties to his subordinate, Ricel, a fair minded Deerait, who left to continue the hearings in another room. Cottis gave instructions that the newcomers were to be admitted to his presence with all possible haste so that he could learn more about them. His interest had been aroused considerably by the news that Felgorian accompanied them for the latter was widely known in the province. Sicruci had been an important centre on the main trade route from Deerait through the forests to Rionder before the small city had been seized by Baron Enmarkan's dragoon squadrons from the Central Plains.

The yellow skinned district military commander was forty eight years of age, approximately half the average span of his race. He was acquainted with Felgorian, not only from the recent visit which the Riondese ambassador had made to Estyork and the interesting discussions which they had had together, but also from his youth, when he had been in charge of several mercantile expeditions to the kingdom of Rionder. He sincerely regretted that these missions had ceased because of the bitter conflict in the forests, for he had enjoyed the beautiful city and its environment.

Once they had fastened the reins of their heculs to hitching rails in the courtyard of the fortress, Quinton and his companions were conducted up broad stone steps and through a large carved wooden doorway into the great judgment hall of Estyork. Stolid green-liveried guards holding spears were stationed in alcoves at intervals of ten yards along both walls. At the far end on a wooden dais was a large chair, flanked by two more sentinels, where Cottis sat attended by four scribes, awaiting the approach of the strangers. Behind the governor and around the walls, magnificently woven tapestries depicted scenes from the history of the Deerait nation. High above, situated midway between each alcove was a large window with shutters opened for ventilation. Daylight streamed down, alternated by shadow to give a pleasant, mellow sensation.

When Quinton, Ontar, Admaria and their companions halted before the dais, Cottis greeted them courteously, saying, "Hail, strangers, and you too, Felgorian, my friend. As you may have conjectured, I have been informed of what occurred outside. I realise it may inconvenience you. Nevertheless, my officer acted sensibly in asking you to remain here until the Relyanese depart on the morrow. You will be lodged and fed. I do realise, without the need to be told, that the incident was not your fault. Far too much trouble has been caused since Reorgin and Kinerth arrived here a few days ago.

"Perhaps, Felgorian, you would be so good as to introduce the leaders of your company and tell me the reason for their presence in Estyork. Since I hold the positions of district commander and governor of Sicruci it is my duty to learn all matters which may affect the people in my jurisdiction, especially in these troubled times."

The handsome Riondese looked at Ontar and Quinton for guidance and the wizard stepped forward to say, "I am one of the leaders of our company. This is another whose name is Quinton. Mine is Ontar. We're travelling through Deerait, as many do, on business which we shall reveal to you only. I suggest that our escort, your guards and scribes retire. Then we can discuss our affairs in private with you personally. If you wish, our guards can withdraw to the courtyard. Your own can remain in the hall out of earshot."

"Mmm, I think your suggestion most acceptable.," the stout grey haired Deerait with kind, black eyes concurred.

Quinton commanded his escort, except for Hanshair and Perlow, to leave while Cottis advised his guards and scribes to remove themselves down the hall. The governor also requested that the man and the woman remain, since he was intrigued by the hoods which concealed their faces and by the black veil which Reorgin had rashly attempted to remove. Admaria stood close to the couple who had been rescued with Hanshair just behind her. Once all the Deerait guards and steppe warriors had withdrawn the discussion commenced.

"Now, pray tell me your business," Cottis smiled, leaning forward in his high chair.

"Firstly, I must emphasise that we are not prepared to permit the perpetration of injustice if we can possibly prevent it. It's not in our nature to stand idly by and allow a wrong to be committed. That explains our resistance to the Adiorenji. Secondly, Felgorian is still the official ambassador of the Royal House and Realm of Rionder to Deerait." Ontar paused to permit Cottis the opportunity for comment.

"I grant your first point, with reservations. My patrol would have dealt effectively with the Adiorenji. But I do concede my squad might not have arrived in time to prevent harm befalling the two hooded persons. Regarding your second point, I am aware, as is the entire Deerait nation, that Rionder fell about two decades ago. It was during the time Enmarkan expanded ostensibly to secure his territorial limits. We received an embassy from Broechnaar some months after he had accomplished the conquest of Rionder. The official news was brought by sea to Hesion and thence by courier from the High Council to my predecessor, whose legal adviser I then was. We already knew of it. Our merchants had been turned back by Broechnaar troops on the battlements of Rionder itself when they went to trade that year.

"We were truly sorry to learn of the disaster which befell Rionder. The Riondese were, and are, still highly respected and remembered amongst us for the learning they gave among other things. Yet, with respect, I don't really understand your remarks that Felgorian is still the official Riondese royal ambassador, when none of the reigning family of Rionder survived the assault. At least that's what we were told," Cottis stated.

"You mean that without a reigning monarch there would be no necessity to have a royal ambassador," Ontar

41

acknowledged.

"Precisely. We do know of the bitter conflict between the Riondese and Enmarkan's troops in the forests. This also regrettably helped to stop all trade between Deerait and the Rionder Valley. Our merchants have not risked travelling that way, partly because of the fighting, but also because of the demons and spirits lurking in the woods. The Riondese, and Polingsi, too, provided some sort of protection, or so we always felt.

"Incidentally Enmarkan was against our merchants also, although he didn't actually say so. He signed a Treaty of Neutrality. It became understood, if we refrained from going into the forests, he would not bother us. Our policy from Hesion was to remain neutral. Broechnaar was very strong then, and so were we, before these troubled times fully split our national feeling for union. You probably know about the treaty anyway. But my point is, there is no King of Rionder," Cottis stressed.

"We did know of the treaty, but only because Felgorian told us about it from his recent travels through Deerait. As to Felgorian still being the official royal ambassador of Rionder, that is true. My companion, Quinton, is the son of King Quintar and Queen Vialo. He was saved, unknown to Enmarkan and Tarvokel. I with some companions took him to the Mescarg steppes. He was brought up with the Nai-Zind tribe.

"He has returned, not to commence war against Enmarkan, although this may occur at some future date. The warriors in our bodyguard are Mescarg steppe tribesmen," Ontar stated dramatically, watching the reactions of the provincial governor, whom his instincts indicated to be a man of the highest honour and integrity.

"Mmm, now I understand why Felgorian wondered about the ancient Treaty of Matheird. You probably know the terms provide for us to repel any Mescarg tribesmen coming over the mountains, whether in small or large numbers. The Riondese were engaged against the Empire in the Casman war. They fought valiantly in all the battles."

"Yes, my people did," Quinton commented with pride. "Remember how they formed the rearguard in the battle of Ensselaer?"

"Their valour will never be forgotten. A handful of men

against overwhelming odds permitted the Deerait army time to reform. Even though we were defeated the next day, we were not annihilated, as would have happened but for the Riondese. It was a great pity that your race was not represented at Matheird," Cottis recalled with regret.

"The Riondese were indeed valiant. Their bravery has never been forgotten. The Adiorenji should have remembered that when they fought them in the forests after the war ended," Ontar remarked.

"Have you any copies of the treaty?" Quinton wondered.

"Not here. Hesion's probably the best place for that. The original is no longer in existence because of natural deterioration, but copies were definitely made down the centuries. The High Council has one framed in the meeting chamber. Look, your presence with steppe tribesmen, even if only your escort, means I should take steps to implement the conditions of the Matheird Treaty. Yet, I shall delay any action for the time being.

"A small force like yours should not mean trouble with the Casman Empire, even if Heolanwertin is such a stickler for ancient traditions. I guess you'll have more steppe warriors in the forest. Well, provided you don't possess too many, I don't see any section of my nation even considering action against you in these days. Sorcerers would have to be found to deal with demons and evil spirits. Besides your tribesmen could be anywhere in the forests. That's how the problem would be regarded.

"You won't be ignorant of this fact, namely we in the Deerait section of our nation are on the brink of civil war. We may have to battle with an alliance of the Dariondi, the Adiorenji and the Vilatmori. In fact, tomorrow I have to leave my deputy, Ricel, in command here. I've been summoned to Hesion to discuss the state of anarchy in our unhappy country. If war breaks out, Sicruci is the first province likely to be assailed. It's hardly sensible at this time in our history that I leave Ricel to handle the additional problems of organising an expedition up the Rionder Valley to expel alien tribesmen," Cottis shrugged.

"There's another factor," Quinton pointed out very shrewdly.

"What can that be?" the governor asked appraisingly.

"The Broechnaar garrison in Rionder. They won't like it one

43

bit if you do send forces up there. When Enmarkan learns that such a thing has happened he might seize on it as an excuse to make war, provided he's not involved in another revolt. Your troops would be from the Deerait tribe. The Baron might simply contact the other three tribes, promise them anything, and form an alliance against you. Of course, he'll simply smash them in turn when you Deeraits have been vanquished," the young King of Rionder explained.

"Mmm, I hadn't thought about that. More problems! Listen, I have to organise matters for my departure. In these circumstances, would you consider accompanying me to Hesion?" the governor of Sicruci wondered.

"Yes, we shall," Quinton smiled. "On the way we can talk things over. You will have a lot to do before you leave."

"Thank you. I do appreciate that. I don't suppose for a moment Broechnaar will have a notion that you've passed through the forests. I also assume you've not attacked the garrison in Rionder."

"You're correct on both assumptions," Ontar nodded.

"I've also assumed you do have more steppe warriors. I would like you to tell me their number, since this does involve the Casman Empire and the possibility of its massive armed forces being mobilised. Are you prepared to tell me your numbers?" Cottis asked in the tranquil, mellow surroundings of his judgment hall.

"I wondered when you would come to that question. Before I answer that, how many do you think we might have?" Ontar smiled disarmingly, making a strange motion with his right hand.

"If you came over the mountains, a most difficult feat, and brought a few tribes with you, perhaps three thousand people in all. Say one thousand warriors, fifteen hundred at the very most. We don't know anything about events on the great plains. We're content to leave that savage inhospitable area to itself. It's far too wild. Anyway, it's understood to be under Casman imperial mandate. The Empire's policy for the Mescarg steppes is no secret. So, my estimation of your numbers is fifteen hundred, probably less." Cottis smiled before adding, "Am I anywhere near?"

Quinton and Admaria were content to leave the conversation in Ontar's capable hands at this juncture. However, Felgorian was becoming concerned about the

44

governor's reaction. The Riondese ambassador had temporarily forgotten that the eminent mystic was quite capable of performing a simple spell to cause the district commander of Sicruci to forget anything he had learned, or to make him keep the information divulged to himself.

"We have an army of nearly a quarter of a million men, of whom about one hundred and thirty eight thousand are Casmans. Through force of circumstances we were compelled to form a union of steppe tribes. This summer we had to face the Jaddair army corps which we defeated. The Casmans joined us, because of an ancient law of theirs. Does that answer your question?" Ontar asked.

Cottis slumped in his chair; a poignant silence lasted for several minutes while the Deerait attempted to digest the almost unbelievable words of the handsome stranger with the wondrous gray eyes and mystical aura. The governor did not doubt that the revelation was true; his mind reeled as he tried to concentrate on what the intentions of the newcomers might be. It suddenly dawned on him that Ontar was the name of the renowned Ulgruffi who had founded the Sacred Islands of Wizards on the archipelago of Ordlansa in the Chofanrit Ocean to the west of the continent of Rontmethar. The beautiful woman in the tunic and Deerait skirt had to be his wife, Admaria, and a powerful magician in her own right. He remembered that the couple attended the Kings of Rionder.

The district commander felt weak, wondering what was really taking place. He tried desperately to grapple with the enormous problems now confronting him. He thought about the treaty with the Empire and recollected that his nation was supposed to expel steppe incomers. Then he realised that even without the threat of imminent civil war in his own country his whole nation would be hard pressed to defeat such a huge force. The army commanded by the King of Rionder must have been efficiently organised to defeat a Casman army corps in full battle order; that fact spelled of superlative training and magnificent troops. He looked at Hanshair and Perlow, and was impressed by the stature and obvious military resolution of the Nai-Zind and the small Chofir.

The governor's next thought was that if his nation refused to deal with the steppe forces, the Casman Empire would decide to invade Deerait by land and sea. All this was possible in a time of internal hostilities. He glanced at the sage again and noticed the latter making a casual motion with his right hand. Suddenly Cottis, whose mind had been spinning with almost insuperable difficulties, felt slightly exhilarated and then relaxed. He resolved to shelve his problems temporarily.

"I shall have to ponder these matters. Now, concerning the trouble with Reorgin and Kinerth, you were absolutely correct in your actions. The veiled woman with you is probably from one of the Civilised Nations in the north. Some regions require their women to be veiled in public. So, it might be better if you were to remove your veil while travelling in Deerait," the governor said, looking at Admaria's two companions. "Again, your long cloaks and hoods do tend to provoke interest. It is my recommendation that you change your apparel, but the choice is entirely yours. However, I would very much appreciate there being no more trouble in Estyork or Sicruci because of your dress.

"Ontar, I have to make final arrangements for my journey to Hesion. I've also to arrange for transfer of authority to my subordinate. He can complete the judgments for today. How many warriors do you have in the vicinity of Estyork?" Cottis enquired, rising from his chair.

"About three hundred, including those here. Why?"

"That could be quite useful. Look, if you will trust me, I would like you to provide the escort to Hesion. I normally take about that number with me to signify my office. Your three hundred would do excellently. On the way I shall try to reach some conclusion about your revelations. If I decide in your favour, I shall try to arrange a meeting with the High Council. If I decide against you, I shall allow you to leave and return to the Rionder Valley without fear of arrest. I give my word as provincial governor of Sicruci," the Deerait stated solemnly.

"Thank you. We shall provide your escort. With your permission I shall send three of our bodyguard as messengers. They will inform the remainder of our troops to be at the east gate at dawn tomorrow," the sage said.

"Excellent! I'll only need to take a nominal personal bodyguard from here. If war does break out in my absence Ricel will have three hundred extra soldiers available. Excuse me, I must leave you," Cottis declared courteously, before descending the steps of the dais and proceeding down the long hall.

Chapter Three
Allecenia

Felgorian remained silent for a few moments. He watched the yellow skinned governor of Sicruci striding towards the doorway. The ambassador felt extremely anxious. Although he knew Cottis to be a man of honour and integrity he realised that the Deerait would now be even more concerned about the welfare of his tribe and nation, which would be paramount in his thoughts: his reactions and conclusions were extremely important to the future of King Quinton.

"Excuse me, Great Ontar, but will all be well?" the Riondese asked with respect, his expression revealing the reason for his question.

"Indeed, all will be well, my friend. You may have noticed that I made two signs. The first caused Cottis to keep his counsel to himself. He won't reveal his thoughts to anyone, unless I release him from the spell. The second, a few moments ago, was to calm his mind. What he was told considerably added to his existing worries. With civil war imminent, disturbances in Estyork, and probably trouble elsewhere in Sicruci allied to our revelations, the poor fellow could almost have had a brainstorm," the sage replied.

"I did not mean to be impertinent," Felgorian apologised.

"You most certainly were not. Your concern is most laudable. I am not infallible. I could have forgotten to cast the spell very easily. Gordan once called the weather to my attention when my thoughts were elsewhere. His common sense saved many lives. Admaria and I had to complete a magical ritual to protect the Nai-Zind and ourselves from a terrible tornado.* No indeed, Felgorian, never be afraid to ask questions. Besides, we may have an audience with the High Council if Cottis decides for us," Ontar said, giving the Riondese a most wonderful smile of reassurance.

"You were quite right to ask," Quinton praised. "Hanshair!" he called, beckoning the Nai-Zind over.

---

* Chapter Eight — The Great Storm, Quinton, Vol. 1 of the Historical Beginnings of the Admarian Empire.

"Yes, Sire," the guard commander spoke courteously, delighted to be able to address his beloved paramount ranxem and King by his title once more.

"Appoint three warriors to ride back to camp. Instruct the force there to be ready to march on the morrow. They are to reach the east gate of Estyork just before dawn. They are to be prepared for a long journey. They must all wear Deerait clothing and let their hair hang free. Their turnout is to be of the highest standard," the monarch commanded.

"At once, Sire. With your permission, I'll obtain an escort of garrison soldiers through the town to the north gate for our couriers. It will prevent the possibility of trouble from those Adiorenji," Hanshair said, evincing his ability to foresee and deal with future difficulties before they arose.

"Good. Cottis doesn't want trouble either. Those Adiorenji would attempt revenge if they get the chance," Quinton concurred.

"And they would find out that it was their blood being spilled," Hanshair stated simply and honestly, without any trace of bombast, which Felgorian remarked. "I'll leave you, Sire, but I'll return to ascertain if you require anything."

"You can bring some guards to our quarters after everyone's eaten. There's no treachery here," the young King declared frankly, confirming what his intuition revealed.

"In that case, Sire, I'll pass on your orders. Then I'll see about quarters for the guard. And Perlow is with you."

Hanshair bowed to his monarch and strode off to the courtyard where his fellows waited patiently, watched by the curious eyes of the Sicrucian soldiers on duty. The tall handsome Nai-Zind snapped orders which were promptly carried out. Colmar, the Melcogh, and two others prepared to mount while their commander spoke to the same officer who had been in charge of the patrol which had brought his monarch and companions to the fortress. The white skinned Deerait had already been personally informed by Cottis to ensure that the King of Rionder and his entourage had all their needs tended. He immediately delegated a squad of twenty men to escort the three couriers to the north gate.

Once they had departed Unyamed conducted Hanshair and the remainder of Quinton's bodyguard to quarters within the garrison, near which stabling facilities were provided for their heculs. The steeds had never been accustomed to stalls but

48

the spell which Ontar had cast before dawn prevented any commotion by the fierce creatures. When they had fed and watered their mounts the plainsmen were given food and drink: they settled down to await their next instructions, musing on the wonders of Estyork, the first town they had ever seen.

At the same time as Unyamed was delegating the mounted squad to escort the couriers Quinton and his companions were being shown to rooms a short distance from the judgment hall. A guard in the dark green livery of the garrison conducted them along a broad passage to the left, and then through a pleasant cloistered courtyard with a pool and fountain in its centre. Small multi-coloured ferns and shrubs flourished in the mild climate, even though the terrible blizzards of winter were lashing the vast Mescarg steppes across the mountains to the north-east. It was evident from the neatness of the garden plots that considerable care was lavished upon them, for this was where the governor of Sicruci often sat with his two wives and five offspring to contemplate the administrative problems of his province.

To show that he realised both the rank and importance of Quinton and the two Ulgruffi, Cottis had them taken to very elegant apartments overlooking the courtyard. The district commander of Estyork had also assumed that there would be no objection to the hooded couple sharing accommodation with them. Servitors in dark brown uniforms waited to learn their requirements and provided facilities for bathing.

Once he had completed his toilet Quinton returned to the very tastefully furnished dining room with drapes over the doorway, carpets of intricately woven patterns and fine furniture. He found his foster parents, Perlow and Felgorian already there. They passed the time until their midday meal discussing the events of the morning and contemplating what future might result from them.

When the Sicrucian servitors appeared with trays on which were salvers and dishes of food, the man who had been rescued came through from another room where he had obviously been chatting with his female associate. He had removed his cloak to reveal a beige tunic and matching trousers tucked into black boots. After filling a plate with food he took it through to his companion before returning to join the young King, the two Ulgruffi, Perlow and Felgorian.

Quinton's deduction, that his foster parents knew the

49

strangers, was fully confirmed just after Admaria had given thanks to the Great Power. Before they began their meal Ontar introduced the man as Olluinan, a member of the Sacred Order of Light which the two Ulgruffi had founded centuries before on the beautiful island of Ordlansa and its archipelago of the same name on the Chofanrit Ocean. The youth greeted him courteously, recollecting that his foster parents had oftimes mentioned Olluinan as a very capable scientist, mystic and magician who was assisted in his endeavours by his wife, Artzcellia, and their daughter, Allecenia, the latter having accompanied her father to Deerait.

Olluinan was just over eight feet in height, a few inches less in stature than Ontar and Admaria. He was very handsome, with high cheek bones and the same aloof bearing which the two Ulgruffi and Quinton possessed. This mien is born not from snobbishness or arrogance, but from the study of mysticism which sets the sincere followers of the Mystic Way apart from their fellows on the myriads of inhabited worlds of the Universe. He had brown hair, green eyes and light brown skin, and impressed both Quinton, Felgorian and Perlow considerably. Although he greeted the two Riondese and the Chofir with courtesy and a friendly smile, Olluinan gave no indication of the reason for his unexpected presence in Estyork.

Once their meal was finished and the servitors had withdrawn Ontar turned to Quinton and said, "Olluinan, Admaria, Allecenia and I have much to discuss. Would you leave us for the present and ensure that some of our own guards are posted on the doors to these apartments? No one is to enter unless I give permission."

"Of course, I shall. You and Admaria are my foster parents. I love you dearly. Your request for privacy will find full compliance in me. Until later. Farewell for now," the young King smiled, before rising from the table to leave the room accompanied by his ambassador and personal bodyguard.

"He is without doubt a very fine person. Entirely worthy of you both. We did know what he might be like from the revelations of the Great Power. But now that I've actually met him in the flesh . . . . well, I can only say that I feel privileged. Almost as if one of the Hidden Servants had appeared on this physical plane," Olluinan declared in thoughtful tones.

"I know exactly what you mean. Quinton's in his final incarnation. He's like no one else you've ever met. His effect on battle hardened veterans of steppe warfare is quite something to see. They become like children gazing in wonder at their first sight of Ilix and Selix and the stars. They'll follow him anywhere, because they love him," Admaria said with a gentle smile.

"What's more, he loves them in return, and they know it." Ontar declared before adding softly, "So do Admaria and I. He's like a son to us, and what a son!"

"I am really very impressed. Like I was especially during his actions when Allecenia and I were assaulted. He stood there, so young beside you, ready to face the world. He's very resolute, courteous, understanding, with very high principles. Suitable indeed for the one who is to be the ruler of our world. Quinton of Phentara has a musical rhythm to it. Still, there are many years to pass before our dreams for Phentara reach fruition. No one knows for certain how events may turn out, even if foresight and planning are excellent," Olluinan averred.

"Yes, that's certainly true. Do call in our god-daughter and we'll have a long discussion," Admaria smiled.

Quinton, Felgorian and Perlow descended the wooden stairs, and strolled along the paved cloisters where they met Hanshair approaching with four steppe guards. The Nai-Zind had come to fulfil the orders of his paramount ranxem. Once he had posted the sentinels outside the doors leading to the apartments of the two Ulgruffi and their visitors, Hanshair returned to his overlord in the main courtyard to ascertain if the latter had any further requirements.

The youth thought for a few moments; he looked at the bustling market beyond the fortress gate before deciding to organise a training session. With the willing co-operation of Unyamed a sufficient number of heavy sacks of grain were obtained from the stores. Quinton and his fifty four guards were watched with intense interest by Felgorian, the white skinned Deerait officer and others from the garrison. None of them had ever seen such dedication to exercise. The observers stared at the participants, who performed elementary gymnastics before trotting at a fast pace around a large inner courtyard where recruits were put through basic training. While they ran each carried a huge sack of grain on one shoulder for five minutes before transferring it to the other.

Round and round the courtyard they continued, until forty five minutes had elapsed. The warriors were tired but could have continued much longer: hard training, combined with a sensible nourishing diet to improve health and stamina, had become an essential part of their daily activities ever since Quinton, Ontar and Gordan, the captain of the royal guard and supreme general, had assumed the leadership of the diverse Mescarg steppe tribes. The wizard and his wife had been instrumental in instructing the grassland peoples and their Casman allies in both matters of hygiene and nutrition. The young King of Rionder knew that the highly efficient army which followed him would be performing similar physical exercises every morning, in conjunction with martial activities later in the day and a period set aside for academic education.

Gordan, with Casterandir, Turubin, Shlasmil and Sleworivan, went to considerable lengths to ensure that their training programmes were not permitted to lapse. Each individual soldier, no matter how humble his rank, was made to feel that he was an important integral part of the armed forces on whom his leaders depended; in return the commanders did not spare themselves, so that a mutual respect and love existed in the forces of Quinton, King of Rionder and paramount ranxem of the Mescarg steppe peoples, something in which their Casman allies were enjoying full participation.

When they had completed their training Quinton asked Unyamed that they be given facilities for bathing. In response to his request the Deerait officer conducted them to a secluded garden near the main barracks. Several shady trees and clumps of large bushes surrounded a smooth lawn, in the centre of which a subterranean spring bubbled to the surface to form a large pool. The water disappeared beneath the earth once more on its way to join the broad River Avidnive where it flowed past the southwestern corner of Estyork.

The steppe warriors were all able to swim. Quinton and the Nai-Zind warriors in his contingent had been taught this invaluable accomplishment during the summer months of childhood spent on the banks of the Dentworl. The Great River was now totally frozen under the ice and snowstorms sweeping the Mescarg plains. They bathed twelve at a time, cleansing the perspiration from their bodies with soap processed and manufactured by the steppe women from bison fat. Unyamed had servitors provide them with towels. The Deerait officer had determined to obey the strict instructions of his garrison commander, that all their needs were to receive every attention; the provincial governor of Sicruci attached considerable importance to their presence, far more than he dared admit even to himself.

"What now, Sire?" Hanshair enquired in a low voice on their return to the inner courtyard, accompanied by Felgorian and Perlow. "We can hardly practise swordplay, archery or any riding manoeuvres, even if there is sufficient room here."

"You're right. The Deeraits are watching everything we do. We don't want them to realise how efficient we really are. At least not at the moment. Remember, we may have to do battle with them," his monarch answered softly.

"That is so, Sire," Hanshair concurred, while they waited for the other royal guards to join them, for the quartet had bathed in the first batch.

"Quinton, may I mention something which has just occurred to me?" Perlow asked in his shy manner.

"Certainly."

"I've a peculiar feeling. Those Adiorenji this morning won't allow us to move freely outside the walls of Estyork. They will attempt to avenge themselves for the loss of face they've suffered. The two leaders struck me as very vindictive persons," the Chofir declared seriously.

"Mmmm. I agree with you there. The one named Reorgin especially did strike me like that, exceptionally vindictive and arrogant. Cottis, the district garrison commander, as you heard in the judgment hall, has requested that we remain within the confines of the fortress until tomorrow morning. He's leaving for the port of Hesion on the coast. Although he didn't actually say so directly I believe that, besides our acting as his escort, he wishes to have our protection to assess how effective we are. Again, he can keep an eye on us.

"There's the possibility you just mentioned. Those Adiorenji may attempt to waylay us on our journey. Still, we can deal with that circumstance if and when it does occur. They'll have to gather forces to do so. Their homeland's to the west of here on the borders of Sicruci, not too far distant. If it does come to a fight, you, Hanshair, my friend, will have to act as third in command under Ontar and me," Quinton smiled.

The Nai-Zind felt much pleasure from the remarks of his King, but enquired courteously in his own tongue, "What about the Lord Felgorian, Sire? Should not he take command with me as his subordinate?"

The Riondese ambassador was standing beside them, listening, and received a nod from his King to answer the question of the guard commander. Felgorian looked extremely puzzled for several moments before saying, "I'm sorry, Sire. I realise you wish me to respond, but Hanshair was conversing with you in a strange dialect."

"I do apologise. Hanshair was talking in Nai-Zind. There's two Deeraits standing over there. If we continue to keep our voices down they shouldn't be able to hear our conversation," Quinton remarked softly in the Common Speech, before going on to explain what the steppe warrior had been asking.

Once Felgorian had learned the topic of their conversation he smiled at the guard commander and said, "Hanshair, my friend, you are very courteous. I do appreciate your kindess, completely devoid of rancour or jealousy, in offering to serve in a subordinate capacity to me. However, I must refuse. The main reason is, you know precisely what to do in a conflict. You comprehend the revolutionary tactics of our armed forces. Also, although I do feel fit, I haven't had the training and exercises in both physical and martial arts which you have had. Again, you have a knowledge of strategics which I can only guess at. I am fully prepared to serve under you and your section leaders."

The tall handsome Nai-Zind acknowledged Felgorian's remarks with a slight bow, while Quinton, who had already guessed his ambassador's response, nodded and said, "Thank you. You were totally honest in your remarks. You can act as standard bearer if we do have to fight. That's Hanshair's official position in battle. It will allow him freedom of movement. It will also keep you in a position of comparative safety, and that's essential."

"But, Sire, I want to serve you in an active capacity; not remain in a position of safety. With all due respect, I know that Hanshair received this position as a reward for actions performed on the steppes. Adrigal and Onlestic mentioned it yesterday afternoon when we were riding through the forest. I was asking about the battle against the Jaddair corps. I feel I would like to fight," the Riondese pleaded.

"I know you would. But you're forgetting one important detail. Perhaps you can advise Felgorian," Quinton addressed the Nai-Zind as several more of his bodyguard entered the courtyard from the garden.

"Lord Felgorian, the standard is always well protected. It has to be. It's our principal rallying and command point. I know how you must feel. You wish to serve and not have the stigma of cowardice. I was awarded the honour of standard bearer for services rendered to my King. You feel you haven't earned this privilege because you were travelling through Deerait when we fought the Casmans. In the event of a skirmish or pitched battle in the next few days, if that does happen, you feel that all the bodyguard except yourself will be fighting for King Quinton. You wish to show your loyalty in a similar manner. These must be your thoughts," Hanshair stated.

The Riondese nodded with a serious expression, and the steppe warrior continued, "We all serve our King and paramount ranxem. I am a soldier, but behind me are women who sew clothes, old men who fashion weapons, children who collect hecul chips. Nearly everyone does several duties. Of course, there are a few who are essential for the performance of only one or two. Mirchanrope and Forsever command the scouts. They excel at this duty, and it's their principal concern.

"Gordan, our supreme general, is totally involved in running the army. So are our four Polingsi commanders. Lord Elmendor controls the commissariat. He's very efficient, but has no time to perform other duties. Perlow's main function is to protect King Quinton. There is no one better than he for this duty. His swordplay and courage are beyond description. You, Lord Felgorian, are the ambassador to Deerait, and to other peoples too, when the time comes. You have experience and contacts in this country which no one else has. Your political and economic knowledge is absolutely vital to our cause. If you fall in battle then we lose a valuable asset. We need you. We also respect you highly. Now do you understand?" the Nai-Zind asked earnestly.

The Riondese thought for several moments, before nodding and saying, "Thank you very much. I really do appreciate your remarks, and I do understand."

"I'm glad. You are no coward. I remember how valiantly you fought when Rionder fell. Gordan told me. Hanshair, since we have to remain within the garrison walls, tell our men to relax and rest until dawn," Quinton commanded.

"Yes, Sire. I've arranged for the guards on your apartments to be changed at regular intervals," the Nai-Zind said, before bowing and striding across to muster his command, the majority of whom were now in the courtyard.

"With your permission, Sire, I'd like to accompany Hanshair and learn more about your battle tactics," Felgorian requested.

"Certainly you can. He's very good at strategy. Oh, you probably won't know but, like all our steppe peoples, he can read and write in the Common Speech and do mathematics. The Nai-Zind are the most advanced tribe as regards education. Ontar and Admaria were responsible for that. I'll see you later at the evening meal," the King of Rionder smiled.

"I'm glad Hanshair spoke as honestly and frankly as he did. Till later, Sire," the Riondese ambassador bowed, before leaving to join the royal guard commander.

The young king, accompanied by Perlow, turned and slowly retraced his steps through the garrison fortress. When he reached the main courtyard Quinton paused to look through the entrance at the bustling market square where the stalls were thronged. Customers came and went, haggling, purchasing or examining merchandise. A few pickpockets moved among the crowds, plying their trade with caution; but woe betide any who were caught. A first offence meant a public flogging of twenty lashes; the second incurred fifty; if this did not deter the criminal, then he faced the loss of one hand, a punishment which a thief was seldom rash enough to court.

Vendors strode between the lines of stalls, selling hot drinks and food. The inns did a roaring trade occasionally interrupted by violent disagreements between customers who had imbibed too freely. When such a disturbance occurred the landlord's hired help usually dealt with it, simply ejecting the over exuberant drinkers into the street. However, if matters seemed to be progressing too far, the garrison patrols would be called: all brawling immediately ceased, for Cottis did not approve of such conduct.

Quinton eventually turned away from the gate and walked slowly in the direction of the cloistered garden. As he did so he pondered on the journey to Hesion, which would increase considerably the distance from his base in the forests of the Rionder Valley. Communications could be maintained by courier, but a chain of riders would be difficult to keep up in a country on the brink of civil war; again there was the time factor for delays of many days would occur before answers were received. However, there was a direct occult means of contact with Likans the Polingsi wizard, which involved using Ontar's crystal. This invaluable method had been used before when they had been contemplating the withdrawal of the steppe peoples over the Mescarg mountains.

Quinton was still musing on this and other matters as he and the Chofir approached the cloistered courtyard. He remained uncertain about the length of time his foster parents would be closeted with Olluinan and Allecenia. The youth did not wish to appear rude by interrupting their discussion. On emerging from the cool passageway into the warmth of the day Quinton crossed over to sit down on a wooden bench in the garden. Nearby grew a sweet scented shrub with long vermilion and green leaves. The monarch motioned to Perlow to join him.

Overhead, the afternoon sun shone brightly in the azure sky, where it was sinking from its zenith towards the western horizon. Quinton watched the insects humming and buzzing amongst the plants; this caused him to reflect once more on the startling contrast between Deerait, with its milder climate, and the fierce blizzards rampaging across the vast undulating Mescarg steppes which had been his childhood home.

Having time to spare, the young King of Rionder decided to meditate. He closed his eyes to commence the esoteric procedure which Ontar and Admaria had taught him. Relaxing his body entirely, he simultaneously performed rhythmical breathing exercises, until he felt himself gradually merging with the eternal fluctuating essence of the Universe. The divine vibrations of the Cosmic flowed harmoniously through and around him. The wondrous Inner Light and Revelation began to permeate his consciousness. Once more the youth sensed the beautiful mystical union with the Great Power and allowed his thoughts to drift along the path he intuitively desired.

Time passed imperceptibly. On concluding his arcane exercise, Quinton opened his eyes to discover that the westering sun had caused the mellow shadows of evening to fall. The sound of footsteps from the passageway made him turn to see who was approaching. He smiled when he saw the tall reassuring figures of Hanshair, Adrigal, Onlestic and Felgorian, accompanied by four guards striding towards the apartments where his foster parents and their visitors were closeted. The young paramount ranxem speculated that the two Ker-Mantids were going to reinforce the sentries, who were obviously about to be changed.

Once more he wondered whether the discussion above him would soon finish, but felt no anger or resentment at not being a party to the meeting. Quinton knew that foremost among the subjects of conversation would be the scientific advancements made by the learned sages on the Sacred Islands of the Ordlansa archipelago. He had been told by Ontar that this knowledge would be given freely to Phentara at the appropriate time. Programmes would be devised so that the peoples of his world would be thoroughly educated in the advanced techniques developed. However, his foster parents had told him nothing of such discoveries and he was content to be guided by their wisdom in this.

Quinton thought how resolute Olluinan seemed, resembling Ontar and Admaria in having a hidden majestic mien. His thoughts turned to the mysterious Allecenia and the concealment of her face. Suddenly, a slight movement at one of the apartment windows above caught his eyes and he momentarily glimpsed the veiled woman gazing down at him. Before she moved away he noticed that she no longer wore her hood, but, in the shadow of the room, he had not been able to perceive her features.

More sounds from the cloisters caused him to turn. He nodded on seeing that Adrigal and Onlestic had taken up positions to protect him while Hanshair and Felgorian were returning to the quarters allocated to the rest of his efficient bodyguard. The two vigilant Ker-Mantids stood together, discreetly watching their monarch and the Chofir whom they admired. They glanced occasionally along the passageway which led to the main courtyard past the great judgment hall and also towards the stairs which permitted access to the apartments of Ontar, Admaria and their two companions.

Several minutes passed peacefully in the waning afternoon before a voice called,"Quinton! Come up here! Perlow, please wait outside the door!"

The youth rose to his feet with a pleasant smile on his handsome face, acknowledging the request from his beautiful foster mother. Within a minute he had seated himself at the table where he had dined earlier. The room was exactly the same except that the Deerait servitors had just departed after lighting several candles. Although Admaria, Ontar and Olluinan were present, Allecenia was absent. The Lady had obviously decided to retire to the privacy of her own quarters from the window of which she had been briefly observing Quinton. The Ulgruffi sage apologised for the delay in asking him to return but, as his foster son had already surmised, the quartet had been engrossed in discussing the scientific experiments and knowledge amassed by the Order of Light during the absence of its illustrious founders.

"Olluinan generally reports to Admaria and me on progress on the Sacred Islands. This occurs approximately every four years if we are absent from Ordlansa for long periods. The last time we saw him and Allecenia was in Hesion shortly after you were born. Once Rionder fell, they obeyed standing instructions and did not undertake further quadrennial journeys, although we meet on the astral on occasion. By means of the Master Crystals in Hesewoner, my fellow sages have watched your progress with intense interest. They were able to deduce from our activities this past spring and summer that Admaria and I would be in the Rionder forests about now. Our meeting in Estyork was purely coincidental," Ontar explained.

"I see. What about a crystal? Doesn't Olluinan have one like you and Admaria?" Quinton enquired.

"Both Allecenia and I do possess crystals. We did scry the Rionder forests until recently. That's where we saw your party coming south. You travel very quickly. It was quite a surprise to find you in Estyork this morning," Olluinan commented.

"If Reorgin hadn't been dissuaded by me from snatching off Allecenia's veil, she or her father would have been compelled to employ magic. This would have been very effective but would have brought too much attention. Deerait magicians in general are not as capable as the Casman sorcerers Perlow, Adrigal and Onlestic slew," Ontar stated.

"How long will Olluinan be remaining with us? I assume that he will probably be coming to Hesion. Allecenia and he can hardly have advanced beyond a brief outline of the news they brought from the Islands," the young man remarked.

"I told you he was very shrewd," Ontar raised his eyebrows in the direction of his visitor.

"You're quite correct, Quinton. Both of us will be accompanying you on the journey to Hesion. It was quite a fortunate coincidence meeting Ontar and Admaria here in Estyork. Allecenia and I were about to purchase supplies when we saw you riding along the northern boulevard," Olluinan explained.

"The ship which brought our friend and his daughter to Hesion will be anchored out in the bay for several weeks. The crew will be engaged in marine biological experiments. They expect Olluinan to return to Ordlansa with them at some future date. So, our travelling to Hesion means that Olluinan and Allecenia can continue their discussions with Ontar and me both during the day and when we camp at night." Admaria smiled before saying, "Now I'll go and fetch Allecenia."

The beautiful Ulgruffi walked over to the door giving access to the room where Olluinan's daughter had her quarters. She knocked and entered, closing the door behind her, while Quinton continued his conversation with the two mystics.

"I am sincerely pleased to have the honour of providing the escort for you and your daughter tomorrow. It is a singular honour to be able to perform a service for members of the Order of Light. Everyone works unselfishly for the benefit of Phentara. I only hope the inhabitants of our planet will appreciate the knowledge you have amassed."

"We hope so too. One day, many years hence, you will became the Emperor of Phentara, provided of course that you overcome all the difficulties before you. You should succeed if you continue as you've been doing. Ontar told Allecenia and me how well you thought out the long term strategy for uniting the free steppe tribes. Destiny was assuredly abroad that day when the Ker-Mantids and their allies captured the Ouselorns. Your strategy was exceptionally well done. It demonstrates that you not only possess the capability and talent for organisation but can employ them effectively.

"Destiny has marked you for its child. Therefore events will occur involving your direct participation. The happenings on the steppes are indisputable evidence of this. Yet, from what I know and can sense intuitively, you are the one who will succeed where others would fail," the emissary from the Sacred Islands stated sincerely.

Quinton inclined his head and voiced his thanks. The future before him was awesome and momentous. He realised the Order's expectations for Phentara and hoped that he would accomplish a permanent, peaceful and prosperous union of its peoples before his transition to the Higher Planes. He was aware that the years ahead would bring wars and similar troubles for which there would be no necessity to search. Still, with Ontar, Admaria, Gordan and the four Polingsi beside him, he would possess an enduring warmth and love, which few ever have in their lifetimes.

Some moments later, Admaria reappeared accompanied by Allecenia; the latter wore her elegant cloak of a dark brown material, its hood effectively combining with the black veil to conceal her face. Quinton, who had risen to greet the two Ladies, looked at Olluinan's daughter once more, and began to wonder what she thought, a damsel so mysterious: what was her face like, and why was it concealed?

"Father, we shall have to send for our belongings from the hostelry where we stayed last night," she spoke for the first time in his presence.

Quinton felt her voice thrill him. Its tones of gentleness and resolution somehow reminded him of clear streams rippling in the forests to the north in the Valley of his birth, and the gentle summer breeze blowing across the undulating steppes of his childhood.

"Ah, yes. In the excitement of finding Ontar and Admaria, I'd completely forgotten about that. Perhaps you can help in this, Quinton. I probably require an escort lest our Adiorenji acquaintances find the opportunity to attempt another assault," Olluinan addressed the King of Rionder.

"Mm. Sorry. Certainly," the handsome youth responded, shaking himself from the reverie which the beautiful voice of Allecenia had caused. He turned and called, "Perlow! Adrigal! Onlestic! Please come in!"

The two Ker-Mantids, who had accompanied their ruler from the cloisters to the door of the apartments, had remained with the guards already posted there. They entered with the Chofir in response to their paramount ranxem's request.

"Sire, what do you require?" Adrigal asked courteously.

"Take twenty of our guard with an officer from this garrison. Preferably the Deerait Unyamed if he's still on duty. Go to the Lord Olluinan's lodgings. Help him collect his belongings and heculs," Quinton ordered.

"At once, Sire. Will you come with us, sir?" Adrigal enquired.

"Yes," Olluinan nodded, striding towards the door. "Wait here, my daughter. I shan't be long," he smiled towards the hooded figure.

61

"Oh, Onlestic!" Quinton called.

"Yes, Sire," the other Ker-Mantid replied as he was about to close the door.

"No trouble in the streets of Estyork whatever the provocation. Perlow will be in charge."

"No trouble, Sire," the warrior affirmed.

"That rascal. Adrigal too," Ontar smiled with affection after the three guards had departed with Olluinan.

'Yes, those two would not have stood for any insults against you, Quinton. It was just as well you cautioned them. They're absolutely obedient, but if the Adiorenji were to insult you or us those two would react unless Hanshair or a superior officer or Perlow were there to stop them. You were wise to caution them. They'll keep the peace because of that," Admaria averred.

"They're a pair of lovable rogues. I like the friendship they have with Hanshair," Ontar commented.

"Quinton, what are your feelings about the journey to Hesion?" Admaria asked, while Allecenia sat quietly opposite the youth.

"We'll just have to wait and learn Cottis' intentions once he has thought things over. I do believe, or rather I feel, that Destiny has once more taken a direct hand. We are meant to travel with Cottis to Hesion," her foster son stated emphatically.

"Yes, we feel it too. Allecenia and her father also. This is because the five of us practise mysticism and study the arcane secrets of life. Such benefits are obtained by the sincere student," Admaria declared in serious tones.

"I trust our three messengers reached the camp all right?" Quinton enquired.

"They did. I checked in my crystal earlier. Everything's satisfactory there, and in the Rionder Valley. I even saw Gordan and Sheralex with our godchildren. Rahamb and family too," Ontar smiled reflectively.

"I miss them, you know. Especially Gordan and our four Polingsi friends," Quinton said softly.

"They miss us also," Admaria nodded. "They remember the long years we lived together and the love we have for one another which binds us for always."

"You are fortunate to love and be loved by such friends," Allecenia spoke gently, once again in the tones which charmed all those fortunate to hear them uttered, every syllable evincing a musical quality.

"Indeed we are," Ontar concurred emphatically. "Oh, Quinton hasn't been told you'll be remaining with us, not sailing back to Ordlansa with your father."

"That's because Allecenia will assist us immensely. Her magical and mystical abilities are considerable. She'll be able to expound on the theories behind the knowledge amassed since we last saw her and her father just after your birth. Much has been discovered which Ontar and I have to comprehend. Some of it extremely vital.

"When time permits, you will also be taught by her. She has many lessons to supplement ours. Your own knowledge and advancement are considerable. What Allecenia can teach you will prove invaluable when Phentara begins to advance from its present state of ignorance. Ontar and I decided this afternoon that it is time for you to learn what has been discovered on Ordlansa. Allecenia knows where to commence your programme of education. Needless to say, none of this must be revealed to others yet," Admaria admonished.

"I don't know what to say. I feel excited and stimulated. Humble, too. Thank you sincerely. You too, My Lady Allecenia," Quinton expressed his gratitude.

"And I thank you too. It shall be my pleasure to teach you," the beautiful voice spoke again.

About three quarters of an hour later Olluinan returned, assisted by Perlow, Adrigal and Onlestic, who easily carried the large heavy hide articles of baggage containing the belongings of the sage and his daughter. Both the latter retired to their rooms to change into more suitable clothing before the evening meal. Shortly afterwards a message came from Cottis to apologise for neglecting his guests, but his time was fully occupied in superintending the final arrangements for his departure on the morrow; the provincial governor did not intend to leave Sicruci without having the best administration possible during his absence, especially when the Adiorenji, Vilatmori and the Dariondi were causing so much dissension.

With the advance of evening the westering sun finally sank in an orange crimson glow which was reflected on the gray stones of the cloisters, bathing the area in a warm irradiance. Gradually, as it began to die, the stars appeared, first singly, then in twos and threes, until the night sky was carpeted with twinkling lights. The luminaries prepared for the rising of the first moon of Phentara, Ilix the Enchantress, to begin her walk over the spangled heavens. Eventually, as the beautiful planet revolved in its course around the distant sun, the second moon, Selix the Panther, would emerge to continue his relentless but futile pursuit of Ilix.

With the marked increase of the mellow purple evening shadows the servitors in their dark brown uniforms reappeared to light the small torches hung in wall brackets throughout the apartments. When they had completed this duty the sturdy Deeraits prepared the table for the meal of their overlord's guests before courteously withdrawing to leave the strangers alone. A few moments later Felgorian appeared, having thoroughly enjoyed the hours which he had passed in the company of Hanshair. Once more only the six of them, including Perlow, sat at the dining table while Allecenia ate alone in her room. Quinton wondered again at this strange occurrence but politely refrained from enquiring the reason. If this were the desire of their new acquaintances then it was not for him to voice questions about it.

However, when the others had retired for the night Ontar did comment on the veil to his foster son. The wizard explained that there was a most excellent reason for Allecenia keeping her face hidden from the view of others on Rontmethar, except for her father, Admaria and himself. In due course of time Quinton would understand why this should be so, and realise that the adoption of the veil by the Lady was most sensible. Until she chose to remove her facial covering in his presence the youth affirmed that he would ensure that no one attempted to do so. The King of Rionder resolved not to speculate on this strange matter.

Shortly before dawn the garrison was astir to bid farewell to its popular commander. Cottis was abroad early. After saying fond goodbyes to his wives and family he mounted his fine hecul, and saluted his troops. Next, he gave a command; the column clattered out of the fortress and proceeded across the deserted market square before turning along the boulevard which led to the east gate.

The provincial governor had already been informed by the sentinels on duty at the west gate that Reorgin, Kinerth and their entourage of house carls had departed half an hour earlier; the Adiorenji party had been observed riding at a rapid pace towards Relyan. Cottis, who had signed an order granting the unwelcome visitors special passes to leave Sicruci, told Quinton that they would be heading for the nearest town, Imexcajm, approximately seventy miles distant.

Already a faint saffron glow on the eastern horizon indicated the approaching dawn. The air was chill; there had been several squalls during the night, but the advent of the sun gradually dispelled the cold. Light came rushing over the vast snow covered steppes, and sprang across the mighty Mescarg mountain range to strike the fertile land of Deerait. It revealed the freshness of the countryside. Tilled fields and green meadows contrasted vividly with the darker clumps of bosques, the leaves of which glistened and sparkled with dew and raindrops.

"Here comes the rest of my guard, Cottis," Quinton indicated, as mounted warriors appeared from the northern side of Estyork. The newcomers hastened to join the smaller party which had travelled about sixty yards from the city walls.

The proud soldiers had indeed accomplished an excellent turnout. Their weapons and shield bosses were highly polished; the harness and saddles of their sturdy yellow beaked steeds had been thoroughly cleaned with bison fat. Each warrior wore a dress similar to that generally adopted by the Deeraits, all identification of his individual tribal origin having been removed. In addition to a long sword, every trooper bore a stout bow and a full quiver of arrows, and carried a long spear in his right hand. Pride in themselves and in their youthful ruler became wholly evident to the governor of Sicruci and his personal guard when the steppe troopers rode up in a column of threes.

Quinton nodded to Hanshair who snapped efficient commands. In response to his orders a squad of warriors dismounted and unloaded the pack heculs bearing the shields, spears, bows and quivers of those who had entered Estyork. The two giant linz stood motionless, looking disinterestedly at the activities of the humans, their reins firmly held by a warrior. The Sicrucians gazed at the magnificent creatures with awe, mingled with the thought of how fierce the animals were known to be.

While the distribution of the weapons was being conducted, the remainder of the newcomers followed Hanshair's precise instructions and promptly split into sections, two of which flanked Cottis and the party from Estyork, while a third took up the rear. Concurrently, scouts galloped off in different directions to assume the protective positions they had been taught so well, and which were second nature to them. Colmar and three comrades hastened away in response to a request from their liege. The garrison commander had agreed with Ontar that the King of Rionder was to be in absolute charge of the entire force, but would consult with him if danger loomed.

"Why have you sent scouts out? There's no need," the Deerait asked.

"Just standard procedure. Remember, our peoples are at war with the Casman Empire," Ontar replied, knowing that the guards from Estyork were out of earshot.

"Yes, of course. Nevertheless, Deerait isn't at war with you. We're hardly likely to be attacked today by the Adiorenji, the Dariondi or the Vilatmori, or at least I think so. Again, such a large armed force will be able to travel through the Wilderness without hindrance."

"You may be right. Still, we've decided not to take any unnecessary chances. Your nation is troubled by internal dissension among the peoples who compose it. Open warfare is not too far away. That you have to admit. Yesterday, when we rescued our friends we almost crossed swords with Reorgin, Kinerth and their house carls. Felgorian informed us that

66

Reorgin is quite capable of deliberately ambushing us on the journey to Hesion, if he can gather enough men. Consequently we intend that our usual discipline be maintained. No assault will be attempted against us unless we do know about it well in advance."

"I understand, and approve. Your warriors do seem to be highly trained and competent," Cottis remarked in the early morning light.

"They are. They have to be. Not only for their own safety, but also for their freedom," Ontar replied.

"How do they actually feel about being at war with the Casman Empire? To be truthful, the thought dismays me," the provincial governor commented seriously.

"They trust Quinton without reservation. Believe me, they are devoted to him. The steppe clans know the odds against them. They are also aware that their paramount ranxem — that's the title of a supreme steppe overlord — would lay down his life for them. They would do the same for him, unquestioningly. Let me show you. Adrigal!" the Ulgruffi mystic called to the Ker-Mantid, sitting astride his hecul, close to Quinton, Admaria, Felgorian, Perlow, Olluinan and his daughter.

"Yes, Great Ontar," the warrior acknowledged, turning his steed aside to trot over to the sage and his companion.

"Cottis, the district commander of Estyork and governor of the Deerait province of Sicruci, wishes to know what you think about being at war against the mighty Casman Empire. It's quite in order for you to tell him your personal thoughts."

"Sir, none of us wished war with the Empire, but imperial policy gave us no choice. We just wanted to live in freedom, but they wouldn't let us. If King Quinton goes to war with Casman or anyone, no matter how strong they may be then, for good or ill, to the end of all things I shall follow him. That is sufficient for me. He would never make an unjust war," Adrigal stated, simply and emphatically. "Nor would Great Ontar and our other commanders," he added with sincerity.

"Thank you," the sage said, and the devoted Ker-Mantid rode away to resume his former position as the column began to move off on the long journey to Hesion.

"I begin to comprehend," Cottis nodded, wonderingly.

"You couldn't know, but Adrigal originally came from a tribe which was one of our bitterest foes. They were punished severely by Quinton for their cruelty. They accepted their sentence, and fought valiantly in the battle against the Jaddair corps this past summer. Now they are devoted to their paramount ranxem. Adrigal and his fellow tribesman, Onlestic, attained their positions in the guard by performing an act of supreme bravery during a night assault on the Casman encampment.

"Perlow, the small man with the light skin, fought in the same action. He is Quinton's personal bodyguard. I can sense your surprise. He saved Quinton's life in the battle and is one of the finest swordsmen I have ever seen. He has the privilege of calling all his leaders by their personal names," Ontar declared.

The rising sun brought warmth to the cavalcade riding along the broad trail which ran from Estyork to Troldaart, the capital of Chellene province, two hundred and thirty five miles to the east, almost half the distance to Hesion. About a mile on their right the River Avidnive flowed on its long journey to the sea. Although several barges were visible to people on the banks, sailing downstream with produce from the market on the previous day, the vessels remained hidden from the view of the party because of the gentle folds in the land.

On either side of the highway were orchards and fields, the latter of which had just been planted with winter maize and vegetables. This beautifully tended agricultural area ended approximately eight miles from Estyork. It degenerated into the region known as the Wilderness which stretched for many leagues. Its woods, scrublands and hills had once been the home for large marauding bands of brigands. In bygone years the bandits had often assailed the traffic on the River Avidnive, almost causing trade between the hinterland and the coast to cease.

A few years after Cottis had been appointed provincial governor, he had boldly launched several campaigns against the cut-throats, which had achieved major successes. It had also been widely believed in Estyork that the Adiorenji from Relyan had had dealings with them, for the merchandise of the latter had never been seized, nor had any barges transporting their produce downstream ever been assailed.

The fine warm morning passed without incident. Quinton found himself riding beside Allecenia, who was delighted to have his company. Her father was fully occupied in discussing matters of occult ritual procedure with Ontar and Admaria, so she took the opportunity to learn more about the youth and his childhood. When she thought about this afterwards the veiled Lady felt pleasantly surprised, for she had intended to commence her tuition of the King of Rionder. All too soon for the couple, Hanshair galloped up to request permission to halt for the midday meal.

Quinton nodded his acquiescence, for the spot chosen had plenty of fresh water from a large stream for both riders and their steeds. The efficient Nai-Zind, who was closely watched by Cottis, organised his subordinates so that two minutes later their mounts had been hobbled and were being led to quench their thirst. Shortly afterwards the entire party was seated on the ground or on flat rocks, munching bread and meat. They drank water and finished their repast with fruit supplied from panniers brought from Estyork at Admaria's request, for she fully believed in the valuable nutrition obtained.

The column was preparing to set off when a scout came galloping from the direction of Estyork. He reined up fiercely, dismounted and ran over to Quinton to whom he bowed with respect, before speaking rapidly and succinctly. During his narration he occasionally indicated with his left hand towards the direction from which he had ridden. The King of Rionder listened attentively to every detail and then snapped out terse commands. Warriors leapt to do his bidding. His force was being organised for battle.

Quinton strode over to the provincial governor, who was standing with Felgorian, to explain. "Cottis, there is a large force of Adiorenji hastening this way. They're coming from the direction of Estyork. They avoided the town by keeping to the north. Colmar, the rider you saw arriving just now, has informed me that Reorgin, Kinerth and their companions joined up with a large party some miles west of Estyork.

"I didn't mention it earlier, but Colmar was present when we had the confrontation with the Adiorenji yesterday morning. He and three comrades were delegated by me to follow them when we left Estyork at dawn. I wanted to be certain they wouldn't attempt to follow us and cause trouble. They met this force of their countrymen. About eight hundred as far as can be estimated. Tell me, where would a force like that be going? It was travelling in a southerly arc. That should have kept it several miles west of Estyork."

"The Adiorenji often ride the old boundary marches nowadays. They used to do this long ago, before our nation united in face of the threat from the young Casman Empire. The custom was resurrected a few years ago to irritate us and to assert their independence. It's usually done four or five times annually. Reorgin and Kinerth are the sons of Koreorgin. He's the horbspan, the supreme ruler in Relyan. So they have the authority equivalent to their status. That would be sufficient for them to commandeer the march riders to pursue us," the Deerait explained.

"How would they know we're your escort? Probably the rumour of it would spread through the town," Felgorian answered his own question.

"I agree with that. You seem to be preparing for battle. Is that wise? Eight hundred, fully armed march riders are a considerable force," Cottis remarked thoughtfully to Quinton.

"We have no alternative. Sooner or later a major incident was bound to occur. The Relyanese are evidently intent on forcing a conflict on us. Reorgin and Kinerth will not desist, you know that. Perlow pointed this out yesterday. I do not wish to fight, but shall do so. From memory, there are no towns until we leave this Wilderness region. Only a few scattered dwellings. No forts or military installations. We can't return to Estyork because the Adiorenji are between us and the town. So, we shall be prepared for battle at any time. For the present, we shall proceed until we find a suitable position for defence. Remember, there are only eight hundred of them. We shall manage them very nicely," the paramount ranxem of the forces serving under the magnificent green and white banner of Rionder spoke with confidence, totally devoid of bombast.

For some reason the garrison commander of Estyork, the virtual ruler of the province of Sicruci, did not demur. The aura of leadership and obvious ability which radiated from Quinton caused Cottis to have faith in the youth, similar to that which the steppe tribes and the Jaddair corps possessed. The odds against them began to appear more of a nuisance than fearsome. The royal guard had already taken up battle positions with their monarch and his companions enfolded in a large square. They maintained this formation when the journey recommenced along the broad trail.

Ten minutes after they had set off Ontar signalled to Quinton to join Admaria, Olluinan, Allecenia and himself. The youth, who had been conversing with Hanshair, rode over to his foster father: the latter dismounted and asked the quartet to do likewise. The wizard commanded the warriors to proceed for three hundred yards, declaring that it would not be long before they could resume their square. Perlow, Hanshair, Adrigal and Onlestic were told to remain about twenty yards distant, with the mounts of the eminent mystic and his companions. Cottis was accompanied by his personal escort and Felgorian to where the main body was to wait.

The monarch wondered what Ontar was about to attempt, and deduced that the sage was going to survey the Adiorenji. He noticed that there was no sign of his foster father's crystal, but refrained from making any comment. The sage requested that they all join hands and form a circle.

"Excellent! You are holding Allecenia's right hand, Quinton. That is important for this purpose. Admaria, Olluinan, Allecenia and I have performed this ritual before. Allecenia will assist you. The aura and vibrations from the right side of her body are invaluable. Allecenia, My Dear, commence the exercise," Ontar spoke in his vibrant tones.

Quinton glanced at the slim cool hand of the hooded Lady with the black veil. He saw that her fingers were long and elegant with neatly trimmed nails. The colour of her skin was a soft golden brown, lighter than his own. For a moment she turned her head towards him and the youth received the impression that she was smiling at him in a gentle fashion. Olluinan's daughter then looked straight ahead and uttered a short word of four syllables in mellow tones. She next spoke a brief mantra, and told her companions to close their eyes, which they promptly did.

A few seconds later, the sounds of the birds and the gurgling of a nearby stream vanished. Quinton saw only the normal amount of light behind his eyelids, which he could have anticipated. Nevertheless, he concentrated on the exact centre of his forehead when Allecenia requested him to do so. Suddenly, to his astonishment, he saw a vivid clear scene in which he was fully able to discern the approaching Adiorenji force. He felt as if he were floating disembodied above and in front of the latter. From the invaluable esoteric training of his foster parents, he realised that he had performed an astral projection. His consciousness had left his physical form and was travelling in his psychic body.

71

He felt a sudden pressure on his left hand, and looked to where Allecenia hovered. Again the youth was amazed when Admaria, on his right, together with Ontar and Olluinan, disappeared, apparently leaving him and the veiled Lady alone in a warm mist. His perplexity at his strange surroundings, and the fact that he no longer seemed to have contact with his foster mother, was immediately dismissed from his mind for, in a brief instant, the hooded cloak and the facial covering vanished. He was taken aback to see a perfectly exquisite young woman smiling at him.

Thus it was that Quinton, King of Rionder and paramount ranxem of the Mescarg steppe peoples, first beheld the divine features of the Lady Allecenia, the virgin daughter and only child of the sage, Olluinan and his wife, Artzcellia. He gazed with an awe and wonderment, tinged with reverence, at the face of the most beautiful woman ever to be born into the world of Phentara. The Lady smiled at him through gentle gray blue eyes, the same shade as his own. Her countenance was wholly perfect with high symmetrical cheekbones. Her shimmering hair was dark brown and hung in waved tresses to her shoulders, while the texture of her skin was sheer. She wore a robe open at the throat, fashioned of a white smooth material which clung majestically to her very shapely and well proportioned figure.

"Perhaps now you can understand why I have to keep my face covered. I have always done so when I travel abroad in the Outer Lands, ever since I was a girl centuries ago. My parents, and those who belong to the Islands, have been the only people to see my face uncovered. My mother is back there on the Ordlansa archipelago and works, like we all do, for the benefit of our whole world. I too possess powers taught to me by Ontar and Admaria.

"They desired me to show you this esoteric mystery of collective astral projection. Only those far advanced along the Mystic Way can conduct it. However, they have to experience personal projection first. Admaria told me you'd successfully completed this some years ago but were kept within specific bounds by Ontar and herself. What happens in collective projection is that an advanced mystic controls the projection for all those in a closed circle and projects them all to the same place. I shall go into the necessary rituals and preparations for this occult operation in the near future."

72

"Thank you, My Lady," Quinton bowed graciously.

"Please call me Allecenia. Brave Perlow can do so too! This applies to my father also. We all owe him your life. Ontar and Admaria also wished me to show my face to you, the time to be at my personal discretion. You are to be the First Emperor of Phentara. From you will come the Empire among the innumerable stars in the future, if all comes to fruition.

"I took the opportunity just now of allowing you to see my face. It's the first chance I've had. You will be totally unaware of this but you are very dear to all of us on the Sacred Islands. Many desired to come with us to meet you in the flesh. They envied my father and me in a most friendly manner. Like my mother said, we may toil with our scientific and occult experiments to obtain knowledge in safety, but you are the Chosen One. You have to battle valiantly to overcome the massive problems of our anarchic planet. Ontar and Admaria spoke to me at the midday meal. That was when they said that if I wished to show you my face I was free to choose the time. I would never have done this without their permission. Both of them are wise beyond mortal comprehension," the Lady stated categorically.

"I sincerely thank you, Allecenia, for your honour to me. You are indeed so perfectly beautiful, divinely exquisite beyond the measure of mortal pulchritude. I shall ever treasure your gentless and courtesy in my heart. And for me, it shall be eternally in my living memory. You are like unto the goddesses of yore in the legends of Rionder. Yet, even these would bow their heads in very homage should you pass by, and the very angels of the Great Power would sing your praises," Quinton spoke with total sincerity for he knew that words could not describe her unique loveliness.

"I thank you, Kind Sir. Never have I had such a beautiful compliment," she smiled enchantingly, her face radiating a warm glow which appeared to emanate from and around her. "We must return to our physical bodies. These will be standing erect, precisely where we left them."

A brief moment later Quinton felt the ground beneath his feet. He opened his eyes at the bidding of the Lady. Allecenia released his hand, but not before she had given it a gentle squeeze. Ontar, Admaria and Olluinan, with wisdom of the interlude, talked in Ulgruffi with the couple. They discussed the Adiorenji, while they walked over to their heculs. The youth shook his resisting mind away from the wondrous vision he had seen and joined in the conversation.

The quintet concurred that a suitable position would have to be found to prevent unnecessary casualties being suffered by their own forces. There was no doubt that the Relyanese commanded by Reorgin and Kinerth meant to assail them, even though they were accompanied by Cottis. Such a heinous intention represented a dramatic increase in the hostile attitude of the three tribes towards the Deeraits themselves, and an abrupt violation of the uneasy peace extant in the country. Open civil warfare could not now be far behind. However, as Quinton remarked, such an eventuality might prove to be advantageous in their long campaign against the Casman Empire. Divide and conquer was an adage well known to Ontar and his foster son from their studies of the history of their planet during the long winters on the undulating Mescarg steppes.

The two Ulgruffi allowed Olluinan and Allecenia to ride ahead and reach the square of guards in order that they could have a private conversation with Quinton. The youth sat astride his fine hecul, his linz and that of Felgorian being led by mounted guards. He looked at Admaria and Ontar, whom he loved and who were devoted to him. Quinton was not really surprised when the sage spoke to him about what he had witnessed.

"You saw Allecenia when we were in our psychic bodies observing the Adiorenji. She chose to do so freely. I am content she has done so. In time you will learn how to manage and control a collective astral projection. You now understand why Allecenia has to keep her face covered. Her beauty is divine. If Reorgin or Kinerth had managed to tear off her veil there might have been a terrible fight. Each would have wanted her for himself. They are base, with many incarnations ahead to improve their soul personalities."

"Quinton, you are very privileged to have seen her face. No outworlder has ever done so before. You are the first. The majority of the adult members of the Order are married. They have all been tried and tested. They are able to perceive the aura and inner soul in an individual. Thus they can ignore the physical attributes although, naturally, these do play a not unimportant part. It is a great privilege for you to have seen her. She has, of course, realised that you have the sense and

74

innate honour not to act as those of a base nature might. I am really proud. I know Ontar is too," Admaria said with a smile on her beautiful face.

"I know you both are. She is unblemished. No facial lines. She said she was centuries old," Quinton commented in wonder.

"She is. Remember, Admaria and I are thousands of years old, and will live as long as you. We are the last of the Ulgruffi, formerly the longest lived dwellers on Phentara. Olluinan and his wife, Artzcellia, like our sages, were selected by Admaria and myself to assist us on the Ordlansa archipelago. Our choices came from all over the world. Because of the knowledge they and we possessed we are able to increase a person's lifespan considerably although death, the great mystery to those outside our Order, does occur. This extension of mortality is only done when the Hidden Servants give their approval.

"As a matter of interest, Admaria and I still have one more important initiation to face. When, we don't know. Anyway, those of the Order who reach perfection will continue their evolution on the Higher Planes. The remainder will be reincarnated on the physical plane in due course of time so that they can complete the development of their soul personalities.

"Nevertheless our vast store of knowledge will be given judiciously to you and your descendants. No, don't look surprised! You will have heirs to govern your Empire, and to keep your subjects under the aegis of a benign dynamic rule. Especially the fierce Zancericts on the continent of Abdur-Timil. Marriage will come to you one day, but not for years yet. This we do know, but not precisely when. We don't know to whom, for we have never once received a single clue to the identity of your bride," Ontar averred.

"Perhaps that's as it should be. I did suppose I would have a wife and children, like the Polingsi, or like Gordan and Sheralex with our two godchildren. I must confess I've often thought Sheralex to be the prettiest woman I've ever seen, except for you, Admaria. Now, I've seen Allecenia," Quinton mused.

"We, too, have often commented that Gordan's wife is the most beautiful young woman we've ever seen. The beauty of Allecenia is divine. The Hidden Servants concur with that. We have never attempted to compare anything to it. It is beyond comparison. Anyone we think of as handsome or beautiful we judge by the standards of the outer world, not our home on the Sacred Islands. There are many very beautiful women in the Ordlansa archipelago, such as Allecenia's mother, Artzcellia. But no one approaches Allecenia's beauty," the sage declared categorically.

"As Ontar has just affirmed, Allecenia is beautiful beyond comparison. She has shown herself to you unselfishly and she is very modest. It will give you a divine memory upon which to dream when the road ahead is harsh. Such may occur if we and your friends are separated from you. Allecenia is very wise, which must also be remembered. Ontar and I are her godparents," Admaria said with much affection.

"Then I am doubly honoured, for she is worthy of you," Quinton acknowledged, looking at his handsome guardians.

"Her revelation was private, for you alone. Otherwise she would have included us in it. That is very remarkable in itself. Let's attend to the dangers of the present. This unexpected threat from the Adiorenji may prove to our advantage. It may indeed augur a means of advancing our eventual attainment of the Deerait nation, as our allies and as your subjects," Ontar declared thoughtfully.

"It may prove to be so. Let's therefore concentrate on finding a suitable place where we can defend ourselves. They must make the first hostile move. We cannot, and must not, let ourselves be accused of being the aggressors," Quinton stated, focusing his mind on the urgent situation.

"While you were alone with Allecenia, I projected further in my psychic body. There is such a place. We should arrive there just before sunset. It's unlikely our pursuers will attack today, or even be aware of our position before dawn. It's not the Deerait custom throughout the nation to attempt battle after a long journey if at all avoidable. Mind you, they did break the custom very reluctantly during the Casman Imperial War. This will give us an excellent opportunity to impress Cottis most forcibly," Ontar smiled grimly, undeterred by the odds against them which caused no concern or carelessness in the elite guard of the King of Rionder and paramount ranxem of the Mescarg steppes.

Once they had rejoined the column Quinton commanded that their rate of progress be increased. Cottis did not question the orders given by the youthful monarch, which puzzled Unyamed in charge of his personal escort; yet even the latter were unconsciously beginning to accept the leadership of the handsome capable Riondese. Ontar stopped occasionally to scry behind while the scouts began to use the signalling system devised by their ruler and his Inner Council. The boss on the hide shield of each warrior was highly polished, so that on bright days it could be used to reflect the rays of the sun and flash messages; however, when necessary, standing orders permitted every soldier the authority to conceal its brilliance, thus avoiding detection.

The Adiorenji neglected to send any scouts forward, nor did they have the least indication that their quarry was not only aware of their whereabouts but also surveying them closely. The Mescarg steppe tribesmen utilised every clump of bushes and bosque, every fold in the land and every conceivable hiding place so that their pursuers were completely surrounded by vigilant watchers. The training on the vast undulating grasslands and in the forests of the Rionder Valley proved invaluable, for the observers remained undetected throughout the afternoon. When the sun sank to rest on the Chofanrit Ocean the hostile force of march riders halted to pitch camp. They believed that they would surely catch up with the strangers in the morning and punish them harshly for the slight caused to Reorgin and Kinerth. The sturdy Relyanese remained oblivious of the fact that their quarry was already in position on a high hill about a mile from their own tents.

With the fall of evening a cold wind swept down from the north, heralding rain. Nevertheless before dusk Quinton and Ontar began to lay out their defences. Each soldier received his orders, the Deeraits also being pressed into service. Watches were set; sentries patrolled ceaselessly, keeping their eyes on the glow of the fires from the Adiorenji encampment.

The weather proved extremely changeable during the night; its vagaries resulted in the Deeraits being afraid of the anger of their gods. Superstition was a valid factor in the lives of the races on Rontmethar and throughout the other continents of Phentara. Every inexplicable factor caused the peoples to worry about which deity they had offended and how he or she could be propitiated. The Mescarg and Phlorcartid steppe tribes had many gods. Even with the coming of Quinton as their paramount ranxem their belief in wraiths, ghosts and evil spirits had not waned; notwithstanding, the knowledge that Ontar and Admaria were their principal wizards had relaxed their general dread because of their absolute conviction that the two Ulgruffi were far more powerful than the beings in whom they believed.

Unfortunately the four tribes which composed the Deerait nation had no such patronage. The intermittent nocturnal showers, combined with savage gusts of wind, caused the provincial governor of Sicruci and his personal detachment to doubt the advisability of remaining to face the Adiorenji. They thought that the hostility of the elements represented bad omens, indicative of certain defeat on the morrow. Consequently Cottis proposed to Quinton and Ontar that they attempt to outdistance their pursuers by riding off before dawn.

"I disagree! We have to face them! If we don't and escape, they may sack some small cottage or settlement. Innocent people could suffer. We can and must stop Reorgin and Kinerth here!" the King of Rionder declared in resolute tones.

"These changes in the weather show that the gods of the air and the spirits of the rain clouds are against us!" The Estyork commander spoke with concern.

"Are not all your deities similar throughout your entire nation?" Quinton asked shrewdly.

"Yes, that is so," Cottis affirmed, surprised that the youth should even be aware of Deerait pantheism.

"Then, if your gods and spirits are similar, can you truthfully say whether they are angry with us or with the Adiorenji around the campfires over yonder? Is not rain falling and wind blowing over there too?"

"That is a fact. I see. We shall follow your strategy. I'll explain things to my personal guard," the governor nodded pensively before striding off towards his worried soldiery.

"Well done, young man. That should keep them quiet until the morning at least," Ontar remarked.

"I hope so. By then we shall be committed to battle, provided the Adiorenji decide to fight. Let's go and check the state of our defences once more. Selix is rising." Quinton indicated where the Panther had just emerged serenely over the distant dark mass which was the edge of the Riondese forests.

Under the bright glow of the second moon of Phentara which shone, albeit intermittently, through the scudding wind-driven clouds, the youth and his foster father strode around the area selected for the approaching conflict. When they had completed their inspection Quinton and Ontar returned to where Admaria awaited them in the shamianah. After greeting her loved ones she advised them that her scrying had revealed no hostile movement in the Adiorenji encampment. The extremely beautiful dark haired woman knew that on the morrow her foster son would probably have to fight a battle, more a skirmish in comparison to the momentous engagement on the Mescarg steppes that summer; yet its outcome was just as vital for it would demonstrate to the Deerait governor of Sicruci the efficiency of the military forces under the command of the King of Rionder.

"Our defences are completely ready. Hanshair and his subordinates have worked hard and know our strategy. The contours of this hill won't impede our movements. We'll have to ensure none of our animals is hit by stray arrows. They're far better mounts than the average Deerait steed. We'll require every single one of them for our journey to Hesion, especially if we have to return quickly to Estyork. Besides, we'll have to use them in the charge tomorrow," Quinton said reflectively from where he sat beside the fire in his large tent which had been pitched on a flat area on the slope behind the hill.

"Yes," Ontar concurred, adding, "and we have a plentiful supply of arrows."

"Our warriors will fight valiantly. The odds are against us numerically, but we'll win," Admaria stated with assurance.

"I want you, Allecenia and Olluinan to be safe," Quinton remarked with concern.

"I can fight as well as Ontar. Don't worry, we women will help with the wounded," his foster mother smiled, touched by his affection for her.

"Thank you." Quinton looked tenderly at her.

"You know, with this battle imminent, I'd meant to mention this before you both left to make the inspection. We've often talked about armoured protection for our troops. Now we're in Deerait on the way to Hesion. South of the capital are iron ore workings and quarries. The Deeraits manufacture agricultural implements and other metallic artifacts. The Hesion garrison has armour and helmets. So does the Estyork garrison," Admaria pointed out.

"We'll certainly require protection when we attempt to take Choolsay. The imperial troops there wear armour. Jaddair and some of the outlying provinces don't have any. Heolanwertin commandeered the lot. The Emperor and his predecessors for the last millenium have tended to neglect these regions. Probably afraid of rebellion. There was a period about eleven hundred years ago when several major revolts occurred. They were organised by relatives of the imperial family," Ontar said.

"I was relieved Terfieldst's corps didn't have armour. Gordan said our losses could have been higher, and our victory more difficult in proportion."

"He was right, Quinton. On the Islands we do experiment with many things. We have gained a considerable knowledge of metals. Also we have Olluinan here. He and I will draw up the necessary plans with explanatory diagrams. We'll show the Deeraits how to construct blast furnaces and increase production. That's provided they become our allies. Allecenia will tell you about them. We'll keep such information secret until we learn the thoughts of the High Council in Hesion as regards our army and our war with Casman," Ontar declared very pensively.

"You see, Quinton, our researches will prove useful. They are meant to be used, even for warlike purposes. Regrettably, war is with us, and it will be thus for a long time. Inventions and discoveries should be for days of peace but, until men gain sufficient wisdom, they will be misused. You'd better have some rest. Tomorrow has to pass before further consideration can be given to anything," Admaria nodded.

The youth retired to his section of the tent. After he had knelt to give thanks to the Great Power for His daily gifts and had offered himself in humble service during his hours of sleep, Quinton undressed and climbed into his cot. The warm furs felt cosy and he snuggled down, while his foster parents discussed the revelation which Allecenia had made to their charge. The two Ulgruffi expressed considerable surprise that Olluinan's daughter had done so at the first opportunity.

"We only suggested it to her at the midday halt. Then she does it. That's not like her at all," Ontar shook his head.

"Hopref has been after her for a long while, and a few more of our young men on the Islands. She treats them with firmness and kindness without hurting their feelings. Yet, along comes Quinton, and she reacts differently," his spouse smiled.

"Even Olluinan was surprised. You could tell the way he mentioned it privately to us just before our evening meal. He couldn't understand it. He said it was so unlike her."

"If we hadn't known her so long, I would think that she had fallen for Quinton. I wonder whether she has."

"The thought had crossed my mind too," her spouse concurred, adding, "but she's never fallen in all the years."

"We always said it would have to be someone very special. Quinton certainly is that. Ah, we'll just have to wait and see. They do like one another's company. Allecenia is very sensible, and would never take advantage. Olluinan was only too happy to have Perlow address him and his daughter intimately. He knows the debt we all owe him."

"He was kind. Just think. One day you and I will be grandparents. I do like the thought," Ontar smiled.

"So do I," nodded his wife. "It seems just like yesterday that Quinton was a babe in arms. Cryenig and Zolamina are now walking and chattering in childish fashion. Children are only young once. Parents should make the most of them. Oh, spoil them a little, but teach them the true value of things. Let's go to bed."

"Yes, let's. Tomorrow will be a hectic day. Another stage in the advancement of Quinton's world Empire," the sage said.

Chapter Five
Friends left behind in the Forest

The descent of mellow evening on the day when Quinton, Admaria and Ontar had set off to meet Felgorian was welcomed by Gordan, on whose massive shoulders the total awesome responsibility for command of the mighty army had fallen. Three of the Polingsi, Turubin, Casterandir and Shlasmil, were fully occupied in training the Jaddair corps in cavalry manoeuvres and tactics. Although most of the Casman infantry had ridden heculs for the first time on the long journey from the Mescarg steppes to the haven of the Riondese forests, they still had to be shown how to care for their ferocious steeds. The imperial soldiery evinced an eagerness to attain the high military standards of their new allies and willingly attempted anything demonstrated to them, no matter how tedious the task.

Gordan's burden of communication with the vast force was much alleviated by the invaluable assistance of the more advanced races in education. The Riondese, Nai-Zind and some of the others, like the Polingsi and Zugars, wrote instructions in the Common Speech, which were passed around the entire army to literate officers. Several chains of command had been created, each supplementing and complementing the others, so that military efficiency was maintained at all levels.

The ordinary private soldier was kept active, mentally and physically, and made to feel an essential part of the whole. His superiors always listened to any suggestions made and, if thought apposite, these were forwarded to the Inner Council for consideration. Additionally, selected teachers from the Riondese and the steppe clans assumed the task of teaching their Casman colleagues the basics of reading and writing in the Common Speech.

The supreme general and captain of the royal guard of Rionder missed those who had departed for Sicruci; this circumstance was fully realised by his beautiful Nai-Zind wife Sheralex, when he entered their spacious home shortly after dusk. She lifted Cryenig and Zolamina from where they were playing with toys under the watchful eye of their nurse and passed them to her husband. He seated himself beside the fire and looked up with a smile. With his offspring snuggling into his arms, Gordan began to tell them a story of the wicked steppe ratchans. The wolves had stolen a baby boy from its parents but the child was saved by the giant bison which carried him safely home.

When he had finished, the mightiest warrior on Phentara gazed down at his children and smiled. Both had fallen asleep and were beautiful in the flickering flames of the fire. A serving woman came in to lay the table while the nurse assisted Sheralex in putting the infants to bed. Gordan rose, stretched, and walked through to the basin of warm water in his bedroom. He bathed his hands and face before drying himself with a soft cloth. An intense feeling of loneliness came over him. Although he knew it to be essential, he hated being separated from Quinton, Ontar and Admaria. Their love and companionship meant a great deal to him.

Sheralex entered and spoke gently, "Husband, I know how you feel. You miss them. So do I, far more than I ever thought possible. Yet I know in my heart that they love us, especially you. Remember how Quinton called here last night and played with Zolamina and Cryenig?"

"Yes," Gordan smiled, "and Ontar, Admaria and Perlow came with him. Admaria, you, I and Perlow sat talking, while Ontar and Quinton played heculs and warriors with our two children. To think that the mightiest wizard on Phentara pretended to be a hecul and screeched like one while our King and paramount ranxem scampered on all fours with Zolamina on his back."

"Yes, and do you remember how we all laughed when Cryenig ruffled Ontar's hair until it was like a tangled maze? And the expression on Ontar's face when he looked round far too solemnly at his rider? And how Cryenig chuckled?"

"That was memorable. Then the four Polingsi walked in with their wives and Turubin looked at the proceedings and stated frankly, 'I don't know. I just don't know. If I were Heolanwertin I'd go and hide in a closet.'

"Then Casterandir said 'With a head of hair like that, you'd just need to stick Ontar out in front of the army and he'd cause all the enemy heculs to stampede. Mind you, ours would have done so already.' That's what life is all about. The poignant sadness of parting shows the joy in one's friends. I'm glad I feel sad. But I've got you and our two children and I do love you all. Especially you with your green eyes," Gordan said softly, taking his wife in his arms.

After they had kissed, Sheralex whispered, "I feel that our four Polingsi friends will call this evening."

"They're supposed to be miles away in the forests for the next few days. Mmmm. Knowing them, they'll ride over after completion of today's duties. Say, let's set the table for them!" Gordan exclaimed.

"I've already seen to it. You didn't notice the number of place settings. You do have a smart wife," Sheralex declared.

"I know. Sometimes she tends to get impertinent. Oh, there's someone at the door!"

The knocking was followed by the entry of Beltarik, the Polingsi caranxem, who apologised for his intrusion. The chieftain explained that he had been talking to Likans a short time before; the latter had been about to send a courier to Gordan with the news that the party on the journey to Estyork had camped for the night. The wizard also confirmed Felgorian was safe and that although there was some activity in the Ebrordin mountain region of Deerait no massed gatherings of the Adiorenji were being organised.

"I said I'd bring the message to you. It was on my way in any event. I'm returning a courtesy call on Rahamb and his family. My own family's just outside. Any messages for your father-in-law?" Beltarik asked.

"Just tell him we're all fine. We'll come out and greet your family," Gordan responded courteously.

The Riondese and his beautiful dark skinned wife spent a few minutes chatting with the family of the Polingsi caranxem before the latter departed. Gordan and Sheralex watched them disappear in the gloom of evening and were just about to cross the threshold when the sound of heavy hooves caused them to turn round. The four guards stationed in front of their dwelling were immediately on the alert but relaxed when they recognised the tall figure of Turubin riding towards them on his linz. The Polingsi hailed them before dismounting and fastening the reins of his mighty steed to a tree a few yards from the cabin.

"Thought I'd come and visit for a while," Turubin commented.

"Sheralex thought you would. You miss them too," Gordan

remarked, leading his friend inside.

"I certainly do. It feels as if your heart's been torn out. I know, and you know, that we'll get over it. Oh, Casterandir and Shlasmil should be here in about ten minutes. They've gone to see Elmendor about some routine matters. By the way, I'll bring the construction regiment to your headquarters tomorrow about mid-morning," the Polingsi remarked, glancing around the room.

"Very good. Quinton's suggestion that we check the state of the main trail from Rionder to Estyork is an excellent one. Once it's cleared all the way to the edge of the forest in Deerait we'll be able to send troops south very quickly."

"Mmmm. Estyork is the fulcrum in Sicruci and the northwest. The first attack in this region has to be concentrated there. If we have to face the Adiorenji, Vilatmori and Dariondi at Estyork, a quick route south is essential," Turubin nodded.

"Whatever happens, it's vital that we control Estyork," Gordan affirmed.

"Say, isn't Sleworivan here? I thought he would be."

"Did you expect him to arrive before you?" Sheralex asked.

"Yes. I was busy at my command headquarters when he passed by. Naturally I assumed he'd ride straight here. We'd already told our wives not to expect us. We meant to surprise you, even if you did guess we'd come to visit," Turubin smiled.

"He's probably gone to see Mirchanrope and Forsever about scouts for the shock troop regiments. Rahamb's certainly licked them into shape. Souriin's performing well as his junior officer. Sleworivan did mention he'd require six dozen more scouts for the shock troop courses in view of the numbers now attempting it. He certainly likes supervising Rahamb and his command. One shock regiment is off on special manoeuvres in two days. By the way, where's your escort?" Gordan asked, as they sat in comfortable chairs before the fire.

"The four of us decided to give them the night off. We felt this was a special occasion when we should come alone," his friend answered.

"I understand," Gordan nodded contentedly.

Within a few minutes the two comrades were joined by Shlasmil and Casterandir. Almost immediately, Sleworivan rode up. When the visitors had finished their toilet, the party took their seats at the table. After Gordan had given thanks to the Great Power for His Beneficence, Sheralex called to the attendants who served a delicious meal. Large platters of braised haunch of venison and cooked vegetables were followed by cheese and bread. Fruit was also available in a large bowl and there were jugs of rotar milk to which the warriors helped themselves.

None of the servants thought it odd that such important commanders did not partake of ale or wine for it was known abroad that they followed the teachings of Ontar and Admaria. Whilst on the Mescarg steppes, the quintet had been admitted into the Mysteries of the Sacred Order of Light. They had been exceptionally well educated by the two Ulgruffi and possessed a good basic comprehension of mystical and magical operations. Since both the latter were more effective when alcoholic beverages were not imbibed, the five men now totally abstained from such drinks.

Such a circumstance had not gone unremarked throughout the army and a considerable number of the steppe tribesmen followed their example. This might have provoked snide comments from their fellows, but Quinton did not partake of alcohol either; consequently the preference of those who did not indulge was fully respected.

When they had finished dining, the servant women cleared the table, leaving Gordan, Sheralex and their companions alone. They did not talk much at first, obtaining comfort from the proximity of close friends. Their thoughts drifted down the years to the steppes and before that to the sack of Rionder, fifty miles to the east of where they were seated. Much had happened since then and future events would bring them into the centre of political and economic affairs of their entire continent. Quinton was destined to become the Emperor of Phentara, and they were determined to serve him to the utmost in his endeavours.

Gordan, who sat holding his wife's hand, smiled and remarked,"I was just thinking about how much Admaria accomplished here in the forests with her willing helpers. Everything was ready for nearly quarter of a million soldiers. The army arrived here from the steppes utterly exhausted. Yet comfortable quarters were awaiting them. The workers here really did excellently."

"Everyone certainly merited the praise Quinton gave them. All those who left the steppes in the spring. Especially the Phlorcartids who herded the heculs and rotars we brought with us. Others started to repair the wagons while we rested, except for Ontar and Quinton," Turubin nodded.

"Those two were up and about early the first morning speculating on the situation in Deerait. Never mind learning the disposition of the army in the forests. That's the advantage of advanced mysticism for you," Casterandir smiled.

"It took less than a week before word got about that the troops wanted to start work again. I thought it amazing. I reckoned it would be at least a month before they became bored. So did you, Shlasmil," Sleworivan commented.

"Yes, that was about the time Rahamb first suggested the shock troops. Quinton told everyone to be patient for another week. He organised entertainments. The Casmans did enjoy the Riondese music and steppe dancing. Their own is quite good. Say, Gordan, I meant to ask you: the third week, when the training started, you, Ontar, Admaria, Sheralex, Quinton, Perlow and some guards were absent for nearly two days. I believe you went to Rionder. That's the time I was touring all the commands," Shlasmil said, looking at his friend.

"Yes, we did. Ontar thought Quinton would like to see the city of his forefathers. We travelled from here and took the forest paths until we struck the main trail down to Rionder. Ontar did make a slight detour for old times' sake. He visited his old home. You know, where I took Quinton after Rionder fell. It was just the same. Empty, of course, but not overgrown or dusty. Simply clean and tidy like the morning we left it. Then we continued on to Rionder.

"We reached there in the late afternoon. Enmarkan's guards were visible on the battlements but the gates were tightly shut. I suggested we ride round the city staying within the trees at the forest's edge. This took us until sunset when we rode back in this direction, making camp about four miles from Rionder."

"How did Quinton take it?" Turubin asked. "For that matter, how did you?"

"I think both of us were filled with sorrow for the events of the past. Quinton, naturally, because he had lost his parents. I, because I could recall them in all their beauty and glory in the last days of Rionder. I told him how his parents embraced me and how his mother kissed me on the cheek on the day they both perished. And how beautiful they were. And how I had to force myself not to weep then.

"We were really saddened. But suddenly both of us

experienced an ineffable soothing influence as if Quintar and Vialo were aware of us and were with us and loved us. Ontar and Admaria had the same sensation. Admaria said that their souls had left the Higher Planes to be with us. She said she knew this intuitively. Quinton did most definitely. Shows you how advanced he is in psychic matters. Even Sheralex and Perlow felt something too."

"I did. There was a wondrous feeling of love and happiness," his wife concurred.

"I'm pleased. Really pleased that King Quintar and Queen Vialo contacted you in some manner. They were beautiful people, always kind and courteous to the Polingsi," Shlasmil smiled reflectively.

Some time afterwards, the visitors rose and took their leave, feeling more contented. Gordan and Sheralex watched their friends ride off through the trees in the crisp night air. Overhead the stars spangled the heavens in which the Enchantress was now sinking to the west. The couple entered their home, closed the door and smiled at one another.

"I feel much better. I'm glad they came," Gordan said, as they undressed and climbed into bed.

"I know you are. I also know that's exactly how you felt when the children and I left you in the spring to cross the steppes and come to Rionder," Sheralex whispered.

"I did," her husband admitted freely while she lay in the crook of his right arm.

"So did I. We'll always feel this way. The hurt will come time and time again down the years. It won't stop until the last battle in the last war. Then, if the Great Power permits, He who is all the gods of my people in One, as Admaria has taught me, we can spend our lives together in peace and harmony."

"Yes, we shall, when all is over," Gordan murmured.

"And that will be centuries ahead. Quinton is no ordinary person. I believe in my heart that he was born to rule our world," Sheralex stated solemnly. "And it is right that he should be the one to do so. Within him is the majesty of Ontar and Admaria."

Gordan was absolutely astounded. His King's destiny was known only to a select few beyond the realm of the Sacred Islands in the Chofanrit Ocean, and they were sworn to secrecy. He was amazed his wife had the prescience to know that it could come to fruition. Although the mighty warrior did not pass any comment, he resolved to mention what she had said to the two Ulgruffi. Sheralex snuggled up to her husband and they both fell asleep.

The next morning, just after sunrise, Gordan left for the supreme command headquarters. His escort of twenty soldiers followed behind their chief general as he trotted his linz down the forest trail. His household guards were warriors in their prime, chosen from a broad cross-section of the Mescarg steppe tribes. Gordan knew that at this very moment Quinton and his party would be heading southwards and also that the four Polingsi would be attending to their duties. Throughout the vast Riondese forest the army was astir, ready and eager to meet the challenge of the new day.

When he reached his destination, Gordan dismounted, unsaddled his mighty steed and turned it out to pasture. He entered the large wooden hut specially constructed for the administrative headquarters of Quinton's forces. Inside were several clerks, copying out the duty rosters on parchment, which was made by the Riondese people, to be transmitted to the various regiments for the following day. These would be handed over to Elcharn the Nai-Zind and Telriche the Zugar, both sub-chiefs of their respective tribes, for checking before the general signed them.

Once this had been accomplished swift couriers would speed the long miles to the central command posts. Casterandir, Shlasmil, Turubin and Sleworivan would already be dealing with the orders received the previous day. Their junior officers would follow the written instructions without hesitation. A complete chain ran from the highest to the lowest.

Any break, such as might occur in battle, would not prove disastrous for every single officer was taught to think for himself and to react promptly and effectively no matter what the circumstances. The lower ranks of the steppe army were also capable of functioning with the same precision, should their superiors be killed, incapacitated or absent for any reason. Each soldier had physical and martial exercises to perform and, besides receiving an invaluable education, was also versed in the science of strategics.

The supreme general settled down and began to deal rapidly and efficiently with his workload. He had just completed everything outstanding when Elcharn entered to say, "Excuse me, Sir, a courier has just arrived from Commander Turubin. The construction regiment should be here within five minutes."

"Thanks. I'll be straight there. Have a hecul saddled for me. Also send a clerk in with the written orders for the construction regiment," Gordan acknowledged.

"Yes, Sir," the Nai-Zind sub-caranxem said respectfully before leaving to perform the requests of his superior.

Turubin rode up with his personal guard at the head of the large force which was under the command of a very capable Zalsremin, Jamborajd. Gordan mounted a fine racing hecul; his headquarters' staff and duty personnel were already drawn up in perfect formation. When the regiment halted it was inspected by the highest ranking officer in the forces of the King of Rionder and paramount ranxem of the Mescarg steppes. The chief general expressed his pleasure, for the turnout was perfect, the normal standard for his army.

When he returned to the front of the long column he addressed the officer in charge, saying "Jamborajd, you've already been advised by Turubin what is required. Here are your written orders. They should cover every foreseeable contingency. Remember, keep away from the city of Rionder. No contact with the Broechnaar garrison is to occur. It's unlikely that any of Enmarkan's troops will travel too far from the town for any reason. But take no chances. Maintain regular courier reports."

"Yes, Sir," the Zalsremin nodded seriously. "We'll do our best. We're expecting four Riondese scouts to accompany us."

"They'll meet you about two miles along the trail. Men, what you are going to do will be arduous. Nevertheless, it is absolutely essential. King Quinton requests that it be done. He believes it will prove to be of the greatest importance in the future."

"Then, Sir, if our King and paramount ranxem requests it, it will be done," Jamborajd stated emphatically.

"Thank you. I assure you, your task is vital to our ultimate victory. It will save valuable time. If war breaks out in Deerait, Estyork will be the first place to be attacked in the northwest. We have plans to prevent it falling into hostile hands. The Adiorenji, Vilatmori or Dariondi must not be allowed to capture it. Battles, fighting, victories are one thing. But behind success there is always hard work and preparation. May the

Great Power go with you."

"And with you, Sir," the Zalsremin courteously bowed from the saddle before turning and riding off at the head of the long column.

Turubin sat astride his linz beside Gordan, watching the steppe warriors from different tribes going past. At the rear of the regiment came large wains drawn by powerful rotars while a screen of scouts surveyed the forest. Ahead of them the four Riondese waited to guide the construction soldiery safely around the city of Rionder and down to where the old trail from the Valley to Deerait ran. When the last wagon and trooper had departed the two comrades dismounted and men from their escorts ran over to hold the reins of their steeds.

Turubin's linz suddenly became agitated and reared its head back. It was about to attack when its master uttered a low trilling sound. The huge charger immediately became docile and the warrior holding the long reins relaxed. Turubin smiled at his Riondese friend, for the four Polingsi, Quinton and the latter had been taught this method of controlling the giant shaggy beasts by Ontar.

"Handy thing that," Gordan commented in Ulgruffi.

"Yes. Magic and mysticism are certainly hard work but the results can be efficacious," his comrade declared thoughtfully. Turubin reflected momentarily on the occult and esoteric knowledge which the two Ulgruffi had demonstrated to him and his comrades on the distant Mescarg steppes and during their sojourn in the forest.

"We'll start with the reports on the shock troops. Once they're done we'll move on to the other forces doing the shock programmes," the supreme general said, leading the way to his office.

"What about the comprehensive progress survey and the weekly reports from the commanders?" the Polingsi enquired.

"You can glance through them later. I've been through them already to save time."

The two friends settled down in chairs at Gordan's desk, selected writing materials to make any relevant observations, and began to read the most recent details concerning the two five thousand shock troop regiments. Quinton and Ontar, together with the other members of the Inner Council, had decided to form this special force. The revolutionary idea had originated from Rahamb about a week after the army had successfully reached the Rionder Valley. In consequence, the Nai-Zind caranxem had been appointed temporary commander of the new formations and had worked closely with the Inner Council in their inception. The soldiers chosen were all single men; they were to be trained as an elite prepared for instant action at any time.

Although all the steppe troops were highly experienced in the art of warfare, the shock regiments had to surpass the normal military standard required for the army. Tests were imposed, which at first only the single men were permitted to attempt; again, if a warrior were the only child in a family, his admittance was barred. Quinton had determined that no family would become extinct during any of his campaigns if such a tragedy could at all be avoided. Once Gordan and the four Polingsi, together with Quinton, Ontar and Admaria, were satisfied with the results of the selection made by their subordinates, they gave Rahamb the authority to form the new regiments.

Shortly afterwards, Hanshair proposed that not only should future members of the royal guard be chosen from the ranks of the new force, but also that the present members should pass the shock regimental tests. The Nai-Zind explained that it was only fitting for the paramount ranxem to be protected by the finest warriors. Admaria concurred with this wholeheartedly and the entire guard — both the royal, Gordan's and the four Polingsi household — spent weeks in the most intensive training.

A totally unexpected consequence occurred when the four Polingsi were approached by deputations of officers from their commands, the subordinates having been requested to do so by the lower ranks. It became evident that although the two shock regiments were accepted without rancour as an elite, those not eligible to join, whether through having been failed by the selection boards or disqualified because of family reasons, wished to have the opportunity of attempting the new courses. Similarly the Casmans, who had commenced the basic training of the steppe soldiers, also requested that they too be considered when they were suitable for screening.

The Inner Council discussed this turn of events in private and decided to inform the entire armed forces of their conclusions. They called a special meeting, requesting the presence of Rahamb, Souriin and many officers from the steppe army which included members of the Riondese and Polingsi peoples; Terfieldst, Ceanill and their general staff, with several subordinates, represented the Jaddair imperial corps.

One bright afternoon everyone gathered in a large clearing at the apppointed hour. Benches had been laid out to accommodate those attending while the Inner Council was to be seated at a table on a small rise, overlooking the assembly. The day was warm; even though it was winter, leaves still adorned the trees with the wondrous myriad tints of mellow autumn; small and large birds chirped and flew to and fro, unconcerned by the human activity beneath them.

When Quinton and his friends arrived the soldiers ceased talking and stood at attention until their monarch and the rest of the Inner Council had seated themselves. There was a most respectful silence before the King of Rionder arose to address the assembly. He told his audience that he and his companions had been heartened by the loyalty of his followers and by the multitude of requests for permission to try for the shock regimental standard. Their youthful overlord averred that he especially was very touched by their devotion to him and by their sincere desire to increase their already formidable military capabilities.

"I personally wanted you all to be here. Your presence is very much appreciated by the Inner Council, as we have come to be known. Many of you have ridden long distances from your camps and homes to be here this afternoon. I felt I had to thank you sincerely for your requests and ask you to express my gratitude to your troops. Such interest in what was only a proposition by Rahamb not so long ago emphasises that we are all one in our endeavours.

"Without further preamble I'm going to tell you what the Inner Council has decided. This is open to discussion. However I must stress that entrance to the shock regiments themselves is still restricted to single men who pass the selection tests, both written, oral and physical. Any who fail will be allowed to apply again after an appropriate interval.

"One point from which the Inner Council will not deviate is to insist that admission to these shock regiments is never, and I repeat never, to be granted to the only child of a family, lest that family perish. Having said that, I have to contradict that statement slightly. An only child will have to serve in the other regiments for the duration of the Casman campaigns,

93

since every one will be needed against the imperial corps. Although none of you may have realised it this condition already applies in general to the members of the guards. The majority are single men with brothers and sisters. Valour is important but the family is the foundation of civilisation.

"My next point is to confirm that when our Casman allies complete their training satisfactorily they too shall be eligible under the same conditions to apply for entry to the shock regiments. By the way, our eventual intention is to have at least eight of these regiments. For the present we shall only form two. The formation of the rest will depend on what we learn from their performance during training.

"The Inner Council has further decided that all single men, who are barred from admission to the new regiments, and all married men will be allowed to experience the training of the shock regiments. We in the Inner Council should have guessed the reactions of our troops.

"The royal and household guards and the scouts are also included. The physical training courses are exceptionally arduous and will take several weeks. We have prepared timetables for all regiments other than Casman or those employed in training the Casmans, to commence within a few days. The shock regiments have already been training for three weeks.

"Some of you will have remarked the absence of the royal and household bodyguards and their temporary replacement by soldiers from Shlasmil's command. Well, they are training with the shock forces. Unfortunately for the guards, they have to complete the programme in a shorter time. They can blame Hanshair for that. It was his idea," Quinton explained, pausing with amusement when he saw the grins on the faces of his attentive audience.

"To continue. Souriin, whom some of you may know as one of Rahamb's subordinate officers, is a member of the Nai-Zind, as well as the Hedunon tribe. He made a proposal, which we thought to be a most excellent one. This was that every regiment should have its own medical company, fully equipped and trained.

"Ontar, Uppetshar and our present medical staff will supervise the formation of this essential service. We have quite a number of warriors and Casmans who, although able to move around quite capably, are not up to the physical standard necessary for acceptance into the armed forces. They may have received wounds causing some incapacity or, because of an accident or deformity, were never thought of as being suitable for active service. If any of them wish to join the medical corps on a permanent basis, they are free to apply.

"Remember this. Every one of us lives with the dreadful thought of being wounded and not receiving prompt treatment. If a soldier knows that swift medical treatment by highly trained personnel will be available, then his battle morale will be high. I wish this to be known abroad: no matter how humbly anyone serves, no matter how menial his task, that his King is very grateful to him.

"In addition to the individual medical companies at regimental level, the existing overall one will continue to research and serve. It is our further intention to have the healers visit each regiment, so that every soldier will fully understand the elementary procedures of first aid. Classes will be instituted. Such knowledge will be invaluable both on a personal level and for assisting others if and when the medical orderlies are occupied elsewhere.

"The commissariat under Elmendor is being expanded to cope more efficiently with our immense logistics. They have received orders to issue every soldier with a basic medical pack. Also we must ensure that our forces are fed, and fed well. Good hot food regularly available also sustains morale. The Inner Council will be working diligently with Elmendor and his subordinates in preparation for the Deerait campaign and also for the assault on the Casman mainland. Accordingly we have been revising some of our contingency plans. These were formulated during the past winters on the Mescarg steppes. You will be given details in due course. They should cope with and cover most of the likely eventualities when we march south.

"You are all aware that we have to control Deerait before we can launch our campaign against the Casman mainland. An effective and efficient supply chain is essential. I have no wish to alienate the Casman peoples by plundering and seizing food and fodder unless absolutely vital. Deerait ships will land troops to seize a major Casman port. Once this is secured we shall have a base. Fleets will have to supply us initially with food and weapons until we can capture a Casman fortress arsenal.

"Now I'd like to clarify the idea behind the shock troop training programme. You may have heard various rumours that the shock troops are to be used only as infantry. This is only half the truth. They are definitely to be trained as infantry. The programme is very intense. Nevertheless they will return to mounted duties when their courses are finished. The Inner Council has decided that the shock regiments are to function effectively both as cavalry and infantry, depending on circumstances.

"The Jaddair corps was not permitted to use its cavalry force efficiently in the major battle this summer. Terfieldst will confirm this. On the other hand the steppe army did perform like infantry with a small proportion of cavalry in support. Cavalry tactics are very important to each Casman provincial army corps. The odds facing us are very high even with a Deerait alliance. The Empire can field another one million, three hundred and fifty thousand troops.

"There are some very hilly and mountainous regions in Casman where cavalry tactics would be pointless. In such regions the infantryman is the prime factor. The shock regiments are primarily intended to spearhead any such action. As I mentioned earlier they will also be used as cavalry if and when required.

"It is our intention to combine the shock troop training with raiding and infantry tactics. We will become fully adept at guerilla warfare. In simple words, depending on the terrain, our men will use their heculs to transport them to a given point. On arrival, they will dismount to carry out their mission, secure in the knowledge that their steeds are available when they have to withdraw. Again, though we may be emphasising infantry tactics at the present, cavalry tactics are just as important and will be used to advantage.

"Finally the shock regiments are intended, as their name suggests, to be our spearhead. Any solder in such a formation will be capable of surviving because of intensive training. Remember any one of your troops and yourselves who has sensible suggestions must be listened to attentively. Rahamb's sensible suggestion proves this point. Likewise that of Souriin. Any questions?" Quinton asked with a magnificent smile on his handsome countenance.

The Inner Council quickly discovered that they had successfully managed to cover all the points in the minds of the audience, for no one responded. The paramount ranxem of the Mescarg steppes then declared the meeting adjourned and he and his companions walked down to chat with the soldiery. The latter still found themselves entranced by their leader and the two Ulgruffi. Gordan, the four Polingsi and Perlow were pleasantly surprised to discover that they too were held in high regard, far more than they had ever anticipated.

Quinton and his foster parents favoured such informal gatherings and, whenever possible, they visited villages and encampments near and far. They had even sent for companies from the various regiments, officers and ranks alike, spending time with them and taking a genuine interest in their lives, problems and affairs in general. Such was the manner in which they demonstrated their love for their fellow humans, especially their faithful adherents.

About the same time as Rahamb proposed the concept of the shock regiments the young King of Rionder instituted a custom which was to prove very popular indeed: he embellished on Perlow's original suggestion. Every new member of the royal guard was to have the privilege of spending the whole of his first day on duty in the personal company of his monarch, Ontar and Admaria, whom he was to address familiarly. Little did Quinton realise that this tradition was to endure throughout the centuries. This practice is still faithfully observed today at the Imperial Court on the Central Planet Esgan-Thal, even when the Admarian Empire rules a third of the Galaxy.

Gordan and Rahamb worked very industriously in planning the programmes for the new regiments. The four Polingsi, Ontar, Admaria and Quinton assisted their Riondese friend and his father-in-law, who wished the shock troops to have the best training conceivable. Four long days and nights passed in intensive discussion before they were satisfied with their endeavours. However, during the evening after the schedules had been completed and passed to the scribes to be copied, the captain of the King's guard had a slightly thoughtful expression on his face which Admaria noticed. She and her spouse regarded Gordan like a son; any problem of his was of concern to both of them and Quinton.

When asked by the beautiful gray eyed Ulgruffi if anything were amiss the giant warrior smiled fondly in the candlelight which illuminated the dining room of his home, and said,

"Dearest Admaria, you do know me."

"Then tell me," she smiled in return, reaching across the table to pat his hand. This kind action delighted Sheralex who was sitting beside her husband.

"We've finished the planning for the shock training programme. The instructions for the protagonists are relatively simple to grasp as we know. Also, from the brief personal talks I've had with Rahamb, he and his subordinates should have no difficulty in carrying them out," Gordan spoke with satisfaction.

"I agree with you. Actually, Souriin called on me earlier today, just before breakfast. He was wondering about that too. I put his mind at rest," Quinton nodded.

"Good. In a few weeks the royal guard will attain shock troop standard. By the way, that was certainly an excellent suggestion from Hanshair. The royal guard will be off as soon as the assault courses are ready. The reserves and the household guards will go with them. Men from Shlasmil's command will replace them temporarily. My point is this. For the first time, significant numbers of our troops are going to perform training exercises in which none of us will probably ever be able to participate. We just won't have the time. I don't like that," the Riondese general stated categorically from where he sat next to Quinton.

"I see what you're getting at. We should be doing these exercises. Every one of us did the novel training ones we used on the steppes," Sleworivan pointed out, his pigtails bobbing.

"Like I just said, we don't have the time. The Casmans have to be trained, and trained to our present steppe standard. We'll require them for the major Deerait campaign. Besides supervising them, we have to administer a vast army. I'm not complaining, but face this fact. Up to the moment, each one of us is physically fitter than any one of our troops. We have the advantage of Ontar and Admaria's invaluable teaching in mysticism. But I still feel rather perturbed. What will happen if any one of us has to command a shock regiment personally, or fight with its soldiers? We'll manage, but we may lack something essential. Oh, we'll know what they are capable of doing, once the reports come in. But . . . ," Gordan's voice tailed off.

"I understand what you're getting at," Admaria declared.

"I do. Turubin, I can see you do also," Ontar nodded, noticing comprehension in the eyes of the Polingsi. "Do you, Sheralex, my dear?" the sage smiled at the beautiful Nai-Zind.

She was one of the very few people who could address her paramount ranxem and the two Ulgruffi familiarly. Quinton and his foster parents loved Gordan's wife because she was a very sincere genuine person and had made the Riondese general one of the happiest men on Phentara. Although she was not officially a member of the Inner Council and did not attend its meetings, Sheralex was often asked her opinion on various topics, for her intelligent suggestions often provided a fresh train of thought.

"I can see what Gordan means, Ontar. You men are the principals in commanding the army, administering it and guarding all our peoples. I personally think every one of you should experience the training programmes for the new regiments. Your problem is time. Time for you to learn the new tactics, while supervising the running of Casman training and preparing for the Deerait campaign. And that may commence sooner than we think. My husband wants to ensure that you'll continue to have that perfect instinct of command you all now possess. Gordan does not wish to imperil that instinct. He feels this might happen to a small degree if you don't do the shock training. As a matter of fact, I'd like to learn it too," Sheralex spoke confidently.

"That's right," Turubin agreed. "The problem is how do we manage it?"

"We can't. We've over thirty thousand Casmans each to supervise," Casterandir remarked.

"And that's vital," Sleworivan said quietly. "Mind you, I'd really like a chance at the shock troop training programme."

"So would I," Perlow said. "But I have my duty."

There was a thoughtful silence for several long minutes, during which time Sheralex and Admaria left to look in on Cryenig and Zolamina. Casterandir accompanied them, for he too had twins, two boys, Sulawend and Olimankyn, twelve years of age. When they returned to the main room, Ontar glanced pointedly at his wife, while Quinton sat silently, fully aware of what his foster parents were thinking. There was a solution, but the Heads of the Sacred Order of Light had to give their permission for such advanced esoteric knowledge to be demonstrated.

When the two Ulgruffi nodded simultaneously the youth

99

smiled. The wizard rose and helped his wife to clear the table, for Sheralex had dismissed her attendants an hour before so that they could spend the evening with their families. Once the dishes had been removed Quinton carefully wiped the table with a clean moist cloth. The four Polingsi, Gordan, his wife and the Chofir wondered what was about to happen but politely refrained from making any comment.

The wizard glanced briefly around and was satisfied with his inspection. The doors to the front and the other quarters were closed, while the curtains had been drawn tightly, so that the interior was invisible from the outside. Admaria replaced one of the candles on the table while Quinton extinguished the remainder. The Ulgruffi mystic commanded all of them to be seated and join hands. It was immaterial where anyone sat.

"You too, Sheralex. And you, dear Perlow," Admaria nodded with a pleasant smile to the surprise of Gordan and the four Polingsi.

The only sources of light in the room emanated from the hearth and the solitary candle in the centre of the table. They caused mysterious shadows on their countenances. Ontar bade them all close their eyes before intoning a prayer to the Great Power to request His aid in the operation which he was about to perform. The wizard declared with absolute humility that only Good was behind his intention.

When he had finished, Ontar chanted four stanzas of a mystical poem, which had been much favoured by his own race. Admaria joined in with the words of the last verse and then a silence fell. Gordan felt nothing initially but soon a languorous warmth stole over his entire body: he heard Quinton softly talking, telling the company to relax, and let the vibratory rhythms of the Universal Essence permeate and control their beings.

Chapter Six
Shock Training Courses

The captain of the royal guard suddenly felt his psychic eyes open and focus on a woodland scene. To his surprise, except for shields, he and his companions were fully armed. He thought how beautiful Sheralex was, apparelled like a warrior. Gordan recognised the clearing which had been designated for the commencement of the first shock troop assault course. He was about to express his thoughts and surprise at their environment when Turubin spoke.

"Ontar, Admaria, what are you two up to?" the Polingsi asked in a most friendly manner.

"You all wanted to train like the shock regiments. This is your opportunity," Admaria laughed merrily.

"It's an illusion," Sheralex and Perlow surmised correctly, speaking at the same instant. This caused the two Ulgruffi and their foster son to look at one another with mild astonishment.

"It certainly is. Time has been suspended. Although we shall spend weeks inside this illusion, not a single second will pass. We are still in the sitting room of Gordan's home," Ontar smiled.

"Yes, we are all going to work our way through a shock regimental training programme. Sheralex, you will find that you possess the present military knowledge of the steppe warriors. So you won't be at a disadvantage," the beautiful Ulgruffi stated.

"Ontar, Admaria or I will know at once if we're required urgently. Then we shall all open our mortal eyes and return to normal," Quinton explained.

"Is that how you were able to learn so fast? When you were about fifteen your knowledge increased exceptionally quickly. I remember thinking that at the time," Sleworivan commented shrewdly.

"You're almost right," the youth acknowledged.

Ontar then revealed that their protegé had advanced sufficiently through the esoteric portals of the Sacred Order that, by the age of fifteen, he was eligible for entry into certain of the Highest Realms. After satisfactorily completing the complicated initiatory rituals and tests Quinton had been granted access to the Arcane Methods of Cosmic Learning; these took either the form of instant intuitive knowledge or of working assiduously through a programme on the Higher Planes; the latter process was considerably longer than the former but no time passed on the physical level. The sage further stated that Gordan, Sheralex, Perlow and the four Polingsi had only been permitted to participate in the Ritual of Illusion because their desire was sincere; the presence of a sufficiently advanced mystic was essential for he or she had to vouch for the integrity of those with lesser occult wisdom.

"When the illusion finishes you'll all have the practical knowledge you unselfishly desired. But you may have no recollection of how you obtained it. You'll never question how you received it, except you'll believe Ontar somehow transmitted it to you," Quinton explained.

"I do thank you most sincerely." Gordan smiled his gratitude.

"We all do. Perhaps we may be able to perform this ritual ourselves someday," Casterandir expressed his hopes.

"Perhaps, but it lies within what are known as the High Realms, the most advanced esoteric degrees of the Order of Light. There are only a few who have attained such heights," Admaria spoke gravely.

"And they are taught directly by the Servants of the Great Power," Sheralex said.

"And on the Higher Planes," Perlow stated unequivocally.

"How did you both know that?" Ontar asked, astonished, for Rahamb's daughter and the Chofir knew nothing about what occurred along the Mystic Way.

"I just knew," Perlow affirmed.

"It just came to me. I simply knew too. I hope I haven't done wrong," Gordan's wife answered with complete frankness.

"Certainly not. Since you both realised it intuitively, it's a sign you've advanced through quite a number of incarnations. Also, since it came to you within the illusion, it is a private sign to all of us that you both are favoured by the Dwellers on the High Planes. And that is no small matter," the wizard nodded with reassurance.

The beautiful Riondese forest lay around them, its trees still bedecked with a multitude of orange, brown and crimson leaves. The gentle climate of the Valley permitted such foliage even though the season was winter. Small animals scampered through the bushes while their larger cousins followed game trails, or went about other pursuits. Streams from the Mescarg mountains, in which trout moved slowly in the cooler waters of the season, trilled and babbled over rocky beds. Overhead, hidden in the branches of the trees, a host of birds chirped and sang, ever alert for enemies creeping stealthily up to devour them.

The companions walked for a short distance over the sward to a tall post which marked the commencement of the first course. Gordan looked cautiously about, for the shortness of the freshly cropped grass indicated that linz were in the vicinity: but Ontar confirmed that while in the illusion they would not be assailed by any creatures. As if to prove the truth of his statement, one of the shaggy green animals lumbered out of the trees nearby and began to graze. The beast would have had no difficulty in detecting their presence for a slight breeze blew from behind the humans directly towards it. The scent should have caused the linz to charge or flee, but it paid no attention to the party.

"This is where we start. Let's go," Admaria said, and led the way forward at a fairly fast pace.

During the first six days in the illusion they traversed large and small rivers, climbed rock faces, and dodged arrows with heads covered by a soft wood. They also learned how to avoid lances, and to pull the riders from their heculs whenever they charged. Such battle tactics had been practised before on the steppes, but not so intensively. Quinton and his companions were no slouches in the art of scouting and successfully avoided many but not all of the traps and ambushes which had been very cunningly set.

They were often attacked by odds of seven to one and demonstrated their ability not only to repel their assailants but also to inflict casualties on them with their swords. The blades of the latter had been encased in a most effective wooden sheath which covered its entire length to prevent serious injury.

Dummies, fastened securely to charging heculs, gave them ample opportunity to practise archery against moving targets. Casterandir remarked that the swift hit and run tactics of the cavalry were very helpful. Intermingled with the dummies and human attackers were friendly warriors who wore white armbands above both elbows. Officers appeared occasionally to observe the participants' reactions and reflexes in desperate situations, when it might be difficult to distinguish between friend and foe.

The assault course had a circuit of two hundred miles; they had to average thirty five miles daily to maintain the same rate of progress as the guard companies. An hour after starting on the first day four mounted officers appeared to hand them very basic rations which had to be supplemented from the environment. Although permitted to light fires at night, they had to be cautious, for the programme included repeated assaults during the hours of darkness. Since the participants were allowed to roam within a two mile radius from where they finished the course in the evening they could select any site within that limit which they hoped would prove undetectable.

However, even with their ability, this was not as simple as it might seem. The best trackers, from the regiment commanded by Mirchanrope and Forsever, had been chosen to test those attempting the shock training programme. These capable warriors had hiding places all along the course, in the trees and above and below ground. There was no telling when and where the scouts might be, and the ten companions had to use all their skills in avoiding them, else they would not obtain any sleep.

The first two nights proved exhausting for the trackers and their associates discovered their whereabouts and launched repeated attacks until dawn. Admaria and Sheralex wrestled and fought as powerfully as the men, but everyone was slain at least four times because of vastly superior numbers. However, by daybreak on the second morning they were managing much better and their adversaries began to sustain higher casualties.

Each sunrise brought a temporary cessation of hostilities for officers appeared to question both sides closely. The information gained not only showed the progress of those trying the course, but also provided a clearer picture of what could be expected from future participants. Such knowledge would be transmitted back to Rahamb and his commanders whence it would be forwarded to Gordan at his headquarters for analysis. The officers gathering it also discussed and advised the trainees on how to improve their performance by pointing out any weaknesses.

"We didn't do as well as we should have, even though the odds were so much against us," Ontar remarked, while the officers escorted them back to the course on the morrow after their first night.

"And we thought we were good. We're as good as the scouts in every way. This course is far more difficult than I believed possible. I am pleased. We shall have to do better," Gordan declared.

"In swordplay there's no one in the entire army who can stand against any of us. Especially Gordan, Quinton and Perlow. You too, Ontar. The drawback is their numerical superiority combined with the padded arrow onslaughts. A hail of them must cause casualties when no one has a shield," Shlasmil pointed out.

"What about being struck in the eyes? Padded arrows could damage or cause blindness," Sheralex suddenly wondered as the thought struck her.

"Your father covered that contingency. He asked me if I could assist. Admaria and I performed an enchantment on the regions selected for the courses to prevent harm to the eyes or face from bolts or swords," Quinton explained.

"I like the idea of not having shields. That's an excellent disadvantage, even if our opponents do," Casterandir commented approvingly, adding, "and I am wholeheartedly in favour of that. It compels us to learn."

"It's just as well we've experienced defeat. You remember what Rahamb said at one stage during our planning. He said each member of the shock regiments would receive a shock," Admaria recollected.

"Your father was absolutely right, Sheralex. He also said the shock would be the reaction, when anyone doing an assault course found himself up against fully trained steppe warriors," Quinton explained.

"I see. Our army has always fought against troops without our superlative training. If we ever have to, then we would have immense problems. This must be one basis of the new regimental exercises. Mind you, I also thought we could have done much better," Gordan's wife remarked ruefully.

"We should have done better. But what my cousin contributed, among other valuable suggestions, was that everywhere overwhelming odds should be encountered. We have to suffer defeat, lack of sleep for long periods and continual harassment to disillusion us. That's when we have to find the will to keep improving our performance. By the time we've finished this first assault course we will have improved," Quinton declared emphatically.

The relentless essential onslaught continued; but the third night brought a welcome respite for Perlow successfully located several hidden scouts and their comrades at sunset. The latter were surprised and slain; they praised the victors. As Quinton pointed out to the vanquished, their defeat did give them the opportunity to return to their own encampment for an enforced rest, in accordance with the rules.

Although they succeeded in avoiding detection for the remainder of that night, the following day brought the commencement of another extremely exhausting trial. The observing officers unexpectedly appeared in the late afternoon for the purpose of informing them that they were not permitted to sleep again until they had completed the entire course.

"One of Rahamb's little variations. He promised he would treat this extremely seriously. He's keeping his word. I think it's a fine idea," Gordan remarked.

"Yes, it certainly is. We're all fatigued, but at least the observers brought us a good hot meal. The least they could do," Quinton smiled, pulling a face.

"One thing I want to mention. I'm certain none of us has used mystical knowledge since we began this course," Shlasmil said.

"And no one was asked not to. It will give us an excellent insight into the physical and psychological effects of such a programme. The exhausting hours. The interrupted meals, when we have to beat off attacks. The traps and ambushes. The objectives to be secured," Sleworivan smiled wryly.

"Next time my father has any more silly ideas, you tell him his favourite daughter won't speak to him," Sheralex declared to grins from her companions.

"Shall I tell you what else your dear father dreamed up, because you don't know all the details of this programme?" Turubin said, finishing a large plate of stew and vegetables.

"If it's bad news, don't," the beautiful Nai-Zind responded.

"I'll tell you anyway. You'd only worry if I didn't. When we finish this assault course, we have a day's rest. Then we repeat it again for a second week. After that we have two weeks on an even more difficult course. I don't mean we do the second course in a week and repeat it the week after. Oh no, it's a single course of six hundred miles. Then we have two whole days off," the Polingsi explained, breaking a large piece of bread from a crisp loaf which had been baked at a field kitchen.

"Turubin, you stop it! You just want to tease me!" Gordan's wife bantered. "All right, tell me what happens for the last three weeks. You're just bursting to make me happy."

The warrior attempted to preserve a solemn countenance, but failed miserably. His handsome dark brown face crinkled into a broad smile and then he began to laugh infectiously. Turubin was so carried away that the others felt obliged to join in his mirth. Eventually Ontar revealed the programme for the last three weeks. The sage said that the final stage was a thousand miles, consisting of the first course followed by the second and finally two hundred miles of an entirely unknown course.

"Ah well, why should you men have all the fun," Sheralex declared resolutely.

When they had finished their repast, they were permitted to lie down until sunset, a brief interval which passed far too quickly. Rahamb himself rode up and told them that the time had come to continue. The Nai-Zind caranxem was very satisfied with their performance. From the reports of his subordinates, he knew that his King and companions had fared far better than anyone else who had attempted the course and had reached their present stage.

Although they were under the illusion, Ontar, Admaria and Quinton had not revealed that the time chosen was many weeks ahead, when the guards would have completed their programme and the majority of those selected for shock regimental training would have successfully striven likewise. The extra three weeks required by the forces under Rahamb's command included an extra week to complete the second course on both occasions, and a week for rest and debriefing.

Because they were responsible for protecting the paramount ranxem and the Inner Council, the guards had been given a shorter time. They had to prove themselves the finest troops in the steppe army. Little could Rahamb have guessed but his thoughtful suggestion of an assault course is still remembered today, when the final selection of new bodyguards for the Imperial Household is made on Esgan-Thal.

Quinton chatted softly to his companions as they ran off into the night, saying that their worst enemy would be lack of rest and food, for no more supplies had been or would be given to them. The constant attacks by mock hostiles and scouts were launched to cause mental disturbance and disorientation through fatigue and hunger.

Gordan concurred, and affirmed his thoughts that they should try to halt briefly every four hours under the cover of darkness. Food would also be a major problem; they would have to spend valuable time in hunting or fishing, for fruit was not available on any trees because of the lateness of the season.

"They won't be able to track us easily if we remain in the shadows during the night," Sheralex murmured.

"That's providing they aren't in the shadows waiting for us," Admaria responded.

Although they had been told that no hostile attacks would be launched against them for the first three quarters of an hour, to give them a chance to overcome any obstacles immediately in front of them, they did not relax their vigilance for an instant. Their eyes became accustomed to the darkness of the forest and they moved very stealthily, taking every precaution to maintain complete silence.

Twenty minutes after they had started Quinton, who was in the lead, raised his hand and pointed ahead. There was an almost insignificant ripple running across the trail. It appeared to be a natural contour of the land. However, the youth was suspicious, for his instincts told him that all was not as it should be. If they had been travelling in daylight they might have been able to examine their surroundings more closely, but the night shadows beneath the trees tended to deceive the eyes.

"I think it's one of Rahamb's surprises. I'll crawl ahead and see what it really is," Quinton whispered, while his companions watched the vicinity most carefully.

The others concurred with his suggestion and he lay down, before beginning to wriggle forward cautiously. When he reached his objective Quinton used both hands to edge the soil gently aside. He exposed a taut rope running from one side of the trail to the other. The strong cord was an eighth of an inch above the ground, ready to trip up anyone whose foot touched it.

The problem was to discover what type of artifice it was.

Quinton crept back to the others and whispered what he had found. They all concurred that it had to be sprung. Gordan glanced about and saw a large branch with a fork at the end lying nearby. It was almost twenty feet long and the giant pushed it along the ground before him. When the end caught the rope it acted precisely as if a human foot had tripped it.

There was a swishing sound and arrows rained down from all around, both from the trees and tall bushes close at hand. Fortunately the area which they encompassed was not as far as the end of the branch so that none of the watchers was hit. It had been a very neat ambush intended to catch the unwary, its purpose being to sharpen both powers of observation and anticipation.

"We'd better be careful. That might be the only trap, but we can't be certain," Ontar murmured.

"Yes, anyone discovering it and neutralising it might just feel he had been wholly successful. Such elation could cause a drop in his guard. Say, what's that?" Turubin declared, pointing up to a branch on a tree to their left.

"It looks like a rope. It goes upward and vanishes into the branches. I'm not certain where it comes from. There's too many shadows. Those tall bushes are thick enough to prevent us seeing where the other end goes," Sleworivan muttered.

They walked warily, watching every single step they took. The area was strewn with branches and twigs, the remnants of a storm. However it was now blatantly obvious that there was a trap somewhere. Suddenly Perlow raised his hand and the company halted. The handsome Chofir pointed to an eight foot wide broken piece of tree trunk which lay across most of the trail fifteen yards in front of them.

"That's the trap. We would naturally make a detour to avoid climbing over it," he explained.

"You're right," Turubin concurred.

"Let's see what happens when we throw this log," Shlasmil said, picking up a heavy piece of wood.

The Polingsi swung his right hand back, mentally forming a picture of the spot which he wished to strike. He threw the log through the air so that it landed at the end of the tree trunk. Immediately there was movement in the ground. A noose flashed from beneath the soil to seize the piece of wood, whipping it about fifteen feet in the air. If anyone had inserted his or her foot into the trap that person would have been suspended by an ankle until released.

"All sweetness and light. That's your father, my cousin," Quinton grinned.

"I'll father him when I see him," Sheralex threatened with a smile.

The remainder of the night was spent in avoiding similar traps. Indeed they managed to use one of the hidden rope snares to overcome a squad of mounted warriors waiting in ambush for them. Quinton sprang the trap and emitted a yell as if to indicate that he had been swung off his feet. The hostiles, who had been detected about sixty yards ahead, galloped quickly to the scene, only to discover that they had become the victims. Their quarry loosed such an accurate hail of padded arrows at them that they conceded they had been slain.

In accordance with the rules Gordan searched their saddlebags and found sufficient food for two days. Although the giant Riondese could not remember because of the illusion, this action was precisely what Rahamb wished to happen. The Nai-Zind caranxem wanted to encourage initiative, that essential characteristic of being able to act with decision. Even the archery attacks had been devised with that factor in mind; it was thought it might be possible to hone the instincts of the majority of participants to such an extent that dodging arrows would become a natural function.

Since they now had sufficient food to see them through to the end of the first course, if the rations were eked out carefully, the friends began to enjoy the challenge. Although they rested, but did not sleep since the rules did not allow this luxury, they did not permit the enforced fatigue to pervade their capacity to think. One suggestion made by Admaria was adopted immediately; she proposed that whenever possible they bathe their faces in cold water, especially their eyes, which would feel refreshed instead of heavy. If there were no streams in the vicinity a finger moistened in the mouth and rubbed gently on the eyelids proved a satisfactory substitute.

On the morning of the last day they made the astonishing discovery that their natural instincts were operating at a peak of efficiency. They knew beforehand where a trap was to be found, where an ambush was laid, how to climb a difficult cliff face, and looked eagerly forward to the next problem awaiting them. When they reached the end Rahamb greeted them affectionately. He expressed his satisfaction at their progress,

110

for among other things they had managed to finish the course four and a half hours earlier than the normal average.

Once they had bathed and eaten they were shown to comfortable beds in huts not far from where the circuit ended. After breakfast the following morning Quinton and his companions spent a long period with the Nai-Zind caranxem, Souriin and other officers from the shock troop regiments. Everything pertinent to the course was analysed in detail. The aches, pains, times of reaction in different situations, the disappointments when they were defeated, the elation in victory after a skirmish, all these matters and others were fully discussed.

Rahamb admitted that every member of his shock regiments had discovered the superlative use of his instincts on the first course. Those who did not seldom found it on the second and third circuits with their more intensive programmes. Although all those who failed were allowed to perform the course at some indeterminate future date, Souriin had proposed that a select few be permitted to do so after an interval of a week to ascertain what proportion achieved success on their second attempt.

The Hedunon put this idea to Rahamb and the Inner Council. The Nai-Zind caranxem and the others concurred with his suggestion. None of the first group selected was advised that he had been chosen to repeat the programme until the night before. Each was naturally surprised, but did not refuse the sudden unexpected opportunity, although he had no conception that he was about to be involved in an experiment. Gordan, with the permission of Ontar, Admaria and Quinton, met those chosen and hypnotised the warriors into consciously forgetting that they had already completed the courses. However, a subtle suggestion was implanted in their minds, so that the knowledge amassed would automatically filter through when required.

The results proved very interesting. Almost eighty five per cent of those specially chosen developed the fine instinct which Rahamb was seeking. Indeed, the Nai-Zind had originally proposed his programme with such a revolutionary idea in mind, only imparting it to the Inner Council, who requested that it remain secret. Quinton and the two Ulgruffi, with their immense esoteric wisdom, had the acquiescence of Gordan and the Polingsi in authorising the formation of the shock regiments. Except for the Inner Council and Rahamb, only Souriin ever learned the startling truth as to why the Nai-Zind caranxem had been given temporary command of the new formations.

The second and third courses were nominally more arduous to conceal the purpose of the first. If this fighting instinct were revealed then those continuing with the programmme honed their reflexes on the next two circuits. The royal guard, although such had never been anticipated or even suspected, were all found to possess this vital sense in abundance. As Ontar remarked, when every member of the royal and household contingents had successfully completed the shock training without failure, perhaps such latent ability had subconsciously caused them to be chosen initially for their important duties.

When the eligible portion of the armed forces had attempted the course those who did not pass were expected to apply for another opportunity. When they did so a member of the Inner Council hypnotised them in order that they could commence afresh. It was found that no more than three attempts by any individual was necessary before he was successful. However quite a considerable time was to elapse before the entire force, including the Casmans, attained this standard.

Gordan, Sheralex, Quinton, Perlow, the two Ulgruffi and the four Polingsi duly completed the second and third circuits satisfactorily. While they remained in the dimension created for this purpose none of them recalled the hidden psychological objective behind the first course. They proceeded naturally, like any normal warrior, and were very satisfied with what they accomplished.

After the last debriefing and the congratulations of Rahamb and his officers, the illusion vanished and they opened their eyes to find themselves back in Gordan's comfortable dwelling. When this occurred their new comprehension combined with their mystical wisdom to provide a far higher and better military capability than any other person in their vast fighting machine. Perlow and Sheralex evinced a similar understanding, although to a lesser degree since they lacked practical esoteric experience; nevertheless their knowledge was remarked upon privately by Ontar, Admaria and Quinton.

Although the two Ulgruffi and their foster son had complete recall, Gordan, his spouse, the Polingsi and Perlow did not remember what had happened. When the illusion ended the mystical process returned them to the moment when Admaria, Sheralex and Casterandir emerged from the children's room. The friends passed a pleasant couple of hours chatting before the guests bade goodnight to their hosts.

As had been explained to those less advanced than the King of Rionder and his foster parents, their only recollection was that somehow Ontar had imparted the information by occult means; they never remembered to enquire how this had been accomplished. Any time Gordan and the Polingsi pondered about it they always forgot to ask, and eventually accepted this knowledge without question or wonder.

It seemed only a few minutes to Quinton before his subconscious mind aroused him to complete wakefulness. Ontar and Admaria had trained their foster son to be capable of performing this invaluable activity and he could rest peacefully with the realisation that he would awaken at any hour he wished. The youth washed himself thoroughly in a large bowl of water which had been left at his bedside the previous evening. Although the liquid was cold Quinton warmed it sufficiently by the method of placing his hands on either side of the receptacle and concentrating on its contents for ten seconds.

After he had completed his ablutions he dressed and walked through to find that Ontar and Admaria were already in the main part of the shamianah with Perlow, who slept in a room next to his liege. Felthim had just finished setting the table for breakfast. Quinton greeted the Nai-Zind woman, his foster parents and his personal bodyguard courteously. The quartet sat down to breakfast, partaking of milk, fruit and bread, the latter article of food having been personally prepared by their pleasant attendant at one of the field kitchens.

While they ate a sentinel was sent to fetch Hanshair who quickly appeared, accompanied by Felgorian and Cottis; the latter was most favourably impressed by the royal guard commander in the performance of his duties. The Nai-Zind and the Deerait were requested to check the disposition of the defences and the morale of the troops.

The provincial governor of Sicruci, in his bright armour with the Estyork insignia of two crossed fiery arrows, did not demur in the least at being given orders by a mere youth; he was simply eager to carry out his instructions. Cottis began to feel a confidence stealing over him, like the warm sun rising to brighten the world after a long dark cold night. Their force might be outnumbered but somehow, as he left with Hanshair, the Sicrucian did not doubt that their foes would be vanquished.

"Felgorian, please remain. You'll act as standard bearer.

Hanshair will be more than fully occupied. He knows what to do. This in no manner detracts from you. You've had hardly any opportunity since my coronation to learn how we train and practise battle tactics. The guard have gone through the exceptionally advanced shock troop programme, and that is very difficult. Besides, I do require a standard bearer, and have to keep you alive as my ambassador."

"Certainly, Sire. Where will the standard be?" the Riondese asked courteously.

"You can fetch it any time before sunrise. Oh, if I know my guard commander, he'll have given it into the keeping of those two redoubtable Ker-Mantids, Adrigal and Onlestic. Those three are as close as conspirators. Have you eaten?" Quinton enquired kindly.

"No, Sire," Felgorian replied.

"Then sit down and join us. There's some spare platters and beakers on your left. I should have asked you before."

"Help yourself to anything you want," Admaria smiled enchantingly.

"Quinton mentioned Adrigal and Onlestic just now. They and Hanshair have a firm friendship. It's been growing since the two Ker-Mantids became royal guards, just before the battle with the Jaddair corps," Ontar remarked.

"You know Hanshair's the commander of the royal guards. Elmendor's the head of the commissariat regiments. You are still my crown bearer and, more important, my ambassador," Quinton stated, helping himself to another piece of bread from the large warm loaf.

"Yes, Sire," the Riondese nodded, wondering where the conversation was leading.

"Your ambassadorial duties are to be in a much higher capacity than when you served my father. You are to be my principal legate to the centres of government in all the countries we pass through. Naturally this will involve a great amount of travelling." Quinton paused to take a mouthful of bread.

"What our foster son is trying to tell you, among other things, is his intention that, as our forces move, their dependents will accompany us, if feasible. But, until we have subdued the Empire and dealt with Enmarkan there will be little, if any, domesticity. When our wars are over then home life must and will come to the fore. A happy and stable family unit with firm roots in a happy and stable state is vital for the future. That must never be forgotten." Ontar raised the forefinger of his right hand to emphasise the point.

"I agree wholeheartedly," Felgorian nodded, sipping some rotar milk, which kept for many days in sealed hide containers.

"When we can you'll be given your own permanent ambassadorial escort of a minimum of a thousand soldiers. They'll all have successfully passed the shock troop programme," Quinton said seriously, handing the bowl of fruit to Admaria.

"Why, Sire? The largest escort I've ever had was ten men," the Riondese averred with surprise.

"Because by the time we've finished our major campaigns on Rontmethar, Rionder and the Mescarg steppes will not be Quinton's only realms. Under the white and green banner will come the entire Deerait nation, the Casman Empire and the Central Plains, with all territories attaching thereto. Your monarch will not only hold the titles of King of Rionder and paramount ranxem of the Mescarg steppe peoples, he will also have those of Lord of Deerait, the Emperor of Casman and High Baron of Broechnaar," Admaria explained with pride.

"Ah, now I understand. On my long journey I often wondered about what would occur when our campaigns were over and we were successful. It certainly is the most sensible solution for you to assume all these titles. You'll be the most powerful ruler on Rontmethar, Sire. Can I make a suggestion?" Felgorian asked in respectful tones.

"Of course you may. It will certainly be a sensible one. You weren't my father's adviser for nothing," Quinton complimented.

"Thank you, Sire. Since you will have to assume all these titles, which is one thing you must do to avoid anarchy, why not call yourself Emperor of Rontmethar? Any nations not under your rule on our continent may grumble but they won't dare do anything more than that. The power you'll have will make you virtually unassailable. If I know Ontar and Admaria as well as I used to, they'll have plans for the good of our whole continent. What do you think?"

Quinton did not answer, but looked at his foster parents. Ontar smiled partly to himself. Admaria did likewise, and it was she who replied to the sensible suggestion from Felgorian.

"We should have thought of such a title before this. The

Emperor of Rontmethar is an excellent suggestion. Your assumption that we have plans for this continent is quite correct."

"I was certain you would. You both come from the Islands of Wizards. They are the very heart of Good in our troubled world. If I may hazard a guess, your presence in the Rionder Valley over the centuries was deliberate. The Riondese are only a small people. Yet renowned personages paid us considerable attention." Felgorian stopped to nod his thanks, when Admaria poured some more creamy rotar milk into his mug and Perlow passed the loaf of bread.

"Go on," she smiled kindly.

"You cast the rune stones for King Quintar. The reading was never disclosed. That was unusual. I conjecture this was because they foretold the disastrous fall of Rionder and, perhaps, a brilliant destiny for King Quinton. I'm only guessing. I trust I'm not offending anyone by speaking thus," the ambassador said apologetically.

"Certainly not. We know you'll keep this conversation and others like it to yourself. Ontar and I often talked with you in the days of Quintar and Vialo. We would not have spoken so openly if we hadn't believed you to be absolutely trustworthy and prudent. You can trust Perlow implicitly too."

"Thank you, My Lady. Again, I mention the puzzling fact, the Heads of the Sacred Islands took a paramount interest in the affairs of a small insignificant kingdom. Why, when there are other larger and more important realms? A point, Sire, which you may not know. My wife, Elestia, and I stood as your godparents. Gordan was also one."

"I didn't know that. Gordan never mentioned it once. I wonder why?" Quinton spoke pensively.

"Your father had a very quiet naming ceremony for you. With Enmarkan's visit approaching, and Great Ontar and Lady Admaria absent on their way to Deerait, he decided to take some precautions. Your mother acquiesced to a private ceremony. When it was over King Quintar asked that the identity of the godparents remain a secret. This would protect them if Enmarkan attacked our kingdom. The Baron might have put them to death," the Riondese replied.

"Gordan never told you. He was content Admaria and I were rearing you. In those days he wasn't married and was in no position to bring up a child. Remember, his orders were to bring you to us in the forests if danger threatened. Also he thought, if you knew before we revealed your identity, you might ask awkward questions about your parents. He didn't want to lie to you," Ontar explained to his foster son.

"Felgorian only mentioned it just now to assure us that he could be trusted. This we know. His integrity is unequivocal. Even when you were told your true heritage Gordan still requested us not to tell you. He's reticent about some things. I left it to him. Am I right about why you told us about your being Quinton's godfather?" Admaria asked in the main room of the shamianah.

"Yes, you are. It's the Riondese custom for godparents to be chosen from among the closest friends or relatives of a family. King Quintar was an only child. So was your mother, Sire. She came from the forests to the far north of Rionder. At least her parents did, when they joined our people. Queen Vialo was born in Rionder. What's more, your own parents were very fond of Gordan," the ambassador averred emphatically.

"We shall reveal to you the destiny of this young man who is your King. It is essential for you to know this. You are our ambassador. Whatever you do, your actions will be governed by this knowledge. Quinton is to be the first Emperor of Rontmethar. It is sensible to adopt your suggestion. We did not think of that, because his ultimate title is to be Emperor of Phentara. It is his destiny to become the ruler of this whole world, bringing justice and peace to all peoples and nations. His is a freely chosen path. Believe me, Ontar and I had no notion of how his first steps would actually occur. They did through his own strategic proposals at a time when he did not have prior knowledge of his lineage or future."

"I see, My Lady, and I understand. I'm glad I'm only one hundred and thirty two years of age. I should be able to see most of this happening. It seems a pity there are so few races, as far as I know, who live as long as the Riondese. Still, on reflection, King Quinton will have the opportunity to see five or six generations of those who only live about eighty to one hundred years. They'll be using wisdom given freely from the Sacred Islands?"

"Felgorian, I'm glad you're on our side. With so many shrewd guesses, my godfather, it's just as well. I think Ontar and I had better go and visit the troops while you find the standard," the King of Rionder smiled kindly.

"I am honoured to have been told Quinton's destiny. I shall keep it to myself. It does give me more responsibility," Perlow said with humility.

"I know, and thank you, my dear friend," Ontar smiled graciously, for all of them had grown to love the small Chofir whose integrity was unequivocal.

The four men rose and left the table. Admaria called loudly for Felthim. The Nai-Zind woman came through from the back of the tent to clear the dishes from the table, while Ontar's spouse went to waken Olluinan and Allecenia in their quarters at the rear of the shamianah. When the couple from the Sacred Islands had eaten the table would be prepared to receive any wounded.

"Hail, Sire," Hanshair approached his monarch as Quinton and his three companions emerged from the tent. "All is as ready as can be. Everyone, other than the sentinels, is relaxing at present."

"Excellent. How are our few Deeraits?" the King of Rionder asked, while Felgorian strode off to find Adrigal and Onlestic in order to obtain the standard.

"Not too bad. They're rather nervous. I stationed them in the second line, like you suggested, right next to where the standard will be."

"Good. Felgorian will take charge of the standard. You'll have to function as my chief officer, like Gordan would in similar circumstances. Remember, we did tell you that you'd be given opportunities to assume high command. Ontar and I know you can do it," Quinton declared with confidence.

"Thank you, Sire. Do you wish to inspect the troops? Oh, by the way, Adrigal has the standard. He's just around the hill yonder. There, where the Lord Felgorian has gone," the Nai-Zind warrior indicated.

"We did assume Adrigal or Onlestic would have it. I'm sincerely pleased you and the two Ker-Mantids are friends. It augurs extremely well when our enemies of yesteryear are our fast allies of today and tomorrow. And also that you trust them with the standard. I concur with your judgment. Let's get on with the inspection of our positions. At the same time, we'll run briefly through the battle plan with each section commander," Quinton said, motioning to Hanshair to precede them.

119

Overhead the stars still sparkled in a tantalisingly cloudless sky, for the wind had finally succeeded in chasing the rain to the north. Selix had vanished westwards in his eternal pursuit of the Enchantress, but the heavens were still beautiful and mysterious. They had remained an enigma for millenia to the vast majority of Phentarans. Although the learned sages in Hesewoner on Ordlansa had advanced far in the science of astronomy, their knowledge had never been revealed to the superstitious inhabitants of their planet; it might perhaps have dispelled many erroneous suppositions and groundless fears; alternatively, it might have caused considerable disruption.

Ontar accompanied his foster son and listened while the capable youth discussed the battle strategy with the section commanders. Helijaw, Portarid, Quirgid and the other officers were awed by the presence of their dynamic paramount ranxem and the eminent mystic. Nevertheless, they were able to demonstrate to their monarch that every single soldier knew precisely what was required of him.

The stars began to vanish as Phentara spun on its axis to bring the land of Deerait on the continent of Rontmethar into the light of day. A glow in the east heralded the approach of the sun, the life giving orb of all habitable worlds. Hanshair sent word to every contingent to be alert and remain as quiet as possible.

The sounds of men and animals moving to and fro were now faintly audible from the Adiorenji encampment, which could be distinguished by the glow from several fires. There were several bosques between the Relyanese warriors and their quarry. None of the carls realised yet that Quinton and his column were a relatively short distance away. Indeed, it was not until they had loaded their pack heculs and were extinguishing their campfires that one of them caught sight of their quarry.

The Adiorenji had ridden forward to water his steed in a stream about two hundred yards from the defensive position assumed by the forces under the King of Rionder's command. He happened to glance to his right at the moment his mount began to drink its fill, and caught sight of them waiting silently on foot, their spear heads glittering in the new day.

The carl gaped for several moments before wheeling his hecul about savagely and galloping back to inform Kinerth and Reorgin. The two vicious brothers did not ponder the strange attitude of their quarry, for revenge remained uppermost in their minds. Orders were snapped and the march riders formed ragged lines before trotting forward. They believed that their superior numbers would bring swift victory. Their forefathers in the time of Dinmonad would have told them that reality was totally different when fighting against the Riondese and their allies.

"Here they come," Quinton murmured from where he stood on the hillside.

"The fools. Such folly. Lives thrown away for nothing," Ontar sighed sadly, to the further surprise of Cottis just behind, who realised that defeat was not even anticipated by those in charge of his escort.

Above their heads the mighty banner of Rionder fluttered proudly in the breeze. The giant green linz, symbol of the forest kingdom, seemed animated against its white background. The standards of the Adiorenji were dwarfed by its shining magnificence for it glittered in the morning sunlight in all its glory. It was the representation of the power, majesty and wrath of the small realm, as Enmarkan had discovered over twenty years before and which the evil in Broechnaar was to face in the future, when the youthful Emperor of Casman, Supreme Overlord of the United Deerait Nation, King of Rionder and paramount ranxem of the Mescarg steppes, put an end to the vicious tyranny in that unfortunate and unhappy country.

Kinerth and Reorgin scoffed at the resolute lines on the hillside. They possessed superior numbers to smash through the opposition. Appearances were obviously deceptive; Felgorian had been boasting about his friends' prowess in the square in Estyork two days before. The brothers anticipated an easy victory and charged recklessly forward, not even bothering to consider the elementary military strategy required for such an assault.

"Olluinan, you will remain here. You are too valuable to lose," Admaria commanded, standing in front of the shamianah in the light of day.

"Yes, My Lady," Allecenia's father acknowledged with the highest respect, for she spoke not as his friend, but as one of the Heads of his Sacred Order.

"But Ontar is in danger, Godmother. And what about Quinton?" Allecenia pointed out with concern in her voice.

"Ontar will be all right. My intuition tells me this, though

121

there are times when I receive no such esoteric reassurance. Quinton will be, too. Besides, he has Perlow. Olluinan, you've had no military training. Quinton, Ontar and the royal guard have. We have ten thousand shock troops in our army. To join their elite ranks requires severe training, among other things. None will believe you to be a coward.

"Look yonder. Those twenty guards on top of the hill will not fight either, unless matters turn drastically against us. Their duty is to watch for any wounded and bring them here. They want to fight but they have been specially trained as medical personnel. Even though they are not primarily cast in the role of fighting men, they are essential. Like you are," Admaria explained kindly.

"Thank you," Olluinan nodded with a smile in his green eyes.

"Prepare to receive charge!" Hanshair's powerful voice rang out over the clamour from the Adiorenji: a large number of the latter were firing arrows which were easily deflected by the shields of their adversaries.

When the enemy reached the gentle slope of the hill the speed of their heculs began to slow down with the ascent. Standing beside his King, the Nai-Zind commander watched their progress carefully. Hanshair suddenly raised his sword. The guards in the front rank immediately dropped to their knees and put down their shields. They unslung their bows, selected arrows from their quivers and notched them. Their comrades in the second row did likewise, but remained erect.

The Relyanese did not attempt to withdraw in face of this threat. They rashly continued to advance in a ragged undisciplined horde. Their archers fired ineffectively, for they were unused to performing this action from the saddle while climbing. The carls had no comprehension of how highly trained fighting men would react, but they were about to find out.

Quinton nodded reluctantly to Hanshair and the latter shouted, "Fire! Independent firing!"

Almost two hundred arrows flashed through the air to strike into their marks. Heculs and carls crashed to the ground. Even before the shafts had wreaked their deadly havoc, further missiles were swishing towards the numerically superior force. More march riders and their steeds were slain. Men crawled about with pain from wounds surging through their bodies. Heculs lay writhing and kicking, the majority of their riders in a similar or even worse condition.

Those unscathed wrenched savagely on their reins. Their only desire was to escape from the deadly hail scything down their comrades. Suddenly, from the right and left sides at the base of the broad hill, steppe lancers thundered forward to smash into their flanks. More carls were speared by effective thrusts. Simultaneously half of the supporting infantry raced over the top and leaped into the saddles of their tethered steeds before galloping to assist in the final stage of the strategy.

Quinton's remaining archers showed that their intensive weapon training had been worthwhile. A continuous flow of shafts was directed towards the midst of the enemy and was maintained until the supporting cavalry arrived. Then Hanshair signalled for it to cease. By this time their adversaries had had enough and did not need to be asked to surrender.

Quite a number did succeed in effecting an escape; but all were captured within half an hour by contingents of the royal guard on their fleeter heculs. When the prisoners returned to the scene of the battle they were promptly pressed into service to assist their fallen comrades. The carls numbly gazed at the carnage, unable to grasp the appalling disaster which had overtaken them. One moment they had been eight hundred fairly determined warriors about to inflict a savage revenge on those who had slighted their overlords; then, within a brief space of time, their total disregard of basic military principles had resulted in absolute defeat, almost bordering on annihilation.

Admaria, Allecenia and Olluinan found that only four of the royal guard had sustained minor arrow wounds. Once the shafts had been removed, the gashes were cleansed and bound. It was expected that the soldiers would be able to resume their duties very shortly. However, the steppe physicians became fully employed in dealing with the casualties sustained by the march riders.

Ontar and Quinton estimated that almost three hundred Adiorenji had been slain, while another two hundred and fifty had been wounded. Squads of the royal guard rode to fetch the pack heculs belonging to their adversaries. When they returned, the fit carls were ordered to erect tents immediately so that the injured could be placed inside.

The tall resolute steppe warriors were alert for any

treacherous act, but none was forthcoming. The savage disastrous defeat had completely demoralised the force commanded by Reorgin and Kinerth. They were pathetically eager to obey any instructions given them. Fires were laid, and water was brought from the stream to be boiled and used for cleansing wounds.

The Deeraits from Estyork were astounded by what had taken place. The King of Rionder had placed his command in an excellent position and, when attacked, his contingent had reacted with a deceptively devastating ease against superior numbers. Cottis now wholly comprehended how the mighty imperial Jaddair corps had been vanquished by the steppe tribes. The governor of Sicruci realised that his country, even if it were united, could hardly hope to repel such an invader.

Quinton, Ontar, Admaria, Allecenia, Olluinan and the steppe physicians toiled for long hours to help the wounded. Arrows were removed; lance and sword gashes were cleansed and stitched; broken limbs were set in splints. Every single piece of clean hide bandage in the emergency packs of the royal guard was used; even then there were still not enough dressings. The house carls were told to hand over all the spare clothing they had.

"Everything's filthy. The material's not suitable either. It's too coarse," Hanshair said to Ontar, looking at the pile of garments on the ground.

"I know. I'll perform a spell to change and cleanse this heap," the wizard nodded, still angry at the utter disdain shown by Kinerth and Reorgin for the lives of their inferiors.

The Ulgruffi sage raised his hands to the sky before chanting several phrases in his native tongue. A pleasant refreshing perfume arose; the texture of the clothing altered to become suitable bandaging material. The latter was quickly distributed to the field stations where it was cut into adequate lengths. This extra supply sufficed to meet the needs of the emergency and to provide a reserve when dressings had to be changed.

The physicians laboured until mid-afternoon before the last casualty had been tended. Quinton and his foster parents were only too glad to finish. They joined Olluinan, Perlow, Felgorian and Cottis at the table in the shamianah for a hot meal. Allecenia ate in her own quarters. By this time, the King of Rionder and his foster father had overcome their wrath at the inessential slaughter, and only felt sorrow for the hapless

Relyanese.

"We'll deal with Kinerth and Reorgin in the morning," Quinton stated grimly, rising from the table.

"Reorgin is dead. One of the lancers killed him. Kinerth was wounded. I tended him. He'll recover. That brings the problem of what to do about him," Admaria said seriously, as they walked to sit outside the shamianah in the saffron glow from the westering sun.

"Sire, Reorgin and Kinerth are the sons of Koreorgin. He's the principal Adiorenji chieftain in Relyan province. He has great influence and authority. When he learns what has occurred here, and he will, he'll want vengeance. It won't matter to him that his sons were in the wrong. The death of Reorgin will inflame him," Felgorian nodded.

"I was about to mention that too. I think I'd better return to Estyork. Koreorgin can raise over a hundred thousand men. He'll blame me, as well as you, Quinton," Cottis declared with concern.

The King of Rionder did not respond for over a minute, during which time he thought rapidly. The journey to Hesion was essential, for it provided the opportunity to meet the High Court. If, in the meantime, Koreorgin were to learn of his son's demise and attack the capital of Sicruci, a very long delay could result before his party was able to return there; Estyork was the fulcrum of the northwestern region of Deerait, and whoever controlled it dominated that area of the nation. Indeed, with civil war imminent, they might never reach Hesion. The difficulty was to decide what steps to take to counteract this situation.

"Cottis, Felgorian, we shall continue our journey in the morning. Don't worry about Koreorgin. Ontar will deal with that eventuality." Quinton spoke with such absolute confidence that his ambassador and the governor felt no doubt that his course of action would not imperil Sicruci.

The sage looked over at his foster son with affection. He suggested that it was time to visit the wounded for several of them had sustained very severe injuries. Quinton concurred; he, his foster parents, Allecenia and her father spent two hours with the steppe physicians tending the Adiorenji, changing their bandages where necessary, and ensuring that they were being well cared for by their fellows.

When they had finished Quinton found himself walking

beside Allecenia in the mellow twilight. She had asked to accompany him when he did the rounds. A few paces behind, Perlow, Hanshair, Adrigal and Onlestic followed discreetly, entranced by the wondrous voice of the veiled Lady. Olluinan's beautiful daughter watched while the youth, on whose shoulders rested the future of Phentara, chatted to his troops. He praised them for their actions and took a sincere interest in their welfare.

When he had completed the rounds, Quinton continued on to the Adiorenji lines which were being patrolled by squads of alert steppe tribesmen. The carls and march riders wondered why he had come into their midst. They were surprised when they found out that this dynamic youth, who had led their adversaries to such a brilliant victory, wanted to check on their personal well-being.

The Relyanese crowded around the King of Rionder. Perlow and Hanshair began to have qualms about the safety of their monarch; but their tension relaxed when they saw the awe and reverence on the faces of the carls. Even those who had been in the square with Kinerth and Reorgin the previous morning started to wonder what madness had possessed their masters to wish the death of their courteous visitor.

When he had departed from their encampment they felt a personal loss and wished that he had remained longer. They did not know what the morrow would bring but felt more content. The King of Rionder had expressed his sorrow at their losses in the skirmish: they believed him when he had said that he wished it could have been avoided. Several thanked him for the considerate manner in which his warriors had let them bury their dead and chant their death songs.

Shortly after sunrise Allecenia, her father and godmother left the shamianah for the hospital tents while Ontar and Quinton, accompanied by Perlow, strode directly to where Kinerth lay recovering from an arrow wound in his left leg. The Adiorenji glared balefully at his visitors but the latter sensed his fear, no matter how bombastic he attempted to be.

"You were warned unequivocally by Felgorian three days ago in Estyork of what would happen if you tried to attack us. Your brother paid for his folly with his life. Your military knowledge is absolutely appalling! Your followers suffered a terrible loss of life through your crass stupidity. I could not face my own troops if I threw their lives away in such an arbitrary fashion!"

Quinton snapped.

"Pah! My father will avenge my brother's death! He will destroy Rionder and Estyork and slay you and your comrades! You can do what you like with me!" the Relyanese snarled.

"Don't you ever speak like that in my presence again! Anger I can understand. Your total insensitivity and callous disregard for the lives of your carls, that I will never condone. Now, be warned! If you or your father ever attempt to make war against me your armies will be smashed like you were yesterday morning. Perhaps it would have been better if I had let my personal bodyguard and good friend, Perlow here, single-handedly slay your party in Estyork," the monarch spoke coldly, his tones suddenly terrifying the wounded man.

"What are you going to do with us?" Kinerth managed to splutter out nervously, gaping at the Chofir.

"Nothing. Except we are commandeering three hundred of your heculs. There are sufficient left for your purposes. But you will remain here until all your wounded have recovered. No one will be sent in advance to Relyan. When you pass Estyork you will not enter the town. You will go home without causing any trouble. The march riders won't be missed. I believe the riding of the marches takes several weeks in any case," Ontar declared, making several mysterious passes with his hands.

"Yes. I will do as you ask," Kinerth nodded, without complaint.

"Good. There is ample game in this neighbourhood. Your carls have sufficient supplies of other food stuffs. Our physicians and my wife will leave instructions with your followers on the tending of all wounds," the sage said before he and his foster son left the hospital tent with Perlow.

Eighteen casualties had died during the night. However this misfortune had been expected for their injuries had been far too severe for them to recover. The remainder were progressing quite satisfactorily and it was anticipated that the majority would survive. Six Relyanese had a working knowledge of healing; Admaria gave them instruction in the art of medicine beyond anything they had learned or been taught before. She placed them under a light hypnosis during which trance they remembered everything she both told and demonstrated to them. This invaluable comprehension remained in their memory for all the days of their lives, and many of their fellow tribesmen benefited from it.

Four hours after dawn the uninjured carls and march riders watched the column commanded by the King of Rionder depart on its long journey to Hesion. When it had vanished from view they felt a loneliness but turned to tend their injured comrades. What none of them realised was that the Ulgruffi sage had placed a blocking spell in Kinerth's consciousness so that the latter would remain encamped until all his wounded had recovered, nor would he send any couriers to inform his father of the disaster.

"Apart from the enchantment on their leader I also went round the other Adiorenji. They won't reveal anything to passers-by. When they reach home they'll remember everything, but not before," Ontar explained to Cottis and Felgorian, who felt very much reassured.

"What will you do if we're in Hesion and Kinerth starts for home?" the Riondese ambassador asked from the height of his linz.

"We'll keep a regular watch on him. Don't forget, it'll take Koreorgin some time to amass sufficient forces to assail Estyork. Constant crystal surveillance will be maintained. Likans, the Polingsi wizard, will also be scrying both Relyan and us. So, if we are delayed, Gordan will move south with a large enough force. He'll catch them by surprise even if they have already seized Estyork," the sage stated with confidence. He looked at the governor of Sicruci who happily accepted the prospect of an alien army defending his capital. Cottis was still under the influence of the spell cast in his judgment hall.

Chapter Eight
High Crystal Magic

The column continued on its journey for several days without incident. The Wilderness stretched about them on all sides for their route had swung away to the northeast. The River Avidnive was left far behind although they would rejoin it a few miles before Troldaart. Their rate of progress was beyond that which the Deeraits would normally have attempted but Cottis did not demur; he was content to leave everything in the hands of the young King of Rionder, and was pleased with the friendliness between his personal bodyguard and the steppe warriors. The governor of Sicruci was particularly impressed with Hanshair's efficiency and often conversed with the Nai-Zind.

The scouts were ever vigilant and since no danger appeared to be imminent Ontar and Admaria were able to hold intensive discussions with Olluinan about the scientific discoveries on Ordlansa. Allecenia took every opportunity to talk to Quinton, whom she had discovered to be an excellent student. The youth listened attentively to everything she said, asking pertinent incisive questions on both exoteric and esoteric subjects for he was eager to learn.

The veiled Lady caused considerable polite comment among both the steppe warriors and the Deerait soldiers. Although she realised this, Allecenia did not know that some of the royal guard were kindly watching her closeness to their monarch. Ontar, Admaria and Olluinan also commented privately to one another on it. The Lady herself wondered at her increasing fondness for Quinton, little realising that these stirrings were the beginning of a deep love. Her pupil too was becoming very attached to his teacher and often thought with tenderness about her.

One afternoon, when they were two days distant from the capital of Chellene and about fifteen miles from the end of the Wilderness, Colmar emerged from the undergrowth. He trotted his hecul over to his monarch, who was conversing with Cottis and Felgorian. The Melcogh informed Quinton that he had found the spoor of a strange animal. The creature was approximately the size of a linz, judging from the length and depth of its tracks, and the gaps in the brush through which it had thrust its violent passage.

"If it keeps going in the same direction it will arrive in the middle of a small farm, Sire. Great Ontar advised the scouts about the whereabouts of that steading this morning. I believe the creature's on the rampage," the Melcogh declared succinctly as the two Ulgruffi rode up to hear his tidings.

"Yes, it could well be. It's a ysdarculd. It will have to be turned back. We'll tell you about it later. Pass the word for everyone to have lances at the ready in case it swings back this way," the King of Rionder commanded.

"At once, Sire," the guard and relief scout acknowledged before riding off to find Hanshair.

Ontar, wearing an elegant light blue cloak which he had donned that morning, thrust his right hand into his saddle bag. He withdrew the beautiful box containing his crystal. Unfastening the clasp, he handed the receptacle to his foster son before concentrating his vast mental power on the ball. The orb quickly cleared under his gaze and the wizard scanned the region around. He soon found the ysdarculd and affirmed that it was heading for the farmhouse.

The animal was just under twelve feet tall and had eight feet with long dark green claws. It had a very powerful body covered in coarse thick yellow hair, a shaggy tail four feet long and a large square head, around which four turquoise eyes were spaced at regular intervals, enabling it to see in every direction simultaneously. Unlike the hair on its body, the covering on its head was short. Its nose was long and pointed, an advantage in raiding the nests of hornets, the stings of the insects proving inefficacious on its tough hide.

Normally the animal was placid, living mainly on grass and roots. However this particular one was on the rampage and the reason for the drastic change in its nature was not apparent. Although the creatures were not in danger of extinction their numbers were not large. Quinton and Ontar were determined not only that this ysdarculd should be saved but also that it would not be allowed to wreak havoc on the unsuspecting farmer and his family. They were resolved that the beast should be examined to find out why it was acting in such an unusual manner.

"It's about three miles from here. We won't be able to catch

130

it in time. I'll have to use a spell through the crystal," the wizard declared, dismounting from his hecul.

"That's High Magic," Quinton commented in Ulgruffi.

"I'll assist," Admaria said, climbing down from her saddle to stand beside her spouse.

"Good," Ontar smiled tenderly at his beautiful wife whom he loved dearly, which he had ever done throughout the long millenia they had been together. He thought how attractive she appeared in her tunic and trousers matching his own attire. Admaria smiled in response, and recollected that her spouse had complimented her on the long wide skirt she had worn to enter Estyork.

The wizard commanded the guard to take their eight steeds and wait four hundred yards further along the trail. They were again told to have the long spears which they used as lances ready, in case the huge animal decided to veer in their direction for its speed could be phenomenal. Hanshair sent several squads to find and return with the scouts ranged about the column lest they and their mounts be attacked and slain. The pack and Adiorenji heculs were enclosed in a ring of resolute soldiery.

Ontar placed his crystal in a groove on top of a large rock of suitable height beside the dusty trail. Before doing so he had made a gesture with his left hand to cleanse the stone of all impurities. Next he and Admaria held hands around the wondrous globe. The wizard uttered a brief prayer to the Great Power for His assistance in their endeavours. When this was finished Ontar and his spouse closed their eyes and chanted several sentences in Ulgruffi.

Quinton stood beside Allecenia with Perlow, Cottis and Felgorian just behind, while Olluinan on his left watched the Heads of the Sacred Order most attentively. The veiled Lady expressed surprise at the manner in which the occult operation was being performed. She whispered to the youth that normally those attempting it would have traced a magical circle on the ground and placed special herbs at regular intervals around its circumference.

"What's puzzling you?" the King of Rionder asked, a gentle smile on his handsome face.

"Such occult operations can be accomplished just as my godparents are doing just now. But crystal spells are difficult to perform without diagrammatic or other aids. Like the time

131

Ontar told me about, when you contacted Likans in the Rionder Valley. It took three of you. That's the usual number," Allecenia said, looking into his gray blue eyes.

"That's right. They must have increased their knowledge. Cosmic Masters. Hidden Servants," Quinton murmured.

"Of course. They'll still receive instruction from those on the Higher Planes. Have they appeared any different during the last few months? They do appear so to me but I haven't seen them for twenty years."

"Mmm. Let me think. Yes, I do believe they have changed, ever so slightly. Their intuitive faculties have increased. This occult operation without herbs or a diagram is an indication that they've gone further down the Right Hand Path," the King of Rionder declared astutely.

Since Ontar and Admaria had progressed sufficiently in their search for wisdom, and had learned all that they could on the physical plane, the only possible teachers for further knowledge and advancement were the Hidden Servants of the Great Power who dwelled on the Higher Planes. These Cosmic Masters had instructed the two Ulgruffi for centuries; the abilities of the latter had now reached such a peak that a final initiation was necessary for the attainment of perfection. This test would prove to be very difficult; what it would entail was concealed from them but they would face it with humility and resolution.

The Heads of the Order of Light stared unblinkingly into the orb, the contact of their hands and the incantation causing their minds to merge. The combined power generated was transmitted through the wondrous crystal towards the huge ysdarculd, still charging relentlessly in the direction of the small steading. It smashed through bushes and undergrowth. Birds and animals fled before its onslaught for none could stand against it.

The globe concentrated the mental energy, and the invisible beam struck the creature forcibly on the head, penetrating to its brain. The beast still raced onwards but its speed was beginning to decrease. The ysdarculd felt bewildered and ran in large circles for several minutes before slowing down to the pace of a racing hecul. It then galloped off in the direction of those who had taken control of its mind.

It was not long before the sounds of crashing in the scrub caused the mounted steppe warriors to level their spears. Ontar and Admaria still maintained the vital contact with the yellow coated animal. As the creature approached the trail it slowed down to almost the average walking pace of a Phentaran. When it emerged from the undergrowth about ten yards from the crystal it bounded forward to halt beside the handsome couple.

Both left the globe and went to examine the unfortunate beast. The huge animal was now standing hypnotically on its eight feet. It did not resist or protest at the two humans touching its massive frame. Quinton, Olluinan, Allecenia and Perlow hastened over to assist. It was the King of Rionder who found a small branch embedded in its hirsute body just above the inside of its fourth right leg.

"Well done. That's the trouble. It's poisonous. It's a twig from the jemiluin bush, a common but dangerous form of plant life. The sap from that stick is more than sufficient to slay several men. A creature as large as this has more resistance but the pain generated by the poison is terrible," Ontar told his foster son.

"You remove it. I'll apply some herbal ointment," Admaria said to her spouse.

The mystic gently but firmly began to pull the offending branch out. This was not as simple as it appeared. A jagged spur had wedged itself firmly inside the body of the ysdarculd behind one of its sixty ribs. Bloody scratches around the wound indicated that the animal had vainly used its claws in an attempt to remove it but the awkward angle of insertion had defied its every effort. When the pain began to increase, as the poison coursed through its veins, it had run amok.

The enchantment held the creature in a trance, where it became and remained insensitive to its agony. Ontar deftly twisted and turned the branch until he felt it yield and was able to withdraw it. He handed it to Quinton who glanced at it briefly. The youth then threw it away into a nearby stream, for water destroyed the poison in the wood.

Admaria had removed an unguentarium from her saddle bag before the guard had left taking their mounts. Dipping her fingers into the ointment, she smeared a quantity of it around and over the wound. This unction was very effective for the treatment of bruises and more serious injuries, being manufactured from a compound of several common herbs. Besides healing, soothing and cleansing, it also had the property of drawing out any poison and suppurating pus.

Some drops of dark blue blood still flowed from the open

wound, causing the long yellow hair beneath to become more matted. The sage pressed his hands on either side of the gash and breathed deeply. Ontar remained motionless for almost a minute before standing back. Olluinan, Quinton and Allecenia looked significantly at one another for the deep cut had healed to leave a thin line where the wizard had joined the flesh together.

"Fine. It should survive now. The laying on of hands will have eliminated the toxic effects of the jemiluin," the Ulgruffi explained with a smile, for he loved Nature in all her wondrous profusion.

Admaria was equally pleased. She watched while her husband clapped his hands thrice in response to which the four eyes of the ysdarculd brightened considerably. The huge creature turned and trotted back into the scrub, the sound of its passage gradually receding into the distance. The company stood silent for a few moments, entranced by the turquoise eyes on the back of its head which appeared to be evincing its gratitude.

"Half an hour and the hypnosis will wear off." Admaria answered the unspoken question from her foster son and his companions.

Ontar picked up his crystal. He replaced it in its container, which Quinton had just passed to him, before waving his hand. This signal caused Hanshair and a squad of the guard to bring their steeds. When they had mounted the governor of Sicruci was rather surprised for the Nai-Zind requested in a most courteous manner that the wizard indulge the royal escort. The sage nodded graciously and the warrior bowed before riding off to send the scouts out once more.

"What was that about?" Allecenia wondered.

"Of course, you, your father, Felgorian and Cottis wouldn't know. Every now and again Ontar gives natural history lectures. They are extremely popular. The guard have seen a ysdarculd for the first time so they want to know more about it. I'm certain Onlestic would prompt Hanshair to ask. Hanshair would have done it anyway. They really like the discourses," Quinton explained.

"Onlestic? That fierce looking warrior is interested in Nature?" Olluinan spoke with astonishment.

"He certainly is. It's surprising but he can tell you the name of every bird and animal on the Mescarg steppes. When he plucks up the courage to ask Ontar he's a most attentive pupil," Admaria smiled as the party continued its interrupted journey.

"There's only one other I'd put ahead of him for interest in natural history. Do you agree, Quinton?" the sage asked.

"I most certainly do. That's Gordan. His knowledge is phenomenal. He can remember the most minute details," his foster son replied.

Cottis shook his head in mild astonishment. Both the supreme general and a member of one of the most warlike tribes on the distant grasslands were nature lovers. It sounded unbelievable, but the provincial governor recalled that everyone in the royal guard was far better educated than the most knowledgeable Deerait. They could read, write, perform mathematics, draw maps and had been trained in the science of strategics. Their attitude to life was one of inquiry and harmony.

After the evening meal the Sicrucian strode over to where the members of the royal guard not on duty sat on the ground, ready to listen to a lecture from the erudite mystic. He was accompanied by Quinton, Admaria, Allecenia, Olluinan, Felgorian and Perlow. His own Deerait escort were also present; they sat beside the tall steppe warriors whom they had found to be kind and considerate on the long journey from Estyork. The dramatic defeat of Kinerth and Reorgin had increased their respect for the strangers from the grasslands to considerable heights.

Ontar was already standing in front of his audience. He waited for a few moments until everyone had settled down. The sage smiled before speaking. "I am glad to see you all here. Welcome to our Deerait comrades also. Nature is an integral part of our existence. Animals, reptiles, plants and insects can harm and even kill us. However, they are all part of the Creation of the Great Power. We should never slay for the sake of killing. Food is necessary but inessential slaughter is reprehensible. Again, if a tree is felled for wood, its seed should be planted to ensure that its species never vanishes from our world. Remember, it provides sanctuary and food for other creatures and is a welcome part of the environment.

"Let us talk about the ysdarculd. It is a distant relative of the linz. Unlike the latter, which today is found only in the Rionder Valley, the ysdarculd inhabits many parts of

Rontmethar. The main regions are scrub lands like the Wilderness. It is a shy creature and likes solitude. The only other creature of comparable size is the linz. There are valleys to the far northwest of Rionder where both creatures live in harmony. These havens are very remote and almost inaccessible.

"It is mainly herbivorous but with a taste for small vermin. Its powerful claws are very useful for digging holes to secure its prey, and also for breaking into hornets' nests. If the nests have been built inside a tree trunk of sufficiently strong wood to resist its efforts the animal will use its long tongue to gather its food. It pushes its pointed nose into such crevices and then proceeds to flick its very long tongue to gather its prey. The end of its tongue secretes a sticky substance. Once the hornets adhere to this they are doomed.

"Naturally when a hornets' nest is attacked the insects retaliate with terrifying ferocity. Such action has no effect on a ysdarculd. Its entire body, even if it were to be denuded of hair, has a hide impervious to the stings of such insects. In addition to its normal function the body hair is so thick that it traps many hornets, thus providing the animal with an extra source of nutrition.

"It is a very clean creature and will spend hours in a pool, washing and preening itself. Admaria and I once observed a ysdarculd doing this. At any one time it uses the claws on four of its feet to remove any twigs and leaves entangled in its fur. Its turquoise eyes, which have a clear second lid to protect them, enable it to see to clean its chest at the same time as its hindmost legs range up and down its long back.

"The one you saw this afternoon was a full grown adult, almost twelve feet in height. However, it is only very rarely that a baby ysdarculd is seen. The creatures are only capable of reproduction every four years unless they are rearing offspring. The period of gestation is two and a half years, each cub weighing approximately one hundred pounds at birth, and an exact miniature of an adult.

"Their mating habits can be unusual. If two are present, they copulate in the normal fashion. However, if only one inhabits a region it mates with itself. In other words the creature is hermaphroditic. Single parents are as attentive to their young, of which there is only one, as are pairs. The adults remain together until their offspring has reached eight years of age.

The lifespan of a ysdarculd is sixty to seventy years.

"The young are able to walk and fend for themselves from the moment they are born. Each possesses a wonderful knowledge of everything it encounters. Its parents, or parent, are very protective and very hostile to any creature coming near a cub. Even the linz, which is probably the most fearless animal in our world, will not approach any adult ysdarculd with young. At other times the two creatures occasionally feed side by side and have been known to cavort and play, extraordinary as that may appear. Like the linz, the male and female ysdarculd move singly, except when a cub is involved.

"When it is about to give birth the beast will find a cave. It gathers a huge quantity of grass, partly to provide a comfortable bed and partly for food. The creature conceals the entrance with bushes and branches, weaving them into a strong mesh. This barrier is wedged firmly into the entrance of its lair and can withstand exceptionally strong winds.

"During the last eight weeks of pregnancy the ysdarculd spends most of the day in the open, devouring acres of grass. It will not eat anything else during this period. Its average weight of eight tons increases by almost eight hundred pounds and, of course, the animal has made provision for this vast increase in girth when selecting its lair. This excessive eating is to provide nourishment for the cub.

"Both parents, or parent, as the case may be, spend four weeks in the lair, never moving outside. During this time the young ysdarculd is fed entirely on milk. This natural product is very thick and creamy and full of essential nutrients. You may think it peculiar that the cub is kept inside the cave for such a long period when it could actively move about and feed itself on the outside.

"The reason is that the milk contains vital ingredients. These give the offspring the thick protective hide of its parent or parents, for its skin is very tender at birth. Admaria and I once used occult means to examine a cub immediately after it was born. We observed its daily progress and discovered that its skin was toughening. By the time its parents took it out of the lair its hide had the resilience of an adult.

"To verify our findings we cast a spell to prevent the cub from being fed for four days during the third week of its life. It did not suffer but its hide became noticeably tenderer than it had been from the moment we commenced the experiment.

We concluded that approximately eight hundred gallons of milk have to be ingested before a cub's hide is strong enough. The parent or parents know instinctively when the safety point is reached. There are very few things capable of penetrating the hide of a ysdarculd. The viciously sharp branches of the jemiluin bush are one example."

Ontar continued with his lecture, describing other interesting habits of the square headed animal. When he had finished he spent quite a while answering questions from his audience. Olluinan and Cottis observed the eagerness of the steppe warriors to learn and discuss new things. They particularly noticed how enthusiastic Onlestic was, and listened to the Ker-Mantid putting forward very intelligent queries.

That afternoon the column had left the sprawling Wilderness region behind. The following morning found the cavalcade travelling through the vast region of farmlands on the borders of Chellene province. Cultivated fields, sturdy manor houses and stout serfs working on the land were to become common features for the greater part of the remainder of their long journey to Hesion.

Since they maintained a rapid rate of progress, the column reached Troldaart just before sunset the next day. Quinton called a halt beside the Avidnive two miles from the city for the purpose of giving the royal guard and the Deerait escort sufficient time to clean their uniforms and equipment. While they were occupied in this task Cottis sent Unyamed and two of his personal escort ahead to advise Governor Wercyn of their imminent arrival.

When the main body neared the city walls a party rode out to meet them. A very elderly black skinned Deerait smiled with pleasure at seeing the commander of the Estyork garrison once more and the latter was pleased to introduce Quinton and the other dignitaries accompanying him to his friend Wercyn. The elegantly dressed governor of Chellene was entranced by the two huge linz. He was also very impressed by the tall dark soldiers who formed the major part of the escort from Sicruci. He could not identify their origins but knew that these were fighting men of the highest calibre.

Troldaart was a sprawling city which did not have the boulevards and amenities of Estyork. Its first line of defence was a massive wall on which many guard-houses had been built. The gates were as strong as those at Estyork but the garrison, although reasonably turned out in a beige livery, did not have the efficiency of their counterparts in the capital of Sicruci. Ontar shuddered to think what would happen during a major assault on the latter town if Cottis' troops had been of a similar military standard.

Once quarters had been established for his royal guard and he and his companions had been shown to rooms inside the castle, Quinton found time to relax in the room which he shared with Perlow. No one begrudged the Chofir this honour for the elite guard knew that their monarch could not be better protected. He bathed and changed his clothing; a servitor came and removed his soiled garments for cleaning. The youth felt refreshed and was about to leave his room with his bodyguard to walk along the corridor to find his foster parents, when a knock came at the door.

"Please come in," the King of Rionder called.

In response to his command Felgorian entered, followed by Hanshair. Both appeared excited and the Riondese was the first to speak.

"I've some good news, Sire. Actually Hanshair is responsible for it. There was a copy of the Matheird peace treaty hidden in the wall of the room he is sharing with Adrigal and Onlestic."

"Well done, Hanshair. How did you discover it? What made you curious?" Quinton asked with intense interest.

The commander of the royal guard explained that he had discovered it purely by chance. There was only one large window in his room through which a cold breeze was blowing. While Adrigal and Onlestic were unpacking fresh uniforms, Hanshair lit two wall torches, before crossing over to close and bar the shutters. After he had done this, he was about to talk to his two friends when his sharp eyes glimpsed the end of a very thin metal rod protruding about an eighth of an inch from the stonework behind the alcove for the right hand shutter.

"It seemed rather odd, Sire. Hardly noticeable in the dust. So I gripped it between my thumb and forefinger and gave it a pull. It didn't move. I'm afraid my curiosity was too much. I desperately wanted to see why it was there. The sealant between the stones had crumbled."

"I see. Let me guess. You prised the small square stones at

139

the end of the rod to permit you access," Quinton smiled.

"Yes, Sire. I also replaced them and removed all traces of what I had been doing. Adrigal and Onlestic thought I had gone crazy. What I'd noticed was the end of a scrolling rod, very much thinner than the ones we use for rolling up manuscripts. Around it was a thick document which the stones had concealed. Words were written in large black letters on a yellow hide parchment. I could read them for they were in the Common Speech. I just glanced briefly at it and made it out to be a treaty of some kind," the Nai-Zind stated.

"That's when he came to my room next door. It's the Casman treaty with Deerait when the Empire made peace long ago. It will help us immensely," Felgorian enthused.

"It certainly will. Well done again, Hanshair," Quinton praised.

"Thank you, Sire. But it was just pure chance," the royal guard acknowledged.

"Perhaps. Or perhaps you were meant to find it. Oh, not by the Deeraits, but by the Great Power beyond." The King of Rionder pursed his lips thoughtfully before intuitively saying,"I suppose you've given it to Ontar."

"Yes. He'd just left his room. He was about to come to you when we met him. We told him quickly and he glanced at the scroll. Then we heard several Chellenese approaching down the corridor. So he told us to ask you to come to his quarters as quickly as possible. Then he went back into his room before the Deeraits could see what he was holding, Sire," Felgorian explained.

"Right. Hanshair, behave normally. Tell Adrigal and Onlestic not to mention it to anyone. Felgorian, you and Perlow come with me," Quinton commanded.

Within half a minute the Riondese ambassador, the Chofir and his monarch had entered the comfortable room allocated to Ontar and Admaria. A log fire crackled in a small hearth, augmenting the illumination from a torch on the wall to the left of the shuttered window. There was a large comfortable bed, a small table and two chairs, while several mats covered the stone floor.

"This is a most excellent find. We won't have any time to discuss it at the moment. I've just read through it. Here, have a look, Quinton," Ontar said, passing the scroll to his foster son.

140

Quinton held the manuscript in both hands, rolling it adroitly at a quick pace. When he had glanced briefly at its entire contents he handed it to his foster mother, who performed the same operation. Admaria returned the artifact to her spouse who went over to one of his personal chests and placed it inside. The wizard then made a strange motion with his right hand, which the ambassador correctly assumed to be a spell to prevent anyone opening the trunk.

"We'll keep quiet about this. You can study it when we camp tomorrow evening, Felgorian," Ontar stated.

"Good. Thank you. How did it come to be there, if I may ask?"

"Just chance. Who knows? Wercyn may," the wizard speculated.

"When I passed through here on my way back from Hesion the governor gave me his hospitality. Naturally I directed our conversation to civil war, the steppe tribes and the Treaty of Matheird. I'm certain Wercyn mentioned a copy of the treaty had been kept here about two hundred years ago. Then it vanished. I didn't enquire further. Perhaps I should bring it up in conversation at our meal?" Felgorian proposed.

"Why not?" Admaria smiled.

The governor of Chellene had been very impressed by the royal guard and was even more so during their dinner when Cottis disclosed details of the skirmish with the Adiorenji. Wercyn expressed his admiration, reflecting that such a regrettable incident was bound to happen. He then declared that Kinerth and Reorgin had forgotten the lessons of history by attempting to attack those from the Rionder Valley.

"They should have recalled the forest war when their forefathers were thrashed by yours long ago. We here in Deerait have never forgotten the courage of your people in the Casman War," Wercyn bowed slightly from where he sat next to Quinton.

"Talking of the Casman War, Sire. Did you know that there was once a copy of the Treaty of Matheird here?" Felgorian asked blandly.

"How very interesting. What happened to it?" the King of Rionder wondered disarmingly.

"No one's certain. Some say it was stolen. Others that children of the then governor hid it for mischief two centuries ago. There is an unsubstantiated story that they hid it somewhere in the garrison quarters. No one missed it for a while. Everyone thought it had been removed to have a new frame. About the time they realised it had actually disappeared the city was in the throes of a plague. The death toll was enormous. The children were among the dead, and that was that," Wercyn shrugged.

"We'll never know. Your explanation seems quite likely," Quinton agreed, glancing briefly to where Allecenia sat beside him, her face concealed in her hood.

They were dining with Wercyn and his three elderly wives in a room just off the main hall. It was homely, with soft chairs and couches placed around the large fireplace. Eight servitors in yellow livery stood four paces behind the large table at which their overlord was entertaining the governor of Sicruci, the King of Rionder, his ambassador, Perlow and the quartet from the Ordlansa archipelago. To his personal surprise Hanshair had also been asked to attend in his capacity as commander of the royal guard and sat next to Unyamed opposite his paramount ranxem.

The company spent a most enjoyable evening and, whenever Allecenia spoke, a hush fell while everyone listened to her wondrous tones. Like his fellow provincial governor, Wercyn was very impressed with the King of Rionder. Indeed, on their departure just before dawn, the elderly black skinned Deerait dressed in crimson robes requested that they all be certain to visit him on their return journey for their brief sojourn had been so delightful.

"We certainly shall, my friend," Quinton smiled benignly, before nodding to Hanshair who snapped commands to the guards to begin their journey once more.

Wercyn looked after the column as it clattered over the cobblestones on its way to the east gate of Troldaart. He wondered about the enigmatic youth and his eminent handsome companions and felt a gladness that he had met such people and conversed with them. His tribe and nation were facing perilous times, but Quinton of Rionder could represent a haven, although he did not know why he thought thus. Nevertheless the Chellenese recognised another sign that the times were troubled for his Sicrucian counterpart had brought no wagons. This demonstrated that Cottis was prepared for a swift return to Estyork should war erupt.

Felgorian took every opportunity to study the Treaty of

Matheird. He spent a portion of each night poring over every paragraph. What he did not realise was that Ontar, Quinton and Admaria, like Olluinan and Allecenia, possessed eidetic memories, such a wonderful talent having been given to them because of their advanced progress along the Mystic Way.

The two Ulgruffi and their foster son spent many hours with the Riondese ambassador discussing the terms of the treaty. The nearer they drew to Hesion the more Felgorian comprehended every minute detail, and how the latter would be regarded by the different cultures of the Casmans and the Deerraits. Quinton and Ontar intended that they all would be fully capable of responding to any questions from the High Council.

About eighty miles from Hesion the broad trail left the fields behind and the column entered a sandy desert region. The land was infertile with very few trees and bushes. Ontar remarked that, apart from the milder climate, the area resembled the Hiclecine Desert which effectively sealed off the Central Plains from the Mescarg steppes.

One evening the Ulgruffi mystic addressed the steppe warriors with the news that they would see the sea on the morrow for the first time. The words of the sage had an unforeseen effect on the royal guard. They were so eager to reach the ocean that next morning they rose an hour before the normal time, dismantled their tents, saddled their heculs and prepared their breakfast. When Quinton, his foster parents and their companions left the shamianah so that it could be taken down, they were astonished to see their escort waiting patiently. Cottis and his troopers were equally amazed when they too emerged from their own shelters.

"I never expected this. As long as they never lose their wonderment they will enjoy life to the full," Admaria remarked as she mounted her hecul.

"That is absolutely true," her spouse concurred.

Chapter Nine
Hesion

Almost two hours after the magnificent saffron fingered dawn the cavalcade rode along the broad dusty trail up a rise and emerged onto the brow of a small hill to catch their first view of the rolling Chofanrit Ocean. The huge expanse of shimmering azure water was an astounding revelation to the warriors from the Mescarg plains. They had heard about the sea from discussions with the Deeraits in Cottis' personal guard, which supplemented the general knowledge of their continent learned in lectures written by Ontar and Admaria. However the descriptions given by both the latter sources were essentially inadequate regarding the vast stretch of glittering water on their left hand side about quarter of a mile distant.

"There's a convoy of ships yonder," Ontar indicated to the northeast.

"About twenty or so. Probably been trading with the Zancericts at Pherign on Abdur-Timil," Cottis remarked. "I believe that's the course they usually take coming home. They occasionally call in at Matheird to trade with the Casmans on the return voyage."

"Pherign is a commercial centre and port. The Deeraits barter grain for woollen materials and spices. Zancerict chirts have the finest wool on Phentara. It is very highly prized. The clothes woven from it are of a high quality, most comfortable and very durable," Admaria said to Quinton.

"It's a most important part of the Deerait economy. The ships will be sailing on to Hesion, I presume?" the youth enquired.

"Yes, they are," his foster mother affirmed.

Over on the right the landscape gradually changed as they proceeded to the main Deerait seaport and administration centre. The slightly hilly region of the past few days levelled downwards to a wide flat plain which was entirely cultivated; in the fields workers were employed at their daily labours. Small stone dwellings with thatched roofs, which clustered around the larger central farm buildings, were visible in the distance in several places. Each manor house was the dwelling place of a landowner, responsible to an Elder of the Court at Hesion for the output of the area under his control. He owned the land but was always supervised so that it was not misused.

A great landowner might rent acreage to tenant farmers with sufficient capital. The latter were required to take care of their property; this entailed hard work, but most landlords were fair and appreciated diligent lessees. The main factor governing any immense agricultural industry is the weather; fortunately for Deerait it seldom varied, with hot summers and warm winters, bolstered by an adequate rainfall. The soil itself was rich and fertile and, if ploughed, planted and harvested carefully, yielded an abundance of food.

The vast vegetable and grain produce of the Deerait farmlands was well known to Quinton and his foster parents. Ontar and Admaria realised that, although the four tribes supported themselves and ate well, in the future Deerait would be the central granary for the entire united continent of Rontmethar. Fresh vegetables would be kept in good condition, utilising methods already perfected on the Sacred Islands, to maintain an even temperature on board sailing vessels. However, this improvement might not be made available for years to come; such revolutionary processes could only be put into operation when Rontmethar and the other continents of Phentara had accomplished sufficient strides forward in education to cause their diverse races and nations to differentiate between technical adancement and what, at present, would be regarded as evil witchcraft.

On all of the great estates there were serfs who toiled directly for the landowners themselves. In return for their labours in the fields these humble peasants received food, shelter, clothing and protection. Their life generally tended to be harsher than those employed by the free tenant farmers; nevertheless they were fairly content with their lot. This villein class was expected to furnish troops when their lord rode to war in answer to a summons from the High Court.

Because of the influence of the young vibrant Casman Empire, the rulers of united Deerait had commenced the practice of appointing governors for the various provinces of their own territory. Although the Adiorenji, Vilatmori and Dariondi had initially concurred with this custom, they now adhered largely to the ancient practice of having local chiefs for each district, with a consequent family dynasty.

Cottis, in his capacity as governor of the province of Sicruci, was really the overlord or representative of the Deerait Court for his region. He had the duty of supervising the landowners and seeing that they not only conducted their agricultural responsibilities properly, but also cared for their serfs. This did not mean that the latter throughout the northwest had an easier life, for their days were filled with hard labour: however, they were not permitted to be exploited like they had been in the years before the national union of the tribes. This factor was often a source of considerable disagreement between the Deeraits and the other three peoples in the High Court, for the Vilatmori, Dariondi and the Adiorenji mainly disregarded the welfare of their villeins, treating them little or no better than slaves.

The peasants were still called upon to perform martial duties; these usually consisted of two days' military service each month, training in the use of swords, spears and archery. The entire nation had maintained this activity for many years after the treaty with the Casman Empire; but, with the passage of centuries, the rulers had been lulled into a sense of false security and landlords and governors for the most part had ignored or forgotten about it entirely. Nevertheless, with the present continual agitation between the tribes, a few sagacious landlords had resumed martial programmes, even before recent word came from Hesion to provincial governors that it was imperative that it be conducted on a regular basis.

Crop cultivation continued throughout the whole year because of the climate. Dairy produce was also a major industry, with rotars being reared to provide milk and cheese; the animals were also bred for draught and meat. In addition to the produce of the fields the Deerait nation also kept orchards which supplied them with an abundant variety of fruit. Vineyards provided wine, not only for domestic consumption, but also for export. Fishing was carried on all around the coasts, both inshore and deepsea. The catches were not only for the home market, for many vessels plied further afield along the imperial coastline, selling the results of their endeavours to the Casmans who were renowned for their reluctance to engage in maritime activities.

As the sun strolled up the clear sky to its zenith, the column coninued along the trail which was now only a hundred yards from the sea across a golden sandy beach. The steppe soldiers gazed at it continuously, marvelling at the high combers which undulated from the distant horizon. The sight of the powerful waves, crashing and cascading in a white bubbling foam onto the shore utterly entranced the warriors. They were like little steppe children, gazing in innocent wonderment at the golden moons and the silvern stars in the firmament for the first time. Each felt closer to the divine, infinite rhythmic essence which permeates and is the basis of all things, emanating from the Great Power.

"I know how they feel," Quinton spoke softly, having seen the rapt expressions on the faces of his guards.

"Yes. As long as one can find awe and harmony in the beauty of Nature and the Blessings given us, then there is no need to doubt the existence and love of our Creator," Allecenia responded from where she rode in her accustomed position beside the handsome youth.

"Look yonder. There are the ships we saw earlier far behind us. They've passed us in the distance out there. I'd thought that they would have travelled closer to the coastline on their way to Hesion. The sea is fairly deep inshore here. Oh, I remember now. It's to do with what Ontar taught me, about the movement of the tide being subject to the positions of the moons. It must be ebbing, isn't that so?"

"That's correct. When you come to the Sacred Islands you'll be shown how the tides are controlled by the passage of Selix and Ilix. We have instruments there to demonstrate tidal motions. I personally shall be most pleased to demonstrate them to you," Allecenia said gently in her beautiful tones from behind the veil which concealed her features.

"I shall look forward to that immensely," Quinton smiled.

Since the column was drawing nearer to Hesion it began to encounter travellers and more workers toiling in the fields. The villeins especially stared in amazement at the large well armed company and the magnificent linz. The steppe contingent, tall powerful and erect in their saddles, were garbed like ordinary Deerait soldiers but they exuded a confidence and martial knowledge which was definitely far superior to that possessed by any warrior in the four tribes. This naturally provoked the questions both to their identity and place of origin. If the curious observers had known what Cottis did, namely, that in the distant forests to the north there was a force of nearly a quarter of a million highly trained fighting men, then their unease would have been not inconsiderable.

After a short halt at noon near the beach for a cold meal they pressed onwards and finally came in sight of the capital of the Deerait tribe and nation just after mid-afternoon. The sprawling town lay beside the Chofanrit at a point where not only was there an excellent harbour, but also the Avidnive reached the ocean, dividing Hesion in two. Both parts of the town were connected by four bridges. Each was a strong wooden construction approximately a mile in length, supported by twenty equidistant stone pillars two hundred and ninety feet in height, thus permitting the tallest vessel to sail beneath it. The building of the wide-spanned bridges was the result of many years work and, besides being a most remarkable achievement, had been completed three centuries before to give access to both parts of the capital.

Estyork, whence the party had travelled, was a well laid out town with broad boulevards and reasonable sanitary facilities. Ontar and Admaria recollected that the Deeraits from the capital of Sicruci had modelled many aspects of their town on Rionder, for the capable citizens of the latter had erected their sylvan city in a similar fashion. Hesion, like the remainder of the population centres of the agricultural and maritime nation, had had no particular architectural plan: it had merely sprawled wherever its inhabitants had felt like building. Sanitation was very primitive; outside most of the residences it was not uncommon to see piles of ordure; ordinances were frequently posted, or called by town criers, for their removal lest fines be levied.

The streets were narrow with buildings rising to heights of two to three storeys. Passers-by had to be cautious, for often no warning was given when rubbish or less desirable substances were summarily thrown out of upper windows. Small yellow and green omniverous dogs, or lours, slunk from heap to heap dragging garbage all over the thoroughfares, the majority of which were paved with cobblestones, the latter being either dusty or muddy, depending on the weather.

Since it was the centre of government for the Deerait nation, in addition to being the major port on Rontmethar, Hesion was a thriving vibrant community. Ships brought merchandise from many lands, taking away grain and agricultural implements; the Deeraits excelled in the manufacture of such tools because the best quality high-grade iron ore deposits were located to the southwest of the town. Men toiled there day and night, fashioning metallic articles; the glow from the forges was clearly visible in the sky after sunset.

Every street in the business district had shops which advertised their wares by signs. The latter were extremely large, often stretching from high above the doorway over half the narrow thoroughfare. The candlemakers had ordinary sized candles for sale in their establishments but outside the signs, if they were to be believed, showed that their produce was at least five feet long and two feet in diameter. Similarly, the premises of cobblers appeared to serve customers with feet belonging to giants.

Business was of paramount concern in the town of two hundred thousand inhabitants. In addition to ships, the wealthier merchants owned several establishments and were generally the leaders of their respective guilds. To learn a trade an apprentice was obliged to belong to the appropriate guild for his calling and the latter looked after his welfare. His wages and conditions of employment were of prime importance and a trainee was far better cared for than the serfs who toiled in the fields. Yet the lot of the farm labourers was beginning to improve almost imperceptibly in the Deerait tribe; perhaps this was due to the troubled state of national politics and the realisation that the villeins might be required to march to war; indeed there seemed to be a change abroad, as if Phentara were awakening from a long slumber in anticipation of momentous times and events ahead.

The cavalcade finally reached the outskirts of Hesion and the riders saw the sprawling metropolis laid out before them. In the clear air they perceived miles of rooftops, the massive bridges over the River Avidnive and glimpsed ships and barges, either sailing or berthed. They rode down a long gentle slope to arrive at the fortified north gate.

The Deerait capital was enclosed by a wall fifty feet high with guard-posts at regular intervals. Although this protected the city, many houses had been built outside the south gate to accommodate the increasing population. The massive stone defence ran all around the town as far as was possible. However it ended on reaching the river and the shore on both banks where armed vessels took over. Since the mouth of the Avidnive was very wide, several warships patrolled from there out to sea and along the coast. Where the river flowed from the countryside to pass between the two sections of Hesion its depth was shallow, and huge barges with a single giant sail kept watch.

"Halt! State your business, strangers!" a Deerait sentinel with shining peaked helmet and breastplate, and wearing a gray and yellow livery, called down to them from the guard-post above the massive archway.

"Hail! I am Cottis, governor of Sicruci province and district commander of the garrison at Estyork. This is my escort."

"Sir, where is your standard?" the sentry asked courteously, his eyes straying to the huge linz.

"It was accidentally destroyed by fire in the summer. Regrettably, it has not been replaced," Cottis answered. "Now, can we enter Hesion?"

"Forgive the delay, sir. In these days of unrest we have been ordered to check on the identity of all large parties who wish to proceed within the walls," the guard called down respectfully. "Can you help me in this? Is there anyone here who can vouch for you?"

"I approve of your caution, and applaud it sincerely. Is Ilixiod still the north gate commander? He is my cousin."

"Yes, sir. He is still our commander. He's also on duty. Please attend while I send for him, sir."

"This is a new matter since I was here last. Then there was free access in and out of Hesion any time, day or night. It does reveal how extremely delicate the present situation is with the other sections of my nation. There certainly must have been considerable discord at the High Court meetings if the Elders have felt obliged to pass a decree to check on the identity of strangers. I don't believe this has ever happened since the Casman War centuries ago," Cottis remarked to Ontar.

"You're right. Perhaps it might be better if you were escorted into Hesion by your own bodyguard. If permissible we'll pitch our tents yonder where that small stream flows to the River Avidnive. It might be awkward for you to acquire accommodation for three hundred strangers in the town barracks when we are not Deeraits like your personal escort. I hope you can arrange this for our party. We have no desire to offend your people by not accepting their hospitality. Yet we do not wish to impose ourselves on the capital garrison," the sage declared.

"When Ilixiod comes I'll explain matters to him. He'll make

all the necessary arrangements for supplies to meet your needs. Your heculs will find ample grass yonder, but supplementary fodder will also be made available. The area here is common ground used by the citizens of North Hesion — that's the section of the town between here and the river — for general activities. Ah, there is Ilixiod!" Cottis exclaimed with genuine pleasure.

"Greetings, cousin! Your entry to Hesion is granted. Forgive the understandable delay in these doubtful times," the guard commander of the north gate called down from the battlements.

When asked by Cottis, Ilixiod assented to the King of Rionder and his company being allowed to use the common ground for camping purposes and affirmed that he would have provisions brought out to them. The governor of Sicruci and his personal bodyguard were accompanied by Felgorian when they entered the town while Quinton and his party turned aside to pitch their tents. The yellow skinned guard commander was most efficient in attending to their needs. Within an hour wains were bring driven out by extremely curious Hesionites desirous of seeing the contingent, which Ilixiod had remarked as being one of exemplary military bearing and efficiency.

The drivers and their assistants expected to perform the unloading by themselves. However, they were very pleasantly surprised when a handsome youth requested the strange soldiers to assist them. They wondered at the deference shown to one so young, especially when a humdrum task was carried out with evident keenness. The carriers also marvelled at the ease with which the newcomers tossed heavy sacks to one another, when it would have taken two of them to move the large awkward containers. The Deeraits did not recognise the peculiar accents of the warriors who conversed courteously with them in the Common Speech. They were very impressed by the proficient manner in which the camp had been laid out and the tents erected.

Food and wine were quickly distributed; and it was not too long before Quinton, his foster parents, Olluinan, Allecenia and Perlow had been served by Felthim, assisted by Onlestic, in the large shamianah. Each hoped that Felgorian's presence with Cottis, which the latter had requested, would impress the High Council. The Riondese ambassador would act as a liaison between the governor of Sicruci and his King. An additional factor which might prove helpful was that Felgorian had been well received at the Deerait Court a few months previously when he had been sounding out the general feeling about the ancient treaty with the Casman Empire.

"Shall we let our troops sample the fleshpots of Hesion?" Ontar asked with a smile.

"They have done well, but I don't believe we should let them do so at the moment. Firstly, we may have to depart from here very quickly. If they are scattered about inside the city there could be long delays before they are contacted. Secondly, the pleasures and deceits of a more sophisticated and hedonistic society might prove to be more than they are prepared to cope with. If someone did try to cheat them our men would not stand for that. A fight would inevitably result. The Deeraits would find them quite a handful. I am against it," Admaria declared firmly, looking at Quinton for his comments.

"I agree with you. Food and wine are to be brought to us from the city so there's no need to go into Hesion for supplies. Felgorian will send word or come himself. We could have an emergency. Civil war could break out in Sicruci. Estyork is the key to the region. I want to be there if the town is attacked.

"Of course, our troops could and should try the fleshpots. But not until the future. Besides, they don't have any money. They've never required it. Bartering was the normal way of trading on the steppes. Money will have to be obtained and distributed among our people in time," the youth stated.

"Yes. Our Casman troops are acquainted with a monetary system. Likewise the Riondese and the Polingsi, from trading with the Deeraits before Rionder fell. The steppe peoples have had the basics of monetary theory explained to them in our lectures, but they have not had any practice," Ontar said.

"What do you think will happen next?" Allecenia asked.

"I assume you're referring to a summons from the Court. I hope we'll have word tomorrow. Cottis will settle down in his quarters first. Tonight he'll probably be summoned to report on hostile activity on the borders of Sicruci. So, Felgorian should be back with us tomorrow, hopefully with news of when we are to attend the High Court," Ontar answered, before filling his beaker with water.

"When do you want me to set sail for home?" Olluinan said, glancing at the Heads of his Order.

152

"Tomorrow. The autumn winds will still be favourable. They should remain so for the next few days. But don't risk anything. Have a safe passage to Ordlansa," the wizard replied.

"Of course, the winds! I'd forgotten about them. I do remember a time many, many years ago. Allecenia and I were about a week late in returning to Hesion after a visit to you in your hut in the Rionder Valley. What happened, Quinton, was that the winds had changed drastically. Beyond the western coasts of Deerait the tides and winds are favourable to mariners most of the year. Sailing is relatively simple. However, towards the end of spring, and again about this time of year, the relative positions of Phentara, the sun and the two moons cause the tides and winds to change for several weeks. Gales and storms arise at sea and passage thereon can be perilous. We were delayed for quite a while on that occasion."

"Mmm. I see. Why didn't you use magic to calm the elements?" the young King of Rionder wondered.

"Two reasons. Firstly our ship was docked here in safe harbour and time was not precious. Secondly, this is a Deerait port. If observed, our use of magic might have terrified the Hesionites. They are very superstitious. They believe wizards shouldn't thwart the natural manifestations of the gods."

Olluinan paused and his daughter spoke, "We hold this to be a truth. White Magic is given to us from above. It must be used judiciously. So, Quinton, we followed our intuition on that occasion and set sail when the sea was relatively calm. Mind you, if an unexpected storm arose and we could not save ourselves from death, then it would be correct to practise magic in such a case."

"I understand. There is a great mystical and universal law in what you've just said. I shall meditate upon it carefully," the youth nodded with sincerity.

"When do you wish to board the ship?" Allecenia asked her father. "Not tonight, I hope."

"No. About midday tomorrow. The early afternoon tide is most favourable," Olluinan smiled gently.

"Excellent. Then we shall have the pleasure of your company this evening," Admaria said kindly, before adding, "and you can summarise your report to us."

"I shall. We've gone over everything very closely. There are only a few minor odds and ends to clarify. Shouldn't take long," Olluinan commented.

"It's almost dark outside. If you will excuse me, Perlow and I had better go and do the rounds," Quinton remarked, rising from the table.

The King of Rionder and his personal bodyguard left the huge tent and strode off to find Hanshair. The Nai-Zind, who happened to be nearby, was pleased to see his monarch approaching and greeted the latter courteously. At that moment Adrigal and Onlestic appeared from behind a tent; the Ker-Mantids promptly moved into positions to escort their paramount ranxem while he conducted his inspection of the encampment. Quinton had no difficulty for all was in order, which was only to be anticipated, since the steppe tribesmen were fiercely proud in their resolve never to fail their liege.

The camp had been laid out efficiently with the tents in four straight lines. The heculs, linz and rotars had been hobbled before being turned out to graze in the afternoon. In accordance with their guard commander's instructions, the animals had been herded together just before sunset and were being tended by several warriors. Other sentinels maintained a watch on all approaches to the camp, a matter which was noted by both the Deerait soldiery on the battlements and some curious civilians; the latter had made a circuit of their position in the late afternoon, ostensibly on the way to exercise their mounts.

When the inspection had been completed Quinton and his four bodyguards walked slowly beside the small stream between the tents, listening to the noise of the town. The sounds of revelry were borne to them, with cries and shouts both in the tongue of the Deeraits and in the Common Speech. Bright torches flickered and illuminated the battlements where sentinels were visible walking to and fro in the performance of their duties.

"Extremely vociferous people, Sire," Hanshair remarked very respectfully.

"They certainly are. Mind you, I can recall several occasions when a similar noise occurred in the Nai-Zind camp during a feast, especially when we celebrated Hedunon day. Perhaps they're trying to enjoy themselves as much as we used to," Quinton smiled at the pleasant memories.

"Yes, Sire. Still, they are townspeople with perhaps not the closeness to Nature we have had all our lives. Friends, some I've made among our Casman allies, have mentioned to me how townspeople partake of their enjoyment. I do not begrudge

154

them their relaxation at all, but I think a lot of them may go to excess," Hanshair commented, making a wise observation.

"I think they probably do. Like you've just said, they may not be as close to Nature and the essence of things as we are," Quinton responded thoughtfully.

"May I speak, Sire?" Onlestic asked with humility.

"Certainly."

"Perhaps they lack a comprehension of what really matters in life. The three of us have been conversing in our off-duty hours about such matters. When Unyamed told us about the busy merchants of Estyork and the even busier trading of Hesion, we all thought that too much emphasis was being placed on the accumulation of wealth. Although money has its place . . . ," the Ker-Mantid paused shyly.

"Pray continue. Don't be embarrassed, any of you. Ontar and Admaria, Gordan and the Polingsi commanders would be delighted to have you talk thus with them. I am very pleased," their monarch praised in the early starlight.

"We concluded that the first thing in life should be the Great Power and His Works. Then, the mental and physical health of the individual. Next, helping one's fellows. Lastly, wealth, but that is the least," Onlestic said, while Adrigal nodded his concurrence.

"And what have you to say, Perlow?"

"My comrade forgot to mention Love. Somehow I feel that there is a Love permeating everything. This Love is another name for the Great Power. It is He. It comes from Him, and is one with the Source of All. The Hesionites in general may have a lack of understanding of what really matters. It may cause the majority of them to miss out on the important things in life. I think that's what Hanshair meant, Quinton," the adopted Chofir tried to explain.

"Yes, it certainly is. We must all enjoy ourselves within reason, but we must never forget to thank the Great Power for His Beneficence to us. Our life was hard on the steppes, but in general it was of a better, intrinsic quality than in the towns. Townspeople, especially in the so-called Civilised Lands to the north and in the Casman Empire, tend to indulge themselves far too much, thus really spoiling their enjoyment of life. However, we must never look down or despise townspeople, for we too can learn from them. Likewise, can they not also learn from us if we are patient with them, and most of all with ourselves?" their liege stated.

"Yes, Sire," Hanshair and the Ker-Mantids concurred in unison, while Perlow nodded.

Quinton remained chatting with his devoted guards for several minutes before he and the Chofir returned to his shamianah. Olluinan had just finished his discussions with Ontar and Admaria and the remainder of the evening was pleasantly spent talking about the beauties of Ordlansa and its archipelago. The youth mentioned the very sensible attitude of his four guards which he hoped would prove to be a general one among the remainder of his escort. His foster father concurred, but tempered his approval by cautioning him that the pressures of town life might prove too much for some of their troops.

At dawn the following morning Quinton sent Hanshair to the north gate. The Nai-Zind asked the officer of the guard to grant permission for his King to enter Hesion. The reason for such a request was that one of the party of notables desired to take ship from the port on the early afternoon tide, and that only seventeen persons wished to traverse Hesion for this purpose. Ilixiod readily assented, for his cousin had advised him that all courtesy was to be extended to the visitors. Consequently, later that morning, Quinton, Admaria, Olluinan, Allecenia, Ontar and Perlow, escorted by eleven guards, rode under the archway into the sprawling city.

The outer north gate itself was fashioned from the very strong wood of the urtoz tree, and was approximately two feet thick. Across and down it ran wide metal bands for added strength and protection to reinforce the two massive beams which were used to bar ingress to hostile forces. The archway was eighty feet long; sixty feet from the outside there was a second gate with the same dimensions, providing an additional obstacle to any attacking force which might attempt to gain access that way. At the end of the archway on the street steps went up on both sides to the guard-post and the battlements.

Houses ran along the bottom of the dull red walls all around the city; these dwelling places were interspersed with shops, taverns and stables. The streets were crowded, thronged with citizens and visitors going about their daily business. Women shouted to one another from the high windows, gossiping in the bright morning sunlight. Men chatted or discussed various activities in the thoroughfares, while pedestrians, wagons and mounted travellers moved along. Boys hastened on errands for their masters and young girls learned the art of housekeeping from their mothers.

Quinton and his party looked with interest as they rode down a street with a sign indicating the North Harbour. The bustle and activity of a thriving township were still relatively new to the young paramount ranxem and his steppe troopers, for they had had little experience in either Estyork or Troldaart. In their turn the Hesionites scrutinised the small cavalcade passing by, remarking how fierce and strong the soldiers of the King of Rionder appeared; word had gone throughout the entire city the previous day regarding the identity of those who composed the escort of the Sicrucian provincial governor.

The street was very long: eventually they crossed a busy junction and rode down a thoroughfare in which the majority of the establishments were taverns. The atmosphere was slightly menacing but all was peaceful. Suddenly Ontar pointed out two Zancericts strolling from the direction of the harbour. The sage and his foster son knew that those approaching belonged to the fiercest race on the continent of Abdur-Timil. They were tall broad shouldered men with very high foreheads and dark green skins; their hair was wiry and combed into a peak, around which a maroon ribbon was tied tightly so that the ends sprouted over it in a small even fringe.

Each wore a long curved sword in a leather scabbard and had a sheathed dagger on his right hip. They were dressed in crimson knee length cloaks over an orange shirt and dark green trousers bound by a white belt, to which their weapons were attached by thongs. On their feet they wore black shoes. Their mien appeared haughty but respectful; this natural attitude occasionally led to trouble with others who did not realise that the Zancericts were an innately shy and modest people.

"So that's what they look like," Quinton said when they had gone past. "You mentioned once or twice that they could be formidable foes, if I recall correctly."

"Yes, they can be. In the days of the Ulgruffi Empire, it took a few years to subdue their ancestors. You'll remember from your geographical lectures that they're a race of approximately three million people. Their home is the Ceitswand region on Abudur-Timil. It is very arid. You have to be hardy to survive. There are four principal cities, one beside the bank of each of the main rivers.

157

"The majority of the Zancericts are nomadic, herding flocks of chirts, the source of the finest wool on Phentara. I'll tell you about chirts sometime. The other races on Abdur-Timil leave them well alone, except for trade of course. Occasionally they hire themselves out as mercenaries. Once, long ago, the Zancericts were assailed treacherously but their resistance against superior numbers was so fierce that their attackers were glad to withdraw."

"Perhaps, one day, they may be our allies," Quinton murmured in Ulgruffi.

"If we are fortunate enough to accomplish that then you'll find yourself served by warriors as loyal as your steppe tribesmen. Believe me," the mystic nodded.

"Very interesting thought," Quinton smiled. "This must be the harbour. Yonder is the sea," he indicated the end of the street.

"And this is the wharf where Olluinan will take a boat to the ship. That's it anchored about half a mile out there. The one with the two masts. Would you like to go aboard?" Ontar asked.

"Oh, please. I would like that very much," the youth smiled eagerly. "It'll be my first experience of a ship."

The wharf stretched for a considerable distance on either side of the street opening and was a scene of hectic activity. Sailing vessels were being loaded and unloaded; among the latter were some of those the column had seen at sea the previous day. Several of the huge flat bottomed barges, which regularly plied up and down the River Avidnive, were also moored. These had been accustomed to sailing beyond Estyork to the Ebrordin mountains in more peaceful times; but, since the increase in argument and dissension between the Deeraits and the other three tribes, their owners had thought it advisable to cease this traffic and only allowed their transports to proceed as far as the principal town of Sicruci.

Some Deerait warships were visible anchored in the delta. These were large vessels, about a hundred and fifty feet in length with four masts. They had three decks: the first was where the captain and his officers had their cabins; the second had the quarters for the crew and the store rooms; the bottom deck was for the giant oars, these being used when the wind failed or to obtain greater speed in battle. Unlike the vessels belonging to the Adiorenji, Vilatmori and Dariondi, the

Deeraits did not employ galley slaves, having abandoned this heinous practice after the Casman War; a roster system was utilised to advise the sailors when they were required to serve as rowers.

Hovering or gliding lazily above the busy harbour aysmoers with crimson plumages and light green beaks watched the water below for indications of fish. If any were sighted they were immediately swooped upon and swallowed whole in as short a time as possible. The birds also scanned the quays for any boxes of fish left unattended, which might furnish the wherewithal to assuage their perpetual hunger. Woe betide anyone foolish enough to leave his catch unguarded for even a few moments; this would be more than sufficient to invite a host of the screeching gulls to dine with zest and amazing alacrity.

Chapter Ten
The Rolcharacs

Ontar rode in front of the party of strangers whose presence was attracting much attention. The Ulgruffi mystic appeared to be searching for someone or something, so Quinton thought as he watched his guardian. At last his foster father smiled, before nodding to a tall handsome red skinned man, sitting in a large boat about ten yards from the quay. The latter acknowledged the arrival of the wizard with a cheerful wave. He then commanded his companions to pull on their oars to bring their craft to the steps which led up to where the sage and his companions were dismounting.

"Hanshair, Adrigal, Onlestic, Perlow, you will come with us. Colmar, you and the others remain here with our steeds. The locals will not trouble you at this time of the day. We shall return in an hour or so," Ontar said before beckoning those who were to journey with him to the ship.

As he descended the steps Quinton thought how martial and capable his small force of guards looked. The hardy Deeraits in the vicinity of the wharf were no fools either; they fully recognised first class fighting men and had no desire to provoke them in any manner whatsoever. The Melcogh and his command collected the reins of all the animals before leading them over to a large hitching rail with sufficient room left to accommodate their chargers. They tied the animals securely before relaxing and taking full advantage of the opportunity given them to study the activity in the harbour of North Hesion. To the Deeraits this was merely another day filled with toil; to the men from the vast Mescarg grasslands of Rontmethar it was one replete with wonderful sights to observe.

"Hail, Great Ontar," the handsome red skinned man with the shock of light blue hair spoke courteously in Ulgruffi and bowed before extending his left hand to assist the wizard aboard.

"And hail to you, Hopref. It is good to greet you once more. Olluinan has been telling me how excellently you captain the ship," the mystic complimented.

"Thank you. Praise from you is an honour," the other

160

acknowledged.

The young King of Rionder was the last to be helped aboard the large boat which had ten strong oarsmen dressed in white tunics. Hopref stared intently into Quinton's eyes momentarily before bowing low and saying in Ulgruffi, "Hail to you, Expected One. I am here to serve you as I do the leaders of the Sacred Order."

"I thank you sincerely," the youth responded, not certain what to do about this totally unlooked for greeting.

"You are the one for whom we have waited. I am grateful to the Lord Olluinan and Allecenia for allowing me to captain their ship. It is only thus that I have been honoured to meet you." Hopref spoke with kindness in his voice while obvious sincerity coupled with admiration shone from his brown eyes.

"And I am honoured to meet you too. My visit to your ship is short. I hope we shall meet again at some future time," Quinton responded kindly. His personality charmed its way into the heart of another person from the Sacred Islands, and also entranced the rowers, who conversed amongst themselves.

"Now, Sir, we shall be off," Hopref smiled and nodded to his crew.

Oars were pushed against the dank wall of the quay until the boat floated over into a position from which rowing could be commenced. Powerful shoulders hauled back rhythmically while aysmoers screeched overhead in the bright sunlight. As they began to move the travellers were able to perceive the ships and wharves of busy South Hesion in the distance to their right. The oars splashed in perfect harmony and the boat was propelled swiftly over the water.

"Admaria, how did Ontar know where to find Hopref? There was no communication from our camp last night, at least as far as I know, unless astral projection was used. How was it done?" Quinton asked his very beautiful dark haired foster mother, who was sitting beside him on the bench in front of their vessel.

"Not really a mystery. The Master Crystals at Hesewoner function in part like scrying globes. They can also send pictures to receivers capable of translating their vibrations. Of course, knowledge of such instruments is kept absolutely concealed from outworlders. They'd find it terrifying. They'd believe it the work of demons. There is such a receiver on the Erlean,

161

the ship we are being rowed to yonder," the handsome Ulgruffi woman explained in her native tongue.

"The Master Crystals watch us all the time. So the Islanders would know where Olluinan was and send a message to the ship," Quinton deduced.

"Precisely. When our party arrived yesterday outside the north gate, this would be advised to the ship. Knowing about the seasonal vagaries of the tides and using the ship's crystal, Hopref would conclude that Olluinan would be leaving today," Admaria smiled.

The powerful oarsmen pulled vigorously and the distance to the Erlean diminished rapidly. The rowers were from the same race to which Hopref belonged, as was evidenced from the colour of their skin and hair. Admaria confirmed to Quinton that they belonged to a people called the Rolcharacs who had originated on the continent of Iursorle on the opposite side of Phentara to Rontmethar. Each belonged to the Sacred Order and had special scientific work to investigate when on Ordlansa.

Ontar, Olluinan, Admaria, the crew and the steppe warriors were much amused by Hopref, who had moved down the boat to sit beside Allecenia. Quinton watched with interest, devoid of jealousy, while the handsome Rolcharac attempted to court her. The hooded Lady treated her suitor with firmness; the latter, fully aware that she had often informed him of her feelings as regards marriage, smiled tenderly.

"You are breaking my heart, Allecenia!" Hopref cried in the Common Speech, while he knelt in front of her and held her right hand.

"I'll break your neck, you rascal. You never take no for an answer, do you?" she laughingly responded.

"While you are unattached? Never!" came the resolute reply.

Quinton noticed the amused grins on the rowers' faces and the nearest one leaned over to say in Ulgruffi, "Expected One, Hopref has no hope with Allecenia. She does like him, for he is a very kind and generous person. He realises his position in her affections, but has to try. Oh, forgive me for speaking to you thus. My name is Arginirg."

The youth was about to reply when Admaria said, "Arginirg, and the rest of our friends here, please do not be afraid of talking to Quinton. He has often mentioned his longing to meet more people from Ordlansa."

"I most certainly have. Arginrig, I am very happy to make the acquaintance of you and your comrades. I thank you for your courtesy. I hope one day I'll fulfil all the aspirations each one of you has," the handsome youth smiled. His shining aura suddenly radiated from him, and this was noticed by each of the mystics aboard. It caused the rowers and their captain to realise that Quinton was indeed very far along the Mystic Way, much further than they themselves had yet progressed.

Hopref kept up his good natured banter with Allecenia until they reached the Erlean sitting at anchor in the bay. Rope ladders were dropped and the party climbed aboard the fine trim vessel, which was ninety feet in length with two masts and two decks. To Quinton it appeared to travel entirely by sail for no other means of propulsion were visible. The entire crew and officers were drawn up in two straight lines, and Ontar introduced his foster son to every one of them. The wondrous youth clasped their hands and in turn they felt his majesty.

Long afterwards each could recall the sensation experienced and knew in his heart that this indeed was the Expected One; feelings of gladness and an eagerness to serve the future Emperor of Phentara were mingled with solemn thoughts about the immense labours which the King of Rionder would have to face. These engendered a resolve to work industriously at their own projects, no matter how tedious their tasks might seem on occasion.

Quinton, Ontar and Admaria spent the entire time on board the trim vessel chatting with the crew who came from all over Phentara. The conversation was conducted in the Common Speech for the benefit of the steppe warriors. The excitement of the Sacred Islanders was wholly evident. They delighted to honour Hanshair, Adrigal and Onlestic, and praised Perlow without reservation, for they knew of his heroic deed. The Heads of the Order of Light had intended to take their foster son below deck, but the keenness of their people to meet him could not be denied.

Allecenia and Olluinan withdrew to a quiet corner and spent the time in private discussion. Her father was amazed by something his daughter said towards the end of their talk. He looked at her with delight and surprise, before embracing her.

"Your mother will be pleased. I am. But what about Quinton? Does he know?" Olluinan asked.

"I doubt it. His feelings towards me are most affectionate. I can sense them. But he hasn't made any declaration of intent," the Lady answered.

"Remember, we don't know whom he is to marry," her father cautioned.

"Yes. I'm prepared for that. It will be a very grievous hurt. But I'll serve him whatever the cost. I love him. I really love him, more than life. Am I foolish, when he is a mere youth?"

"Certainly not. He is no ordinary youth. We all know that. He has a maturity far beyond his years. Almost as if his last incarnation had continued directly into this one without a break for transition," Olluinan declared with sagacity.

"I shall just have to wait and see what happens. Poor Hopref. I wonder what he'd think if he knew," Allecenia said.

"Hopref is kind and noble. He will be sad, but wholly devoted and delighted if you are the one who is to be Quinton's spouse," her father nodded.

"Anyway, when he's not courting me he's always been interested in one or two other pretty girls on Ordlansa. He'll be all right," Allecenia smiled.

"Yes, he will. When will your mother and I see you again?"

"Ontar has given no definite time. Oh, here he comes now," she motioned towards the wizard striding resolutely across the deck.

"I happened to overhear your last remark, God-daughter. For once I am unable to say. My intuition normally advises me. This time nothing. Except that you're to remain with Admaria, Quinton and me. Nevertheless we shall meet astrally with your father and mother," Ontar spoke quietly.

"That is a privilege," Allecenia said with gratitude.

"Yes, a privilege of the Great Power that we know how to project. I've also come to bid farewell to you, Olluinan, my very dear friend. The time for parting is here. The shore party must depart now, or the boat crew will be late in returning and you'll miss the tide," the wizard explained.

"Then the time for parting is assuredly here. Mind you, I'm glad I met Quinton in the flesh. So is everyone aboard. It gives us a more definite feeling that he really exists. Beyond doubt, he is the Expected One," Olluinan nodded as they walked over to the large group listening and talking to the King of Rionder, his foster mother and the steppe warriors.

A few minutes later Olluinan and Allecenia embraced and

parted. Her father naturally felt sad, but somehow believed that this was to be an essential part of her life. On his return to his home in Hesewoner, Artzcellia surprised her spouse by stating that such exceptional beauty had not been given to a mortal woman without there being a divine reason behind it. When pressed further she merely smiled and bade her husband to be patient, advising him to trust in a mother's instinct.

Ontar quickly organised matters. In a short space of time Olluinan and the crew were waving farewell, while the Rolcharac rowers, who were as broad as the steppe warriors although on average four inches smaller, pulled mightily at the oars. The boat passed swiftly over the calm sea. Quinton sat quietly, thinking about how pleased the Islanders had been to touch him and talk to him. More than ever he felt humble, and resolved to follow his destiny, for he sincerely wanted to bring their hopes for his planet to complete fruition.

The youth had been embraced by Olluinan who had looked at him gravely and lovingly. The depth of the handsome sage's feelings had taken Quinton totally unawares, especially when Allecenia's father had whispered, "Take good care of my daughter. I entrust her to you." He glanced at Allecenia who was conversing with his foster parents and Hopref, and wondered what was behind the soft spoken words.

At last the boat bumped against the wharf and the captain of the Erlean leaped out to assist his passengers. Ontar, Admaria and Allecenia bade a fond farewell to the Rolcharacs, and especially to Hopref. The latter helped Quinton out. The youth, who was the last to leave, looked into his brown eyes once more.

"Thank you all for a safe journey. I sincerely look forward to seeing every one of you again. Take care of yourselves. You too, my friend."

"And you, Quinton, in whom the hope of our world rests. May the Great Power protect and keep you always. Praise to Him. He sent you Perlow," Hopref said in Ulgruffi, with tears in his eyes. "It has been a privilege to meet you, and hold your hand in friendship."

With these courteous words the noble kind Rolcharac climbed back into the boat. Quinton ascended the steps and, on reaching the top, turned and waved to those below as they commenced the long row back to the ship. Colmar and his company came across and looked down at the red-skinned men pulling strongly. They little realised how the latter envied their positions. The King of Rionder and his companions stood for a long time until the Erlean had moved away into the distance.

"I'm glad I met them all," Quinton said as they mounted their heculs.

"And they're glad they met you. You do mean a lot to those on the Islands," Ontar averred.

"I know that beyond all doubt. It makes me feel humble that they care about me as a person. I shall do my best for them," his foster son said softly in Ulgruffi.

"Where to now, Sire?" Hanshair called.

"Back to camp," the paramount ranxem of the Mescarg steppe peoples commanded, turning his capable mind back to the present.

The party proceeded along the wharf which was very quiet with only a few Deeraits about, and turned along the Street of the Taverns. They clattered over the cobblestones. Quinton had just commented to Ontar on the number of drinking dens when his foster mother riding behind spoke.

"Yonder are the two Zancericts we saw this morning. They likely had business with the wool merchants in a city quarter not far from here. That's their ship docked on the far side of the wharf. Further along the quay than we went," Admaria commented, showing her knowledge both of Hesion and of maritime vessels.

"They shouldn't be in this neighbourhood at this time of day," Ontar spoke seriously to his foster son. "The wharf is empty of all activity, as you no doubt noticed. This is the time when bands of thieves and rogues begin to foregather in many of these taverns. An armed party like ours won't be assailed. Two Zancericts with fine clothes are targets too difficult to resist."

"No militia?" Allecenia enquired. "I'm sure I've seen them in this district on occasion."

"Yes, in the late morning perhaps, but not from about this hour until dawn. The Deerait militia tend to avoid this area unless a full scale riot develops. When that happens a regiment from the town garrison turns out in force to support them," Ontar replied, before adding, "because things can be pretty grim."

"In other words, a full scale riot is required to bring the rule of law here. That's a bad situation. The gangs avoid that state of affairs if they possibly can. They like to be left to their own wicked pursuits," Admaria said.

"I know what I'd do, Sire," Hanshair spoke frankly.

"Exactly what I would too," his liege averred, showing the resolute side of his nature once more.

There were only a few passers-by in the thoroughfare, warily eyeing the well armed party. Quinton noticed one further along making a surreptitious signal to an evil-looking Deerait who was leaning against the dirty wall close to a tavern door. Almost immediately the ruffian shouted inside and a score of cut-throats rushed from the inn, armed with swords, clubs and knives. They hastened towards the Zancericts about twenty yards distant. The latter quickly drew their scimitars and stood steadfastly side by side, determined to defend themselves in the face of what appeared to be certain death. They were totally oblivious that assistance was coming forthwith.

"Admaria! Allecenia! To the rear! Hanshair! Guards! Draw swords! Charge!" Quinton bellowed without hesitation.

His voice resounded in the street even as his faithful warriors hurtled after him and his foster father. The sound of clattering hooves thundering towards them made the villains scatter for doorways and alleys to avoid being trampled by the fine heculs. The Zancericts looked up at their rescuers in wonderment, and were astounded to hear Ontar speak reassuringly to them in their own tongue.

"Remain with us! We shall protect you against such infamy," the sage said in his wondrous voice.

"Our gratitude and sincere thanks to you, Sir, and your valiant companions. We are strangers in a foreign land. We've been here before. We are aware of the perils of this wicked Street of the Taverns and its neighbourhood. Our business took much longer than anticipated. We foolishly believed we'd attain the safety of our ship in the harbour without being molested," one replied shyly.

"I shouldn't make a habit of forgetting the passage of time in places like this," the wizard smiled kindly.

"Archers on the rooftop yonder!" Perlow called, ever alert, pointing upwards.

"Draw your bows! Independent firing!" Quinton snapped his orders in the Common Speech. Then he shouted in Ulgruffi to prevent their assailants learning his intentions, "Admaria! Allecenia! Make a detour! Ride back to the harbour! Get to

167

the north gate. Tell Ilixiod what is happening. I believe it's long past time for this street of evil to be purged. Whatever happens, bring the guards!"

"If Ilixiod needs time to organise the militia and garrison troops we'll have to ask his permission before we bring in the guards," Allecenia said to Admaria as they wheeled round and galloped back towards the harbour.

"No matter what Ilixiod says, we shall bring in our own guards. You can go through the courtesies of asking him. I shall simply race through the north gate for our troops. We need them! That's all that matters! They would have it no other way!" her godmother stated unequivocally.

"Ah, I'm beginning to understand more fully. On the Islands we tend to become lulled by our pleasant surroundings. You are more dynamic, like Quinton and his soldiers. They are so decisive and resolute," Allecenia nodded, the sudden thought striking her mind forcefully.

Back in the Street of the Taverns five sturdy Deeraits had climbed onto the roof of the hostelry, from which the abortive assault on the unsuspecting Zancericts had been launched. They had hoped to slay some of the riders below before their position on the parapet was detected. Unfortunately, for their own survival, they had no inkling of the comprehensive training which instilled vigilance and decision into the troops of the King of Rionder.

Even while they notched arrows to their bowstrings their adversaries had already launched cruel shafts in their direction with deadly accuracy. Three were struck in the chest and toppled backwards while their other two comrades pitched headlong over the side of the building to crash bloodily onto the cobblestones; one had received an arrow in his throat, which had penetrated through to reappear from the back of his head; the other, who had sustained a shaft in his left eye, screeched horribly before lurching in his final death throes and tumbling over the parapet.

"Dismount! Let's clean out yonder lair of evil!" the wizard commanded in his vibrant tones, his height appearing simultaneously to increase in majesty, to the utter astonishment of the Zancericts.

"Squad, dismount! Your steeds will be safe! Great Ontar has attended to them with a spell!" Hanshair snapped, having seen the sage making a magical sign with his left hand.

168

Although still startled by the momentous turn of events the two natives of Ceitswand did not hesitate. They were ready to assist the valiant warriors into whose midst circumstances had brought them. They had no time to ponder the apparent rashness in assaulting the tavern before them; not until much later did they remark to each other that the more sensible course of action would have been for them and their strange allies to beat a hasty retreat to the harbour and the sanctuary of their vessel.

Quinton leaped from his hecul and was second inside the tavern behind his foster father, closely followed by Perlow, Hanshair, Adrigal, Onlestic, the guards and the two Zancericts. The first impressions which the Nai-Zind commander momentarily had was that the shadowy entrance of the Harbour Tavern was the gateway to a veritable nest of devils: but his beloved monarch had entered and he would follow him no matter where he led or what was to be encountered. Similar brief thoughts ran through the minds of the Chofir and the two redoubtable Ker-Mantids who were both looking forward to the ensuing battle, if the truth were to be admitted.

The dingy interior was reasonably well lit with torches in brackets around the walls of a large room. Several tables and chairs were spread about and a fire burned fiercely in an open hearth in one corner, its flames casting further flickering shadows. A staircase led from the right of the fireplace to the upper quarters of the establishment where the brutal innkeeper and his cronies had their rooms. A vile putrid stench of rotting meat and vegetables permeated the decidedly insalubrious atmosphere, a breeding ground for the disease and pestilence which often spread throughout Hesion.

Quinton, Ontar and their companions had little time to survey their surroundings for they were immediately faced with thirty heavily armed Deeraits, wielding swords, clubs and knives. Instantly the royal guard sprang into action without waiting for their King's command; this was their duty, to protect their monarch with life and limb, having no regard for their own personal safety. Twelve powerful resolute Mescarg steppe warriors strode in front of their beloved paramount ranxem, his foster father and the two Zancericts. Reckoning that they would be fighting at close quarters, the royal guard had discarded their bows, quivers and shields, throwing them down against the wall inside the entrance to the tavern; their huge lances had been left behind in the camp for it was thought that they would not be required during their visit to Hesion. Perlow, Adrigal, Onlestic and Hanshair smiled briefly at one another before advancing with keen blades which glittered in the flickering light.

"Take them! We'll teach a lesson they'll never forget!" the white Deerait innkeeper snarled in his native dialect.

Although Quinton and Ontar were fully aware of what had just been said, the guards and the two Zancericts possessed no knowledge of the Deerait language. However a translation was unnecessary; the meaning was only too obvious. Hanshair and his two Ker-Mantid associates did not hesitate. Passing their swords to some of their fellows, they threw the nearest chairs at their adversaries before lifting an enormous heavy table and tossing it in the same direction. The Deerait thugs had no time to marvel at the strength of the strangers for they ducked to avoid the lighter missiles, from which they sustained a few minor bruises. However, the effect of the massive table inflicted far more harm, for ten of their number were felled.

"Now we'll take them!" the Nai-Zind commander shouted, seizing his sword.

His companions in the guard did not waver for an instant. They were outnumbered but confident in their ability and prepared to lay down their lives, if such were required, to obey the youth who was their liege lord. For a fleeting moment, Hanshair cast his mind back to that beautiful day several months before when Quinton had crowned himself. He had felt very proud then, and did so now, advancing to assail the ruffians. His two Ker-Mantid friends and Perlow flanked him. The fight within the tavern erupted into a pitched battle.

"We must help! Your guard is outnumbered," one of the Zancericts said to Ontar, "but they appear so dynamic and efficient."

"They are. We four shall remain here behind them covering the door. We'll keep watch for any more rogues coming to assist those Deeraits. We can also take the opportunity to assist, should it arise," the sage replied. "As you've observed, Quinton has a bow and some arrows. Perhaps we should get some also."

"They are outnumbered three to one. More ruffians may come from the other taverns to help their comrades," the other Zancerict spoke shyly.

170

"Do not concern yourselves. They shall manage very well," the wizard said with assurance.

His words were soon to prove correct. The training and exercises devised on the Mescarg steppes had developed muscles and fitness seldom seen in Deerait. The cut-throats were powerfully built but, against the royal guard of the King of Rionder, they might just as well have been sickly children. The fighting was at close quarters. Swords clashed and rogues began to die. The powerful hacking and thrusting of their resolute adversaries forced them back, leaving several of their companions on the filthy floor. The club wielders fared little better. They lashed out but the guards easily avoided their blows before either chopping off their wrists or felling them with sword pommels and fists to send them reeling unconscious.

Hanshair, who was in the forefront, was attacked by five thugs. His reactions were prompt. His flashing sword blade not only halted their attempted advance, but slew two. Adrigal and Onlestic roared the Ker-Mantid battle cry and dispatched the other three with terrifying speed. Colmar and Perlow were in the thick of the fray, using their swords, fists, feet and any crockery or furniture available.

Quinton watched closely. His sharp eyes glimpsed a figure on the stairway with a knife in its hand ready to throw. The King of Rionder did not hesitate. His hands quickly notched an arrow. He loosed the strong shaft over the head of the antagonists. It sped to its mark, struck a cut-throat below the chin and emerged bloodily from the far side of his head. He crashed to the floor as the youth ran to one side to climb on top of a table beyond the fighting.

Again his fingers moved faster than sight. A second assassin was struck in the heart, his dagger tinkling down the stairs, while its owner vomited blood and tumbled after his weapon. Simultaneously Ontar and the Zancericts found themselves occupied. The sage had noticed a fallen Deerait roll over to the side and rise to his feet. The latter held a poniard which he was about to throw at Hanshair. Ontar's right hand flashed across to the weapon sheathed on his left hip beneath his cloak. Before the Nai-Zind could be struck, the wizard's long bladed knife seemed to sprout from the centre of the ruffian's chest.

The two Zancericts heard footsteps running over the cobblestones and notched arrows to their bowstrings. Four swarthy unclean Deeraits burst through the doorway. Their intentions were hostile, such was evident from the swords in their hands. Both Zancericts reacted promptly; they loosed their shafts and two of the newcomers lost their lives. Ontar had just turned round from throwing his knife when a bolt flashed by his head to strike a third ruffian. Almost immediately Quinton released a second shaft at the doorway, where it ended another evil life.

By this time almost two thirds of the gang inside the tavern were either dead or unconscious. The remainder panicked and fled out of the side door, some leaving a hand behind on the floor. The Zancericts gazed in astonishment at the scene, scarcely able to believe what they saw. The speed with which Quinton had fired his arrows had exceedingly surprised them. For the first time they began to have hopes of escaping with their lives.

"We have completed the task in here, Sire," Hanshair said, turning to his King. "Thank you for watching our backs."

"My pleasure. Mind you, Ontar knifed a Deerait about to slay you," Quinton smiled, stepping down from the table.

"Thank you, Great Sage," the Nai-Zind bowed.

"My privilege, Hanshair," the wizard acknowledged the courtesy.

"What kept you so long?" Quinton enquired of his guard commander.

"Those two lazy Ker-Mantids and that Chofir, Sire," Hanshair quipped in return, to which remark Onlestic immediately pulled a most ugly grimace to the amusement of all present.

"Well done, every one of you. They'll be back with reinforcements. Find the cellar. Seven of you, remove the corpses down there. Put the unconscious thugs there too. Collect as many arrows as can be found. Adrigal, Colmar, check upstairs. Barricade the door to the roof, if you can. Hanshair, you and our Zancerict friends, drag those corpses in here. Close and bar the door. Perlow, attend to the side door and the windows. Then assist the others. Once this area is cleared of bodies, jam tables against the doors." Quinton snapped crisp precise commands.

A warrior retrieved Ontar's knife and wiped it on the tunic of its victim before handing it back to the eminent mystic. While Quinton and his foster father supervised the proceedings on the ground floor, Adrigal and Colmar sped up the filthy broad stairs with drawn swords. The Ker-Mantid and the Melcogh looked into every single one of the various rooms, but all the apartments were empty. They reached the top and were about to close the open door to the roof when a very slight noise caught their sharp ears.

Adrigal nodded to Colmar, who broke open a large cupboard. Both warriors relaxed, for inside was a Deerait girl of about ten years of age with a grubby face and grimy yellow skin. The child was absolutely terrified and, while Colmar barred the door to the roof, Adrigal sheathed his sword and stooped to lift the girl into his arms. She did not struggle for the fierce warrior smiled gently and chattered utter nonsense to her.

"Take her downstairs. I'll follow," Colmar said.

"That door fastened securely?" Adrigal asked his comrade.

"Yes. It's very thick. There's three bars across it. I'd have liked a large table to jam against it, but there's no furniture of any kind on this floor."

"The stairs are far too narrow to bring one up from beyond the first floor," Adrigal stated. "Look, I'd better take this child to King Quinton and Great Ontar."

"Don't take her to the ground floor. They won't have finished clearing up yet. Take her into one of the first floor rooms. She's terrified. There's no need to frighten her further. I'll find her some food and ask the King and Great Ontar to come upstairs. Wonder what she was doing, locked in there," the Melcogh remarked as they descended.

"Whatever the reason, no child should be treated in such a manner. Oh, Colmar, thanks for telling me not to take her downstairs. Would've terrified her," came the grim reply, which was replaced by a smile and the uttering of soothing phrases.

"What have we here?" the sage wondered when he and his foster son entered the room where Adrigal had seated himself on a bench with the girl on his knee.

Quinton nodded to Colmar, who had brought up a piece of bread and some meat from a recess near the fireplace. The child snatched at the food eagerly, sensing that the tall strangers intended her no harm. While she ate, still sitting on Adrigal's knee, Ontar questioned her gently in the local dialect. He learned that her name was Vlamar; she had been kidnapped several days before near the house of Ihlden, a prominent and

173

noted citizen of Hesion. In addition to being the little girl's grandfather, this particular personage was also a most influential member of the High Court or Council. Both the wizard and his foster son already knew about this Elder, for Felgorian had mentioned his name during his report in the forest.

"Have you come to rescue me?" Vlamar asked in a small voice.

"We didn't know you were here. But we'll see you're taken home as soon as possible," Ontar said kindly, his marvellous voice calming the child.

"What do we do with her when the fighting starts, Sire?" Adrigal enquired quietly in his native dialect.

"Either Ontar or I will put her to sleep. She won't see what happens. We'll keep her here with a spell of guard for added protection," Quinton answered, touched by the concern of the battle hardened warrior.

"Thank you, Sire," the Ker-Mantid acknowledged courteously, still in awe of the youth who was his overlord.

After the Deeraits had been expelled from the Harbour Tavern they fled to the Aysmoer Inn, the largest, busiest and most notorious in the neighbourhood. The dramatic events were related to the principal kemarr, or baron, whose name was Riekou. The latter was the undisputed ruler of the district, and his word was law. His place of business was only a hundred yards further up the street from the Harbour Tavern, which he also owned. Unfortunately, the underling in charge of the inn had been slain by Hanshair, and Riekou was enraged when this news was broken to him.

The kemarr resolved that the strangers must not be allowed to escape. Riekou worked on the principle that no slight, however small, was to be endured without the perpetrator being savagely punished. He therefore commanded the deaths of those who had interfered with the activities of his henchmen. No one, not even the militia, was going to thwart him. The news that it was the King of Rionder and his escort who had rescued the Zancericts did not abash the baron. After all, was not Rionder a sacked kingdom, with its people living like animals in the vast northern forests? Who would complain if its ruler were slain?

Within five minutes of the conclusion of the fight inside the Harbour Tavern, gangs of rogues, ruffians and cut-throats were pouring into the streets surrounding the inn. Over five hundred were present, clamouring and cursing, while almost the same number of their associates were being summoned from further afield. Riekou had immense influence. None of the lesser kemarrs dared ignore his commands. His vengeance would be swift and violent against those who refused to assist him.

The shouts of the approaching mob reached the keen ears of Ontar and Quinton. The youth leaned forward to trace a magical symbol on the forehead of the girl who immediately fell asleep. Adrigal rose and placed her gently on a bed near the door. Once they had left Ontar uttered a spell of guard, so that no one could enter the room and harm the child. He followed the others down the stairs to where the rest of the guards and the Zancericts waited.

"Listen! We have to hold this place for another ten minutes. Then our comrades should be here. We've managed to secure the doors. The windows, narrow as they are, will be their first main approach. A Deerait can climb through the aperture. There are four windows, all facing the front. Hanshair, you, Ontar, Perlow and I shall be the reserve. The rest of you, split into threes and take a window. Be ready when they smash the shutters. Make every arrow count. Onlestic, you accompany our Zancerict friends," Quinton ordered.

Chapter Eleven
The Cleansing of the Street of the Taverns

Admaria and Allecenia reached the harbour without hindrance. They turned to the left; their strong steeds with the splayed hooves apparently sensed the urgency of their riders. The two women galloped for about fifty yards before turning left again up a thoroughfare parallel to the Street of the Taverns. There were comparatively few citizens about. The honest Hesionites in the district sensibly began their work very early; they endeavoured to have their daily labours completed before mid-afternoon when the gangs usually appeared in the vicinity.

The thundering hooves caused anyone in the path of the fine racing heculs to jump aside. Allecenia and Admaria raced neck and neck to the north gate which they reached within a record six minutes. While Olluinan's daughter called for Ilixiod the beautiful Ulgruffi galloped under the mighty archway to rein up moments later in front of the encampment. A warrior ran forward to grasp the bridle of her steed, while a squad of guards rushed over to obey her every wish.

"Quirgid! Helijaw! Portarid! All section commanders to me! Ontar and King Quinton are in peril! Turn out the entire royal guard immediately! All weapons except lances to be borne! Bring two extra quivers of arrows for each soldier! Arms for me too!" she called in a strong resolute voice.

The news that their monarch and his foster father were in danger animated the steppe warriors. Half of them hastened to saddle their heculs while the remainder gathered sufficient weapons for the entire force and the Lady Admaria. Within three minutes the royal guard was mounted and galloping after the beautiful Ulgruffi. The encampment stood empty except for Felthim, looking after them with a very worried expression on her face. The Nai-Zind woman spoke a silent prayer to the Great Power and did that hardest of all things when friends are in peril, which was to wait anxiously.

At the far side of the north gate, Ilixiod listened intently to Allecenia's request that permission be granted for the royal guard of Rionder to enter Hesion. The Deerait knew the dangers of the Street of the Taverns, but his authority was

176

limited. He could not send his own troops to assist without direct authority from the Castle. However the entrancing voice of the veiled woman touched his heart.

"I shall grant you leave. I should not do this without informing the garrison commander. Yet time is short. Take your troops! Do what you can! I'll personally be the courier with the message that there's a riot outside the Harbour Tavern. That will bring in the military. I hope your companions can be rescued by your guard and that your guard can hold out until a regiment comes from the Castle," Ilixiod declared.

"How long will that take?" Allecenia asked, looking up at the north gate commander who stood on the steps above her.

"Probably at least half an hour before help reaches your King. The city militia will take slightly longer. Cottis said that he was very important and had to be honoured. Like I said, I shall go personally to the Castle. I'll bring out the regiment and the militia. May the gods defend you and yours, Lady!"

At that moment Admaria galloped back under the archway, followed by almost three hundred grim faced warriors. Allecenia pulled her steed out of the way of the cavalcade before digging in her heels and hastening after them. Ilixiod ran down the steps and shouted for his mount which was swiftly saddled and brought from one of the nearby stables. The sturdy Deerait urged his charger forward in the direction of the Castle, which stood about fifty yards from the River Avidnive in North Hesion. As he rode he doubted whether the King of Rionder or any of his escort would survive for the kemarrs were capable of mustering almost a thousand cutthroats from the drinking dens around the waterfront.

Inside the Harbour Tavern, Quinton, Ontar and their companions listened to the howls of the mob surrounding their shelter. The hostelry stood on a corner. The front and side doors were being assailed by battering rams in the shape of long benches. However the steppe warriors had securely jammed tables and other heavy furniture, so that nothing short of burning could give access through either entrance.

Riekou's lieutenants urged the rabble to smash the shutters and force their way through to slay the interlopers. Neither the principal kemarr nor any of his underlings had thought it necessary to climb across the rooftops to descend through the door there to the floor of the inn. After all, there were only

177

sixteen persons inside the Harbour Tavern, not including the kidnapped child. These fools would be killed. Their demise would be held out as a warning of what happened to anyone daring to thwart the principal baron who controlled the Tavern district. Riekou fully realised that someone was bound to inform the Castle that a riot was occurring but, by the time the military arrived in regimental force, they would only find his dead adversaries. The chief kemarr also anticipated that the Riondese soldiery would attempt to interfere, for he had been advised of the flight of the two women. He had over a thousand villains on hand. They should have no problem in dealing effectively with the opposition of the royal guard.

The thugs used clubs and axes to smash through the shutters. They anticipated that they would soon be able to climb through the openings and overwhelm the King of Rionder and his friends. However, those inside the inn were not about to yield to certain death without a fight. It took about three minutes before cracks appeared in the shutters, and another two for the weakest bars across them to buckle and give way. Several of the ruffians smashed determinedly at the doors but, since the wood was very thick and strong, their frantic efforts made no impression other than to mark the entrances slightly.

A deep animal roar arose from the evil horde when the first shutter and its wooden bars crashed inside. An eager villain scrambled through to be despatched immediately by a swift sword thrust from Colmar. Fortunately for the defenders the width of the window was only sufficient to allow access to one person at a time. The Melcogh withdrew to one side and his two fellow warriors fired swift shafts through the opening. Ten arrows swished through the air and a corresponding number of rogues perished.

Similar events were now taking place at the remaining windows. The press of the mob, viciously eager to slay those inside, had the disastrous effect of causing their fellows nearest to the Harbour Tavern to receive volleys of shafts from the interior. Within two minutes of the last shutter being smashed eighty cut-throats had been killed or wounded. Consequently their cronies were most reluctant to proceed with the assault.

Reikou, mounted on a large hecul, hovered on the fringes of his horde of underlings. When he saw the deaths of his henchmen the kemarr decided on a change of tactics. He would burn them out, regardless of the danger that a fire could spread and destroy innocent people and other buildings. The important thing was to ensure that all Hesion continued to realise that he and his fellow kemarrs absolutely controlled the affairs of the Tavern quarter.

The robber baron, a fat black skinned ugly personage with bejewelled hands and the wealthy clothing of the merchant class, snarled his orders. Although it took only a short time to enter one of the other hostelries on the Street of the Taverns to obtain the necessary combustible materials, the minutes were slipping past. The mob continued to jeer and utter vile threats while many of them battered futilely on the heavy doors which protected their intended victims.

"What about sending some of the lads across the roofs to try and smash a way in through the door there?" a lieutenant suggested.

"No. That's too good for those scum. We'll burn them out. When they leap out with their clothes aflame we'll pour oil on them. We'll roast the lours," Riekou leered cruelly.

The ruffians who had been sent to collect the oil duly returned, but time had now run out. Simultaneously, several of their comrades, who had obtained lighted torches from another hostelry, were on the point of approaching the front of the Harbour Tavern. They were cautiously keeping out of the range of the archers within when the Royal Guard of Rionder came charging along every street to hem them in a ring of steel. This was part of the strategy organised by Admaria. Ontar's beautiful wife was in the forefront; she bore a shield, a sword, a bow and a quiver of arrows which she knew how to use very well.

The cut-throats were assailed by what seemed to them veritable demons from the Pit. The steppe warriors bellowed a new battle cry, "Rionder! Rionder! Quinton for Rionder!" as they dismounted quickly and formed lines of archers.

Admaria had ridden with the contingent down the Street of the Taverns from the north gate and demonstrated her competence in battle. She proved that she was as brave and as qualified as any member of the Inner Council. Her tactics were to pour a relentless hail of death-bearing shafts into the masses of villains who had been desperately attempting to slaughter her loved ones.

The first battle cries signalled relief to those inside the

Harbour Tavern. The constant battering on the doors suddenly ceased. Outside the bands of ruffians began to receive exactly what the law-abiding citizens of Hesion had hoped they would for many years. The cut-throats discovered that their every avenue of escape was covered for the beautiful Ulgruffi had given precise instructions to the guard, providing the section commanders with the battle positions for their squads.

Riekou roared at his henchmen to attack and the latter raced at their adversaries. In each street and alley the steppe warriors had swiftly drawn themselves into resolute lines. In the north of the Street of the Taverns Admaria stood at one side of the leading rank which knelt. She shouted the order for independent firing and the mighty soldiers who served under the magnificent banner of Rionder launched swift deadly shafts into those who had dared raise their hands against their beloved King and the Great Wizard Ontar.

Allecenia had also followed her godmother's contingent, but was not allowed anywhere near the scene of battle. She was protected by four valiant warriors who kept her safe at the rear. They bore no resentment at not being given the honour of fighting to save their King. Admaria had commanded them to lay down their lives before any person laid hands on the veiled Lady. Indeed the quartet were among those who sensed that Quinton and Olluinan's daughter were perhaps becoming more than friends.

"Everyone! Up on the roof! We'll be more help there. They won't bother with us in here," Quinton ordered, running for the stairs with his foster father.

"We've got to stop any of those rascals climbing up to fire down on our men," Hanshair declared.

"Precisely, my friend. My Dear Wife will already have taken steps to lessen any such casualties. But our presence will help reduce the risk to our troops," Ontar smiled grimly.

"We still have quite a number of arrows, Quinton. The ones in our own quivers and those we acquired from the Deeraits downstairs," Perlow said, following at the heels of his overlord.

"I know, but they won't last for ever," the youth agreed with the unspoken thoughts of the Chofir.

"We shall make every single shaft count," Adrigal called.

"If you don't Gordan will be extremely angry," Onlestic grinned.

"All his training to go for nothing? No! By Selix, Gordan is

180

bigger than I. I'm not going to let him down. I'm not going to miss with one shaft," Colmar joined in the banter.

"Gordan's bigger than you. He's bigger than anyone, even a green linz, and twice as strong," Caejkan, a Jeghular, commented.

This remark brought smiles to the faces of Quinton and Ontar who had reached the top floor. They quickly removed the three bars and opened the door. Sunlight came slanting from the west as the sixteen men stepped around the sloping black slated roof to reach the front of the building. They spread out to peer over a parapet to obtain a view of the conflict below.

"There are a lot of them," one of the dark green skinned Zancericts said. "Can your troops contain them?"

"Certainly. Remember the Hesion garrison will be here shortly. With such a disturbance they can do no other," Quinton replied with his wonderful enchanting smile.

"I hope they can," the other Zancerict spoke shyly. "We have brought terrible trouble on you and your comrades."

"We could do no other than assist you. I believe it is the time of reckoning for the wickedness in this area to be crushed underfoot and the cankerous evil removed," Ontar spoke calmly, while the steppe warriors loosed shafts into the melee below.

"If the garrison doesn't arrive soon, Hanshair, what do you think will happen?" Quinton asked pointedly.

The Nai-Zind, cognisant that his monarch wished to allay the fears of the two strangers from Ceitswand, and thinking momentarily of the shock troop training, calmly said, "If the garrison doesn't arrive soon, Sire, there won't be a single one of our foes left alive."

The two Zancericts looked at one another in disbelief. The strange warrior had spoken his words in a matter of fact manner. They realised that Hanshair was speaking the simple truth and not for the first time did they wonder who these allies were. One was about to speak when Caejkan bellowed a warning.

"Roof opposite! Some have come up!"

On all sides of the villains in the thoroughfares the steppe warriors loosed their shafts once their attackers were within close range. Deeraits perished with arrows sprouting from their chests. The royal guard had had superb training: their captain and supreme general would have been delighted by the military bearing of his troops. He would have applauded the cool manner in which they faced and repelled the horde of thugs and ruffians, the present members of the vicious gangs responsible for terrorising Hesion for centuries. Their crimes were legion — the commission of assassination, murder, torture, robbery, kidnapping, rape and extortion. The majority of these crimes went undetected: if a trial ever did come about witnesses were either killed in their homes or in the streets in broad daylight; some were even found floating in the harbour.

The lesser kemarrs shouted orders for their respective gangs to charge and deal with the newcomers. Many of the villains bore bows and drew shafts from quivers. On all sides where they discovered themselves faced with enemies large numbers of thugs rushed towards their new adversaries, uttering curses and dreadful threats. They erroneously believed that the King of Rionder's guard would flee because of their superior numbers and ill-famed reputation. Even before Quinton and his companions reached the first floor, a full scale battle had developed outside.

"Fire at will!" Admaria commanded in a vibrant voice, loosing a shaft into the chest of an unkempt ruffian, while on the other thoroughfares similar orders were being given by the section leaders.

A veritable hail of arrows swished in deadly fashion towards the wall of human targets. Down crashed the first line, then the second, third and fourth, riddled with scores of bolts. The corpses and the wounded littered the streets, impeding the progress of those behind. The latter, unable to guess what was occurring in front, pressed and pushed forwards, unwittingly driving their comrades to certain death. Within a minute almost two hundred of the tavern gangs had been slain or incapacitated.

"We're lost!" a kemarr snarled at Riekou. "Let's get out of this mess!"

"We shall not admit defeat! We rule Hesion!" the underworld overlord spat vehemently. "Pull our men together! Ignore all the blocked streets except the north! We'll break out and reform!"

Riekou was totally unmoved by the suffering of his adherents. His only concern was to prevent his wicked rule and power from being imperilled. It was quite simple for him to issue commands, but another for them to be carried out. The baron had not considered the fact that his adversaries had no intention of allowing his men to break through their lines. Indeed, Admaria and the royal guard were fully prepared to prevent such an eventuality.

Quite a number of the rogues had begun to respond to the archery fire; their resistance would have proved more effective if their shouting comrades had not jostled and pushed them about. Notwithstanding, shafts were falling on all the strategic positions of the royal guard. Although this had been anticipated, casualties were being sustained in spite of a shield roof barrier brought into play at the discharge of the first hostile arrow.

Above the conflict Quinton and his companions dealt swiftly and effectively with any enemies who appeared on top of the buildings opposite. Certain of Riekou's more intelligent underlings had hoped to wreak havoc among the ranks of the newcomers, but found themselves either slumping in death on the parapets or toppling over to crash down on their comrades in the Street of the Taverns below.

"They're about to rush Admaria's position!" Ontar called.

"I know. Some of our warriors are down too," Quinton stated angrily, looking to where his foster mother directed her troops.

"Guards, fire every single shaft against the brigands moving towards Lady Admaria's position," Ontar ordered. "We must prevent them from escaping."

The Zancericts watched with silent admiration while their rescuers loosed every arrow in their quivers with an accuracy born of long practice. The speed with which the shafts were launched was very fast, Quinton being the quickest, his nimble fingers notching, releasing and inflicting death on those about to attack his beloved foster mother. Over a hundred missiles hailed down into the thoroughfare. Simultaneously the guards on the other approaches, cognisant of the gangs' intentions, increased their rate of fire, aiming upwards so that their bolts scythed down into the mob.

The archers on the parapets of the Harbour Tavern, including the two men from Ceitswand, watched while Death reaped a rich harvest. Riekou's hecul was struck in several places; its master received arrows in his left eye, his throat and chest. The slaughter was intense, almost seven hundred perishing, for none of the villains had brought shields. The remaining thugs begged for mercy and threw down their weapons, thoroughly demoralised. Quinton raised his rotar horn to his lips and blew the ceasefire. The loud blasts echoed throughout the neighbourhood and across the city. The faint sounds reached the ears of Cottis in the distant High Court chamber. The governor of Sicruci had not forgotten the rich notes and knew the identity of the owner of the horn.

"Admaria! We're all right!" Ontar called. "We'll be right down."

"When you've rounded them up, search every building! There'll be quite a few hiding in them! Also downstairs in the cellar of this tavern!" Quintin shouted.

Shortly afterwards they reached the street where the full impact of the hideous carnage forcibly struck the Zancericts. Corpses and wounded lay strewn everywhere in grotesque attitudes. The tall determined steppe warriors had already begun herding the survivors of the mob together. Several squads were about to commence the search of the buildings indicated by their paramount ranxem when the sound of clattering hooves reached their ears. Moments later the first of two thousand garrison troops appeared, ready to quell the riot and save what they could of the King of Rionder's bodyguard.

"Hail, Ilixiod!" Quinton greeted. "Can you organise the disposal of the corpses and tend to the Deerait wounded? Have your soldiers search all those buildings. There are some more of this wicked crew in them. There's dead and living rogues in the Harbour Tavern's cellar, and three dead on the roof."

The resolution and personality of the youth were so forceful that the north gate commander and the garrison officers did not demur. The sight of the slaughter was appalling. The effective manner and the brief period in which the Riondese troops had fought and vanquished a vastly superior force was not lost on any of the newcomers. When Quinton detailed Hanshair, the two Ker-Mantids and Colmar to supervise the Deerait regiment, none thought to object, reflecting afterwards that it had appeared the most natural thing to do.

"How many have we lost?" the youth asked when his section leaders had been gathered together.

"Seventeen killed outright. Twelve wounded who will recover. One wounded about to die at any moment," Quirgid reported.

"Who is the one about to die?" Quinton asked solemnly, stroking his chin.

"Portarid, Sire. He was hit in the chest," the Zugar section commander declared sadly.

"Take me to him," the youth ordered.

The dying Pingalik had been a member of the contingent which had charged from the direction of the harbour to rescue his King; he had received his mortal wound towards the end of the conflict. Portarid lay with his back against the wall of a chandler's shop, the westering sun on his ashen face; blood oozed from his lips and nostrils, while the dark stain on his uniform around the arrow embedded in his chest increased ominously. The steppe warrior felt a gentle night beginning to envelop him, a welcome beckoning blackness in which to forget all his pain. He began to slip away, when a beloved voice called his name.

"Portarid, my friend. My brave Pingalik, don't go yet."

"No, Sire," he muttered, forcing himself back to the searing pain of consciousness. His King, whom he adored, had called him back. He would obey his paramount ranxem, no matter what the cost.

"Just call me Quinton. No more Sire for you, dear comrade," his monarch said, moving down to lie beside the steppe warrior and put his arms around him.

"Quinton, is that you?" Portarid murmured, while those watching felt their eyes fill with tears.

"Yes. I'm here. I won't ever leave you again," his paramount ranxem said, pushing back the warrior's black hair which had straggled across the perspiration on his soaking forehead.

"I love you, Quinton. You gave my tribe back its identity," Portarid sighed, a ghastly bubbling noise emanating from his throat.

"I love you too, my friend. I was honoured to elevate you to the guard after your valour on the plains in the summer. You've given your life for me. I'll always remember your sacrifice."

"Battle, battle. If I were to die, I wanted it to be in an important battle. Like when we defeated the Casmans," the dying Pingalik wheezed. More red blood dribbled from his mouth and nostrils with every gasp for breath.

"This was an important battle. We have cleansed this city of a very great evil, far more than the Casmans," Quinton said softly with emphasis.

"Let us through, please," Ontar's voice spoke.

The sage was followed by his wife, and the two Ulgruffi knelt beside Portarid, each taking a hand of the dying guard.

"Here are Ontar and Admaria," Quinton said.

"Ontar. Admaria," the Pingalik nodded ever so slowly, his breath stentorous.

"We're here," the couple replied in unison.

"Portarid," Quinton spoke, "I promise you no one will ever forget your name from now onwards. What you have done today with your comrades will always be remembered by all the citizens of this great city. And never again will such an evil quarter exist in Hesion. I promise."

"And I promise you, Portarid, that the angels of the Great Power will honour you for your deeds today," Ontar stated in tones which left no doubt that it would be so.

"We love you, my friend," Admaria said with sadness and a sob.

"I am going. I feel and see a light, a bright light," Portarid whispered. "It's full of Love. Goodbye, Quinton, Admaria, Ontar."

His King and the Heads of the Sacred Order kissed him on the temple. Moments later he smiled briefly, before his head fell to his chest. Quinton laid Portarid's body gently on the cobblestones while Ontar removed his own cloak and covered the deceased. The sage, his wife and foster son wept with the guards who were present. The two Zancericts had followed the youth and also shed tears. They felt that they were personally responsible.

"My friends, it was not your fault," Quinton reassured them.

"If we hadn't been so foolish in coming this way at the hour we did this would not have happened. Your valiant guards would not have been slain," one said sorrowfully.

"Listen carefully to what I am about to say. You were meant to come this way at that time. We were meant to rescue you. It was ordained. This I know beyond all doubt, now that it has happened," Admaria spoke firmly.

"I am Ontar, Head of the Sacred Order of Light on the Ordlansa archipelago. This is my wife, Admaria. You will have heard of us. We walked your land long ago, in the days your forefathers were ruled by the Ulgruffi Empire in the mists of time, when Phentara was much younger. We both have been to Ceitswand several times. Our names are in your legends," the wizard said in his vibrant tones.

"Of course we know your revered names. All our people know of you. You are the Blessed Ones of our legends. If you say it is so, then I fully believe you," the same Zancerict said. He paused a moment before adding, "My name is Te-Tell-Il."

"And my name is Ro-Deend-Ie," the other bowed.

"I thank you for the honour. Now, if you will return to your ship, we shall provide an escort," Ontar said.

"We would like to be present at the burial service for your dead, unless this is private," Te-Tell-Il requested.

"Once more I thank you. When this is arranged we shall send for you. Quirgid, organise an escort for these two gentlemen. Until we meet again, farewell," Ontar smiled gravely.

"Until then," Te-Tell-Il nodded.

The two Zancericts were escorted safely to their vessel by a squad of steppe troopers. While this was being executed Quinton and his foster parents went to visit the other wounded who were being tended by Allecenia and their fellows. In the meantime the Deerait regimental commander had sent messengers back to his headquarters to advise his general officers and the Elders of the High Council of what had taken place. They requested advice on what should be done with their captives and the situation regarding their position towards the King of Rionder and his bodyguard, of whom they were totally in awe.

The presence of Quinton, Admaria and Ontar, and their loving actions at the transition of Portarid, remained in the hearts of the steppe warriors at the scene. Their comrades who had been occupied elsewhere wept when the tidings were related to them. The knowledge that the Inner Council cared deeply for them was fully known extant; the beautiful genuine demonstration of sincere affection in the Street of the Taverns increased their love for their King and his closest companions.

The Deerait soldiery, who had often fought mock battles in their manoeuvres both inside and outside the city had never, in their wildest imaginings or even nightmares, believed they would ever witness such an appalling sight of carnage. That a force of three hundred could inflict such terrible casualties on the dreaded gangs was almost beyond the grasp of their mental capacity. Somehow the supervision of the Riondese royal guard on their activities was not resented.

The capable steppe warriors advised and ordered the Deeraits in their duties. Wagons were brought for the dead but first the wounded guards were borne away to their encampment. Ilixiod, although not in overall command of the regiment, was nevertheless very highly esteemed: no one demurred when Cottis' cousin had cots from the nearest hostelries placed in the wains for the King of Rionder's casualties. Whatever his superiors, and that included the High Courtiers, might think, the north gate commander was determined that nothing was to be too much trouble for the valiant men who had been hurt in the Street of the Taverns. Everything possible was accomplished for their comfort; the softest sheets and blankets, hot water and food were promised. A large company from the Hesion regiment was posted around the King of Rionder's encampment to ensure that no one intruded.

Admaria and Allecenia accompanied the injured back to camp while Ontar and Quinton supervised the transport for the dead steppe warriors. The corpses of the latter were reverently placed inside two huge wains which were escorted by two hundred members of the royal guard. Sightseers who had heard about the conflict stood respectfully at the sides of the streets while the procession passed. When it had gone by the citizenry discussed the dreadful occurrence.

On reaching the encampment the bodies were removed to Quinton's shamianah where they were stripped, washed and dressed in clean uniforms. Each individual had his hair fashioned appropriately and, where applicable, tribal identification marks were painted on his face or arms by his fellows. Admaria, her husband and foster son had resolved that their dead were to be laid to rest honourably as if they had perished on the rolling plains of their birth.

The surviving members of the gangs were escorted to the Castle where they were held in dungeons to await judgment from the High Court. The latter had been informed by courier of what had occurred. Three Councillors, accompanied by Cottis and an escort, came to visit the scene of battle. As they neared the Harbour Tavern they passed the garrison troops conducting the sullen brigands to prison.

"By Ilix and Selix, look yonder!" one exclaimed in horror.

He had received his first glimpse of the slaughter. Dead men lay in heaps or individually, arrows protruding from their bodies, mortal agony reflected in the grotesque expressions on their faces. Cottis nodded sombrely; he had seen this happen before and knew the shock it gave. One thing was certain, the provincial governor of Sicruci thought, Hesion would never be the same again.

Everywhere garrison soldiers were employed in the task of removing wounded brigands or corpses into wagons driven from the Castle. The Council members were quick to observe that their troops were being supervised by tall men with flowing hair, dressed in Deerait costumes. It was not hard to guess that these were the efficient bodyguard of the King of Rionder.

If three hundred of his forces had caused such devastation, then the Deerait nation could be thankful that the Riondese were only a relatively small race. The three Elders then recollected the horrific losses Enmarkan had sustained at the hands of the same people. The governor of Sicruci had not yet revealed anything of what he had been told in his judgment hall in Estyork, for he was still under the influence of the spell cast by Ontar.

"Hail, Cottis!" a voice called.

The riders turned to see a very handsome youth with a dynamic personality striding towards them between the heaps of slain.

"Hail, Quinton. Sire, allow me to introduce to you three members of the Deerait High Council."

"Before you do that, my friend, is one of you named Ihlden?" the King of Rionder enquired.

"That is my name," an elderly white skinned Deerait dressed in finery acknowledged.

"Adrigal, fetch Vlamar. Bring her here. Ask Ontar before you go upstairs," the youth called to the guard who was nearby.

"At once, Sire," the Ker-Mantid bowed. He hastened around the corner to the front of the Harbour Tavern where the mighty wizard stood, talking earnestly to several attentive Deerait officers.

The sage was advising them about the permanent policing of the district by the militia, with a special suggestion that the Harbour Tavern itself be altered to become a headquarters for those appointed to perform this duty. When Adrigal appeared the wizard snapped his fingers and nodded to the warrior. The Ker-Mantid smiled respectfully, since he realised that Ontar had removed the spell of guard. He entered the inn and shortly afterwards emerged into the Street of the Taverns to find the wizard awaiting him.

"The child is still asleep," the mystic murmured.

"That is good. It will stop her seeing the horrors of our battle. Can you keep her like this until she is away from here, Great Ontar?" Adrigal asked.

"Of course I shall. Your concern does you credit," the wizard praised the thoughtfulness of his companion, patting the latter's shoulder benignly.

"If I may say so, your own, our King's and Lady Admaria's does you credit also, Great Ontar. You were all very kind to Portarid." The royal guard expressed the thoughts of all those who had witnessed the Pingalik's transition.

"We could do no other. Portarid was a fine person, an excellent section leader and a good soldier. We do not forget these things. Remember always, it is we who have to bear the responsibility for the lives of you all," Ontar acknowledged.

The sage and the Ker-Mantid strode down the side street to where Quinton awaited them. The youth introduced his foster father to Ihlden, Rosmiche and Phorigor, three very eminent members of the High Court. The sight of the unconscious Vlamar caused her grandparent a moment's concern, but Adrigal reassured the latter that the little girl was unharmed and would not awaken until she had been taken away from the neighbourhood. Ihlden dismounted and walked over to where the warrior held Vlamar gently.

"How did your grandchild disappear?" Ontar asked.

"She was snatched in the street near my home, a mile from here. Two servitors accompanied her. They were assaulted by some cut-throats and stunned. That was seven days ago. I did receive a ransom demand but no details of how or where it was to be paid were given," the elderly Councillor sighed.

"I noticed that both Vlamar and you have made no mention of her parents," Quinton interjected.

"They perished four years ago. There was an outbreak of plague. The gods must have been angry with Hesion then," Ihlden replied.

"I am sorry. That was unfortunate. We shall hand her to one of your private escort," Ontar said, motioning to Adrigal, who complied with the mystic's command.

"All rioting and major violent disturbances in this civic district are normally dealt with by the militia. They work in conjunction with the town garrison. And, as you can now observe, the Castle regiment is clearing things up. The militia should be here shortly. They usually patrol during the morning," Phorigor spoke, in a fruitless attempt to excuse the lack of policing in the afternoon.

"That is all very well for the morning. I understand that there are no patrols later in the day," the King of Rionder responded.

"The area is perilous. I am ashamed to admit that no one from the military or militia patrols it then."

"I see. Eighteen of my men have died because this section of the capital has no respect for the law. They gave their lives to save me and my foster father, not to mention two Zancericts unfortunate enough to be assailed. Oh, don't worry, we rescued them! If there had been respect for the rule of law in this neighbourhood, nobody would have been killed, not even those wretches and their kemarrs. This place is cleansed! Let it remain that way! You shall attend the burial service for my warriors," Quinton stated coldly.

There was a poignant silence for several moments during which the High Courtiers looked uneasily at one another. The words of the King of Rionder had struck home. Beside his comments being totally accurate, the Elders had felt as if they were in the presence of an overlord. When he had been much younger, Rosmiche had been the Deerait national ambassador to the Casman Empire at Choolsay. He had witnessed the opulence and splendour of the imperial court; but even the awe which he had experienced then had never equalled that brought forth by the personalities of the King of Rionder and the handsome man called Ontar in whose eyes was lore and wisdom.

"We apologise. Words are inadequate . . .," Phorigor faltered.

"I repeat, we have lost eighteen good men. I want them to be buried in a beautiful spot, preferably overlooking the ocean. They did like the Chofanrit. When we stopped briefly at noon yesterday they hurried to the water's edge. I remember how they laughed and dodged the incoming waves. They were so happy.

"You will erect a monument to their memory. It will be maintained in perfect order, with a garden around it. I shall supply you with the names to be carved thereon, together with an inscription of their deeds today. Every year on this day the High Court and city dignitaries will hold a service of

191

remembrance in their honour. Neither this district nor any other in Hesion will ever again be lawless. This is what I want for my warriors! No less will suffice!" Quinton spoke adamantly.

Without hesitation Phorigor, the Head Councillor of the Deerait tribe and united nation, said solemnly, "It shall be done as you request, Sire. We shall find a suitable place on the morrow and ask you to approve its location. The monument will be built. The city will be law abiding. Every year we shall honour your dead. Their final resting place will be one of beauty. It is the least we can do to atone. We owe you a debt, a great debt."

"Then I am satisfied. We shall hold the burial service in two days' time with full military honours," Quinton emphasised.

"And we shall supply the burial coffins, if it pleases you. It is our Deerait custom," Ihlden declared in apologetic tones.

Ontar looked at Quinton with a nod. His foster son concurred, with the provision that the coffins were to be fashioned from the finest wood. The Courtiers agreed unanimously. Cottis had watched this scene with sorrow, for he felt very attached to the King of Rionder and his bodyguards. Nevertheless he felt considerable pride that such a feat of arms had been accomplished.

Around them garrison soldiers were now being assisted by militia, the latter having brought more wagons. The area was gradually being cleared while several companies controlled the crowds abroad to see the sights. The sun was sinking towards the distant horizon from where a chill wind had risen and was blowing across the harbour, causing waves to lap noisily against the sea walls.

"King Quinton, we shall grant you an audience this evening at the eighth hour. It would be churlish of us to keep you waiting longer," Phorigor said, looking down at the youth from the saddle of his hecul.

"Thank you. We shall attend you then. We shall leave here and return to our camp," Quinton acknowledged.

"Before you go, Sire, I would like to thank you for saving Vlamar. Often the kemarrs never return their kidnapped victims. They never make mistakes. Nobody has ever proved such crimes. Those who are returned have always been kept blindfolded. Was she blindfolded?" Ihlden asked.

"No, she wasn't. They would have murdered her. We realised

that. Perhaps they might have sold her to a ship with unscrupulous officers. They in turn would have sold her abroad," Quinton gave a wry smile. "I'm sincerely glad she was saved. Remember, once she's away from here she'll awaken with no harmful effects or bad memories of her captivity. We must go. Farewell, till the eighth hour."

After they had mounted their heculs the entire royal guard still in the vicinity escorted their monarch and his foster father back to the encampment. The recovery of the steeds under Ontar's spell, including the one used by Olluinan, had proved fairly simple. The yellow beaked creatures with the pointed heads and three violet eyes had remained near an empty hitching rail at the bottom of the Street of the Taverns. Several of the mounted guard had ridden to fetch them once the steppe injured and dead had been removed from the vicinity of the conflict.

Allecenia and Admaria had organised the care of the wounded most effectively. Their injuries had been tended and they were resting comfortably. The new quarters for the King, the two Ulgruffi, the veiled Lady and Perlow had been fashioned by the erection of a clever combination of three tents. When the last contingent returned from the Street of the Taverns a hot meal was ready. However, before partaking of any food, Quinton and Ontar looked in on the casualties, but were careful not to disturb them.

On their return to camp they had both noticed that not only had Deerait soldiers been posted around the perimeter to ensure their privacy, but also that ample supply wagons had been provided by Ilixiod. The wizard and his foster son were content with what the High Council had promised. Although the meeting that night should have provided a source of considerable satisfaction, the loss of their warriors grieved them deeply.

A short time after they had finished dining in their temporary abode, Felgorian returned to the encampment to confirm that the Council was expecting them. The Riondese ambassador expressed his sincere personal regrets that the royal guard had suffered casualties, for which Quinton thanked him. His godfather also revealed that Hesion had been shaken to its foundations by what the King of Rionder's small force had accomplished against such overwhelming odds in so short a time.

"Whom do you wish to accompany you this evening, Sire?"

"Ontar, Admaria, Perlow and Allecenia, of course. You too, Felgorian. Hanshair is organising an escort of fifty guards. He'll command them. I dare say we'd better put on some clean clothes, too, Ontar," Quinton smiled gravely.

"Yes. We washed our hands and faces before our food, but didn't change because the meal was ready. Oh, I see my cloak's over there. Who fetched it?" the sage enquired.

"Helijaw did. He's Portarid's cousin. He was with my section. He performed bravely. Hanshair and I told him how Portarid died. He was very upset when he heard the news of his cousin's demise," Admaria said.

"We'll talk with him tomorrow," Ontar nodded seriously.

"I noticed you cast a spell to keep the hospital tents warm and the air fresh," Quinton smiled at his foster mother.

"Actually Allecenia did," she responded.

"That was kind of you," the youth stated.

"I felt I had to. The night air will be chilly. Any infection will be eliminated too," the veiled lady said in her gentle tones.

"We'd better have a good wash and change. We should have a most interesting evening. I wonder what the High Court will say," Admaria remarked thoughtfully.

"I feel hopeful, but...," Quinton shook his head.

"You think we won't be successful?" Ontar asked, rather surprised by the manner in which his foster son had spoken.

"Not that exactly. I don't know. I have a feeling something totally unexpected may transpire. Something dreadful for Deerait and for us too. Nothing I can actually put into words. Just an intangible premonition. It may be nothing," the young

King shrugged.

"Mmm. We'll just have to wait and see," Ontar stated pensively. He had considerable respect for any views expressed by his foster son. What no one present realised was that Quinton's presentiment was to involve Ontar, Admaria, Allecenia and the youth himself in battling against a most terrible threat, one which Phentara had faced long ago.

Half an hour before the appointed time for their meeting with the High Council, the escort of royal guards rode from the encampment and under the high battlemented archway into the sprawling city of Hesion. The night air was chill, but the west wind had dispelled the few rain clouds. Quinton and his companions wore fresh Deerait styled clothing, while the fifty one warriors had attended conscientiously to every minute detail of their uniforms and equipment.

Even if Hanshair and his subordinates could only guess at the importance of the vital consultation at the eighth hour, they seemed to sense a slight tension emanating from their King and his party. Felgorian, especially, was concerned; he did not wish his monarch to become embroiled by force of circumstances in a war against the Deerait tribe itself. Although his loyalty was unequivocal, the Riondese ambassador had always entertained kindly feelings towards the largest section of the maritime and agricultural nation.

Now that her servitors, the innumerable shimmering stars, had fully emerged to carpet the clear nocturnal sky in wondrous patterns, the golden Enchantress floated serenely in all her glorious resplendence and magnificence above the rooftops. Ilix cast her glittering aurelian radiance in generous profusion over the city causing the myriadfold shadows to ameliorate, and the River Avidnive and the Chofanrit Ocean beyond to coruscate with multitudinous lights. She illuminated the noisome streets of Hesion where the sound of numerous clattering hecul hooves prompted many of the citizenry to peer curiously out of doors and windows.

On the road to the Haromarg, the general name for the central fortress, there were several buildings which boasted no light; this circumstance prompted Ontar to give a discourse. Allecenia and Admaria had heard it often before, the former for the first time from her parents on Ordlansa, the latter millenia before in Inthearna, supreme capital of the mighty Ulgruffi Empire; nevertheless, both women listened closely since the esoteric lecture always engendered new positive thoughts for meditation.

Riding near the head of the column, Perlow, Hanshair, Adrigal and Onlestic also attended to the lesson but remained ever alert and vigilant. The quartet realised that the populace was not inimical; in fact the citizenry were extremely grateful to the King of Rionder and his guard for the drastic cleansing of the tavern district; but the Mescarg steppe warriors never forgot for an instant that they were involved in a war against the Casman Empire, and the drastic consequences which defeat would incur.

In his melodious voice the handsome eternally young looking wizard spoke in the Common Speech saying, "The windows of dwelling places can be likened to the immortal souls temporarily resident within the bodies of human beings. In His Infinite Wisdom, the Great Power has decreed that our souls are to be imprisoned in corporeal form until such time as perfection is attained in our incarnations.

"Take, for analogy, a house with no light on a dark night. It could be said to have a resemblance, either to a new soul or to a person who has fallen into the abyss of evil and self-delusion, wilfully ignoring the Light. The Divine Law of Compensation will inexorably instruct him until he learns to improve. Consequently his house will gain a little Light, perhaps glimmering faintly from a small garret window. With progress more lighted windows will appear. Occasionally, since he is on this mortal plane and therefore prone to fallibility, he may lapse into Error; some of the lights will dim, perhaps even vanishing completely to leave darkened rooms.

"Time will be spent on this physical plane, with incarnations coming and going, until the lights which have been extinguished, or not yet lit, attain their full brilliance. Eventually all the lessons of life will be learned. Then all the lighted windows will shine forth through the eyes and the aura will be fully revealed, when perfection on this physical plane is attained."

The mystic stopped speaking and looked at his foster son. The youth smiled in response, for he too had heard the invaluable lecture several years before on the blizzard swept Mescarg steppes. He was aware that Ontar had related it to cause Felgorian and the four warriors to ponder its significance. Perhaps, through meditation, the quintet might evince indications that they too wished to journey consciously along the Mystic Path.

If pondered in depth the discourse will draw forth thoughts corresponding to the inner development of the person contemplating its message and equivalent to his or her comprehension. Then more esoteric insight will be brought subtly into the objective consciousness; these new ideas will either be dismissed or perhaps cause the search for a portal through which to find the Mysteries of Life. If the desire for Truth increases, the Higher Powers will provide the opportunity; it remains for the seeker to choose to follow these inner promptings in a sincere search for arcane knowledge. However, as often occurs many, having eagerly begun, fall by the wayside, wilfully disregarding the stirrings from within, to remain ignorant until a future life brings wisdom.

"That's a wonderful discourse," Quinton said in the Ulgruffi tongue.

"It certainly is. It was ancient even in the days of my youth. I was first told it as a temple neophyte," Ontar concurred.

"I wonder if our friends will ponder upon it. I sincerely hope they do," Admaria remarked.

"I'd like them to do so, very much. We'll have to talk like this to them occasionally. It'll help to draw them out. Mind you, Perlow, Hanshair and the two Ker-Mantids are progressing. Their conversation with Quinton last evening was most indicative of that," her husband stated frankly.

"Yonder is the Haromarg, Sire," Felgorian called at that moment, when the column turned right at the end of a narrow street and into the large open square in the centre of which stood the fortress.

In the moonlight the Castle appeared a most forbidding place, even with the River Avidnive close at hand. Its layout was similar to the stronghold in Estyork, and indeed to the fortresses in most of the major centres of population throughout the Deerait nation. However, it was twice as large as its nearest rival; inside its walls were accommodations for a garrison of about twenty five thousand troops. Quinton led his column across the cobbled square to where a platoon of thirty guards stood at the main entrance, the portcullis of which was raised.

"Hail, King of Rionder!" a helmeted officer in red livery stepped forward respectfully.

"Hail!" Quinton acknowledged.

"You and your companions are to enter the Castle. The High Council awaits your presence," the officer stated courteously.

"Thank you."

The paramount ranxem of the Mescarg steppes rode his hecul under the massive archway into the courtyard beyond. Torches were hung in brackets all around, while the doorway to the inner part of the Haromarg stood open. The visitors dismounted and attendants hastened over to lead their heculs to hitching posts near the main gateway. Ontar smiled for, like the others, he sensed that the Deeraits were attempting to make amends for the death of the eighteen royal guards.

Word of their arrival was transmitted quickly inside. Ihlden received the tidings and hastened to greet the visitors. The aged Courtier came down the broad steps to meet Quinton and his entire party. He asked that they follow him, before conducting them inside. Hanshair and his comrades looked about at their magnificent surroundings. Elegant chairs and other furniture combined with carpeting and tapestries to form an impressive interior.

"The High Court is gathering at this moment, Sire. Cottis will be present too. It will only be a few minutes before we are sent for. Your escort can remain here in the warmth. Food and drink will be provided for them. You and your friends also, if you wish," Ihlden smiled kindly in the spacious hall.

"Thank you, but we shall be all right. Although I dare say my men will no doubt partake of your offer. Where do you wish them to wait?" Quinton asked.

"We have put tables and chairs in a room just over there. If they will follow the servitors."

"Go ahead, Hanshair. Perlow will come with me," Quinton spoke in Nai-Zind. "We'll be fine."

"Then the guard knows you will be safe, Sire. There is no treachery here," the commander bowed, before telling his guards to accompany him.

"I am indebted to you, King of Rionder. I must express again my thanks and gratitude for the safe return of my grandchild. Not to mention the cleansing of the Street of the Taverns. I thank you most sincerely, Sire," the elderly white skinned Deerait declared, bowing graciously.

"It was an honour and a privilege to be of service," the youth responded.

"You do resemble both your parents. It was many years ago. I've forgotten exactly how many now. I saw them just after they were wed. In those days I travelled on official business between the various centres of our nation. This included an occasional visit to Rionder. Your father's city was most beautiful. It was so well built and laid out with broad streets, totally unlike Hesion. I've often attempted to have some parts of Hesion rebuilt like Estyork and Rionder. But there are too many objections because of the expense and upheaval," Ihlden shook his head ruefully.

"That would be most advantageous here. Wide streets and boulevards with better sanitation would give conditions for improving the standards of health. Then the citizens would develop physically and mentally. Such improvements would mean finer and stronger generations of children," Quinton averred.

"I can see you're highly intelligent. Cottis hasn't revealed anything to us regarding your visit. He's only said that it's essential for you to have audience with the High Council. He is highly respected for his wisdom and judgment. He is the most capable provincial governor in the entire nation. Sicruci is our front line of defence against the Adiorenji in the west.

"If I may hazard a guess, I don't think you've come to ask our help against Enmarkan. We can hardly contemplate advancing against Broechnaar with civil war about to break out. Felgorian will concur with this," the elderly Deerait glanced at the Riondese ambassador. "Besides, Felgorian, you did visit here not so long ago to have a talk with me. The main topics of our conversation were our internal situation and foreign policy. In particular, Deerait's attitude to the Casman Empire and its relationship to the steppe tribes on the Mescarg plains. Is that not so?"

"Yes, my friend. You recall exactly what you well know to have been the most important part of our conversation," the handsome Riondese smiled.

"Perhaps your visit here is further connected with those topics?" Ihlden asked disarmingly.

"You are certainly a fine councillor and statesman. Your political ability is most perceptive in your seemingly innocent questions," Quinton laughed with inoffensive amusement.

"I thank you. You are wise for one so young. I shall not press you further before you and your companions meet the High

199

Court. Tell me, Ontar, how is it that the Riondese always appear to be unaffected by the passing of the years, while we Deeraits have a shorter span?"

"That's simply explained. They don't live in cities like Hesion, but in the fresh country air," the mystic replied.

"Another politician," the Deerait conceded with a merry laugh, the group around him joining in his mirth as a liveried officer approached.

"Hail, Elder of the High Council. Your presence is called for by the High Court. Also that of His Majesty, the King of Rionder and his illustrious companions. The Court is now in session."

"Thank you," Ihlden nodded. "We shall leave for the conference chamber immediately. Follow me, my friends."

The elderly Deerait conducted them across and out of the hall. He strode to the end of a broad passageway lit by torches in wall brackets before turning left. Ihlden walked several yards along a second corridor to a large door on the right-hand side, outside of which two liveried sentinels holding spears stood at attention. This was the entrance to the chamber where the virtual rulers of the Deerait tribe debated the most important affairs concerning their own people. Until several months before, Hesion had also possessed a National Central Council, or Court, where the chief representatives of the four races had carried on similar business: now, unfortunately, only the Deeraits remained for the ambassadors and delegates of the Vilatmori and Dariondi had departed by sea for their own regions, while those of the Adiorenji had travelled overland.

The Deeraits themselves were scattered over a considerable area. Envoys from the various community centres journeyed to Hesion for advice on problems affecting their respective districts if satisfactory solutions could not be found in the courts of their own provincial governors. Cottis had not ridden to the capital at this time for such advice but had been requested to attend the High Court for a consultation on the defences of Estyork and Sicruci: the latter region jutted into the territory of the Adiorenji and was the most probable area for the commencement of hostilities, being strategically situated on the borders of the leading antagonistic tribe.

The High Court and its military advisers anticipated that large naval conflicts would tend to be avoided for the war fleets were evenly scattered along the coasts and had been ordered to maintain stations to protect the most important ports relevant to their respective peoples. The number of battleships of the three tribes was matched vessel for vessel by the Deeraits whose seamanship was slightly better than the rest.

In addition to being the finest administrator among the provincial governors, Cottis was also highly respected by his own people. It was common knowledge that he should have been promoted to the rank of High Courtier some years before but the main obstacle to his election was the difficulty in which his nation found itself. The conscience of the Estyork garrison commander would not let him desert his post in such a time of crisis when his martial and organisational abilities would be required to protect those whom he ruled.

His influence was such that, even in a time of imminent hostilities, his request to the High Court to grant an immediate hearing to the King of Rionder and retinue received keen attention. Cottis had also indicated that this was not simply a visit by a small ruler to ask for assistance: it was a matter of vast importance which would affect the lives of the entire Deerait nation. Although pressed the governor of Sicruci did not reveal anything which Quinton and Ontar had told him in Estyork; however, his evident concern combined with his high reputation and integrity had convinced the High Court to grant the audience. The meeting had originally been scheduled for the following evening but after the battle in the Street of the Taverns Phorigor had brought it forward.

The conference hall was large. It boasted a magnificently carved white oval table in the centre around which sufficient chairs had been placed to accommodate all those expected to be present. Although torches gave ample light, further illumination was provided by a bright crackling log fire which blazed fiercely in a hearth situated between two high curtained windows. A few tapestries adorned the walls, briefly depicting important historical events in the life of the Deerait tribe, together with banners and standards from the various regions under its rule.

Phorigor and his companions greeted the party courteously. The Supreme Courtier asked everyone to be seated. When they had complied with his request he ordered the sentinels outside the room to seal the chamber. They waited until sounds indicated that the bar across the doorway had been put into place. Quinton, Ontar, Admaria, Felgorian, Allecenia and

Perlow sat together to the right of the fireplace.

"King of Rionder and illustrious companions, I greet you officially. The High Court has been requested by our able governor and friend, Cottis of Sicruci, to grant an audience to you. Cottis has not revealed the reason for this request, other than to state that your presence here will affect the future of our whole nation, but his influence is respected.

"However, before we proceed, it is appropriate that we thank you for the rescue of Ihlden's grandchild and the drastic cleansing of the Street of the Taverns, a most noble deed. We, the High Court, can barely believe that Reikou's ochlocracy was destroyed so quickly. The sacrifice of your personal guard will never be forgotten. We are resolved never to permit such an area to exist in Hesion from this time forth," Phorigor declared gravely to nods of acquiescence from his colleagues. "Now, will you kindly enlighten us as to your presence here, Your Majesty"

"I thank you sincerely, High Court of the Deeraits, for your courtesy. It is very gracious of you to grant us an audience especially in these dangerous days. I shall not delay you further, but shall relate the events leading to our presence here," Quinton declared firmly. He felt a tingling sensation all over his body with the realisation that this was a moment of Destiny.

The paramount ranxem of the fierce Mescarg steppe tribes told succinctly how, through force of circumstances, the Nai-Zind had been obliged to unite all the free tribes in the western region of the grasslands. His words assumed such a reality that the Elders could almost visualise the battle on the Garsbut Plain. They learned that the occidental clans had been brought under one ruler, after the defeat of the Ker-Mantids and their allies commanded by Ackhau.

From there, the scene moved to the vast migration of the Phlorcartid nation to serve under the banner of the King of Rionder. This union of the entire steppe peoples caused murmurs from the attentive Councillors; some recollected that Felgorian had questioned them about such an eventuality during his visit to Hesion earlier in the summer. Their personal thoughts regarding their own position were temporarily lulled while the handsome youth continued with details of the advance of the Jaddair corps from Mikghiltherid under the command of the competent governor and warlord, Terfieldst.

The King of Rionder briefly related how the Casmans had been vanquished and had decided to join his own forces. The High Court felt their senses reeling while they attempted to digest the devastating revelations. Here was no deposed ruler of a small friendly kingdom, but the commander-in-chief of a highly trained and efficient army of almost a quarter of a million troops. The defeat of an entire imperial corps, which had never occurred before in history since the birth of the Empire, rammed home the military capability of his steppe warriors; no doubt his Casman allies would be attaining the same high standard in the vast forests to the north.

When Quinton had finished speaking there was a profound silence. Cottis looked at Phorigor, nodding his confirmation that he too had felt dumbfounded by the facts which the High Council had just been given. A few poignant minutes passed during which the Deeraits pondered what these dramatic tidings meant for their nation. Even if they had still stood firmly allied with the Adiorenji, Dariondi and Vilatmori, a quarter of a million skilled soldiers to the north would represent an awesome threat. The combined forces of their four tribes did outnumber those of the King of Rionder, but time would be required to organise an effective defence, if such could be done.

Finally Phorigor spoke. "Your Majesty, Cottis was correct. This matter is of the utmost gravity. We realise that our relationship with the Casman Empire is among your concerns. However, would you kindly inform us of your immediate intentions?"

"We would like the support of the entire Deerait national naval and land forces. We are at war with the Empire of Casman, not because we wish to do so, but because of the dogmatic Casman manner of thinking," Quinton replied.

"Pray continue. Advise us of what will happen if we refuse and resist you?" Ihlden asked, leaning forward to look piercingly across the table at the youth opposite him.

"We could launch our forces south, and easily raid your towns and provincial districts. We estimate, even if you were to inform the Casmans by sea, that the Empire would require at least nine months before it could send the necessary support to you. Your entire country would be devastated by then."

"Somehow I do not think you really wish our destruction," Ihlden commented shrewdly.

"Of course not. You must realise, nevertheless, that the Casmans will inevitably come in pursuit of us. Alien forces will march through Deerait to conquer us. We do not want to retreat too far north beyond Rionder in the face of imperial forces allied to your own. If we did that we would have to contend with Broechnaar and Enmarkan," Quinton replied.

"Yes, Enmarkan. A curse on Rontmethar," Phorigor nodded. "Yet you have made the point that you wish our army and navy. Suppose we of the Deerait tribe alone oppose you. I am assuming in this that you are not thinking of joining with the Dariondi, Vilatmori and the Adiorenji. Hopefully we could resist you until Casman relief arrived. Our fleets would be sent to bring the imperial corps. That would save much time, and possibly counteract the havoc of war on our country."

"Ontar and Admaria, Heads of the Sacred Order of Light on the Ordlansa archipelago, support my cause," the young King of Rionder responded, making a dynamic move in the face of the skilled negotiators.

"In other words, you really mean to have our navy and land forces!" Phorigor snapped, having totally neglected the Ulgruffi in his calculations.

"We certainly do! It is our resolve to defeat the Casman Empire. We have no alternative. You know Casman thinking and policy. Once this is accomplished the combined forces under my command will move against Enmarkan by land and sea. I emphasise this is not merely to avenge the death of my parents and the sack of Rionder. It is to rid our continent of a heinous evil," Quinton nodded resolutely.

"Let's leave the last point for the moment, although we do agree with you about the wickedness of Broechnaar. If we find ourselves ranged against your forces it appears we shall also have to contend with the wizardry of the Sacred Order of Light," Phorigor looked at Ontar and Admaria, sitting beside the veiled Allecenia.

"Centuries ago my fellow magicians and I were responsible for the sinking of many of your ships. That was when your people foolishly decided to invade our Islands to wrest knowledge from us. Your race was cautioned not to assail us but ignored the warnings we gave. Quinton is correct when he infers that magic could be used to make you join with us if necessary. Our first strategic moves would be against your principal towns. If, in the unlikely eventuality that we were

204

forced to withdraw, we had to resort to magic then it would be used!" Ontar stared fiercely at the Elders.

"Indeed it would. From your ancient writings and legends, you will find that for millenia my husband and I have been and still remain the most powerful wizards on Phentara. Forgetting that and the apparent threat which we represent in your minds, there is another factor about which you do not know. Quinton will explain it to you," Admaria said.

"Yes, there certainly is," the young King concurred with his beautiful foster mother. He addressed the influential High Court of the Deeraits in a respectful manner but nevertheless one which caused them to feel as if they were in the presence of the personage who was their own overlord.

"Please tell us, Your Majesty," Phlorigor spoke most courteously.

"Thank you. This brings us back to Baron Enmarkan. You may have deduced from the fact that, since Ontar is a wizard of high ability, he does possess a crystal. He uses this instrument to scry to considerable purpose. For years he has surveyed the nations of Ronthmethar. Broechnaar has had special attention paid to it. You are aware, of course, that Enmarkan and Tarvokel did have a policy of expansion. You probably believe they decided to abandon this years ago."

"Yes, we do. We did sign a Treaty of Neutrality not long after Rionder fell. Since the seizure of your city he has not attempted any military adventures either against us or anyone else. It's impossible to obtain information about events on the Central Plains. Enmarkan does not permit foreign merchants beyond the special trading compounds in his coastal towns. Still, there are stories and rumours, all unverifiable, which have reached us. These relate to pogroms and rebellions," Dyseey, a black skinned Courtier dressed in elegant clothing, said thoughtfully, stroking his chin.

The conference chamber was cosy and warm from the heat of the fire. Logs crackled and burned merrily, emitting an occasional spark which jumped from the hearth onto the stone floor. Although the curtains had been drawn there were gaps at the top of both the high windows which flanked the fireplace. Through these a number of stars were visible, twinkling like brilliant jewels in the velvety heavens; they blissfully watched Ilix on her graceful nocturnal walk through the sky above Rontmethar. A chill wind gusted down the streets and thoroughfares of Hesion, causing the passers-by to pull their cloaks around them: there was probably not a single individual who thought how well they fared climatically, while on the distant Mescarg steppes fierce blizzards lashed the lonely terrain, piling up huge pink snowdrifts.

"Enmarkan doesn't allow anyone to travel within his realm lest they learn what's happening there or foment trouble. However, neither he nor Tarvokel has forgotten dreams of empire. Over the years since the sack of Rionder they have had to put down a determined series of rebellions. Unbelievable cruelty has been inflicted by their soldiery. Such revolts have caused delays in their expansionist policies. But, believe me, they have not been forgotten for one moment!

"At the present time Broechnaar is quiet and totally under Enmarkan's fist. He's now busy preparing ships to turn the Central Plains into a naval as well as a land power. However, it will take some years to complete the building of a large enough fleet and to train sufficient sailors. I know he could hire fleets of mercenaries, but you would be bound to learn of it and be alerted.

"For all his failure, the Baron is wise in the ways of preparing for war. His ultimate aim, which Ontar and Admaria have deduced from crystal observation, is the conquest of your entire country. Rionder was only the first step, a major base. Why bother with a navy for a war against the Civilised Nations, when he can simply march there? They are ready for plucking at any time. It will definitely never be the Casman Empire. But he does have sufficient forces to conquer you. Yes?" Quinton said as one of the Courtiers raised his right hand.

"Forgive my interrupting, Sire, but could you explain further why he is never going to attack the Empire?" Rosmiche, a native of Chellene, asked with a puzzled expression.

"Yes, why not the Empire eventually?" Phorigor nodded pensively.

"Although the defeated Casmans joined my forces, they detest Enmarkan and his forefathers. The Empire may be losing its grip through hedonism, and have lost many of the fine qualities of its early years, but it has never lost its loathing of the evil rulers of Broechnaar, the worst of whom is Enmarkan. The Baron knows this full well. Our Casman allies confirmed it too. If he were rash enough to attack Casman the whole might of the Empire would rise as one to destroy him.

The Casmans would fight to the last man rather than submit to Enmarkan's hideous rule. In the war of attrition which would inevitably result, the Central Plains would lose," Quinton replied, pausing briefly.

"That is why my foster parents have long concluded the Deerait nation is the focus of his expansionist strategy. The remaining continents of Phentara are too far away for the coastal battle fleet he is building. A sudden unexpected naval attack on several chosen ports, coupled with a massive land assault down the Rionder Valley, would defeat you especially in a time of imminent civil war and bitter dissension among your tribes."

"Of course, he would sustain crippling losses in a naval battle with you, but do you really think that he would declare war on you? Never! Enmarkan will simply appear with all his armies and ships and overwhelm you. He won't give you the opportunity to organise a defence. Casman wouldn't worry about your fate. It feels secure against Broechnaar! Also, you are a very wealthy trading nation," Ontar declared vibrantly.

"I'm beginning to see. You mean, even if the Casmans joined with us to defeat your forces, they wouldn't battle with us against Enmarkan at a later date, providing he didn't attack them while they were here?" Phorigor said, pursing his lips.

"Precisely! Heolanwertin and his advisers adhere to a strict isolationist policy. This you know of course. The Emperor of Casman never alters anything. The unintentional slight by the Mescarg steppe peoples will never be forgiven. Enmarkan conquering you would not cause him the least bit of concern. If the Empire did become involved in an alliance with you to defeat us, once we were removed from the scene, the Casmans would go home.

"You may think Heolanwertin could be persuaded to sign a mutual protection treaty with you. But why should he? He believes that no one would dare assail his Empire. He wouldn't think it worth his while, especially when such an agreement would so obviously be for your defence. I emphasise, Heolanwertin has the greatest army on Rontmethar, and Enmarkan will not dare assail Casman. It is quite conceivable, if Casman did decline drastically with provinces leaving the union, the Baron might be tempted to do so in the future. But Enmarkan is growing old. The conquest of Deerait will satisfy him in his lifetime.

"His heir, Count Tarvokel, is certainly rash enough to contemplate the expansion of the Central Plains Empire into Casman. However, Enmarkan's death will precipitate sporadic rebellions against the new Baron. These revolts, both in Broechnaar and a conquered Deerait, will take a long time to subdue. Such is our assessment of historical facts for the future," Quinton stated, while Ontar's eyes gleamed with enjoyment of the discussion.

"Let's assume we decided to ally ourselves with you. Then we would have to face the wrath of the Empire. This also presumes you'd help us against the other three peoples of our nation. What then?" Phorigor wondered.

"I put it to you this way. What alternative do you have? Even if we weren't a factor, in a very short time you will have a civil war raging. Your naval forces are evenly matched with the Adiorenji, Vilatmori and Dariondi. The main conflict would be on land, with you Deeraits being outnumbered. Your military commanders are slightly better than those in the other tribes. Nevertheless, this could give Enmarkan a marvellous opportunity to conquer your whole country easily," Allecenia spoke for the first time in her beautiful voice from where she sat next to Quinton.

"Listen to me! At this moment in time, the instant that you, who are the High Council of the Deeraits, learned our purposes and whence we had come you should have sent messengers to the Imperial Court in Choolsay! Are you going to do so?" Ontar demanded fiercely. "Make your minds up now!"

"Why?" Rosmiche blurted out, startled by the visage of the wizard.

"Because that is required by the Treaty of Matheird. By the way, I thought you had a copy in this room," the sage replied.

"There was until last week. We decided to have a new frame for it," Ihlden explained.

"There must be some Casmans in Hesion. All you have to is to inform them. That will save time. It'll obviate the necessity of sending any of your own people on the long journey to Choolsay," Quinton pointed out cheerfully.

"Yes, why don't you?" Felgorian rapped, his stern face not evincing the pleasure that his youthful monarch and companions were pushing the renowned High Court of the Deeraits into a corner.

"We are discussing matters with you. That is why," Phorigor

explained, floundering slightly.

"All right then. I'll tell you what we could do. You are our hosts. So, to prevent you from breaking your treaty, we could inform the Casmans ourselves. In any event, Ontar and Admaria will not use magic to force you to join our cause, unless powerful magic is used against us," Quinton stated blandly, appearing utterly convincing.

This change of demeanour in the aspect of their visitors greatly puzzled the Deeraits; even Cottis, who nurtured a desire to side with the King of Rionder, was unable to comprehend the turn of events. The High Court were taken aback; Phorigor took the obvious course by asking the reason.

Ontar smiled gently before replying, "We tend not to do things that way. Well, the treaty stipulates that the Deeraits are to repel any ingress from the plains across the Mescarg mountains, by any or all of the western steppe tribes, whether they travel either as far down as Deerait itself or remain in the forests to the north. This action takes immediate effect once you are apprised of such an occurrence."

The Ulgruffi mystic paused, and Ihlden nodded, "I believe that's quite correct. Please continue."

"In a united nation, you might be capable of contending with us. However the treaty was concluded on the hypothesis that only the western steppe tribes travelled over the mountains. It stipulates that the eastern tribes — those known as the Phlorcartid nation — are always under the direct eye of the Empire and that the Deeraits are not responsible for their actions.

"All that is required of you is to chase the western tribes back to the grasslands, and naturally Casman has to be informed. Your supposedly superior forces should be able to accomplish this without difficulty. Present circumstances appear to invalidate the treaty. It was very carelessly drawn up, for only the western tribes concern you, as is stated therein. You are not permitted to deal with the Phlorcartids in any way whatsoever. We've made a thorough study of the treaty.

"So what do you do? You are now faced with a quarter of a million highly trained troops in the Rionder forests. With your entire national military forces you could hardly deal with us without great losses. Indeed, against us, you'd be defeated. This brings in another stipulation. It states that, in the unlikely eventuality that the Deeraits prove unable to perform the duty of forcing the western tribes back over the mountains, the Casmans will advance through the pass from the east, simultaneously landing sufficient army corps on the shores of Deerait to march to the Rionder Valley. Admaria, please continue," the wizard smiled. He tactfully brought in his lovely wife to demonstrate that he was not the only member of their delegation with a grasp of the strengths and weaknesses of the Treaty of Matheird.

Admaria inclined her head to her spouse before speaking. "Your ancestors were very careless about the conditions inserted in the treaty. They were more concerned about repairing the destruction wrought in your country by the Empire when you fought the Casmans so long ago. Your fleets raided up and down the imperial and Deerait coastlines for years, making Casman suffer, in a war which neither you nor they could win. Their failure to win was because of total lack of seamanship. With your bases on the Hayleink island and your complete command of the seas, the Casmans had either to endure the humiliation of endless devastating raids on their homeland and on their Deerait coastal positions, or make peace.

"Reluctantly they decided on peace. War is expensive. The drain on the Empire's monetary resources was crippling. Your blockade of their ports prevented all foreign trade. This was disastrous for their economy and the imperium was realistic. In those days there was no power on the Central Plains except for scattered clans at war with one another.

"Today you are faced with a ruinous civil war. Also you will have no option but to allow Casman troops passage across your own soil to remove us from the Rionder Valley. How many do you envisage? We estimate at least four army corps. That's six hundred thousand men. These troops, under the provisions of the treaty, will have to be supplied and fed by your good selves. Quinton, you continue, please," Admaria indicated.

"Certainly," the youth smiled at his foster mother. "The Adiorenji, the Vilatmori and the Dariondi will not be concerned about this. You see, the best route to the Riondese forests is through your territory, not theirs. They will not antagonise the Empire by warring with you simultaneously, especially when you are forced to feed a massive Casman army. Suppose we are defeated. The war against us will be long. You can believe me in that. It will also be long for you, the Deeraits.

You will be ruined. Your economy will be in shreds. The other three tribes will remain prosperous. They'll wait until the Casmans depart before sending their combined forces to conquer you. Don't forget the Empire will expect your own forces to be committed against us. So, your soldiers will be war weary and ineffective against fresh foes."

There was a silence which appeared to hang almost tangibly while the High Court tried to formulate a response to the points made by the two Ulgruffi and their dynamic ward. At last, Ihlden managed to speak.

"Lord Ontar, why are the other three tribes uncommitted? I thought the treaty bound the whole Deerait nation."

"Felgorian, you answer the question. You visited the centres of the three tribes recently to learn of their understanding of the Treaty of Matheird," the sage said, turning to the Riondese ambassador.

"I shall be most pleased to clarify this point. Every single tribal leader with whom I conferred stated categorically that he could not foresee a steppe migration over the Mescarg mountain range. Each also affirmed, if such a circumstance did arise, the Matheird Treaty stipulated that the Deerait people were responsible for its implementation. This is ambiguous. The three tribes will not hesitate to utilise it as an excuse to keep out of a war against us," Felgorian pointed out.

"Allecenia, you explain how the Casmans will regard such actions by the three tribes," Quinton said.

The veiled Lady smiled tenderly at her youthful companion, which action he intuitively sensed, before she addressed the High Court.

"The treaty was drawn up centuries ago before Casman reached its heights of learning and culture. In other words, before the Empire fully developed its legal system. The present Casman lawyers for the imperial court will recognise the validity of the claims by the Adiorenji, the Vilatmori and the Dariondi and excuse them from any obligation under the Treaty of Matheird.

"You see, the words Deerait or Deerait nation are never mentioned. Regrettably, for your point of view, the terms used are Deeraits or the Deerait people. Again, the actual treaty was signed only by officials from the Deerait tribe itself, probably because your people were then the only ones with a smattering of education in this land. Technically, the Deerait tribe will be held responsible for carrying out its conditions.

"The Casmans are very pedantic in legal affairs. Your argument that you signed for the whole Deerait nation would receive consideration. It's doubtful if they would decide in your favour. But an appeal would take a long time to settle, and the Empire would wish to deal immediately with the problem of hostile forces in the Rionder Valley.

"Our assessment is that Casman will insist on landing troops. You'll have no choice other than to concur with this request. If you refuse, you can be certain that your fellow nationals will be only too delighted to supply the Empire with ships and men to conquer you. If a civil war erupts before the Casman army corps arrive, the fighting will be of no interest to them as long as they receive their supplies. Such supplies will, I must emphasise, be expected to come from you Deeraits alone.

"The three tribes will evade any imperial charges of interference. They'll declare they're prepared to provide the Casmans with whatever they wish if they give them control of your provinces. Your provinces will then supply the Casmans anyway. Can't you just hear the leaders of the Vilatmori, the Dariondi and the Adiorenji telling the Empire how they found out about the steppe tribes in the Rionder Valley and how you Deeraits started a civil war to silence them?

"Whatever happens, you'll lose and become slaves under the other three sections of your nation. In turn, all of you will fall under Broechnaar. Remember, the Empire will not assist you against Enmarkan. The Baron's invasion plans won't be completed for some years. If Casman does defeat us, which somehow I doubt, and we are driven back to the western steppes, then it is more than likely that the western and eastern steppe peoples will be totally enslaved too. Their identities, tribal and individual, will be lost forever. They will become members of the imperial slave caste. What we have accomplished so far is too much for the Empire to forgive."

"As Allecenia has just told you, whatever happens, Deerait will be enslaved under Broechnaar. Its armies are far better trained and far more numerous than yours, even combined with the other sections of your nation. One way or the other, the Deerait tribe and nation will be finished. Incidentally, our defeat will mean the entire Jaddair corps will be put to death because we gained a victory over them. Their families will also be slaughtered. Hundreds of thousands of people will die in the Choolsay arena, men, women and children. Casman law will ensure that. We dare not lose!" Admaria declared, her beautiful dark hair shining in the light from the fire and the flickering wall torches.

"Oh dear. All this and other problems too. Civil war, steppe tribes and the Hedial temple demons," Phorigor sighed with exasperation.

"Hedial! Tell me what that spawn of Darkness and Master of Iniquities has to do with you! Tell me now!" Ontar snapped vehemently, crashing his right hand down on the table in front of him, dramatically altering the calm atmosphere in the chamber.

Felgorian was as startled as the others, with the exception of Admaria, Quinton and Allecenia. Everyone looked at the Ulgruffi mystic, whose countenance bore a deadly serious expression, indicative that the mighty sage was extremely perturbed. The Supreme Courtier and his three fellows quailed under the flashing eyes which demanded to know the connection with Hedial. Gone was the skilful negotiator of a few moments ago; in his place was the most capable and powerful wizard ever to walk the beautiful world of Phentara under the sun and two moons, a personage whose dominating presence radiated like a beacon flaming in the darkest night. The High Councillor felt as if he had been summoned before one of his principal gods, so awesome was the aura emanating from Ontar.

"Um...we...," the elderly Deerait spluttered, terror stricken.

"Relax. Steady yourself. I did not intend to frighten you. I am on your side wholly and unconditionally if you stand against Hedial," the eminent mystic spoke in soothing tones.

"Yes, we all stand unreservedly against the Demon. Some miles from here, not far from the coast just off the southern highway, stands a small ruined temple. It was dedicated to Hedial long, long ago. Folklore has passed tales down the years of the evil once resident inside the fane. Some of our legends tell of ancient seers who prophesied that Hedial would emerge to appear in our world. We think these fables are becoming a reality," Phorigor explained.

"What signs have there been?" Admaria wondered, while Perlow and Felgorian listened intently. The Chofir felt especially honoured at being present, and also that he was trusted with secrets such as the eventual conflict with Broechnaar.

"There is without doubt a heinous wickedness in the temple. Strange lights have been seen at night. They flash in the sky and turn the heavens into garish colours. Our people for miles around shun the area. Animals will not go near the fane. They will not venture closer than a half mile in the daytime. At night they are terrified by the lights I mentioned," the brown skinned Supreme Courtier replied.

"I take it you've sent out patrols to investigate. When was the last and what did they report?" Ontar asked.

"Two days ago. A company of the Hesion garrison was sent to survey the temple area. They left here as instructed in the late afternoon. The company fled back here in panic. The officer reported that shortly after sunset a light emanated from the direction of the fane. It was a ghastly greenish hue. Then dancing demoniacal figures appeared. Our troops fled terror stricken, so their descriptions were very vague.

"The officer stated that his patrol was just approaching the wood. The fane's on a hill in the large clearing beyond. They never even managed to enter the trees. Spectral figures swooped towards them. Fear was all around. Their heculs stampeded immediately. They are stout hearted fellows but they were terrified. The whole area apparently reeked of evil," Phorigor paused.

"I see. I have a grimoire in our encampment. It will provide further advice on this matter. What steps do you contemplate, if any?" the wizard enquired.

"We just don't know what to do. We have magicians in Hesion, but doubt if any has the ability to deal with a Demon of Hedial's rank. They are too scared to attempt anything. In fact," the Elder gave a wry smile, "they have disappeared. Probably in hiding or left the city. Magic is not what it used to be in Deerait. We had thought to send to the Empire for aid as a last resort, although I doubt whether their best sorcerers could do any better than our own. We were going to have a discussion this evening after this conference about sending envoys to Casman for occult assistance. Great Ontar, will you and the Lady Admaria help us?" the Head Councillor pleaded.

"Of course we shall. I made up my mind to do so the instant you admitted you stood against Hedial. Even if you had desired to follow him, I would still have fought. We shall commence our preparations at once. Our assault will begin tomorrow morning. Precisely where is the temple?"

"On the main southern highway. You travel for six miles, then a lesser road to the left appears under a rektur tree. The tree was blasted by lightning. A few hundred yards along this minor road and you reach a wood. Ride through the wood. The fane is on top of the hill beyond. Great Ontar, what do you wish us to do in return?"

"Nothing, except perhaps pray. Hedial concerns all of Phentara. He is evil beyond mortal comprehension. Indeed, that is why the Sacred Order destroyed your fleet centuries ago. Your magicians were intent on summoning the Demon to this physical plane to attack Ordlansa. I shall take Admaria with me, also you, Quinton, and you, Allecenia. While you await our return, please discuss what you are going to do about our forces. If we do not return, then it will not matter. Hedial will appear with all his hellish fiends and our world will be destroyed.

"Nevertheless, we have to take thought for the future. So, if you do decide to join us, we shall use our army judiciously against the three tribes. When Casman discovers this the Empire will declare war upon you. You will have slighted them by daring to become our allies. Make no mistake. This is a fight to the finish for them, until the steppe peoples are crushed. The Empire will risk the danger that your fleets will attempt to repeat what they did in the war long ago. The Emperor and his Court will have no choice. Casman honour, peculiar as it may seem, is not to be sneered at, and will be upheld by Heolanwertin. We estimate two years before the Empire will be in a position to bring its troops here. We must not let them know what is happening in this part of Rontmethar for as long as is possible. Hopefully we shall be on Casman soil by then.

"Briefly, here are further points to which you must agree. Pledges of undying loyalty will be sworn by your most sacred gods. Understand this! What is transpiring is no chance affair! Quinton, the King of Rionder and paramount ranxem of the Mescarg steppes, is no ordinary mortal. He is a child of Destiny! This is no boast for I, Ontar, aver so unequivocally. You will accept him as Supreme Overlord of the entire Deerait nation and all lands belonging thereto. When the Casman Empire is defeated, for it will be — this I know and believe, even in the face of Hedial — he will be the new Emperor. Again, when Broechnaar is liberated and the scourge of the House of Enmarkan removed from that unhappy land, Quinton will be Baron of the Central Plains. He is to be the First Emperor of Rontmethar."

"And that's the least of it," Allecenia, Admaria, Felgorian and Perlow thought to themselves, while the eminent sage continued to speak.

"In return, all his peoples will be educated. They will receive just governors and superiors. Their own customs, if not evil, will not be despised. From lowest to highest, all will be equal in law. Slavery will be abolished completely. This will not be a slow easy life, but one full of dynamism and inner fulfilment.

"Ponder these matters. If we did not have to leave you to face Hedial and his minions, we would have discussed them with you at length. If you wish to talk further when we return, we shall be pleased to do so. If you refuse our proposals, then we shall take our leave as friends. Forgive my haste, but we must depart immediately. Please have the door opened," Ontar commanded in his vibrant tones, simultaneously making a slight pass with his right hand which released Cottis from the enchantment placed upon him in Estyork.

Phorigor rose from his seat, crossed over to the door and rapped twice. In response to this signal the sentinels in the passage removed the bar to permit the King of Rionder and his party to leave. Behind them the High Council had their chamber resealed and settled down to discuss the astonishing revelations of the evening.

"That wizard Ontar, his wife and the youth Quinton are not like ordinary mortals. The veiled Lady seemed like them too. They exude an aura of power and majesty. It makes one feel as if you are in the presence of greatness. Destiny, that's the word I was seeking. Yes, in the presence of Destiny," Ihlden declared.

"That was and is my impression too. I feel as if I want to follow them," Cottis averred, adding, "and I am no traitor to my people."

Phorigor looked profoundly at the governor from the province of Sicruci and concurred, "You are right, absolutely right. If you had revealed to us what you knew of these tidings, we would never have been able to comprehend it."

"Yes, I know. Somehow I felt that I shouldn't tell you myself. There was a restraint of some kind on me. Probably a spell cast by Ontar, now removed because of the discussion he asked us to have," Cottis guessed without rancour.

"Understandable. The wizard would take such precautions. Here are my thoughts. Ontar and his companions are going

217

to face the evil from the temple of Hedial. Their task will be awesome. Failure will result in the destruction of our world. Success will remove a diabolical threat to the existence of Phentara. If they fail, then no one else will ever be able to defeat the Demon.

"It is rumoured abroad that the Sacred Islands, in the western archipelago of Ordlansa, are the havens of Good. Ontar is the Head Wizard. He will be supreme in the magical arts. I remember he said Quinton would be Emperor of Rontmethar. But I don't know. If they fail, then we are doomed to horror beyond our worst imaginings. He and his companions have unselfishly gone to the temple. May the gods be with them," Phorigor shook his head mournfully.

"Like you've just said, he and his companions are going to fight Hedial without asking our promises to join them. They go freely to face a fate far worse than death. If they lose, their souls will be damned for eternity. They asked for no reward. How many would do such a thing?" Rosmiche commented thoughtfully.

"True. Minutes ago, I thought them to be the worst peril facing us. Now, well, they are our only hope," Dyseey murmured.

"If we agree to join our forces to theirs, young Quinton will have to be accepted as our Supreme Overlord. Ontar wants him to be the Emperor of Casman, if we defeat them. Baron of the Central Plains too. Yes, Cottis?" Phorigor looked over at the provincial governor.

"I did not mean to interrupt you but I feel you should know what I witnessed on the journey from Estyork. We were attacked by eight hundred Relyanese. Quinton and his three hundred guards defended me. Their military efficiency is far beyond anything we have, or Casman either, I should think. His men rushed to carry out every order. They evinced a training and willingness to follow their leader which has to be seen to be believed.

"The Adiorenji under Reorgin and Kinerth were not merely defeated. They were utterly crushed with terrible losses, and it was so simply done without any fatalities to Quinton's guard. Also, remember what happened this afternoon in the city."

"You think their military capacity is as effective as they led us to believe?" Ihlden asked.

"Definitely! Even more! I sincerely believe their military

potential and organisation to be such that they could conquer Deerait without difficulty, even if we were one united nation. For many generations our ideas about the steppe tribes have always been that they are a bunch of totally uncivilised barbarians, perpetually squabbling and warring. The warriors I spoke to had obviously received a formal education. They can read, write and perform mathematics. Most of our own people are completely illiterate.

"Their intelligence and interest in life and Nature are phenomenal. They saw a ysdarculd in the Wilderness and asked Ontar to tell them about it. The wizard called the whole guard together and gave them a lecture on the animal's life. He told them facts I had never heard before. When he had finished the members of the guard asked pertinent questions. Their commander courteously thanked the wizard on behalf of his men. They seem to be in harmony with the essence of Being," Cottis stated frankly without bias.

"Your impressions are perhaps from being in the company of the elite troops of the King of Rionder's army?" Rosmiche suggested.

"No! That's what I thought at first. Then Quinton remarked to me that his bodyguard, although an elite, was wholly representative of his forces. Since the great journey across the Mescarg mountains he has changed his bodyguard considerably to give others experience. All those with him are single. They have families, but the other members care for the welfare of the family unit.

"The serving woman with him is also single. I believe she is to be married when he rejoins his main forces. His guards also perform what we term women's work. Each individual does this willingly, even officers. Oh, before I forget, Ontar introduced me to some of his escort who came from the King of Rionder's former bitterest enemies. They are devoted to him, and he fully recognises this. Mind you, he is absolutely devoted to them, and they know it!" Cottis stressed.

"We must reach a conclusion. It is only just. I propose we consult the Seer's scrolls without delay. If they are defeated by Hedial, whatever conclusion we reach will be of no avail to anyone. Death will then be welcome," Rosmiche voiced all their thoughts.

"Nevertheless, let us take a few moments to pray to our gods for the welfare of those who have freely gone forth to aid us.

Then let us assume they are victorious. It would hardly be courteous if we did not attempt to reach a satisfactory solution for our people, and perhaps for those who have given us such succour." Phorigor declared before adding, "In any case, it would be most rude if we were unable to give them an answer, even a negative one. I believe the ancient scrolls may provide the answer."

Once they had left the conference chamber, Ontar spoke quickly to Quinton in Ulgruffi. The youth listened attentively to his foster father while they hastened to the great doors leading to the courtyard where the heculs were tethered. The sentinels marching to and fro on the battlements watched as the sextet mounted up and galloped under the portcullis with all haste. They were followed by Hanshair and his fellow guards who had been called from the side room. The hooves of their steeds clattered noisily on the cobbled stones as they raced down the quiet streets of Hesion under the waning moonlight of Ilix, for the Enchantress was sinking away from Rontmethar. Deerait citizenry heard the urgent sounds of their passage but paid no heed; they continued with their revelry or turned over to find sleep once more.

"Hail, Sire!" a voice called, when they rode over to the encampment from the north gate. "Turn out for King Quinton and his illustrious companions!"

"No need, Colmar! Tell them to remain where they are! Quinton, you must go now. Take the greatest care. Do not, I repeat, do not approach within half a mile of the temple, either in daylight or in darkness. Admaria, Allecenia and I shall follow you once I have done some research. We shall join you as soon as possible in the morning. May the Great Power protect you and keep you," the sage said, blessing his foster son in tones filled with concern.

The youth nodded before wheeling his hecul to the left and riding off quickly into the night. Perlow looked questioningly at Ontar in the light from the campfires, but the latter shook his head to indicate that the King was to travel alone. As the sound of galloping hooves receded, the wizard told the Chofir and Felgorian to accompany him to his tent and led the way with Admaria and Allecenia immediately behind.

The ambassador and Perlow hastened after the Head of the Sacred Order of Light. When the awning of the shamianah had been dropped behind them Ontar commenced to tell the two men precisely what Hedial meant. The danger, which the whole of Phentara faced, was revealed. The Riondese and his steppe comrade had to sit down as the terrible words of the mighty sage shocked them to the core.

"I see. I understand what you meant in the High Court," the Riondese nodded at last. "What do you wish me to do? Can I help? I feel totally inadequate. This is the business of wizards in which ordinary men should not interfere."

"Yes. If meddlers had not interfered or dabbled in Black Magic long, long ago, Phentara would not be faced with doom at this moment. Perhaps Destiny brought us to Hesion in time to repel the Demon. Only time will tell. What you have to do will prove very difficult. In a word, wait. It will be extremely difficult and frustrating. You now realise fully what Hedial means."

"Have you any chance? Can I come?" Perlow asked anxiously.

"You must stay here, my friend. Admaria and I have personal knowledge of the Demon. Down the long centuries, from the Ulgruffi Empire to the establishment of the Order on Ordlansa, we have encountered and fought him and his minions quite often. But, I believe intuitively, never in such terrible circumstances. I am going to check on what I told you in an ancient grimoire. I have not forgotten the legend and history it contains, but I want to study it very closely. Felgorian, you will take overall charge of our contingent here.

"Quinton, Admaria, Allecenia and I will battle with Hedial. If we are successful we shall return here by early afternoon tomorrow at the latest. No, don't be surprised. This is an arcane matter, which must remain so. The business and affairs of wizards, as the ancient adage goes. If we do not appear by mid-afternoon proceed to the High Court and tell them that we have failed. What they will do then is for them to decide.

"Then you and our contingent must hasten home to the Rionder forests for the short time left to you. It may be weeks, months or even a year. Depart after the funeral for the fallen. Tell Gordan and Likans only. No one else. Doom will come soon enough. Go and get some rest. We should be gone by dawn, or not long afterwards. It'll depend on how much research I have to do in my grimoire. Oh, Felgorian, before I forget, send Hanshair to me. I'll instruct him to obey you in all things. He's responsible for our escort, as you know."

221

The Riondese rose and left the tent. His expression was drawn and very serious. Perlow remained haggard and silent. Admaria and Allecenia seated themselves at the table while the wizard began to search through a large chest for the tome which he required. A few moments passed before the guard commander rapped on the tent pole to which the awning was attached.

"Come in," Admaria called.

"Oh good, it's you, Hanshair." Ontar looked round with a benign smile, having just discovered the book in question.

"Felgorian told me that you wished to see me, Sir," the Nai-Zind declared, bowing to the company.

"My friend, I am going to give you an order which you will question in your heart. It will appear very strange, but I wish it to be carried out to the letter," the mystic said.

"Yes, I shall, Great Ontar," Hanshair acknowledged.

"You are to obey our ambassador, Felgorian, absolutely in all matters. Your King has left on a vital mission. My wife, the Lady Allecenia and I shall follow him as soon as possible. If we do not return by mid-afternoon tomorrow, we shall never return. You will do exactly what Felgorian says. He will order you to pack up and return to the Rionder Valley after the funeral in Hesion. You will do this without question. It is a hard matter to ask you, for you have always been, and still are, our friend and faithful follower.

"I cannot yet reveal to you the project in which we have become involved. It is the business of wizards, in which ordinary mortals do not belong or should not even be aware. Do not weep. We may be successful. If we are not, heed Felgorian. Depart immediately for the forests. I know you will do this for us, faithful warrior and loyal companion. Now I must ask you to leave. The Lady Allecenia, Admaria and I have to hold vital consultations," Ontar spoke gently.

"I shall obey you, Great Sage," the tall Nai-Zind said in a broken voice, tears brimming over and running down his handsome face.

"If it is at all possible, we shall return," Admaria smiled gently and reassuringly as Hanshair left the tent.

"They do indeed love you all," Allecenia commented softly from behind her veil.

"Indeed they do. It is an overwhelming responsibility, especially for Quinton. None of us must ever forget that their love and devotion must never be taken for granted or squandered. Here is the ancient grimoire," Ontar stated, sitting down in the glow of the candles on the table.

Shortly after he had passed through the lines of Deerait sentinels and the lights of his encampment had vanished into the night behind him Quinton saw Selix rising in pursuit of Ilix. The second moon shone from a sky dotted with clouds and wondrous myriads of stars. The youth trotted his hecul down a long slope which turned away from the city. Before him the King of Rionder saw the River Avidnive, glittering and shimmering in the mellow beams of the Panther.

The grass softened the sound of the hooves of his mount, while around him night birds called to one another as they hunted small animals or went about other pursuits. The wind had died away, but a slight chill permeated the environment. Quinton was a hardy steppe dweller; the temperature did not affect him in the least, even without his advanced mystical knowledge. He concentrated his attention on reaching the river and finding a safe route down the bank.

"There we are," he thought, glimpsing a dip in the land before him to the right of the pointed head of his steed.

He tugged on the reins and his mount trotted forward to pick its way down the steep bank to the edge of the slowly flowing Avidnive. Without hesitation Quinton dug his heels into the side of his hecul and the animal entered the water. The depth of the river never exceeded four feet in the upper reaches: near Hesion it increased to an average of almost ten, but there were shallow points marked by signposts, one of which the youth had selected, where it could be forded easily.

On his left, about a quarter of a mile distant, he saw the wall of the city end on the bank from which he had just descended. Across the river the wall began again and went round the town on the far side to the sea. The red flickering of torches indicated the various guard posts on the battlements and on the nearest high bridge. Possessing excellent eyesight, Quinton also perceived the shadows moving to and fro where the sentinels were making their rounds, the four barges which guarded the Avidnive between the two sections of Hesion, and the crimson glow in the sky from the iron ore workings to the south.

The water came up to his stirrups, splashing his black boots.

It felt cold, but the sensation only lasted a short while until his hecul had waded quickly across the wide river and gained the far bank. It clambered out and once more increased its rate of progress. Shortly thereafter the youth joined the southern highway, stretching like a white dusty ribbon under the gentle moonlight of the Panther.

With Hesion at his back, the King of Rionder increased the pace of his steed to a gallop. The wide trail passed under the thundering hooves of the racing hecul until finally it slowed down and trotted past the grotesque, lightning blasted rektur. Quinton guided his mount carefully and cautiously along the smaller road to the left until he reached the wood. The atmosphere was gloomy and possessed a latent menace, which malevolent sensation increased with every yard progressed. Suddenly the hecul attempted to turn about, a most unusual action for the highly trained and obedient creature. The youth uttered a spell to calm it before dismounting and fastening its reins to a tree beside the broad pathway.

The animal stood patiently under the influence of the minor enchantment while its master crept forward into the night. Soundlessly, in the manner which Gordan and the four Polingsi had painstakingly taught him, Quinton made his way through the ever increasing gloom to the far edge of the small wood. He noticed the silence which was absolute; gone were the nocturnal noises of birds and animals. The youth dropped to the ground and stealthily crawled the last few yards from the final trees to a clump of bushes. Once he had reached his objective safely Quinton parted some branches to survey the area before him.

The strange eerie gloom hung only over the wood, while the innumerable stars and the second moon of Phentara illuminated the temple on the hill. Nevertheless, the nameless dread still existed. Suddenly Terror struck the King of Rionder more forcibly than before, but his resolution and nerve did not yield to an almost overwhelming impulse to flee. He caused his mind to forget everything, utilising some of the esoteric knowledge taught by his foster parents. Quinton had no intention of disobeying Ontar's strict instructions, for the youth well remembered his lessons on the hierarchy of Hell, especially what Hedial was and the vast powers of the Demon.

All lay deceptively still in the golden moonlight. Nothing moved in the woods or on top of the hill. There was no sign of the dancing wraiths which Phorigor had mentioned, but the fane was unquestionably the source of all the malevolence in the vicinity. Quinton had the sense to realise this and remained absolutely motionless. The night passed slowly with Selix sinking to rest. A saffron dawn fingered the eastern sky before he rose and commenced to scout along the perimeter of the woods which completely enclosed the large clearing where the temple was situated.

For some time the King of Rionder moved swiftly with all stealth; he observed his surroundings with extreme caution. In the morning sunlight he perceived that the birds and animals had returned to the wood. However, no living creature ventured into the open where the fane dominated. Quinton concluded that it was nightfall and the ensuing gloom and horror which caused the sylvan inhabitants to depart.

"There certainly is a terrible evil here. Ontar and Admaria will require all their occult knowledge to deal with Hedial. I must try to recall the lessons they taught me in a time which seems so long ago and far away," Quinton thought solemnly as he rode his hecul out of the wood and back to the rektur tree.

He removed its reins and saddle before unfastening the tough cord on its yellow beak. It made no hostile move against its master for the latter had not removed the spell. The hecul merely lowered its head and began to graze. The King of Rionder watched it for several moments but the animal evinced no intention of leaving him. The vicinity appeared tranquil, but Quinton was not deceived; he did not forget his foster father's admonition.

The handsome youth sat down and lay back on the grass under the warmth of the sun. He mused thoughtfully, beginning to recollect some of the invaluable lectures Ontar had given him during the winter after his eighth birthday. Quinton had been an avid student in the cosy hut, part of the enclosed street structure where the Nai-Zind passed the long months, safe from the howling blizzards of the vast Mescarg steppes. The great sage had revealed certain of the arcane mysteries to his pupil, leading him on the Mystic Way, so that he would advance to perfection and no longer have to be reincarnated into the physical Universe.

While he awaited the arrival of his companions in the assault against Hedial, the King of Rionder obliterated all thoughts of the present. He searched deep into the recesses of his mind where the priceless lessons of his foster father lay dormant. The esoteric teachings awaited the desire of the one to whom they had been communicated so that they could be brought forth. Gradually, with the commencement of the process of recollection, the hidden memories flowed into his waking consciousness. So vivid was the revelation that it seemed once more as if his mentor were actually speaking the relevant words of wisdom to him in their wooden home on the snowbound grasslands.

"Life and Death, Quinton, are cycles through which we commence to comprehend Good and Evil. On Phentara, most of the peoples on the various continents possess some knowledge of the doctrine of reincarnation. On Rontmethar, especially among the steppe tribes, this doctrine is held to be sacred, in fact being incorporated in one form or another in their various religions.

"Reincarnation evolves as a rhythmic cycle. When the Great Power creates each of us as a perfect soul, each soul remains perfect for evermore. However, the soul personality is completely undeveloped with no knowledge of Good or Evil. This is why we are born into the physical Universe. We have to learn the lessons of life through many incarnations in order that we evolve a perfect soul personality. When we finally attain perfection there is no need for us to remain on this physical plane of existence, unless such is required of us. Perfection to leave this plane is one matter, for a higher more refined state of perfection may be required until we can become one with the Great Power absolutely. This is one of the greatest of all mysteries.

"However, my lecture this evening is not so much about the doctrine of reincarnation; rather it relates principally to Good and Evil. Since we realise what is Good, then we naturally comprehend Evil, which is a lack of Good. Otherwise, how would we recognise the wickedness of Baron Enmarkan, the ruler of the Central Plains? Good takes many forms, likewise Evil. Unfortunately, some shapes of the latter are very subtle like opiates; for example, a corrupt religion or government which insidiously changes the lives of a people without their realising what is actually occurring. In the study of magic, in which you have been engaged for some time now, Good and Evil are the paramount influences.

"You have been trained in the study of White, or Good,

Magic. Regrettably, Black, or Evil, sorcerers also exist. There are still many of them abroad but the ability of some is of a low standard. They are content to trick and terrify. There are others with a higher knowledge. They are consequently more perilous: these practitioners deliberately choose the Evil Way. From their number emerge the High Blacks. Fortunately the Evil Way, like the Good, involves considerable training. So, to reach the heights of Evil Magic in one incarnation, unless the practitioner is long lived or finds out how to prolong his years, is extremely difficult. Occasionally, an Evil Black may discover the requisite knowledge to increase his lifespan, or find a short route to his goal of Power. The latter did occur during the Ulgruffi Empire but the White Wizards proved the stronger. The Blacks were vanquished.

"Good and Evil are terms for Light and Darkness respectively. Light is the symbol of the growth of the inner self towards perfection. When that is obtained, the soul personality can dispense with the shackles of the body and reunite with the Light whence it came. This journey is long and arduous, but eventually each of us will accomplish it.

"Magic, whether Black or White, is the Science and Art of Causing Change to take place in conformity with Will. Therefore, by proper application of the correct degree of the requisite Force and utilising the correct channel, a magician can cause the Change he wants. Sorcerers and wizards try to attain the practical ability to set the necessary Forces into action. Success depends on their comprehension of the principles involved. Mistakes do occur, and the magician may perish in appalling circumstances. If the Magic is Evil then he may suffer damnation. On rare occasions, the Evil may remain to further endanger those who dwell on the physical plane of existence.

"There are many types of Magic, both Black and White. However, an important factor is the desire of the magician, that is, whether he wishes to relate to Good or Evil. Consequently, Intention too is vital. Necromancy is the art of revealing future events by calling up the spirits of the dead. A Black might do so for an evil purpose, while a White would do so for a beneficent reason. I repeat, the Purpose, or Intention, is of paramount significance. To use magic for selfish reasons may or may not be judged to be wrong by the Great Power, because the All Highest will be fully cognisant of the reason

227

behind its use.

"Let us consider the planes of the Occult Dimension, where time and space have no meaning as we relate them to the physical universe. Occasionally, the battle between Good and Evil may be removed to one of these realms so that the protagonists may fight without being involved on the physical plane. This can only occur when a White Magician of considerable knowledge utters certain sacred syllables. A Black would prefer to remain in this world to conduct his nefarious operations."

Once he had fully recollected Ontar's words, Quinton pondered them carefully, considering each phrase and sentence in relation to the context of the lecture. The youth was only too conscious of the perils which he, Allecenia and his foster parents might encounter. The two Ulgruffi had often related allegories of occult contests between Black and White: this was a method which they often used to enliven and clarify many of the invaluable points contained in their lectures and experiments. The threat to the Deeraits and Phentara from the fane was like one of them becoming a frightening reality.

A few fleecy white clouds drifted lazily overhead, blown to and fro by the gentle breeze. Birds flew around, apparently oblivious to the evil lurking in the temple on the hill. Insects and flowers continued the business of natural life, while far away terrible blizzards of pink snow blasted and howled across the high Mescarg steppes: such was the contrast between winter at the end of the year in the country of Deerait and the harsh but beautiful environment where Quinton had spent most of his young life.

Chapter Fourteen
The Occult Dimension

Hearing the sound of hecul hooves, the King of Rionder rose to his feet and turned to look in the direction of Hesion. He smiled when his keen eyes caught sight of three mounted figures whom he discerned to be Ontar, Admaria and Allecenia. Olluinan's daughter had temporarily removed her veil and the hood of her cloak was thrown back. She fully believed the words of the High Court that no one dared to approach within miles of the fane of Nuoemove, for such was the terror it generated among the populace.

On reaching the youth the trio dismounted and, once their saddles had been removed, the wizard used his staff to cast a simple spell over the four fine steeds, causing them to sink to the ground in a sound sleep. The animals would remain thus until the sage or one of his companions awoke them.

"We know the lie of the land, Quinton. Our crystals revealed all its features. What sensations of evil or unease have you had?" Admaria asked, while they secreted their saddles behind some large sturdy bushes.

"There was a virulent evil in the woods during the night. Terror was abroad, and also beyond in the open where the temple is," her foster son replied. He was hard pressed not to gaze longingly at Allecenia's exquisite face. "Then this morning, nothing at all. The birds and animals returned to the wood but not to the temple area. I didn't venture nearer than Ontar instructed me. Also, I didn't see any sign or indication of the dancing figures, and I watched till dawn."

"Excellent! The sun is the symbol of Light. It can still force the Powers of Darkness to withdraw. Let us walk from here. The stroll will do us good. It'll give me the opportunity to tell you what I learned from the grimoire. First though, there is a black protective invisible circle in existence around the fane, with a lesser radius than the circumference of the woods.

"The Demon is assuredly behind the evil here. I recollected a tale of the temple of Nuoemove — that's the ancient name for this district. I read it first many centuries ago in my grimoire, which must be at least a score of millenia old. Its pages are fashioned from strong hide. Like I said, I first read it long, long ago, when the Ulgruffi were at the height of their power and majesty, and science, law and love walked hand in hand. Ah, those were the days of glory, a shining glory, but all too fleeting even though they endured thousands of years." Ontar sighed with memory and regret for the country of his youth.

"One of the tales in the tome told of an evil place, the land of Dannim, where sorcerers worked magic to conjure up elementals. These entities were then commanded to give instruction on the manner in which more powerful devils could be brought forth. This took them quite a time but, through spells and other rituals, they succeeded in calling forth the demon god Hedial, one of the principals of Hell.

"Once Hedial appeared the sorcerers swore to serve him faithfully. They bound themselves to the Demon by a pact to sell their souls. Hedial was full of craft and cunning, a master of deceit and deception. He did not attempt to destroy them although the protection they had raised against his power was not wholly effective. He fawned on them and told them his desires, promising anything they wished in return. Naturally the magicians hastened to carry out his requirements, so mesmerised had they become. Hedial never ceased to promise them power and wealth in return for their obedience.

"The Demon's main desire was to remain on the physical plane for as long as he wished, without having to withdraw to the nether regions. Fortunately for Phentara, the necessary vibrations to give Hedial and his horde of devils the capability to walk over the face of the world involved lengthy and extremely complex occult preparations and operations. Often the materials required existed vast distances away. Journeys to obtain them and bring them together in one place took many years. During this time of waiting a fane or small temple was built where Hedial could be worshipped with obscene and blasphemous rites. A ring of power or black circle was placed around the construction.

"The conclusion of the tale related how White Magicians, with the aid of Angelic Powers, destroyed the temple of Nuoemove and banished the evil therein. Indeed, the Black sorcerers had often attempted to bring the necessary materials by occult means; but their White adversaries thwarted their endeavours, leaving them the wearisome task of having to travel to seek them.

"This legend is meant to be a warning from long ago. No details of the actual tactics used to defeat Hedial and his minions are given. Notwithstanding, since the grimoire does contain some of the most powerful spells and rituals known, we can assume the importance of the tale was believed so paramount that some record of it had to be written for posterity," the mighty sage declared.

"Ah, what we have here is certainly a parallel situation," Allecenia remarked in her beautiful voice.

"From your tone I sense you are receiving evil vibrations."

"You know me well, Godfather. Even here still in the middle of this pleasant woodland, I do feel evil vibrations ahead of us. Not too potent because of the sunlight, but a definite evil barrier does exist. The black circle," Olluinan's daughter affirmed.

"I sense them also," Admaria concurred.

"You all believe then that we are about to encounter a situation somewhat similar to the one in the grimoire legend?" Quinton said pensively, raising his eyebrows.

"Yes. When Phorigor mentioned the temple last night, I recollected the region around here was once known as Nuoemove, and that was the name in the legend. So, my suspicions were immediately aroused. That's what prompted me to study the grimoire closely. The description of the fane in the old book was very precise. Naturally, the details of the ruined building and the geography of this area have altered with the passage of time down the long centuries. I also perused other books and consulted with Admaria and Allecenia.

"The three of us concurred beyond all doubt that the fane here is on the very same site where the sorcerers conjured forth Hedial and his minions. From scrying we also concluded that the ruined temple building is not the original but another erected on the same foundations many years later. However, its dimensions are precisely those in the grimoire diagrams. There was also a detailed account of the stars and planets overhead on the day when the original fane was completed and dedicated with the customary obscene rituals," the sage explained before asking his wife to continue.

"The Ulgruffi were very learned in both astrology and astronomy. We devised methods of calculating the positions of stars in the past and the future. You know this, Quinton.

When we established the Sacred Order on Ordlansa we continued such scientific investigations with very advanced techniques. One of the things which Ontar and I once did was to work out the relevant sidereal positions in the grimoire. We had no definite idea until then where Nuoemove was, other than it was somewhere in the land of Dannim on Rontmethar. There were approximations of the date of the magic from other details in the tale. These provided us with a sufficient basis from which to work.

"We did this a few years before Allecenia was born. Her mother Artzcellia assisted us in our task. Once we had calculated and checked our findings, we concluded that Dannim was part of what is now called the land of Deerait. More important, we realised that the temple was somewhere near the eastern seaboard, but the geographical details in the legend were imprecise and we could not pinpoint its vicinity. It was quite by chance during a visit to Matheird that we learned its location. We overheard a Deerait sailor talking about his home near the ruined fane of Nuoemove. He was only too pleased to tell us its whereabouts," Admaria explained.

"I see. The long term changes in the landscape because of time and geological movement," Quinton nodded.

"Exactly. After the destruction of the original temple, the people in the region would hand down the events in their folklore. Superstition would prevail. With the onset of the years the chiefs would decide to build some sort of shrine on the site of the original fane to propitiate evil spirits. Initially, this would be of primitive design. Then a time would come when they were capable of building a more solid edifice. Oh, here we are!" Admaria exclaimed as they left the woodland and walked out into the bright sunlight.

"Go on," Quinton said. "It's very interesting. The more we all know the better."

"Yes. The design of yonder temple is, of course, totally different to the original but the dimensions are the same. That in itself is a most peculiar similarity. Very sinister. Why should the evil arise again? We can only speculate. Ontar, Allecenia and I believe that, although the White Magicians with the assistance of Angelic Powers did succeed in casting Hedial and his minions back to their own circles and destroyed the temple, they erred in not reducing the foundations to dust. The base would still be tainted by evil vibrations. Perhaps some Deerait or Dannimite magician or priest unwittingly attuned himself or herself with the evil and the whole process started again at a much slower rate," Admaria conjectured.

When the quartet had walked about a hundred yards over the grass Ontar said, "We shall halt here. So, Quinton, we have to conclude that the evil has expanded down the long span of years. With its increasing vibrations the local people would feel uncomfortable and move away. The area would become deserted except for animals and birds. The present barrier is in the precise position where the Black Magicians first constructed it. Hedial has erected it once more. We four are faced with a battle on behalf of the Light against this particularly vile Demon.

"Judging from the reports made to the High Council, and from sifting through the information gleaned from the legend and my books, Hedial could almost be ready to emerge into the physical world. Allecenia, Admaria and I pooled the vast knowledge we have and that was our conclusion. This appearance may come at any time but definitely at the latest within a few months," the mystic stated thoughtfully.

"The Deeraits remarked on the strange demonaical dancers. I didn't see any. Why not?" the King of Rionder asked.

"The spectres were an illusion. Their purpose was to deter anyone from approaching first the temple, and next the woods as the evil expanded. Notice how the beasts and birds have ceased to come into this clearing in daylight. Hedial would use that device to frighten the Deerait patrol. Since it was chased off the Demon's power on this plane has increased dramatically. There's no longer need for the illusion. Hedial is now able to use Terror alone to control the area. That's what you experienced during the night. With your training you knew how to overcome the Terror projected. The Deerait soldiers were absolutely terrified. They had every reason to be so. They are a superstitious people. Remember Phorigor's expression, when he spoke of the concern of the High Court regarding the prophecies that a Demon would appear in this area," Ontar said.

"It will be a difficult task for us, if not impossible. We four are the only ones available with sufficient training to face the evil. No one could have anticipated that we were destined to meet such peril. Mind you, success may give us the Deerait tribe for allies. That would be a starting point for subduing the Vilatmori, Dariondi and Adiorenji. More, it could mean the Deerait national fleets and war carried to Casman shores. Before that can become a reality we have to commit ourselves to this deadly adventure," Admaria said solemnly.

"I shall do my best," Quinton smiled, aware of the concern in his foster mother's voice.

"We know that. You are thoroughly accustomed to physical danger but the treachery and deceits you will encounter are contrastingly different," Admaria voiced the thoughts of both her husband and Allecenia.

"This may indeed be a task which the Great Power has specifically designated. It will also prove to be a lesson. If I am to be the Emperor of Phentara, I have to learn to really care for all my subjects. This venture will increase my understanding about how to provide for the welfare of their souls. We can only go forward. If I perish and fall into darkness, then so be it. This evil has to be erased from the fair land of Deerait," Quinton declared reflectively.

His companions smiled and gazed at him. The youth was showing a side of himself which had been fairly well concealed, for it had never been required so obviously. He was prepared to surrender his soul if it would help vanquish Hedial and save the Deeraits and Phentara from the abyss. Quinton knew precisely what such a sacrifice entailed. The two Ulgruffi had instructed him thoroughly in the occult, ever admonishing him about the penalties lying in wait for the unwary.

"Let us begin. First we must prepare ourselves. I shall speak some words to elevate us to a state of grace. Then we shall all pray, before Ontar and I explain our strategy," Admaria said.

The beautiful dark haired woman spoke six resonant words in Ulgruffi, each a palindrome containing six syllables. The quartet remained silent and motionless while the incantation took effect. They felt cleansed and spiritually elevated; their garments and bodies had been wholly purified. Admaria then continued the procedure to complete their sanctification.

"I have uttered the words to cleanse our clothes and bodies of impurities. Now I shall speak a prayer to the Great Power for His aid in our task. Please bow your heads. Clasp your hands in front of your solar plexuses," she directed.

In clear distinct tones, Ontar's spouse humbly besought protection from the Ruler of the Universe and the Realm of

Hidden Things for her companions and herself while they were engaged in the awesome task before them. She began with words of gratitude for their lives and the gracious benefits His Bounty had bestowed on them. Admaria prayed for Divine assistance in the difficulties which lay before them, stating that their only desire was to help their fellow creatures on Phentara and that their reward would be the success of their venture.

When she had finished her orison she told her companions to relax before saying, "Our strategy is this. Inside yonder invisible barrier is the realm of Hedial and his evil cohorts. As was mentioned earlier, they'll soon have the capability to walk abroad in our world. Admittedly they will shun the light of day. Their first endeavour will be to cause gloom and darkness to descend all over Phentara. Such action will assist them when they emerge to begin dwelling permanently on our physical plane. The only effective resistance against them, other than ourselves, would be from the Sacred Islands."

"If they do enter our world, could the Order of Light defeat them?" Quinton asked, looking at his foster father.

"We do not believe so. I am the most adept and powerful wizard on this planet. Admaria is next, almost as good in terms of ability. Our brethren in the Order also have considerable power. Allecenia is probably fourth after you, young man. Yes, God-daughter, Quinton may not have had the experience in this incarnation but his ability is phenomenal. After Allecenia, comes Olluinan and then Artzcellia. The remainder of the Order are capable magicians who could tackle and defeat sorcerers extant. However, if Hedial and his battalions assailed them without warning many would perish horribly. Hedial can call on his equals — entities such as Lubeln, the Chief Prince of Darkness for Phentara, Nathagol, Otasalex and Icardo. They are evil beyond comprehension.

"Even if Allecenia, Admaria and I were with the Order on Ordlansa when these beings attacked, the sight of them in our world, combined with their evil emanations, would drive many insane. The peoples of Phentara would be turned to mindless zombies. Millions would commit suicide. Millions would be slain. Volcanoes would erupt, vomiting fire, ash and poisonous fumes. Vampires, demons, werewolves and other entities would swarm abroad. The destruction wrought by these hellish denizens would turn our world into a replica of their own dark circles. The Order would attempt to organise a defence against them by calling on the Great Power and His Holy Angels. However, this would take time. Don't forget, Hedial knows about us. He would launch an assault without warning. Success for the Sacred Order would be extremely doubtful.

"Should the Order be successful and drive Hedial and his cohorts back to the nether regions, we would probably face a world of zombies. They would be sterile, both men and women. We ourselves would be very few in number, the only rational human beings on Phentara. This planet could be utterly devastated in a battle between the Powers of Good and Evil. That's without the prior destruction caused by the entities of Hell, when they first appeared. Very little plant and animal life would survive. There are an infinite number of possibilities regarding what might occur," the wizard said in sombre tones.

"Our strategy is governed by a fleeting vision Ontar and I had on the ride back to camp last night. We were admonished not to disclose any details until after we had prayed today. The vision decreed that we four alone are to combat the evil. We must not attempt to pierce yonder invisible black circle. We could inadvertently let Hedial out, instead of repelling him. So, we must leave this world, this plane, and battle somewhere on the Occult Dimension. We all know from esoteric studies that this is a realm where time and space have an entirely different meaning, if any at all. Everyone, join hands and form a circle!" Admaria commanded in a strong resolute voice.

Once her companions had complied, she nodded to Ontar. Her spouse then uttered the words of an ancient sacred incantation which could only be attempted by a High Adept. The vibrant intonations caused the atmosphere to change from ordinary sunlight to a warm azure shimmering haze which completely obscured the contours of the landscape about them. Quinton felt as if he were floating in space, for he had no sensation that his feet were touching the ground. He was totally unafraid; indeed, a pleasant glow permeated his being, flowing through and around him. Time stood still; even eternity seemed to have ended.

Almost imperceptibly the blue haze dispersed. This might have taken a second, a minute, a month or a million years, so content were the quartet during the transportation from their physical plane into the wondrous Occult Dimension of the Great Power. When the last of the benevolent mist had disappeared they found themselves standing precisely in the same place where the wizard had commenced the incantation.

"Here we are. The Occult Dimension has been achieved. We are now on our own on one of its many planes. What you see here, Quinton, Allecenia, is a reproduction of the land of Dannim. We are in the ancient time when the Black Magicians were involved in calling forth Hedial. The terrain is slightly different. There are more trees in the open and more foliage on the hill. The temperature is tropical. Ontar and I shall ascend to the temple. We shall attempt to ascertain the extent of the evil," Admaria said.

"What do you wish us to do?" Quinton wondered.

The youth was extremely puzzled by the fact that his sword and dagger, which he had worn before the transference to the higher plane, had been supplemented by a stout bow and a quiver of arrows strapped to his body. He noticed too that the elegant cloak which Olluinan's daughter had been wearing had likewise vanished.

"The incantation I've just used has provided me with intuitive information to assist us in our endeavours. Admaria and I can cross the black circle without detection. Quinton, you will be our warrior. Notice how you've been furnished with a bow and arrows, while my own sword has vanished. You may have to shed blood to prevent the evil conjurations. Such violence is permissible, even here in a world beyond normal mortal comprehension. You and Allecenia are to journey to delay the arrival of a caravan. It's transporting the particular herbs and other artifacts to complete the occult operations to give Hedial permanent access to the physical plane.

"We have been given this opportunity to prevent Hedial from destroying Phentara in our own time. Thanks be to the Great Power, the One! We must be grateful to Him, the Creator of All, that we have advanced to this dimension with His Blessing. Quinton, you and Allecenia should encounter the caravan in about one and a half days' march from here due north. You must prevent it from reaching here. That is imperative.

"Use magic if necessary, but you must not use flight to find the caravan! Be careful! There are several capable sorcerers with the caravan. You should be able to cope with them, if and when you encounter them. Admaria and I will enter the fane. We'll determine how to destroy the evil therein. If all goes in our favour, we shall see you here in two or three days. Follow the trail through the trees yonder," Ontar said, indicating with his staff to a gap in the forest.

"We shall do what we have to," Quinton averred solemnly, with Allecenia nodding her acquiescence.

The two Ulgruffi were embraced warmly by their foster son and god-daughter. They watched for several minutes while the handsome couple strode away in the direction of the trail to the north. The sage and his wife turned and stepped out resolutely towards the temple, which stood dark against the clear sky on top of the hill. They held hands, trusting in their own abilities and the righteousness of their cause; this attitude did not lull them into a false sense of security, for they had no illusions about the terrible perils to be encountered.

Ascending the hill, with soft knee-high yellow and green grasses swishing with their passage, Ontar and Admaria wondered how Quinton and Allecenia would fare. The fane might be destroyed, thus denying Hedial access to the Phentara of their future. The vision received by the wizard and his spouse the previous night had decreed that only four persons were to be ranged against the colossal forces of evil; this appeared too few a number, yet Divine advice had been given and it was to be obeyed. The problem now remained for them to proceed boldly, trusting that they would be successful and that all of them would survive.

Monumental tasks had been ordained for them; they had to press onwards. Since the Powers of Light had decreed that Quinton and Allecenia were to engage the caravan as their principal part in the Occult Dimensional adventure, then this had to be. It may have appeared peculiar that all four of them were not permitted to battle with the hellish, demoniacal wickedness in the temple, but their understanding was limited because of their mortality; the Great Power was infinite and immortal, hence His comprehension of everything.

Allecenia and Quinton entered the luxuriant forest in which an abundance of animal, bird and insect sounds indicated vibrant natural life. The couple were fully cognisant that there would be many strange and dangerous creatures abroad, some species of which would have become extinct during the long centuries to their own era. Consequently they proceeded with extreme caution through the trees and undergrowth, following the rutted trail which ran in an almost straight line.

Strange, multi-plumaged birds chattered and screeched warnings overhead while small yellow and turquoise simians with five arms and two long tails swung with marvellous agility from branch to branch, emitting occasional grunts. Insects buzzed around their heads, but none landed on their skin or clothing; Allecenia had made a precautionary pass with her left hand when they approached the forest to eliminate the possibility of their being stung by any which might prove infectious or poisonous.

The bright sun was considerably warmer than in their own time, and the combination of heat and tropical rain made the atmosphere close and sticky. Despite this, they proceeded at a fair pace for several hours. Quinton was ever conscious of the divinely beautiful woman with the perfect figure walking beside him. He often cast a glance in her direction and, on several occasions, was surprised to discover that she too was regarding him in a similar fashion.

"Shall we try some of that fruit? My intuition tells me it is quite safe to eat," the youth said, indicating the large purple apples on a colam tree, the laden branches of which hung down almost touching the ground.

"Please," his companion concurred, for she felt slightly famished.

The foster son of the two Ulgruffi, with his long black hair and very handsome face, stretched out his arm and plucked two of the delicious apples, one of which he passed to Olluinan's daughter. Allecenia smiled tenderly at him. She bit into the soft succulent fruit and nodded her appreciation. Quinton thought again how very attractive she was, dressed in a light green tunic with trousers to match. She was the same height as he, exactly seven feet tall. He did not realise that he was falling deeply in love with her, nor for an instant did he even dream that Allecenia had already done so with him.

His musing about his beautiful companion did not distract him from the perils extant. Quinton had been excellently trained by Gordan and the Polingsi in the craft of tracking, and being aware of latent threats in the environment. His mind automatically registered the sounds in the vicinity. The warning screeches and calls of the sylvan inhabitants because of human presence did not worry him for they were totally natural. These were to be expected: the young King of Rionder kept his senses alert for any unusual occurrence.

Allecenia pointed ahead to where the trail diverted to the left, while before them was a sheltered avenue almost a hundred yards in length. A most attractive colonnade was formed by tall elegant trees with silvern barks; their trunks thrust long sturdy branches outwards, many of which trailed to the ground and were festooned with green leaves and orange flowers. A soft gentle perfume permeated the atmosphere. The fragrant essence wafted towards the couple, tempting them to stroll under the magnificent canopy.

"Let's walk through there. The trail makes a wide detour on the outside of the avenue. We can rejoin it at the far end. The scent is marvellous," Allecenia smiled.

"No! There's danger!" Quinton replied to her surprise.

"Oh! What do you mean? Where?"

"Look, the trail does not pass under this avenue. It would be easier for it to do so. That's decidedly odd. There are no birds in any of the trees, as far as I can see. Nor are there any animals or even insects between the columns. I don't know the name of those trees. Probably they have changed down the years. But I sense some peril under that archway," he stressed.

"I shall follow your advice," Allecenia said gently.

"The perfume seems like an opiate," Quinton commented, as they proceeded to the left of the avenue.

"Yes, I do believe you're correct. On Ordlansa there are bushes from which we extract a drug for medicinal purposes. In some respects the bushes resemble yonder trees. What's that?" the beautiful woman declared.

"One of the trees just emitted some pods. See! There! On the grass!" Quinton replied, pointing to the right between two trunks.

"Now I understand. Those trees are ancient replicas of curenc bushes. The temperature here is tropical, not temperate as in the Deerait of our own time. Curenc bushes flower every three weeks. When the flower dies within a day of its bursting forth, it emits pods like those. If the forest animals wander by, they may be attracted by the pods and devour them. The pods are poisonous and the animals perish within moments. The same applies to birds. At night the bushes lower their branches and, through countless suckers which contain acid, literally consume every atom of their victim! Those trees will most likely do precisely the same," Allecenia explained.

240

"Admaria once mentioned the bush during a lecture. I recall what she said. They do eat only during the hours of darkness. In the daytime these trees will probably be shunned by all living creatures. Unwary humans would be susceptible to the perfume. If we had gone along there the trees would have emitted sufficient fragrance to cause us to become unconscious. When night fell we would have provided them with dinner. For some strange reason, the curenc always grow in two parallel lines and catch their prey between them," Quinton said.

"You're right," his companion nodded.

"Gordan would have guessed about the trees immediately. He's wholly fascinated by Nature, every aspect of it," Quinton smiled.

"Ontar and Admaria mention him a lot. They're very fond of him."

"Yes. Gordan's like a second son to them. Whatever happens to him, Ontar and Admaria are concerned. They love him dearly, like I do. You'll like him too," Quinton declared as they finished their colam apples.

"I do already. I'm glad you were alert enough to sense the danger from the curenc avenue. You did well. Mind you, I did think it would be most pleasant to walk beneath the archway with you," Allecenia murmured in soft tones.

"There's no one in the whole world I would rather have walk through life beside me than you," Quinton whispered gallantly.

Allecenia placed her hand in his, and they halted suspended in a wondrous moment. The magnificent colours of their environment harmonised with their inner selves, so that they became one with all living things. The essence of life itself flowed through and around them from the heavens above to the ground beneath their feet. The forest creatures were caught by the force of the auras from the handsome couple and their calling and screeching assumed a consonant aspect.

The King of Rionder looked into the gentle gray blue eyes which were filled with gladness. The youth gazed at her in a silence, replete with complete contentment. No words could express the total joy in both their hearts. The golden moment seemed to hang suspended and to endure eternally beyond time and space. A supreme ecstasy swelled their pounding hearts. Quinton and Allecenia remained motionless. The minutes passed by, and still they stood on the soft grass covered with

241

small white flowers beside the broad rutted trail in the land of Dannim created in the Occult Dimension.

The long moment began to slip past to its end. As the spell broke they moved towards one another and embraced. It appeared the most natural thing for them to do. To each of them, their first kiss was unforgettable. Quinton pressed her soft lips with his own. His happiness was like magnificent rolling mountainous combers, sparkling in the sunlight and flowing in an unbroken rhythm across a limitless azure ocean.

Allecenia felt as if she had reached the highest state of mystical ecstasy. She had found someone to love unquestioningly, whom she was prepared to follow through the mysterious occult plane and beyond. If they were successful against Hedial and returned to their own time, she would travel beside him all over the world of Phentara, in rags or riches, in war and peace, while he carved out his destiny and empire. All the virgin Lady desired was to walk through life with her handsome companion.

They clung together for some time before Quinton smilingly said, "We'll have to start looking soon for a suitable spot to camp for the night."

"Mmm. Yes, we should. Do you not think that we should travel through the night?"

"I do not believe that would be advisable. Darkness is synonymous with Evil. Also, once Ontar and Admaria enter the fane, which they must have done by now, Hedial will be aware of them and us. We don't want to be caught in the open, unprepared for an occult assault. We should also gather some fruit for our evening meal," Quinton smiled tenderly. "I do love you, Allecenia," he added.

"And I love you too, Dearest. I concur we should find adequate shelter. There's plenty of fruit around. We shall have to be ready to use magic. When we camp for the night I'll project astrally and search for the caravan," she spoke softly, while they continued on their way, hand in hand.

Chapter Fifteen
Beneath the Temple

Ontar and Admaria passed undetected through the invisible barrier and ascended the hill to the temple of Nuoemove. Their thoughts were with their two companions in the desperate venture. The sage and his wife were fully aware of the growing feelings which Quinton and Allecenia possessed for each other: they had often discussed privately over the years the knowledge that their foster son was destined to create an imperial dynasty. However the identity of his future spouse had never been revealed by the Hidden Servants of the Great Power during the Holy Conclaves on Ordlansa. It was only when Olluinan and his daughter had re-entered their lives in Estyork and their god-daughter had shown her face to Quinton that they had begun to contemplate seriously the possibility of the union of the exceptional couple.

During their climb the two Ulgruffi strode around bushes bedecked with flowers. A multitude of diverse plants was scattered about the hillside in magnificent profusion, making a mockery of the heinous evil within the fane above. Green, yellow, blue and crimson petals fluttered above varying sizes of stalks. The gentle wind caused the blooms to sway and dance as if they were enjoying an harmonic symphony of melodious beauty. Ontar and Admaria glanced to their right and glimpsed the Chofanrit Ocean, glittering and shimmering beyond the expanse of treetops. Nothing in this corner of the Cosmic Occult Dimension indicated other than that they were still on the continent of Rontmethar on the beautiful planet Phentara.

When they reached the top of the hill the temple stood out ominously and starkly against the azure sky. On the side, directly facing them, were twelve uncrowned columns five feet apart and twenty feet high. Each pillar was of primitive design, manufactured from innumerable gray smooth flat slabs of varying thickness. The erection was a square inside the perimeter of which was a stone structure, slightly more than half the height of the columns. It had no windows, only a filthy green wooden sealed door facing the north.

"Shall we attempt to enter, or do you wish to look around first?" Admaria asked.

"We'll enter now and commence the destruction of this hellish place," her husband answered grimly.

A cold shadow suddenly covered the sun and an insidious darkness hovered above the fane. They both sensed the menace but, knowing it would only be of a few seconds duration, did not let it deter their resolution to proceed. Moments later the gloom departed and the sun resumed its place in the natural order of things, bringing back its warmth and life-giving qualities. Nevertheless the two Ulgruffi were not in the least fooled; this was an unequivocal indication that evil existed within the temple of Nuoemove.

"Here we go, My Love," the sage said, raising his staff.

The silvern tip began to glow and a ray of white light sped to strike the sealant around the entrance. Admaria watched while the beam seared through the strange solid substance which offered some resistance, but finally melted. Her spouse lowered his wand, satisfied with what had been accomplished: the spell of guard had been broken. He strode over to push the door inwards on its well greased hinges.

"That is human fat," Admaria shuddered.

"I know. Some poor wretches must have suffered horribly to produce it," Ontar nodded.

The wizard led the way inside, their path being illumined by the light from his staff. A few yards ahead the level gave way to steps which disappeared into an obscene darkness filled with hidden menace. They walked resolutely forward, not being in the least dismayed by the anticipated sudden deafening crash, which indicated that the doorway had been closed behind them.

The atmosphere was dank and musty; moisture dripped down the stone walls. The two Ulgruffi were forced to walk cautiously lest they slipped on the wet stone stairs. The staff showed that they were descending a passage approximately twelve feet high. Their surroundings were totally featureless which added a grimness and latent horror to the loathsome place.

"Here we are," Ontar murmured, his melodic voice sounding harsh and toneless. "We came down thirty four steps. I don't believe there is another level below this one."

"Increase the light," Admaria advised. "We'd better obtain

a view of what's here before we proceed any further."

Her spouse extended the illumination which thrust back the sinister Stygian gloom. They discovered that they were standing on the edge of a wide area, the only exit being the way they had entered. The floor was paved with slabs of the same featureless stone which composed the walls, stairway and exterior. However, evidence of Hell was manifest; designs of an obscene and vile character, painted in garish colours, adorned the ceiling, floor and walls. The four strong pillars which supported the roof of the chamber had the heads of several demons carved on them, with that of Hedial being the most prominent.

In the centre of the columns stood a rectangular stone altar on which lay a large curved knife with a bejewelled handle. The altar itself was of sufficient length to accommodate the body of an adult Phentaran: there were dark brown stains on its surface which could only be human blood. On each side of the base was a malevolent representation of Hedial's face. Crimson eyes glared balefully with a virulent savagery beneath the four black horns of the Demon whose head was crowned with thick green curly hair.

"Ontar, it's becoming colder," Admaria whispered.

"Yes, this is it. We've dared to invade Hedial's temple. An entity is coming to punish us for our intrusion. Be prepared. It may be Hedial himself," her husband responded.

They felt the vitality in their limbs draining away and found themselves apparently rooted to the floor, unable to move. The light from Ontar's staff began to diminish as an evil chuckling emanated from the direction of the altar ten feet distant. The countenance of the Demon nearest to them began to glow and become animated. Above it, near the large sacrificial knife, wisps of acrid black smoke arose, filling the chamber with a stench reminiscent of putrid maggot infested corpses under a hot sun.

Admaria strained every sinew in her body, but to no avail. She felt totally frozen from head to foot. Both Ulgruffi fully comprehended what was occurring. Additionally the searing malevolent eyes which mocked them from the altar were exerting a powerful hypnotic influence. Ontar forced his gaze away from Hedial at the same moment as his wife. The Demon believed that two foolish White Magicians had strayed into his domain. This should provide some amusement. Although the Lord of Iniquities sensed that his intended victims did possess a smattering of Power, else they could not have crossed the black circle without detection, he vastly underestimated their ability.

The two mystics stared at the floor while the icy coldness increased in intensity. The couple were totally cognisant of their present perilous circumstances. However they did not permit the dreadful sensation of Terror blasting towards them from the base of the altar to pervade their minds and paralyse their capacity to think. The glow from the staff had dwindled almost to the point of extinction while, simultaneously, the glowing crimson eyes had increased their potency, causing the chamber to pulsate. The floor, ceiling and walls gave the illusion of movement; the obscene figures evinced the impression of performing grotesque bestial actions.

The blood curdling laughter increased in volume for several interminable moments. Then a silence fell. Seconds later a bitter harsh voice commanded them to proceed to the altar where the pungent smoke had begun to whirl and hideous apparitions gyrated in the vortex. Their feet began to slide forward involuntarily against their wills. The Heads of the Sacred Order of Light on Ordlansa permitted the Demon to control them for four grudging paces before they took swift action. Throwing off the enchantments Ontar and Admaria uttered in unison two words of Power in a tongue which was ancient, even in the time when the Black Magicians had conjured forth Hedial in the land of Dannim.

Within an instant the whole chamber revolved violently. The eerie crimson glow abruptly ceased. A swift shaft of lightning from the sky far above seared through the roof to shatter the altar into fragments. The two Ulgruffi witnessed this spectacular occurrence, welcoming its outcome. They immediately hastened to the stairway and sped up the steps with agility, the restored glow from the silvern tip of Ontar's staff illuminating their egress. The outer door lay broken by the force of the spell which they had uttered. The couple ran out into the golden sunshine and down the grass covered hill, where the myriadfold variegated flowers still waved gently and rhythmically in the breeze under the canopy of the azure heavens.

Quinton's handsome foster parents did not pause until they reached the foot of the slope. Once there they turned in time to witness the temple columns crumbling to the ground to complete the demolition of the evil stone structure. Clouds of dust accompanied the fall of the pillars, heralding the glad tidings that the foundations of the fane of Nuoemove had been totally destroyed and the area purified.

"That will give Hedial a great deal to ponder. We certainly learned what the interior of the temple was like! More important, its malignant atmosphere was more deadly than we could have anticipated. Astral projection inside would not have served us so well," the eminent wizard smiled.

"Hedial won't be so accommodating next time. Nevertheless, the temple can't be restored on this plane without the assistance of his human adherents," Admaria observed.

"He's back in his own circles now. The Black Magicians still have to be defeated. They are the Demon's link to this world. They'll conjure him forth again. We do know all of them are in the caravan. Quinton and Allecenia won't reach it before Hedial returns to this plane," Ontar stressed.

"I know. Hedial will have a familiar controlling the sorcerers. That's where the main threat comes from," his wife declared.

"I agree. You and I have to remain here. That's what I didn't mention to Quinton and Allecenia. Although the temple and its foundations have been demolished and sanctified, I was also told that the Demon has to be vanquished absolutely. Not simply by closing any point of ingress to Phentara, but by inflicting on him such a defeat that never again will he entertain thoughts of entering the physical Universe," Ontar explained seriously.

"I did wonder why you were instructed to send Quinton and Allecenia to find the caravan. Especially when you told them not to fly there."

"I thought you would. They've no chance of reaching it before Hedial returns to this plane. They are a diversion. Hopefully they'll defeat any foes the Demon launches against them. You see, My Love, you and I have been chosen to fight the main battle with the fiend in the Circles of Hell itself. Quinton and Allecenia have an excellent chance of vanquishing the sorcerers and destroying the caravan. That'll ensure Hedial's gateway to the physical plane is sealed for certain.

"Then Phentara has a chance of being saved. The empire

of the future may still come to fruition, even if you and I perish. If we lose, our souls will be damned for eternity. We can't imagine the torments Hedial will inflict on us. Let us prepare ourselves," her husband smiled softly, taking her hand.

"You know how high we have advanced in our esoteric studies, both in magic and mysticism. Both Yolfalthien and Sonalprin did mention that we both had attained all the knowledge and experience to forestall the necessity for further incarnations. Except we have to face one final initiation," Admaria reminded her spouse.

"I hadn't thought about that. This could be it. Whatever happens, I love you. I've loved you ever since I first saw you in Inthearna, long, long ago in the count of years. I've had more happiness than any mortal man has ever merited," the sage said tenderly in the bright sunlight of the mysterious dimension.

"I know. I've never forgotten the first time ever I saw your face. I, too, loved you then. It was on that sunny morning in the busy thoroughfare of Artisans. I'd just left the potter's shop when you came over. We bumped into one another. You remember, My Love?" Admaria said with tenderness in her voice.

"I've never ever forgotten. The scene's imprinted indelibly in my memory. Whatever happens, we've had a wonderful life together. Sorrow has not been absent, but we've belonged to each other for millenia. We've never aged, except in wisdom. Whatever happens, I'd do it all over again," Ontar whispered before kissing his beautiful dark haired wife.

"Yes, I'd do it again too. Never forget that we have Love, and Love is everything," Admaria smiled.

"I believe that we'll be victorious. Somehow, we shall win through," her husband nodded while an unbidden hope filled both their hearts.

The westering sun slipped gradually to the far horizon; its fall caused the trees to cast longer shadows over the forest. The two travellers walked resolutely forward, hand in hand, aware that evening was imminent. When twilight fell Quinton surveyed the glades on either side of the rutted trail and eventually saw one which satisfied his requirements for the night. A stream flowed nearby, gurgling and chattering over the stones in its rocky bed. A cluster of bushes formed a windbreak on the side nearest the trail while animals and birds carried on their natural activities in the tall beautiful trees which bordered the clearing.

The youth smiled and indicated the dell to his exquisite companion, who fully concurred with his choice. During their journey they had collected some fruit and berries for their evening meal. Quinton, helped by Allecenia, swiftly gathered logs, grass and brushwood before using his tinder box to start a small fire. Its welcome glow cheered them, and they sat contentedly in front of it, eating their supper.

With the fall of night a chill wind arose and the King of Rionder threw wood onto the fire to maintain its warmth. As the flames crackled greedily the youth sensed that there was danger in the environment and glanced around, alert for any trace of peril. He immediately noticed that there was no sign of the stars, the heavenly attendants of the Enchantress, and that all natural activity had totally ceased, leaving an eerie silence.

"Allecenia," he whispered, "I don't like the atmosphere here. There seems to be a darkness obscuring the sky. Roughly eight feet above our heads. See, where the reflection from the fire only goes up to that height and then stops. Also the trees are slightly obscured all around."

"Yes. There's something severely wrong. Some element of Black Sorcery," she said quietly.

"I've the same misgivings. Hedial?" Quinton asked, raising his eyebrows.

"Probably not. Ontar and Admaria will have roused and thwarted the Demon this afternoon. His powers are vast. He is thought to be the equal of Lubeln, the Chief Prince of Darkness. Hedial possesses the potential to manifest on this plane. That's because of the materials and the Black Magicians in yonder caravan. I don't imply that he can appear at will yet. He'll certainly have a means of maintaining contact with them, probably through the use of a familiar."

"Ontar and Admaria will then assuredly face his full wrath. I'm inclined to agree with you about a familiar. That is logical. The familiar, whatever creature it may be, must have advised the Black Magicians of the temple assault. I reckon the next move will be for them to assail my dear foster parents. They will be commanded to bring Hedial to this plane temporarily! In that case, why bother about us? We don't represent anything like the threat they do. Oh, are you going to project astrally to overlook the caravan? It may be too risky," Quinton enquired in the dim atmosphere which was becoming oppressive.

"Astral projection at this time may be too perilous. The gloominess here indicates evil abroad. If I were to project my body could be taken over by an entity and the silver cord cut. Nevertheless, we do represent quite a threat. Of course, Ontar and Admaria are the major threat. Hedial will be fully aware of that! They destroyed his temple. We know this through intuition," Olluinan's daughter stated.

"Yes, we do!" Quinton exclaimed emphatically.

"We are only secondary. The Demon will have deduced this fact because we are engaged in a lesser task. Your foster parents, my godparents, are far more dangerous to the Lord of Iniquities than you, or Hedial for that matter, realise. The two Heads of the Sacred of Light have hidden occult powers far beyond anything they reveal in the outworld. Although what they do attempt outside the Islands is always fantastic. Hedial will have more than a glimmering of their ability. After all, they did destroy his fane. The fiend will want swift vengeance on them!" Allecenia stated seriously.

"You're right. The Demon will have concluded we're less dangerous to him else why are we walking to the caravan? You and I are probably being assailed tonight to keep us occupied, even if we are not slain. Hence the darkness keeping out the starlight. But I'm puzzled as to why we weren't allowed to fly to attack the caravan," Quinton remarked thoughtfully.

"I didn't think of that at the time. Now you've mentioned it, it does seem rather peculiar. We can only speculate why Ontar said it. Also he told us back in the camp outside Hesion not to take our crystals. It's most strange," Olluinan's daughter commented.

"It is very odd. Still, Ontar will have a good reason," Quinton nodded. "We'd better stop speculating and be ready for whatever happens."

"I'm making a guess. I believe the Black Magicians will employ the major portion of their talents to bring Hedial forth against my godparents. We'll most likely be assaulted by animals, entities, ghouls and perhaps a minor demon."

"Let's form a circle. Hopefully that will be enough protection. We don't have the time or herbs to form stronger

250

diagrammatical designs," the handsome youth pointed out.

Drawing his sword, Quinton quickly traced the circumference of a ring twenty feet in diameter with the fire as its centre. The line was imperfect but he compensated for the irregularities by chanting a spell which caused it to form a perfect circle. Allecenia watched intently until the operation had been completed before waving her hands to banish all impurities from both their bodies and their newly formed protection. She stood still for several moments before smiling when a pleasant fragrance arose to indicate that her rite had been entirely successful.

"It won't keep out animals. Entities, yes. I'll have my bow ready. The fire's quite high. There's enough wood to maintain it for a few hours," Quinton remarked, glancing around the glade.

The noisome pervading darkness lowered claustrophobically until it was about four feet above their heads. The couple were wholly alert, their keen eyes attempting to pierce the gloom in anticipation of the occult assault which their intuition revealed to be imminent. Quinton expected a physical attack, and selected a long black feathered shaft from his quiver. He held the strong powerful bow in his left hand while his right grasped the arrow, ready to notch it into the taut string. Allecenia was equally vigilant; she had a personal occult protection of which her companion was unaware.

Suddenly a dreadful snarling followed by a deep throated howl startled them. Then the eerie silence returned. Quinton promptly nocked his arrow, ready to propel the shaft at this foe once it appeared, for he knew it well. Allecenia had some notion about the identity of the creature and asked her beloved to confirm her thought. The youth concurred with her assumption; the sounds had emanated from a ratchan, a fierce wolf with which he had become acquainted on the vast steppes of his childhood.

"I didn't think they lived this far south in Deerait," Allecenia commented.

"No, they're only found on the Mescarg steppes of Rontmethar. You're forgetting that we're in a time period many centuries before our own. The climate here is tropical. The beasts and fauna we observed this afternoon have a much greater variety than in the Deerait of our era," Quinton explained.

"I should have remembered. You'll have seen ratchans often on the great plains beyond the Mescarg mountains."

"Especially in the autumn when we slew bison for winter food. Ratchans would come sneaking over the grasslands to filch whatever they could. Fires were built in a large ring. Gaps were left so that the bison carcasses could be dragged through to be skinned and butchered. Nothing was wasted. Hides, sinews, bones, entrails were all utilised," Quinton explained, while Allecenia stood snuggling against his left shoulder.

"Tell me more. Everything is quiet for the moment," she whispered, kissing his cheek as he lowered his bow.

"Packs of ratchans used to chase after the herds of bison and deer to catch stragglers. Bison and deer herds are always found together on the steppes. Sometimes the wolves were fortunate. Other times the bison would mass together and charge. I used to feel sorry in a way for the wolves."

"Why was that?" Allecenia wondered.

"You know bison, heculs, rotars and deer hibernate each steppe winter. Ratchans don't. They have a truly miserable existence until spring comes. They have to kill and gorge themselves each autumn to fatten up as much as possible. If they don't, they perish in the terrible blizzards. When the thaw came and we left our hut enclosure any ratchans we saw were pitiable, just skin and bone, often barely able to stand," Quinton replied.

The youth related to his lovely companion a dramatic event in the life of a particular wolf. It had been observed by Gordan during the autumn hunt eleven years before when the Riondese had been sent on a scouting expedition. He had dismounted, and crept cautiously forward, before peering over the crest of a rise. His purpose was to survey a large bison and deer herd which the warriors were to attack the following morning.

He was accompanied by Forsever, the Nai-Zind sub-caranxem, to whom Gordan pointed out the actions of a lone wolf below them. With the wind blowing towards it, the beast had crawled patiently and silently through the long grass. The two men watched intently, admiring its stealth. The creature made its way with its belly to the ground. Its target was obvious, namely a fawn with a dappled coat which had strayed dangerously away from the protection of the herd.

The six-legged ratchan edged forward, until Gordan and his comrade reckoned that its chances of success were excellent.

The grass was high; the approach of the predator was totally silent, each step being tested before a paw was placed down firmly. The fawn suddenly lifted its head, sniffing the air cautiously. All appeared normal and it resumed grazing. The dark red furred ratchan continued its painstaking progress until it finally attained a position from where it would be able to leap at its intended prey.

The two observers did not desire to interrupt the process of Nature. They had no wish for the wolf to succeed in its endeavours; it was simply the absolute necessity for the bison herd to remain undisturbed by humans before the essential hunt on the morrow. Both believed that the fawn would perish: the ratchan would pounce, break the neck of its victim in its powerful jaws, seize the carcass in its mouth and then race off to consume its prize at leisure. However, for no apparent reason, the sprawling bison herd decided to change direction and turned to wander slowly towards the fawn. The movement of the giant shaggy beasts caused the small deer to scamper to its mother, which stood with others of its kind, mingling unconcernedly with the bison.

Gordan and Forsever, peering through the grass on the top of the rise, wondered what the next action of the ratchan would be. A cold autumn wind began to blow across the steppes from the west where the watery sun was half obscured by dull leaden clouds. Below the two companions the wolf lay motionless, hopefully and patiently awaiting another opportunity. Unlike its human observers it was completely unaware that its position was gradually being surrounded on all sides by the moving herd. When it did realise what had occurred the predator lay as flat as possible. Unfortunately several wandering bison trampled nearby and it was compelled to move.

Its presence was detected at once. The bulls bellowed a warning. The mighty herd charged, both deer and bison, determined to exterminate their common enemy. The ratchan found itself surrounded by hostile animals thundering towards it. A circular wall of powerful shaggy black bison advanced on it, as it raced hopelessly to and fro in the ever decreasing ring. All seemed lost when suddenly it made a fantastic bound, born of utter desperation. It leaped over the heads of the nearest bison landing on the back of one of them. The wolf spun round so that its head was between the horns of its adversary;

simultaneously it dug every single one of the strong claws on each of its six powerful legs through the thick hair and into the flesh of its strange mount.

The astonishing presence of the ratchan, combined with its ferocious snarling and painful claws, caused the bison to stampede erratically through the herd, bellowing frenetically. Its fellows and the deer promptly gave way in a panic at this incredible occurrence, while Gordan and Forsever were enthralled by the drama. They barely refrained from cheering when the wolf and its mighty steed penetrated to the edge of the herd. Once the open reaches of the steppes were in front of it, the ratchan leapt down and raced away as fast as its legs could be propelled, probably resolved never to find itself in such strange perilous circumstances again.

"I can recollect Gordan telling us that night what he and Forsever had witnessed. Ontar, Admaria and I were visiting him in his tent. Sheralex was putting out the evening meal for us," Quinton concluded his story.

"You miss Gordan and your Polingsi friends and the others who follow you. I know," Allecenia smiled softly.

"Yes, I do. Especially Gordan and the Polingsi. As you're aware, Gordan saved me when Rionder fell."

"I saw the sack of Rionder and Gordan riding with you in his arms. The Hidden Servants had advised us long ago that we were not to interfere if Rionder were attacked," Allecenia said.

"You would see this on the Master Crystals in Hesewoner on Ordlansa. Ontar and Admaria have often mentioned them. I'd like to see them one day. Uh, oh. We've got company, very unpleasant company!" Quinton exclaimed, raising his bow.

"I see them. Several pairs of eyes, just beyond the firelight yonder," Allecenia nodded, moving away from her beloved.

Raucous growls split the ominous silence, followed by the sound of heavy movements in the brush. Quinton recognised that the ratchans were capable of breaching the circumference of the circle, thus breaking its protection. Ghouls and other evil entities were from a different plane and consequently would be repulsed if they attempted to cross the line of Power. His every instinct revealed that the ratchans were under the influence of some dreadful occult force, inimical to Allecenia and himself.

The eyes vanished, but reappeared almost instantly. Quinton

drew his bowstring back to its furthest extent and released the arrow. Faster than sight his trained fingers notched a second shaft before the first struck its mark and launched it at another target. A frightful screech, closely followed by another nearby, indicated that his bolts had found their objectives. Terrible nerve-wracking snarls and growls arose from all around but no eyes remained visible in the gloomy environment.

"Throw more wood on the fire! I must slay as many as possible before they charge us!" Quinton shouted, searching for another mark.

Allecenia complied with his request. Dry pieces of wood sparked and erupted into flame, swiftly bringing more welcome light. Although animal movements were apparent in the undergrowth, there was still nothing discernible. However, after a minute a large number of ratchans emerged into the clearing, prowling restlessly. Their dark eyes glinted in a very peculiar manner, indicative that the beasts were under some form of enchantment.

Quinton raised his bow and the string sang. A ratchan perished; the arrow in its chest had pierced its heart. Even while its life fled into the paths of death, its fellows trotted forward, six in the foremost rank, with the remainder of the pack prowling close behind. The wolves advanced from all sides of the circle. The King of Rionder fired another shaft before casting aside his bow and drawing his sword from its sheath. He had no time to concern himself about Allecenia, much as he wished, before he was attacked.

The youth did not flinch. He gripped the hilt in both hands and swung valiantly. A ferocious wolf with slavering jaws leaped into the air, claws fully extended to rip and rend. The six-legged brute received the full force of Quinton's keen blade, which decapitated it. The sudden demise of their leader caused the pack to pause briefly but the evil power controlling their minds impelled them against the two humans moments later.

Allecenia realised that Quinton could not withstand the combined onslaught. A wolf sprang at her and the youth leapt to pierce its side with a valiant two-handed thrust. With a screech of mortal agony the beast crashed into the fire, scattering the burning wood in its death throes. Unfortunately its contortions wrested the sword from his hand. In the meantime, four more ratchans bounded to attack. One made for Allecenia. Quinton drew his dagger and threw it unerringly.

The missile penetrated the right eye of the beast and continued to its brain.

Another wolf sprang at the King of Rionder, but Quinton dived beneath its hurtling body to grasp a burning branch. He thrust this straight down the throat of the brute which had executed a swift turnabout. It screamed hideously and fled off into the gloomy undergrowth, its mouth scorched. The other two ratchans breached the circle and Quinton realised that all seemed lost. He seized another flaming brand in a brave attempt to repel them, but a further ten ratchans were hurrying towards the two humans. From the corner of his left eye he briefly glimpsed Allecenia extending her right hand on which she now wore a silvern ring with a single clear jewel.

Olluinan's daughter uttered a monosyllabic word. A brilliant white light sprang from the ring. It divided into several beams, each of which radiated to strike both eyes of every ratchan simultaneously with such a terrible searing intensity that the creatures were blinded. The pain was extremely harsh and the wolves fled, howling in agony to blunder against trees and foliage. When the sounds of their turbulent passage had receded Allecenia looked at Quinton and smiled.

"Those ratchans won't return tonight. They'll run for miles. Then their sight will return and the pain will vanish," she explained.

"I'm glad you took a hand so effectively. Say, where did that ring come from? You weren't wearing it when the wolves first attacked," Quinton observed, retrieving his dagger.

"No. It was a magical gift Ontar and Admaria gave me when I reached my majority. They instructed me in its use. It's very powerful," Allecenia responded.

"So I saw," the youth nodded.

"I wear it all the time on an invisible chain around my neck. If I'm ever in great danger, an instant's thought causes it to appear on the middle finger of my right hand. Look! Another thought."

"And it returns to the chain once more," Quinton deduced, as he noticed the ring vanish.

"That's correct," she concurred.

"I'm glad you had it. We'd have been swamped by that pack. Did you notice how vicious they were?"

"I certainly did. You had barely time to defend yourself and me. You could have used magic. I should have done so sooner,"

256

Allecenia confessed what she thought to be her failure.

"I was about to when that first ratchan sprang at you. Then things became even more hectic. You did really well. We're still alive. If they return, we shall most definitely use magic. Though I doubt animals will be launched against us again. Our adversaries will be now aware of your ring," the King of Rionder said frankly.

"Yes, I agree it's most unlikely they'll use animals again," she nodded.

"The circle's breached in several places. I'll deal with the carcasses and repair our defence," Quinton said, walking over to pull his sword from the side of the mighty beast in which it had stuck. "We'll have to purify the area and ourselves again. There should be time before the next onslaught," he remarked, wiping the blood from his weapon on the fur of the dead wolf.

"And this time very potent Black Magic will be used. Our survival will depend on the strength of our circle, and the extent of the evil launched against us," Allecenia affirmed.

"And our ability. Ontar and Admaria will encounter far more opposition than we two. On the one hand, we're fortunate that we shall most likely repel any occult attacks. On the other hand, I'd gladly face the entire force of Hedial and his legions and risk eternal damnation to save my foster parents," Quinton stated with absolute sincerity.

The King of Rionder replaced his sword in its sheath. He glanced around briefly before snapping the fingers of his right hand and uttering several phrases in Ulgruffi. The ratchan carcasses, together with all traces of paw marks and other impurities, rose into the air to fly over the trees on the far side of the clearing, before tumbling to the ground. The fire gathered itself together, while the protective circle reformed. Allecenia was absolutely amazed: even though she had been advised that Quinton possessed considerable magical knowledge, she had not been prepared for this demonstration of his ability, and remarked on it.

"That was excellently done! It takes Adepts years to perform that! I can do it, but . . ."

"I know. I am very young. Memories from past incarnations and the teachings of Ontar and Admaria. I do hope they'll be all right," Quinton sighed.

Allecenia crossed over to her beloved who put his right arm around her. She leaned her head against his shoulder, feeling very secure and happy. The light caress of her fragrant hair touching his cheek and her softness nestling against him caused an inexplicable tingling to vibrate through his very being. Quinton fully realised how much she loved him, and the wondrous depth of his own emotions. In his heart he knew that Allecenia would be his wife and the mother of his children.

She spoke, "Dearest, I know how concerned you are about Ontar and Admaria. I am too. Listen. My godparents have performed actions beyond belief on the Islands. Their power is far stronger than all the Sacred Islands magicians combined. I've just seen an example of your magical capability. I realise that you too are in advance of me. Ontar did say so, but I didn't fully grasp his words then. I do now!

"Hearken to me. What I am about to say is not to provide false comfort for you. Hedial has no idea what he has aroused in the two Ulgruffi. Keep this in your heart. When compared to ordinary mortals, Ontar and Admaria, for all that they are human in physical bodies, are almost the equivalent of the mighty archangels who serve the Great Power!"

Quinton looked at her astounded. "I didn't know! Naturally, I'm aware they're wiser in all matters than anyone else. I do believe you! I've never thought of them like that. They're my parents. I think of them as Mother and Father. I'm glad you told me. I feel much relieved, very much relieved."

"We on the Sacred Islands know their capabilities. Outworlders may try to guess the extent of their powers. They fall short. Many spells require herbs and artifacts, even for Adepts, unless they dabble in Black Magic to control elementals. Many spells can be cast without herbs and artifacts, but the mental effort of executing them is extremely exhausting — on occasion even fatal to those not sufficiently trained or advanced. Ontar and Admaria behave like kind gentle humans, which they certainly are, but they have the Power and Knowledge for fantastic occult operations. They are full of love and eternal wisdom. They never flaunt their knowledge, boast or use it for aggrandisement," Allecenia declared in reverential tones.

"In other words, perfect mystics," Quinton smiled. "I wonder how they're faring."

"They will be safe, and prepared," Olluinan's daughter averred emphatically.

Chapter Sixteen
Dannimite Sorcery

Approximately thirty miles distant through the dense forest from the young couple, there was another clearing which extended in a large semi-circle onto a cliff above the Chofanrit Ocean. Huge breakers crashed in a frothy bubbling cauldron of foam against the barriers of rock at its base. Overhead a starry sky sparkled for the resplendent Enchantress, sailing majestically like a spectral ship through luminous clouds. Beneath Ilix, countless treetops swayed in the wind while dark purple shadows mysteriously mellowed the night under the intricate leafy canopy of the magnificent forest adorning the land of Dannim.

However, the intrinsic beauty and grandeur of the environment were entirely lost on the group gathered around and near a huge fire in the centre of the clearing. Although their physiques were more brutal and primitive, the men and women were of the same colours of skin as their descendants in the Deerait of Cottis. Their dress was mainly animal hides although several wore coarse blouses of a crude brown material.

Thirty male and forty female helots stood sullenly while their sorcerous masters held an animated discussion on the most effective method of dealing with the adversaries of their Demon Lord, Hedial. The latter had contacted the High Priest shortly after sunset when the camp was being pitched. Since the communication there had been angry disagreement about the manner of effecting their evil Master's wishes, not that anyone entertained thoughts of refusing to comply with his commands.

"Stop this argument! We are wasting time! Let us decide on a strategy!" a tall angular white skinned magician snapped.

"We have already been told what to do by Lord Hedial," a brown sorcerer sneered.

"Kiltron is right! I agree with him. Lord Hedial has communicated his wishes!" a third snapped.

"It's alright for you lesser magicians, Anacorj! You just spout wind. I am responsible. Lord Hedial indicated two threats. He wishes us to deal with those coming to attack our caravan first.

But he hasn't told us how we are to do so and he will tell us as usual! Look! The lour is about to speak again!"

The malevolent familiar had been lying with its eyes closed beside the fire. It suddenly sprang to its feet and stalked arrogantly over to the argumentative group. Yellow searing orbs, filled with red flecks and virulent malice, glared wickedly at the followers of its demoniacal Master. The sorcerers quailed before its gaze while the helots fled to hide behind the covered wagons. All were terrified by the evil emanating from the possessed creature.

"You fools! You blind, stupid, cretinous fools!" it hissed, froth dripping from its fangs. "You should have begun the basic rituals of obeisance. I always give you the appropriate instructions after the elementary rites. Morons! Do you hearken to me?"

"Yes, Lord and Master," the croaking reply came in unison.

"The two in the forest are a mere youth and a woman. Their task is obviously to assault this caravan. They are of little consequence. However, they are my enemies! I wish them destroyed!" the lour snapped ferociously. "You will launch a pack of ratchans against them. If the couple repel them, elementals and the like are to be sent next. If the second phase is unsuccessful I shall advise you on the next step. I doubt a third will prove essential in any event. But even if it does, they will perish. Their damned souls will suffer the torments of Hell throughout eternity.

"Those responsible for the destruction of my temple and its foundations are also to be annihilated. These two, curse them and their rotten souls, have Power! More than you filth! I shall deal with them myself. Therefore for this purpose you will immediately commence the requisite occult operations. I wish to manifest untrammelled in your world from midnight tonight until dawn. I, Hedial, will crush them! Then I shall return to Hell with their souls. I shall torture and amuse myself with them. When I've finished the High Prince of Darkness, Lubeln, will have them for evermore. In due course you shall rebuild my temple. Then I shall come to your world at will when you have completed the occult operations for me to do so."

There were horrified gasps at this, for the strain of performing the highly complicated rituals was appalling; the Dannimite sorcerers dreaded the thought of the next few hours.

260

When they had originally summoned forth Hedial they had believed that they were in control of the mighty Fiend. However, the latter had watched and waited patiently, obeying their every request and whim; the Lord of Iniquities had flattered and praised their every action, aware that they were bound to make a really fatal mistake sooner or later. Eventually one magician decided to have a familiar; he selected the lour, a creature sacred to Hedial. By chance this particular animal had already been used in other occult rituals, which meant that it would be more susceptible to the purposes of the Demon.

The six feet long cur stood on four short spindly legs, while its tail was a six inch white tuft; it was four feet high at the shoulder, and had a yellow coat, dappled with green spots; two vertical ears dominated a narrow head, which had an eye on each side, ending in the sharp point of a long red tipped nose. The unfortunate animal was drugged before the ritual began. Hedial cunningly acquiesced with the magician's instructions to make the lour his familiar. The Fiend directed the Dannimite through a complex occult undertaking, flattering and praising the latter for his wisdom. The sorcerer was totally deceived and bewildered by the magical instructions. Instead of controlling matters and sensibly terminating the operation, he allowed the honeyed tongue of the Demon to overcome his own judgment, and rashly proceeded to its dreadful conclusion.

Hedial promptly seized his opportunity and dominated the familiar. The lour commanded the contingent of Black Magicians to convene so that it could give a demonstration of its powers. The place selected was the small fane of Nuoemove at midnight. Accompanied by several of their helots bearing torches, the Black Magicians entered the temple, descended the steps and duly approached the underground altar on which the cur sat, malevolently regarding its audience. It did not address them but closed its eyes. Moments later a foul smelling gray mist emanated from its nostrils and rose into the air to form a phosphorescent miniaturised outline of Hedial.

The Dannimites had barely time to adjust to this apparition before it sped towards one of the helots. The latter screamed in terror, dropping his torch to the floor of the dark chamber. The entity flew into his left ear. The slave screeched horribly; his eyes bulged like stalks; his hands tore his hide clothing into shreds. He collapsed to the ground, rolling in mortal agony. A bloody, crimson froth bubbled and sprayed forth from his lips and nostrils. The unfortunate victim writhed tortuously for a minute before welcome death released him from his fiendish tormentor. His cadaver jerked spasmodically. Moments passed until, dramatically, eerie magenta flames erupted from his belly. The burning vapour spread slowly, accompanied by the stench of roasting flesh, to consume the entire corpse and leave a pile of black ash.

When the mysterious fire had finally extinguished itself, the gray mist emerged menacingly from the remains of what had been a living human being. The entity sped back to dissolve into the nasal passages of the lour from whence it had originated. The cur arose and grimaced mockingly at its terror stricken audience. Nothing was said; there was no necessity; the harsh demonstration had been fully comprehended. The Dannimite sorcerers would never again attempt to criticise or control the Lord of Iniquities, for they themselves were now totally at his mercy.

Hedial determined to pursue his personal hellish strategy so that he could emerge and remain at will on the physical plane where mankind dwelled. His reluctant adherents received instructions to journey to certain places in the immense forests which covered the greater portion of Rontmethar for the specific purpose of gathering special herbs. Once every essential item had been collected his intention was that a protracted ritual of an utterly obscene nature, a diabolical blasphemy against the Great Power, would be carried out. This rite would entail several human sacrifices from the helots; the latter would be drugged to ensure their compliance since the shedding of blood provided vibrations of high potency.

The Black Magicians obeyed every command of their demoniacal Master and successfully amassed the required herbs. The return of their caravan to the fane of Nuoemove was the point in physical time selected by the Higher Powers for the Occult Dimensional conflict to save Phentara from Hedial. Although his original intention had been to conduct the wicked ritual at the temple, the Demon determined to employ a portion of the rite to punish the interlopers. The complete ceremony itself took several days, but a shorter version would give the Lord of Iniquities a brief space to annihilate his foes. Once the latter had been overcome the

Demon would retire to his own Circles to await the reconstruction of his temple. When this was accomplished, through the supervision and administration of the familiar, the longer ritual would be undertaken.

In the clearing on the clifftop the base creature glared balefully while it watched its human servants. The High Priest and two of his most adept confederates superintended with alacrity the drawing of a circle to encompass the wagons. Within this vast circumference four separate smaller circles were etched for the protection of the mortals, their heculs and rotars, the animals being put to sleep by an incantation from the lour.

A stone container was taken from one of the wains; each person, master and slave alike, sipped a few drops of a narcotic which dulled their senses without causing unconsciousness. The state of trance induced made each individual more susceptible to any commands from the evil familiar. The helots were enclosed in one of the smaller circles except for eight of their number, two women and six men, destined to be sacrifices. Selected herbs were placed in a large metal bowl, the outer rim of which bore ancient occult designs. The fifteen Black Magicians then dressed themselves in their ceremonial robes, long crimson cloaks bound with a black cord.

The painstaking preliminary preparations took almost an hour and a half. During this time the lour lay with its head between its paws, gazing maliciously at the activity through half closed venomous eyes. When everything had been accomplished to its satisfaction, the familiar sat up on its haunches and ordered the High Priest, Xirtix, and Kiltron to launch the attack against the couple in the forest to the south. This was a relatively simple task which the two Black Magicians carried out efficiently. With a sadistic tone in its voice the cur praised their efforts, not that it felt disposed to be generous, but approbation might prove to be of some value to the Dannimites' performance in the further operations of that night.

The lour advised its servants to check everything again. A short time afterwards it realised that the ratchan attack had completely failed. It felt angry but did not evince its displeasure, merely advising a minor entity assault as the next move to keep the couple in the forest fully occupied. It now knew that they possessed a knowledge of White Magic but to what extent it could only surmise. If they repelled the next attack a demon would be sent, one which should overcome them with ease.

Nevertheless the pair who had devastated the fane of Nuoemove were capable of wielding considerable Power, else they would not have dared to enter it; again the deception which had been used to convince Hedial that they were under his control before their escape had merited them close attention. Once the incantations and rituals for the lesser entities had been completed the more serious complex operation commenced. Through the familiar the Lord of Iniquities delegated specific duties to seven of the sorcerers. The intricate ceremony gradually proceeded.

The Demon reckoned that the couple in the forest might be capable of vanquishing the lesser devils but sincerely doubted that they would defeat the fiend which would follow. Even if they did prove successful Hedial felt certain that once the humans in the temple clearing had been eliminated their companions would be snuffed out like an unprotected candle-light in a violent storm.

A male and a female helot were selected and, after they had copulated frantically, were given a revolting bowl of animal excrement and urine to swallow. While this concoction was being consumed, Xirtix chanted evil spells to retain the vibrations from their union. Next, Kiltron and five of the sorcerers stripped naked and mated with each slave, two at a time, unnaturally. Once this obscene performance ended the slaves were given a few more drops of the narcotic which made them slump unconscious to the ground in the centre of one of the circles.

Kiltron, still nude, stepped in beside them carrying a long sharp knife. When the High Priest concluded his incantations, the Dannimite knelt and castrated the male. The latter did not move a muscle, nor did the female when the sorcerer inserted the weapon deep into her crotch and slashed upwards to her navel. Immediately his comrades, those who had abused the helots, came forward to catch the crimson liquid spurting from the victims in brown clay bowls.

Xirtix took the knife from his subordinate and, with blood spouting over his face and robes, cut out the heart of the male helot and then that of the female. The vibrations from this utterly callous deed increased the potency already engendered by the perverted sexual acts. A portion of the specially selected herbs was removed from the metal bowl which had been placed before the familiar and burned by the High Priest. Two male helots were then brought forward to be sexually abused by Kiltron and his five naked companions; they were then castrated, before having their wrists slashed. Their blood was also swiftly collected.

When the latter slaves were on the point of death their hearts were hacked from their bodies. The sorcerers placed the bloody objects with the other products of their evil surgery into a large cauldron. Xirtix and Kiltron urinated into the foul concoction, which was stirred six times to the left before being consumed in wooden goblets by the entire complement of Dannimite magicians. In such a manner, with more blasphemies, obscenities and human sacrifices, the hours passed until midnight. During this time several imps were conjured forth to assist the preparations for the appearance of their Master, Hedial, Lord of Iniquities.

The mental strain, engendered by participating in such wicked rituals, took a harsh toll. The warlocks aged many years, their faces and bodies becoming emaciated. Nevertheless the lour was totally satisfied with the progress made; at the foulest, most blasphemous point of midnight the mighty Demon would appear with all his hellish legions. As the darkest hour approached, the ground quaked; flashes of lightning momentarily streaked above the trees and clearing in bluish white sheets to the skirling delighted cries of the imps. The latter mocked as the firmament appeared to evince the wrath of the Great Power.

Two minutes before midnight the lour directed the surviving helots to consume more of the narcotic, which caused them to fall into oblivion. The Dannimite sorcerers received a similar instruction and collapsed unconscious to the ground, while overhead the black and red horned imps flew to and fro. Seconds before Hedial's arrival, four of these lesser fiends chanted the final incantation. The time had arrived for the Lord of Iniquities to manifest on the physical plane; a gap was blasted through from the Outer Circles to admit the mighty Demon and his hideous cohorts.

Hedial had determined that the Dannimite magicians were to remain unconscious lest they proved unable to withstand the horror of his arrival on the physical plane. They had been under enormous strain for several hours; this had affected their health, and further stress might cause heart failure or paralysis. Again, they would be required for the final, longer ritual to give him permanent access to Phentara. When they had completed the latter abominable iniquity, the warlocks would receive their reward by being blasted to damnation, their souls being held in endless thrall.

The Fiend had not forgotten for a single instant the White Magicians responsible for the destruction of the fane of Nuoemove. He had resolved that before a single hurt was perpetrated against Phentara they would perish and their immortal souls be consigned to Lubeln for eternity. Then the Prince of Evil and he, together with their followers and minions, would swarm from Hell to establish the rule of Darkness for ever in the physical Universe of the Great Power.

Quinton and Allecenia welcomed the departure of the alien blackness which had lifted with the repulsion of the ratchan pack. They knelt solemnly in prayer to the Almighty beseeching His assistance in their time of need, and avowing their desire to prevent evil befalling their world. Once they had concluded their humble supplication, they rose to their feet, holding hands in love and contentment. This might be their last night alive for both recognised their jeopardy.

In an instant the atmosphere altered dramatically. The gloom returned at its former level accompanied by a stench of death and putrefaction. Quinton released the hand of his beloved and made an occult sign which banished the obnoxious odour, replacing it with a beautiful fragrance. Allecenia smiled her approbation, cognisant that a more deadly peril was coming towards their protection. She looked serene and exquisite, with a dignified bearing acquired from long mystical study while her handsome companion appeared lordly with a similar mien.

"I sense something," the youth whispered, his tones sounding harsh under the gloom, which the flames of their fire were valiantly attempting to pierce.

"So do I. It will be some form of entity, probably minor. At this stage, I think we should be quite capable of repelling anything hurled against us with the protection of the circle alone," Allecenia responded.

"Mmm, I believe instinctively and intuitively that we are known to be the lesser threat. Hedial will launch his major attack against Ontar and Admaria. If we can repel whatever

266

is sent to destroy us, then we can only hope they will too," Quinton commented, his keen gray blue eyes watching their surroundings for the first sign of treachery.

"Indeed," Allecenia concurred.

"No matter what happens, I love you, and always will," Quinton said, embracing her tenderly.

"I love you too, Dearest. If we survive this, I'll always be yours," Allecenia whispered, kissing him on the lips.

An oppressive silence descended. It seemed interminable, but was finally interrupted by the sounds of a slight rustling in the trees facing them. Nothing was visible for the perpetrator of the noises remained beyond the range of the firelight. However there was a dramatic drop in temperature and a menacing chill permeated the environment. Quinton and Allecenia did not allow the iciness to affect or distract them. Their mystical training made them impervious to the debilitating cold.

Several long minutes passed before a malevolent cackling occurred, and a small naked male goblin waddled into sight. The entity was two feet in height with a glowing viscid ochre skin. Its webbed feet left scorched marks wherever it trod; its two long arms, with talons instead of hands, dangled below knobbly knees; its face was a hideous gargoyle in which two extremely large revolving, bulbar, white eyes burned.

The entity chuckled, jumped high in the air and momentarily vanished before reappearing on the opposite side of the clearing. This action was performed several times until it halted a foot from the edge of the circle. A long silence then ensued while the goblin studied the two humans. It appeared statuesque but neither Allecenia nor Quinton were deceived, for the glowing eyes were attempting to hypnotise them and thus compel them to leave their protection.

The couple did not permit themselves to be drawn and took the elementary precaution of staring at the ground. The miniature monster soon realised that its adversaries were not going to look at its features. Indeed the goblin sensed that they had the power to overcome it if they were provoked. Wrath consumed the enitity which spat a large globule of dark green venom at the humans. The vile expectoration sped through the air to be repelled by the circumferential barrier. It rebounded to strike the hideous creature, evidently inflicting some discomfort, for it screeched horribly before vanishing.

"That wasn't too bad. The cold went with it. Lesser elementals and entities tend to be rather foolish, but musn't be underestimated. I'll make my ring reappear," Allecenia smiled pleasantly. "I think I may require it."

"I think you can be sure of that," Quinton acquiesced, noticing it on her finger once more.

Nothing happened for several long eerie minutes, when painful heart-rending moans were heard. The insidious oppressive darkness still hung over the clearing; it stifled the very atmosphere with its intensity: but the approach of someone or something was evident. Finally a figure staggered through the trees from the direction of the trail. It sprawled forward over a small bush, landing face down in the grass about fifteen feet distant. Quinton and Allecenia were startled, for they recognised Admaria. Her face and hands were scratched and bleeding copiously; her hair, which was in total disarray, had turned white in patches, and her clothing was in shreds.

"Quinton! Allecenia! Help me! I can crawl no further! Please come! Carry me into the safety of your circle. We were defeated by Hedial. Ontar is dead. A fiend is behind me," she entreated pitiably through cracked lips.

As if to affirm the veracity of her words, a twelve foot tall monster emerged through the trees. The demon breathed flame and was partly hidden from view in a cloud of pungent yellow smoke. It stalked relentlessly towards Admaria, who begged for assistance. Although the young couple remained absolutely motionless, they were both much affected. Olluinan's daughter waited a few seconds before speaking several words in an ancient form of Ulgruffi. Immediately a red bolt of light flashed from her jewelled ring to sear into the entity.

The fiend bellowed in wrath and pain and spewed forth a long column of flame; the discharge illuminated the clearing and struck the circumference of the circle which immediately repelled it. The evil being roared terrifyingly, its clamour echoing into the night. Every syllable uttered was filled with an awesome virulence but Allecenia directed more red bolts against this fearful antagonist, until it was forced to withdraw and vanished behind the trees whence it had come.

"Help me, Quinton! The fiend will return. I am dying. Let me pass away in your arms. Help me! It's returning," Admaria sobbed, as sounds indicated the approach of the smoke covered demon once more.

"Then perish!" the King of Rionder snapped resolutely, for he had noticed that the deadly flame from the entity had not assailed his foster mother.

A snarl, accompanied by vile obscenities and curses, came from the figure which resembled the spouse of the mightiest wizard ever to walk under the sun and two moons of Phentara. There was a flash of green fire and Admaria became a hellish grinning skull faced gargoyle with snakes writhing in its hair. It hovered slightly above the ground and advanced towards them, its cavernous eyes like burning coals. Its body was naked and of a similar texture to the goblin: however, it was six times the height of the latter and far more deadly.

"Close your eyes! Stare at the ground! Don't look at its face or head! It's a type of gorgon, like those in ancient legends!" Quinton cautioned, having also glimpsed the smoke covered demon re-entering the glade.

"I remember. If we're caught in its gaze we shall be turned to stone. It can do this even through the circumference," Allecenia acknowledged pensively.

"Can your ring repel it?"

"I'll try. I'm just not certain. We both must be prepared to defend ourselves powerfully. I believe this fiend can weaken our circle, even enter it!"

"I know it can! I know its name! This is the worst threat so far!" the King of Rionder averred unequivocally.

The gorgon danced obscenely around their protection, shouting incantations to enable it to penetrate the circle. Allecenia directed her ring at the fiend, transmitting both brilliant light rays and fiery red bolts. This action did indeed cause the monstrosity to withdraw several paces but otherwise proved ineffective. The entity held up its slimy left hand and absorbed the force of the onslaught. Neither of the couple dared raise their eyes for they could still hear its stentorous breathing. However the demon had reminded Quinton of a drawing which he had studied in an ancient tome belonging to Ontar. To the absolute astonishment and horror of his exquisite companion, the youth stepped directly out of the circle. Before his beloved had time to raise her head to ascertain his intentions Quinton uttered the five syllables of a mighty Word of Power, which could only be used by Adepts of White Magic with the highest ability.

A terrific blast of blue lightning sped from the heavens and the flash struck the gorgon. Its form was annihilated; it vanished to its own nether regions along with the other demon, never to assume its evil cloak again and assist Hedial in the Occult Dimension. The force generated by the Word caused the circle to increase its area immediately: its circumference expanded uniformly to enclose Quinton. At the same moment, the darkness was vanquished and a mellow night was revealed in which Ilix was just setting. Several hours had indeed passed since the first assault but, because of the magic employed by their adversaries, the passage of time had been distorted. All had now returned to normal and the couple knew that no further peril would enter their environment for the present.

After Quinton had built up the fire they sat down side by side, smiling at one another. The wood crackled under the assault from the eager flames. Allecenia glanced briefly into them, before speaking the thought dominant in her mind.

"Dearest, you used a High Word of Power, one of the very Holy Ones! Such is normally only attempted by the Highest of Adepts. I doubt if there are a dozen on the Islands who would have dared to use it. I myself would have been apprehensive of doing so, and I do possess the capability. It is wondrous that you can do so. Yes, I should have remembered! Long centuries ago it was advised to us in Sacred Conclaves that you would have superlative abilities."

"Thank you sincerely for your comments. I do have knowledge far beyond my few years. It comes to me intuitively. I know how to utilise it with instruction and guidance from Ontar and Admaria. It was wholly essential that that particular Holy Word of Power be uttered. Our immortal souls would have been badly damaged because of the gorgon demon Wargrickon," the youth explained in serious tones.

"I realise that now. I saw how affected you were when you thought it really might be Admaria," Allecenia commented.

"It did startle and disturb me for a few seconds. When it changed to Wargrickon I knew we faced a dreadful terrible peril. The fiend would have projected its gorgon skull innumerable times. Our circle would have been totally surrounded, from the ground upwards for a hundred feet, by countless writhing snake heads. Remember, where Wargrickon passes, Lubeln has a representative through which to channel evil power. And the gorgon can draw on Lubeln's power whenever it wishes.

"There would probably have followed a peaceful deceptive

270

silence. Time would have been slowed down until either or both of us believed that the danger had passed. We would have opened our eyes and have been turned to stone in an instant. If we had persevered and kept our eyes closed then, with Lubeln's power added to its own, Wargrickon would have begun to erase the circumference of our circle. It would have disintegrated.

"That's why I stepped outside to vanquish the fiend. Our very souls would have been damaged and imperilled if the demonic head had succeeded in destroying us. For that reason, and that reason alone, I uttered the Sacred Word. As you know, I could not say it inside our protection," Quinton explained.

"You are fully versed in the hierarchy of Hell, far more than I. I had forgotten all about Wargrickon. I simply thought that the gorgon head was just a ruse to terrify us, like the smoke demon. I'm glad you were as alert. We had better remain here until dawn," Allecenia smiled. "The Holy Word will have sealed the woods around us. We'll be quite safe now."

"Yes, as long as Ontar and Admaria are safe too. If they fall before Hedial the forces of Hell will be abroad in all their hideousness and malevolence. The High Demons will be able to destroy the power of the Word. We'll be virtual prisoners until our circle is destroyed or we perish from hunger," Quinton stated solemnly, his thoughts, like those of his companion, turning to the two Ulgruffi. Both realised that only the latter had the ability to defeat the foul intentions of the Lord of Iniquities and his wicked adherents.

Chapter Seventeen
Destruction of the Inner Circles

Ontar looked tenderly at his lovely dark haired wife in the pleasant warmth of the afternoon sunlight. She appeared radiant and he loved her dearly. He put his arms around her and they kissed. Admaria read her husband's thoughts and smiled into his gray eyes. She fully realised that Hedial was a Demon of awesome power, ranking with Lubeln, the Prince of Darkness of their world. Yet somehow trepidation did not enter her mind nor that of her spouse: their cause was just, and they would engage valiantly, without flinching, against their evil adversary.

"This reproduction of the ancient land of Dannim is very beautiful. It would be delightful to walk abroad," Ontar said gently.

"First, a prayer to the Great Power for his Blessing on our labours. Afterwards we'll commence the organisation of our protection," Admaria nodded.

The couple knelt on the warm grass, feeling the life-giving rays of the sun on their backs as they bowed their heads. Ontar, the High Wizard of the Sacred Order of Light, spoke the words of the orison to the Architect of the Universe. He offered his life and that of Admaria in sacrifice if such were to be required, and thanked the Great Power for all the wonderful Blessings given to his spouse and himself during their long lives. The sage concluded by affirming that they wished only to serve the All Highest with humility, even if this were to result in death.

When they regained their feet, both felt a brief communion with the Planes of Light, that superlative bonding with the Cosmic Consciousness. Ontar then waved his wand while he and Admaria performed a sacred ritual of High White Magic to purify themselves thoroughly. The next stage of their preparations involved further holy incantations, which caused a golden light to emanate from the end of the wizard's staff. The area chosen for their defence was totally cleansed of everything which the forces of Darkness could possibly utilise in their assault.

The beam was projected to etch out a glowing circle forty-nine feet in diameter, inside of which a square was formed, the corners of the latter touching the circumference. An isosceles triangle was also fashioned, having for its base one of the sides of the square while its apex touched the middle of the side opposite; within this latter construction a second circle was etched, touching each of the three sides of the triangle.

The performance of this arcane ritual took some considerable time. It involved complicated movements combined with prayers to their Guardian Angels of Light and usage of the wand; but the protection which resulted was one of the most powerful known to White Magic.

The westering sun had already set beyond the trees, casting a magnificent orange and crimson glow over the landscape when Ontar and Admaria lay back on the grass in the centre of their haven, very satisfied with what they had accomplished. They rested for a while before discussing what the reactions of the Demon might be and concluded that Hedial would come from Hell through the channel of his sorcerers to attack them. Both Ulgruffi had no illusions and talked over carefully what they would do if they were the Fiend.

"I concur with you, My Dear," Admaria nodded in the mellow twilight. "Hedial will advance his appearance onto this physical plane to destroy us. He will delay a permanent stay to have his revenge for what we did to the temple yonder."

"Yes, once we are out of the way and, for that matter, Quinton and Allecenia, the sorcerers will simply return here to conclude the obscene rites to give Hedial the necessary gateway to our world. They will have to restore the fane first. Oh, the Demon must be aware of our two companions. I hope they'll be alright," Ontar remarked.

"If we survive, they certainly will too. Allecenia should be able to manage. She will be able to repel Hedial for a while. Quinton's ability should give her quite a surprise," Admaria smiled.

"He certainly should! It's one thing for her to have an approximate idea of his ability. It's another for her to comprehend it. They'll probably be assailed tonight but they'll take precautions. Like I just mentioned Hedial must know of them by now. When they vanquish his minions he'll leave them alone temporarily. He'll personally come after us first before he goes for them."

"Ontar, we'll have to use our total knowledge of the highest degree. More than we've ever done before. Hedial can, and will, call on his peers for aid once he encounters our defence and our resistance," Admaria said reflectively.

"Of course, but it has to be thus. It's the only way we can be absolutely certain of sealing the Lord of Iniquities within his own hellish domains. He has to be stopped from inflicting his wrath and vengeance on Allecenia and Quinton. They make such a beautiful couple. I just can't get over the fact that Allecenia, of all people, has actually fallen in love. I'm glad our intuition told us that about her and Quinton this evening.

"Hopref and several others have been keen to have her hand but she's always refused them very courteously and frankly. Then along comes our foster son and lo! she falls for him. Not because of his destiny or anything like that but just because she loves him. And he loves her," Ontar smiled contentedly, pushing away all thoughts of the terrible predicament in which he and his wife found themselves.

"Just think! They'll marry and have children. Their offspring will be handsome and beautiful. They'll continue the imperial lineage of Quinton's Empire to the stars of our Galaxy. It's wondrous to ponder that out there in the heavens there are men and women, probably physically different from ourselves, battling and striving with immense problems and humdrum daily tasks, just as we do here on Phentara," Admaria remarked.

"And most likely thinking they'll never overcome their personal problems. The descendants of Phentarans alive today will travel to meet them in the planets among the stars. It is awesome when you think about it. Vessels, or ships, to travel up there with people aboard, seeking out new worlds with entirely different civilisations. Many of these planets will become members of Quinton's Empire. They'll have his heirs as their Supreme Overlords. Say, we'll have to find a suitable name for his Empire," Ontar said, as the thought struck him.

"We could call it Riondese, Phentaran or something like that. The best idea is to let Quinton decide. It's only fair. After all, it will be his Empire," Admaria murmured, looking at her husband while Ilix floated radiantly above the trees.

"You're right. It's to be his Empire when all is said and done.

He is entirely unselfish. If we suggested a name he would adopt it. Yes, we'll let him choose it by himself," Ontar concurred.

The fateful night drew on. The Enchantress finally set and, shortly before midnight, the Panther appeared to commence his eternally fruitless pursuit of Ilix. The second moon caused the two Ulgruffi to commence their final preparations; they both reckoned the witching hour would herald the occult assault against them; it was also the most potent time for the Powers of Darkness to manifest. They embraced and kissed; the handsome wizard and his beautiful wife held each other close for almost a minute before kneeling in solemn prayer.

Once they had finished their devotions, Ontar and Admaria rose to their feet and looked around carefully. The ruined fane assumed a soft mellow appearance in the moonlight, all sharp edges losing their harshness. Everything was normal, which their intuition verified. However midnight was very near and matters could and did change rapidly. A minute later Quinton's foster mother glanced briefly in all directions and stepped back to back with her husband. A darkness was drifting from the trees to obscure the vicinity. Hedial's arrival on the physical plane was imminent.

In the few brief moments before the conflict to decide the future of Phentara began, the two Ulgruffi chanted a short spell with precise mystical intonations. Although their bodies still touched they had now merged their minds completely so that each understood the other unequivocally. They were no longer two separate beings but one, united totally and indivisibly in perfect harmony, like the ecstasy of the sincere seeker for the Light who has finally attained Cosmic Consciousness.

The Supreme Hierarchy of Hell for their world was to be ranged against the beloved foster parents of the King of Rionder. It appeared that Ontar and Admaria were doomed, but whatever their innermost thoughts might be, they were totally resolved and committed to fight valiantly. If they failed in their endeavours they did not fear death itself, nor the appalling certainty that their immortal souls might be imperilled and damaged for eternity, nor that they would have to endure the damnation and torture of the Innermost Circles of Evil.

They were resolute and placed their trust in the Great Power from whom all their Blessings had come. Even if they perished in success their victory would ensure safety for their wonderful planet, preserving it from the most hideous and awesome threat extant: then Quinton would be returned to his own dimension to continue the task of uniting Phentara under one dynamic rule in which monumental labour Allecenia and the Sacred Order would assist him unreservedly.

The insidious darkness swiftly encroached upon their glowing protection to form an impenetrable noisome gloom approximately fifteen yards distant. Gloating laughter and evil chuckling emanated from all around, combined with a violent chill which Ontar dispelled with a quick wave of his staff. The sounds increased to a cacophony of insane grating shrieks. Admaria made a motion with her right hand; beautiful angelic singing replaced the discord; the darkness vanished and the moonlight returned.

"That will cause Hedial some considerable annoyance," her spouse spoke telepathically in their united minds.

"It won't last long. Oh, the singing's ceased," his wife responded.

The darkness reappeared, heralding the immediate approach of a horde of giant vampires with wing spans of twelve feet. They were featherless and their skin was of a sickly greenish hue. Purple flames spouted from their mouths, while their evil luminous eyes projected loathing and hatred. The emanations from the base creatures were almost tangible. Their bloodshot orbs were mesmeric, attempting to compel the two humans to leave their circle. Such an artifice might have succeeded against ordinary mortals but the Ulgruffi were unaffected. Ontar raised his staff, the end of which glowed brilliantly. A bright, silvern ray flashed streaks of lightning from its tip. The intensity of the beams seared and blasted the sight from the bloodsuckers which vanished with raucous screeches of agony.

"Good. The darkness has gone again. He could bring forth Wargrickon next." Admaria paused before silently declaring, "Oh no, he can't! I know! Quinton has destroyed the gorgon!"

"He certainly has! We know it!" Ontar responded in a like manner.

"Hedial must come soon," Admaria said.

The ground quaked and its surface shattered; the entire region within sight rocked visibly and violently. Several tall trees on the fringe of the forest wavered under the reverberations as large cracks rippled along beneath their roots. They rose into the air and were impelled towards the circle. However Ontar was prepared for such an eventuality. His staff flashed. The light caught the giant projectiles, repelling them to crash back into the woods from whence they had been launched.

Suddenly and horrifyingly the ground beneath their feet became a gaping chasm into which the two Ulgruffi descended. They did not lose their balance since their occult haven formed an impenetrable cover which would guard them even if it were overturned. Down, down, down, they fell at a fantastic rate into a bleak dank void. Glancing upwards the couple saw the starry sky vanish when the surface closed above their heads. The further they descended the warmer the atmosphere became. Bolts of lurid yellow lightning lanced towards them from nowhere but the configuration repelled them with ease. Then an eerie nerve-wracking silence ensued in which they stopped and hovered. Nothing stirred or moved; the air became noisome with the stench of sulphur and rotting corpses. The sage promptly uttered a few words aloud, and they were able to breathe freely again.

"This is merely an illusion. In spite of the apparent motion which has taken place we are still on the surface," Admaria declared silently.

"We most assuredly are. The trees were real enough though. So was the earthquake and the damage to the environment," Ontar acknowledged, his keen eyes waiting for the next challenge, which occurred within seconds.

Their haven seemed to gyrate at a terrific speed but they both closed their eyes, not permitting this activity to irritate them. The couple had no real difficulty in remaining stationary, still back to back, so perfect was their sense of balance. They realised Hedial was toying with them and anticipated that the Demon would continue his efforts to destroy them on the surface. However, should his attempts prove fruitless he would drag them and their circle down to Hell, where his power was at its zenith. He could call on his peers, if necessary. The Demon was no fool. He had witnessed the destruction of his giant vampires and the other actions of his adversaries, especially the devastation of his temple; consequently the Lord of Iniquities was cognisant of their capabilities but remained convinced that he would eventually vanquish them.

Ontar and Admaria attended patiently until, at last, the gyrations ceased. Using their intuition they checked the area beyond the circle to ascertain if any fiend had appeared. Finding that all was safe, they opened their eyes to find themselves standing precisely where they had constructed their protection. However the evil darkness had fallen once more; the sage promptly dispelled it. Moments after this action they both felt vibrations of absolute evil and horror which heralded the approach of the Demon himself.

A large black cloud emanated from the ruined temple. It increased rapidly in size until it towered high into the heavens. Legions of elementals and lesser entities streamed forth from its interior. These horrors took a multitude of forms; giant crimson snakes writhed and slithered across the grass, their forked tongues flickering, hissing and spitting venom which scorched the ground with a wicked stench; lizards and reptiles crawled forward, their eyes, like those of the pythons preceding them, horrible and gloating; black imps flew overhead, each bearing a trident from the tips of which flames shot forth in a variety of garish colours; gargoyles, brown trolls, bipeds and quadrupeds, both the latter ranging from six inches to twenty feet in height with webbed extremities, accompanied by other minor demons and ghastly spectral apparitions, charged against the glowing configuration and the foes of their demoniacal Master.

Grotesque beings with two heads like fish and barbed wings cavorted with the imps above the hellish host still pouring forth from the cloud. Finally, when their protection was totally surrounded by screaming entities, Hedial stepped out. The Demon had assumed the form of a handsome man, dressed in the finest clothes and jewellery. He stood thirty feet high with exquisite but cruel dark features; his eyes were a menacing shade of crimson and on each side of his head, just above the ears, two long black horns emerged from his thick green curly hair.

His hellish servitors had been emitting the most heinous and obscene threats against the two Ulgruffi. Their screeching ceased when their Demon Lord approached, the ground trembling under his carmine boots which matched the swirling cloak he wore. The lesser entities fell back in a frightened silence to permit their Master access to the outer circumference of the occult protection. Hedial looked mockingly at Ontar and Admaria, trying to catch their glance in his mesmeric gaze. However, they were not so foolish as to permit him to succeed in that endeavour; the couple murmured a short incantation and the mighty Fiend recoiled with a venomous snarl. Nevertheless the Lord of Iniquities recovered his composure quickly and decided to employ another stratagem.

In the most silvern, placating tones, he said, "You have caused me considerable inconvenience, far more than any mortals have ever done. I believe you have interfered with my designs before. I can admire your pertinacity and your use of the limited occult knowledge you possess. Look, let's be reasonable. Why don't you abandon your flimsy protection and join me? You are far better than the dolts who projected me here. I will give you immortality, riches and knowledge beyond your dreams. All you have to do is join me."

The voice was totally compelling, hypnotic, irresistible. It held the promise of everything one could possibly desire. All that was required was the simple action of leaving the configuration. The nuances were subtle and almost ethereal. How could any intelligent person refuse such an honest invitation, for to do so would be churlish? Surely no deception was being practised?

"Hedial, Lord of Iniquities, you are the originator of lies, treachery, deceit and vindictiveness! Never shall we bow down to you! Get back to your own Circles! Leave this world of the Great Power alone!" Ontar spoke resolutely in his vibrant tones. "We shall never bow down to you, whatever the cost. Beware, Demon! We are wielders of the Sacred Light and its Servants. Assault us at your peril!"

The Fiend snarled. His handsome face became distorted with rage. Throwing his cloak back to reveal a dark green shirt and black trousers, around which a glittering bejewelled belt was fastened, the Demon raised both his hands. An evil, garish, crimson light flashed from his palms. The beams were directed at the outer circumference and the golden glow there began to diminish. Behind their Master the hellish crew screeched and skirled. Ontar and Admaria, strong in their union, chanted aloud a sacred spell of high intensity. Their pure white auras appeared around their entire bodies. By this time over half of the circumference of the outer defence had vanished and the remainder was dulling with ominous significance.

Within the inner circle, the very heart of their haven, the two Ulgruffi uttered in unison several phrases of high occult White Magic which only the most advanced wizards could employ, the recital requiring precise intonations. From their inner selves, through the centre of their foreheads, a golden divine ray blasted the Demon's hands and repaired the damage to the outer circumference. Hedial was savagely seared by its purity and uttered a dreadful bellow which resounded through the night for miles. The treacherous Devil vanished in a stench of sulphur and black smoke, his minions accompanying him.

The stars and the moonlight remained with Selix floating serenely on his course. The environment was peaceful and relaxing in the warmth of the mellow night. However, the couple knew that the most difficult and hazardous stage of their battle lay immediately before them. They had realised why Hedial personally had come to deal with them. This was not because the Demon had no desire to send a lesser entity but because the Fiend suspected that their Power was such that they could vanquish any being of lesser rank than his own.

"That was quite a strain. If we hadn't been united into one mind we could have perished. Hedial is fantastically strong," Ontar commented with a serious expression.

"We were fortunate that we repelled him this time. He'll certainly try again. I doubt if he has ever had to face such intense Power of Light as we've just demonstrated. If we can endure till dawn, the light of day will cause him to return temporarily to his own Circles. His magicians will have to repeat their dreadful rituals for a second night to bring him back. On the other hand they could attempt the rites to give him permanent access. But that would take too long and they'd have to rebuild the fane," Admaria conversed silently.

"Yes, it would take far too long for the Demon's purposes. If we can hold him off tonight, he must know we'll finish our task here tomorrow before he can be brought back by his sorcerers. Hedial has to defeat us tonight. If he doesn't we will annihilate his adherents and the caravan. Those rash Black Magicians have no notion that their evil Master can bring the whole hellish hierarchy with him. He will decide on his next move very soon. We had better pray to the Great Power again. Hedial will take us down to his own Circles," Ontar said grimly.

Still enveloped by the glow of their own auras, the two mystics bowed their heads in humility, beseeching the Great Power to aid them in their unselfish actions. The Ulgruffi desired no reward for themselves; they merely wished to deliver their world and its inhabitants from the unprecedented horror and dreadful destruction which would be unleashed. They were prepared to descend into the Pit even if their lives and souls were to be forfeit. When they had finished the valiant couple felt refreshed and recognised that the Great Power had touched their minds momentarily.

Ontar and Admaria were aware that their vast ability must have impressed the Demon and that his offer to them had contained some elements of sincerity. There was no doubt that Hedial would have punished them, but once the two Ulgruffi were in his power, he would have manipulated them and their knowledge to his personal advantage. His Dannimite sorcerers would be replaced by them; the gateway to the Phentaran physical plane would be opened far wider than the one to be forged by his present Black Magicians.

However, since they had spurned him so unambiguously the Lord of Iniquities would have gleaned that they were that rarity, Pure Whites of the highest ability, and plan his next strategy accordingly. They anticipated that this would be the transportation of their protective circle down into the realms of Darkness and Evil. Once there, in the very centre of Hell, the Demon could call on his peers, principally Lubeln, Icardo, Nathagol and Otasalex. With their combined strength the configuration would be destroyed, first the outer sections and then the inner, to leave Ontar and Admaria at the dubious mercy of the hierarchy of obscene wickedness.

When this occurred, the two mystics had resolved to speak arcane Words of Transcendent Power which had never been uttered by mortal voices since the beginning of Time in the physical Universe. To perform such a holy incantation required knowledge, study and preparation of the highest order. The Sacred Words had been revealed to Ontar and Admaria several years before the birth of Quinton, when they had both been engaged in instruction and conversation with the Servants of the One during astral projections. They had had to pass the most esoteric degrees with superlative honours before this unique information was divulged to them.

The two Ulgruffi had attained a far higher level than any other mortals on Phentara and to them alone many wondrous things had been revealed. Since they had risen to such a position of arcane knowledge, Divine Masters of the Holy Conclaves, singly or in groups, had instructed them in magic, mysticism and science, the greater part of which was to be freely and judiciously imparted to the Order of Light on Ordlansa. However these Sacred Words and certain others were to be kept absolutely secret, only to be revealed and discussed with Adepts of their own advancement of whom, at the present time, there were none.

Even Allecenia and her parents, high as they were, had no inkling of this hidden mystery, nor had Quinton, for none of them had the ability of the two Ulgruffi. Such holy incantations were not to be uttered unless their immortal souls were in danger and the evil forces arrayed against them were awesome; the Words were intended for use when the desire of the speakers was wholly unselfish, not personal.

Ontar and Admaria understood these laws fully. They had no conception of what might happen since the possibility existed that they might err in the very precise and difficult utterances of the Holy Words. Nevertheless they were absolutely convinced that this was the only way in which Phentara could be saved and Hedial banished to his own hellish domains, never again to find a gateway through to the physical dimension.

Allecenia had been correct in her belief and statement to Quinton that his foster parents, when compared to other mortals, were on a par with the archangels who served the Great Power. Her godparents had never for an instant thought of such a possibility. They would have been totally astounded if anyone had suggested it to them for they conscientiously laboured at their mystical and occult progress with contrite hearts and the humility of the lowliest servants of the Most High.

The Panther passed beyond the tall trees of the immense forests; his final rays glimpsed the couple standing resolutely back to back with their combined auras shining radiantly in their glowing protection. Selix had only his eternal fruitless pursuit of the Enchantress on his mind, if he could think, and the affairs of insignificant humans did not affect him in the least. For once, the Panther erred; if Ontar and Admaria failed, the two magnificent Phentaran moons would become dead rocks, since the Lord of Iniquities would extinguish the life-giving sun. The Occult Dimensional planet turned on its axis, bringing the continent of Rontmethar towards another day which might never dawn.

A violent wind arose and whipped the tops of the trees with extreme severity. A far harsher, bleaker and more impenetrable darkness than before surrounded the protective circle with a malevolent menace. From within the blackness evil voices spoke gratingly, chanting foul spells. Ontar and Admaria did not make a single move for this was what they had been expecting. Imperceptibly at first, then quicker, their circle floated into the air. Their haven was borne by an inimical invisible agency towards the malignant gloom emanating from the fane. A deafening hideous screech occurred twice, followed by flashes of yellow lightning; then total silence descended. The configuration vanished with the darkness from the clearing which was left under the twinkling myriadfold stars of the Galaxy. It was as if nothing had taken place, apart from the devastation of the earthquake.

The instant their circle penetrated the gloom, the two Heads of the Sacred Order of Light found themselves on a black ashy plain under a gloomy magenta sun which emitted evil vibrations. No entity moved or was visible but their new environment was impregnated with a virulent hidden menace. Every single second seemed to hang suspended, mockingly daring another to replace it. Ontar and Admaria waited with practised infinite patience, not permitting the apparently tedious passage of time to frustrate or irritate them. They realised that this strategy by the Demon was to tempt them into making a thoughtless error so that Hedial could pounce and take immediate advantage.

The long moments dragged past without any activity anywhere on the vast black plain. Even the dismal sun was motionless; it merely emitted a steady glow which gave a garish aspect to the flat landscape, stretching on all sides to a distant horizon under the magenta sky. The seconds appeared to assume an invisible physical form, filled with waves of searing pain, which beat relentlessly against the two figures in the glowing protection. Neither made the slightest resistance but weathered the vibrations by closing their minds to them. Once the two Ulgruffi had accomplished this, no mean feat in itself, they knew it would not be long before Hedial tried another tactic.

Some time later, it could have been minutes, years or centuries, so dreadfully did the long moments pass, a multitude of large mounds began to appear on the surface of the flat landscape. Each pulsated and throbbed until it reached the height of five feet. A vile stench erupted from the top as a tentacle or arm clawed through and an entity emerged.

Many were skeletons with luminous bones and horrible flashing eyes; others were huge, slimy decapods which belched clouds of vomit and excrement with every movement of their suppurating feelers. There were floating globules with evil lights vibrating mesmerically. Some of the entities were grotesque hunchbacks, on which black and red horned imps perched; the latter devils tore viciously at their steeds, gouging out lumps of flesh which they devoured with relish. From all over the plain, the monstrosities advanced on the circle while, overhead, huge featherless birds with long beaks and red eyes suddenly appeared, again mounted by wicked grinning imps.

Ontar and Admaria stood valiantly in the face of such wholly evil adversaries which gibbered and capered beyond the outer circumference of their haven. The hideous, nightmarish countenances and obscene movements were combined with subtly performed hypnotic actions and incantations to persuade the humans to leave their configuration and submit themselves to the minions of Hell. The threats generated were more deadly and appalling since their enemies were in the heart of their own dominions.

Giant trolls clawed their way to the surface and lumbered forward on scaly legs, their naked bodies covered in suppurating sores, which oozed a loathsome stench and a dark yellow pus. More and more monsters emerged from the depths to join the leering procession. Disembodied heads with four eyes, limbless corpses and the like grimaced, screamed and spat obscenities without any effect on their intended victims.

Minor horned demons with pointed tails flew swiftly from the distant horizon; their approach caused the lesser entities to withdraw slightly. The newcomers beckoned and called in harsh voices, promising all kinds of rewards if only they would leave the circle. All the threats, cajoling and pleading made no impression, for the two mystics ignored their tormentors entirely. Some time passed: then Ontar and Admaria demonstrated their vast occult knowledge by uttering a powerful spell which shattered the sun, blasted the plain into flames and caused the devilish denizens to vanish or be devoured by a whirlwind of fire.

The resulting cataclysm sent a terrific shock and vibrations of Good throughout the Circles of Hell. Every major Demon was cast to the ground and Lubeln summoned his principal lieutenant. The Prince of Darkness was wrathful that anyone, human or angel, had dared wreak such havoc inside his realm. Never before had such a calamity occurred, either before Time had been created or since the formation of the physical Universe.

Hedial swiftly appeared. He cringed before his diabolical Master, declaring his willingness to destroy the protective circle belonging to the perpetrators of such a heinous action. Lubeln was apprised by the Demon that the White Wizards had already used a most potent incantation to repel his own considerable power when he had put it forth to destroy the outer circumference of their protection. On being thrust back into his own haunts Hedial had initiated the rituals to bring the two usurpers to the black plain. However, although cognisant of their ability he had not expected the cataclysmic spell, which had reverberated throughout their spheres.

The Dark Lord rebuked his lieutenant severely for his remissness and for the harm done to Wargrickon. However Lubeln did not demur when the latter apologised and requested assistance to destroy the two Servants of Light. The Ruler of Hell was realistic and comprehended that his lieutenant must have used vast energy against the occult illuminated circle, especially when the configuration of the latter indicated the protection of White Magicians of the Highest Order. The revelation that the haven had been repaired so dramatically, and that those within its embrace could wreak such havoc in his domain, determined the vengeance of the Principal Demon.

Lubeln was rather puzzled. He could not comprehend why such powerful adherents of the Right Hand Path had not withdrawn immediately to their own physical plane on discovering that they had been brought down to Hell. Such a course of action was the most obvious and sensible; they could have escaped without causing such havoc. It almost seemed that they desired a confrontation with the hierarchy of his realm. This was their first mistake; no mortals could hope to survive such an encounter; obviously the humans suffered from the sin of pride in their achievements and would soon learn the penalty for their rashness and stupidity. Their elimination was essential and immediately desirable.

Back once more in the clearing Ontar and Admaria conversed

silently; not for a single instant did their thoughts dwell on the possibility of failure; such would have been an indication of doubt and therefore harmful to their chances of victory. Their peril was beyond imagination. There was very little time before the final onslaught would take place; whether it would actually occur in their present environment or in the nether regions was still a matter of conjecture. Nevertheless they believed that it would take place within Hell itself when all would be resolved with alarming repercussions, either for the Prince of Darkness, his peers and his realm, or for themselves.

The probability that they would be transported again to the black plain had crossed their minds. It was a very depressing region but might prove more hospitable than elsewhere in the environs of the Underworld. Such a decision was left to Lubeln, who had taken complete charge of operations against the two Ulgruffi. The Prince of Darkness had decided to convey them to the centre of his wicked kingdom. Putting forth his immense power, Lubeln caused them to descend from the Occult Dimensional representation of the physical plane. On the instant that they sensed this transition they silently uttered a sacred spell, which effectively sealed the entrance behind them to their own world against Hedial.

Quinton's foster parents discovered that they were entering a barren ice-covered region. Violent blizzards blew sheets of hail and pink snow across a desolate landscape over which spectral shadows howled eerily. The cold was intense, far beyond anything to be experienced on Phentara. However, their advanced mystical accomplishments proved wholly effectual, for the devastating chill just might not have existed. Likewise, when they were transferred to a contrasting but equally inhospitable desert plateau under two searing suns, the terrible concentrated heat did not concern them at all.

Suddenly the couple found themselves whirling through a darkness filled with foul sulphurous stenches. Ghastly apparitions flew to and fro, uttering horrible shrieks of demoniacal laughter. Terror, a deadly paralysing fear beyond that capable of being endured by ordinary mortals, seeped perniciously all around them. When it was obvious to Lubeln that this device too had failed the Prince of Darkness caused their circle to gyrate at a phenomenal speed and fly to another part of his diabolical realm. Ontar and Admaria did not flinch but had the sensation that they were travelling hundreds of miles through vast and innumerable caverns of the Outer Circles of Hell.

From the walls and roof of each subterranean chamber evil images appeared, glowing luminously, while fiends and entities pursued utterly loathsome and obscene practices all around. Terror continued to throb from the very atmosphere itself. The valiant couple swathed in their brilliant aura were unaffected; indeed, their very passage crushed the evil and brought a cleansing purity wherever they were transported.

In one enormous cavern, the roof of which was beyond sight, black giant fire-breathing dragons appeared from nowhere, accompanied by fiendish spectres emanating violent hostile vibrations. Their protection was surrounded above and below by the drakes while the wraiths weaved to and fro, casting powerful spells. The latter were strong enough to affect the circle, the outer circumference of which did become dim until Ontar and Admaria put forth their power.

Uttering several occult phrases with absolutely precise intonations, in a Divine language taught to them by the Hierarchical Members of the Holy Conclaves, the beautiful couple summoned help. Magnificent angelic beings with a beauty and an aura of Power appeared instantaneously, generating a brilliant devastating Light. The Holy entities wielded swords, the blades of which were wreathed in esoteric symbols and white flames.

The black dragons belched forth smoke and fire in torrents. They lashed out viciously with their immense powerful tails, which smashed the rock of the walls nearby, but to no avail. The angels were unaffected by their vomit and slew them with sight defying swiftness. The corpses of the flying monsters crashed to the bottom of the cavern, pouring out a steaming flow of dark blue ichor which etched into the rocky floor. The wraiths fared no better for they were caught in the Light of their adversaries, and were extinguished like candles being snuffed.

When the subterranean chamber had been cleansed the Holy Beings vanished, leaving behind a scene of devastation which utterly enraged Lubeln. The Prince of Darkness finally realised just how powerful the two White Magicians were. The Supreme Demon, like Hedial, had grossly underestimated the knowledge which the couple possessed. Lubeln was consumed with anger that angels had dared invade his domain and promptly decided to vanquish those who had summoned them, lest they cause more damage to his Circles.

The Prince of Darkness for the whole world of Phentara bent his mind towards their protection. In a brief instant Ontar and Admaria found themselves in a fiery furnace where malevolent flames seared the very atmosphere. The occult configuration did not dull for the Ulgruffi caused its brilliance to increase dramatically and the fires died out completely leaving only a threatening blackness.

There was a dreadful interlude during which silence reigned. The quietness was so absolute that Ontar and Admaria could even hear the blood coursing in their veins. Suddenly there was a peal of mocking laughter, far more insidious than any they had heard before during their conflict with the Powers of Darkness. Quinton's foster parents felt a more malevolent and virulent blast of Terror which heralded the appearance of the hierarchy of Hell.

From pictures drawn in ancient tomes they identified Lubeln, Icardo, Nathagol and Otasalex as well as Hedial. Only the five mighty Demons were visible for their overlord had determined that none of his lesser henchmen was to be present. The Ruler of Hell did not wish the destruction and damnation of any more of his minor adherents. The awesome evil which emanated from the quintet, together with the Terror, was repelled by the two Ulgruffi through the use of counterwords and Ontar's staff.

"You will pay for these rash actions, foolish mortals. You will never escape from here. You could still save yourselves by bowing down to me. The Great Power cannot save you. Hah, where is He? Know that I am far greater than He," Lubeln mocked, his hideous face leering and changing darkly. He raised his left hand with its long red nails. The furnace erupted once more as he and his court advanced on the circle. The Demons towered to a height of thirty feet to dominate the two humans.

"The Great Power is far greater than you! He created the physical Universe in all its multiplicity of dimensions. From eternity to eternity there is the evidence of His wonders. His Higher Planes are far more wondrous, as you well know! Lubeln, all you have is this evil plane, and only because He wishes it!

"Your realms are for only one world in the scheme of

Creation, the planet of Phentara. The Great Power permits your existence as part of His Divine Scheme of Things. His reasons are beyond your comprehension and ours. You are only like unto one small grain of sand compared to the entire volume of the physical Universe. When compared to Infinity, you are less than nothing. We shall never yield to you, for you do not have Love, the reason for all your failures," Ontar spoke in his vibrant tones.

The flames which had enclosed their protection once more were repelled by the utterance of the word Love. Hedial and his associates, although unharmed by the fire surrounding them, recoiled when the beautiful word was spoken. The Prince of Darkness had been fully answered; he was cowed momentarily before hatred and wrath dominated his feelings.

"Your end is here! You should have bowed down to me! You shall pay for your folly!" Lubeln spat venomously, arching his black triangular eyebrows beneath the diadem crowning his black bald head.

"Never!" Ontar and Admaria shouted in unison, their nuances causing their combined auras to increase in intensity.

Yellow-eyed Nathagol cursed, for his preferred regions were those of slime, revolting stenches and darkness. Four-eyed, scale-covered Otasalex snarled, but none of them dared supersede Lubeln for the latter had a fiendish temper and could inflict a dreadful punishment if he were thwarted. The Prince of Darkness vomited a revolting green venom towards the circumference of the circle, but it was repelled and struck the burning ground where it etched into the very stone itself. A sulphurous poisonous odour arose, deadly and insidious, wafting itself in long clutching tendrils around the chamber. Ontar's staff flashed briefly and the peril vanished.

"Prepare to suffer! Your souls will be trapped here for eternity! You damned Servants of the so called Great Power always choose the wrong Path!" Lubeln bellowed, snapping his fingers.

Immediately the flames rose high and the sides of the cavern fell inwards to crush the two occupants of the configuration. Although this occurred instantaneously, the beautiful couple both flashed light from their hands and the threat disappeared; the avalanche of rocks reversed so that each piece, whether large or small, returned to its original position in the vast chamber.

The Prince of Darkness nearly choked on his wrath. He nodded to his followers and all of them combined to eliminate the occult protection by the emission of a repulsive purple ray from both eyes and the centre of their foreheads. In an instant the outer circumference had vanished, together with the square and two sides of the triangle. Ontar and Admaria responded by uttering Syllables of Power. Light streamed from their brows and hands, the wizard having cast down his wand. The force against them was stupendous, but they persevered and did succeed in completing the triangle again.

However they were at a considerable disadvantage in the face of the awesome assault. Lubeln was in the very heart of his realm where his power and that of his minions was at its mightiest. The battle of Light against Darkness was a losing one. The three sides of the isosceles triangle ultimately yielded to the purple rays. The Ulgruffi fought back, briefly repairing it once more, but the next onslaught breached it absolutely and it vanished.

The evil beams carved along the circumference of the inner circle. Although the Light resisted valiantly the final defensive barrier was breached and the last protection became useless. Ontar and Admaria had battled courageously in their attempt to mend the appalling damage to their configuration, but against the Supreme Evil of Hell their resolution proved unavailing; the inevitable had occurred. The inner circle, the strongest part of their occult haven, had been shattered; in consequence their deaths were certain; their souls would be severely harmed, if not destroyed, and they would exist in the form of demented spirits.

The terrible awesome hellish hierarchy hastened forward through the walls of flames, from which Quinton's foster parents were now only protected by the Light and their auras. The two Ulgruffi did not flinch. They spoke the Holy Words of Power, more potent and sacred than any known to or dreamed of by Lubeln and his henchmen. A brilliant, glorious Effulgence seared into the cavern and repulsed the Prince of Darkness and his supreme Demons. Simultaneously Ontar and Admaria felt themselves wrapped within a loving kindness of ineffable poignancy, while they continued with their divine incantation, secure inside their configuration which had been wholly restored.

Hedial was totally blinded and, like his companions, lurched screaming through the cavern. Lubeln fell and writhed on the floor, shrunken to a manikin of three feet in height. All the principal Demons had been reduced to the size of pigmies, sightless and impotent. Their agonised screeches should have brought assistance from myriads of imps, elementals and entities but the latter were being blasted and seared by the Holy Effulgence, which spread quickly throughout the caverns and corridors of the Circles of Hell. During this period the broken foundations of the Lord of Iniquities' temple of Nuoemove were reduced to dust and the entire hill became patterned with flowers and trees.

The Dannimite Black Magicians, the originators of the evil against Phentara, perished. The surviving helots were released from thrall and fled while the bodies of their masters, the wagons and the special articles required by Hedial, exploded into flame. The conflagration reduced everything to fine ashes which the west wind blew to the Chofanrit Ocean. The familiar also became a blazing torch; once the screaming lour had totally perished, a cloud of black smoke rose into the sky, before being dispersed.

Shortly afterwards Ontar and Admaria concluded their incantation and collapsed unconscious to the floor of the furnace cavern where the evil flames of the Prince of Darkness had been totally extinguished. The strain of performing the occult operation to preserve their defensive configuration intact had been stupendous. Their stress had been further increased when they uttered the Holy Words which had been revealed to them privately.

Chapter Eighteen
Supreme Lord of Deerait

The Effulgence which resulted from the divine incantation surrounded and protected them for every cavern and hall in Hell crashed into ruins on being cleansed. The valiant couple who had brought this about were transported out of the furnace chamber once the destruction of the Inner and Outer Circles had been completed. Ontar and Admaria felt a gentle breeze and the benevolent warmth of sunlight on their faces.

They had just realised that they were lying on soft grass when a voice said, "My beloved friends and associates of centuries, awaken! It is I, Yolfalthien, who bid you open your eyes. The danger is past! Phentara has been saved on your mortal plane. Hedial is vanquished and Lubeln thrown down. Soon you will be returned to the mortal plane. Quinton and Allecenia will go with you of course. Awaken!"

Both obeyed the request of the gentle voice. They felt no treachery for the sensation of the protective Light still remained. Indeed, they knew the identity and tones of the speaker: Yolfalthien was one of the Hidden Servants of the Great Power, and had often conversed with the Sacred Order during Holy Conclaves. He was a Cosmic Master who had taught them, in conjunction with his fellows, the Higher Knowledge necessary for their continued advancement. Yolfalthien regarded the two Ulgruffi as his favourite pupils, to whom he had often stated that they would surpass him.

Ontar and Admaria opened their eyes to find themselves in a green dell with tall, light barked, leafy trees and a multitude of flowers and shrubs. The colours of the environment were more intense and vivid than on their own physical plane. An azure sky with a pleasant warm sun was overhead while a rill gurgled merrily on one side. The Heads of the Sacred Order rose to their feet and saw Yolfalthien standing before them. He was ten feet tall with kindly green eyes, a handsome light blue face and long golden hair. His robe, which covered his feet, was pure white. In his right hand he held Ontar's wand which he handed to the wizard, explaining that it had been transported with them from the cavern in the depths of Hell.

"Thank you, Master," the mystic graciously acknowledged the safe receipt of his staff with love and respect.

"You are not to call me Master again, my friends. You have just passed your final initiation. Your courage and unselfish use of your knowledge have merited that you both be elevated to the rank of Cosmic Master, which I am privileged to hold also. You have both been granted the title of archmage, an honour seldom given to mortals. I am truly delighted that this should be so. Have no fear for Phentara. As I said a few moments ago, your world and the physical Universe have been liberated from the heinous threat of iniquitous evil, destruction and abomination. Your strength will be renewed and invigorated during your sojourn on this High Plane. You will also be honoured by Him whom we all serve and love for His Goodness and wondrous Beneficence."

Ontar and Admaria did not know what to say, even when Yolfalthien embraced them both. His happiness was evident, with his pleasure personally overflowing at their elevation. They felt their tension and exhaustion replaced by the sensation of strength and eternal youth, which invigorated their physical and psychical beings. The pure white protective aura which had been so invaluable still remained but was now tinged with blue, signifying the perfect mystic. Their occult union had ceased and they conversed contentedly with each other and their erstwhile adviser and tutor.

"We did not expect to be honoured for our actions. We just wanted to close the gateway to Hedial. Then, if we survived, we would naturally return to our own dimension, and resume our lives with Quinton," Ontar stated candidly.

"I know. I also know that once you entered the realms of Hell you were both resolved to perish and suffer damnation for eternity, if needs be. Such is also known to the All Highest and His Timeless Servants. You will now be transported to a higher plane. Sonalprin herself, our High Grand Master, will conduct you further. I am to attend you here presently," Yolfalthien smiled with benignity.

In the forest clearing Allecenia and Quinton sat hand in hand, alert for any further peril, but nothing happened. Midnight came and a distinct feeling of unease gripped them both. Nothing hostile was visible or heard in their environment. However they both knew intuitively that Hedial had appeared. The handsome couple waited; time passed almost imperceptibly; then they felt earth tremors. After the latter had ceased all was quiet until a horrible agonising bellow echoed from the distance. Although Quinton and Allecenia did not know its cause, it heralded the pain experienced by the Demon when his personal attempt to destroy the protective configuration fashioned by Ontar and Admaria had been dramatically foiled.

Further than that they sensed nothing. Time continued to drag monotonously past and Selix finally set. Quinton was about to remark to Allecenia that dawn would soon be blushing across the eastern heavens when there was a brilliant flash of light and they found themselves at the edge of the forest, looking upwards at the fane of Nuoemove.

"Why have we been brought back here?" Allecenia wondered.

"This is our own time! It's not the Occult Dimension! See, the landscape's different to the reproduction of Dannim. You're wearing your cloak and my bow and arrows have disappeared. Ontar and Admaria must have vanquished Hedial!" Quinton cried with exuberance.

Before his lovely companion could comment the ruined temple on the hill suddenly crumbled to dust. A wind rose from the west to disperse the remains of the evil fane over the Chofanrit Ocean. The foundations had been erased and in their place trees, flowers and grass appeared, more beautiful than any before seen in Deerait. Their colours vibrated vividly, bringing an image from the gardens of the Higher Planes.

"Where are my god-parents?" Allecenia asked with concern in her voice.

"I don't know. I wish I did. They may have perished in their success," Quinton softly replied, trying not to think of such a dreadful consequence.

"I hope not," Allecenia murmured, embracing her beloved.

"It would be too much to bear," the King of Rionder said, his heart cold with the thought that his foster parents might have died.

A white haze, about twenty feet in height and width, suddenly sprang from the direction of the hilltop. It floated for a brief moment, almost as if it were gazing at the beauty which had replaced the evil fane of Nuoemove. Quinton was

294

the first to glimpse it; Allecenia turned round in response to his request to look yonder. The mist flew quickly down to pause a few feet from them.

It vanished abruptly to leave Ontar and Admaria standing, totally unharmed. The two Ulgruffi walked to meet and embrace the couple. Quinton felt a huge weight disappear from his heart, for he loved them dearly. They had cared for him and watched over his childhood, for which he would never cease to honour his handsome foster parents.

"Yes, we are all right. Yes, Hedial is vanquished," Admaria spoke with a smile in answer to their unspoken questions.

"You are both different!" Allecenia exclaimed.

"Your auras are perfect," Quinton stated with assurance, for like all advanced mystics he had the capability to see the personal light which surrounds every living creature.

Ontar nodded and briefly related their battle against Lubeln, Hedial and the hierarchy of Hell. The sage also told them of their having been transported to the presence of the Master Yolfalthien, whom Quinton and Allecenia knew to be one of their personal tutors. They listened attentively while the wizard revealed that both he and his spouse had been elevated to the rank of Cosmic Master with the title of archmage for their courage and resolution.

"Years ago we were advised that a joint test would be required of us. Its purpose was to advance us mystically. What we accomplished was sufficient to pass that test. The Great Power has granted us the mystical perfection for this mortal plane, and for several of the Hidden Planes also," Ontar stated.

"We are not permitted to reveal what we saw beyond the plane where we met Yolfalthien. However, we can tell you this. Our powers of both mysticism and magic have been vastly increased. Yours also, My Children. You will discover that you too have been rewarded," Admaria smiled, her face radiant.

"I am glad you're both safe. That would have been sufficient reward for me," Quinton declared modestly, after congratulating the two Ulgruffi on their elevation.

"Bless you for that, My Son," his foster mother said, giving him a kiss on the cheek while her husband squeezed his arm most affectionately.

"You will discover that the four of us can now communicate telepathically with one another, no matter how far apart we are. That will help our personal communications immeasurably," Ontar remarked.

"You won't have noticed it yet. Oh, we do know that you love one another, and unreservedly approve. As I was just about to say, you won't have noticed yet, but the two of you have increased in majesty and personality. And your auras have advanced. Now, we must return to Hesion to learn the decision of the High Court," Admaria said without speaking.

"We can hear your voice in our minds," Allecenia shook her head in amazement, responding in a similar fashion.

"It's amazing and wondrous!" Quinton averred silently.

"It certainly is. We four have been honoured by the Great Power, and have found favour in His sight. Therefore, let us pray and give thanks to Him for our survival and that of our world and Universe," Ontar spoke solemnly.

The quartet knelt on the grass while the sage spoke words of gratitude and praise to the Maker of the Cosmos. When he had finished they rose to their feet and walked away from the hill of Nuoemove. With that deep pleasure found in the company of dearest friends, Quinton, Allecenia and the two Ulgruffi did not converse until they reached their heculs, which were still lying dormant under the wizard's spell.

"It seems as if we've been away for centuries," Allecenia commented aloud.

"We've all been through a terrible ordeal. Failure on our part would have meant worse than death," Ontar nodded wisely, snapping his fingers to awaken their steeds, which immediately clambered up to stand erect.

A few minutes later the quartet had saddled up and were heading for Hesion at a brisk gallop. Allecenia refastened her veil and drew her hood over her head. Quinton smiled at his beloved with contentment, before remarking to his foster parents that everything in the landscape was moving in harmony with and through him; also the colours of the environment had assumed a more poignant reality, behind which was the Light and Source from which All Being flowed generously. Each of the others had a similar sensation and felt that he or she was actually seeing the marvellous hues for the very first time.

"It's part of our reward. We will all find that we're in harmonic rhythm with the Divine Cosmic Essence, the centre and origin of everything. We will sustain this feeling and be sustained by it. If only more people would seek the Way. By perseverance they could attain the heights," Ontar observed.

"That's what I was thinking," Quinton concurred.

"Perhaps we should ride for our encampment before we attend the High Court," Admaria suddenly said.

"Why should we do that?" her foster son asked.

"Oh, you wouldn't know. We gave Hanshair and Felgorian strict instructions. They were to depart immediately after the funeral service for the dead tomorrow, if we didn't return by this afternoon," Admaria replied.

"I understand. Hanshair would be very upset when you told him that. He is a dear soul. We certainly shall return to the camp first," Quinton smiled, his mind filled with fond memories of childhood summers beside the Great River Dentworl. Then he asked, "Oh! What about Perlow?"

"He was totally devastated. His face was ashen. Admaria and I had to console him. He wanted to come. He must've thought he'd lost his new family," Ontar replied.

"He was very upset. But it's only about two hours since we dismounted to fight Hedial. That's all. Although we did spend a much longer interval in the Occult Dimension," Admaria explained.

On approaching Hesion Quinton led the small party to the ford which he had used the night before. Shortly afterwards they passed through the Deerait sentinels around their encampment to hear Adrigal's welcome voice bellowing, "Turn out the guard for King Quinton!"

Felgorian, Perlow and Hanshair had just ridden in from the north gate and trotted over to dismount beside their monarch and his companions. The Chofir and the Nai-Zind gazed at them and wept, as did the Riondese ambassador, to the utter astonishment of the royal guards nearby. To their further wonderment, the paramount ranxem walked over to embrace Perlow most affectionately, which caused more tears.

"I thought you would never return, Quinton. I thought all four of you would perish. Oh, we've just been to survey a most beautiful spot for the grave of our fallen. I spent quite a time last night with Hanshair. He was remembering when you were a child on the steppes."

"And I remember too how he was kind to me. He taught me how to catch a xolger. It was marvellous fun to be towed up and down the Great River Dentworl by the pythons. Dry your tears, my dear friends," Quinton spoke gently, before hugging the Nai-Zind.

Perlow and Hanshair were embraced by Ontar and Admaria also, to the further amazement of the royal guards. The sage praised them while Admaria kissed their cheeks. Allecenia squeezed their arms affectionately. Felgorian was also clasped by his monarch and foster parents and greeted by the veiled Lady. When their private conversation had finished the archmage turned to the other warriors.

"Loyal friends, only Perlow, Hanshair and Felgorian were told, when we departed so abruptly last night, that none of us might ever return. I shall briefly tell you the reason. Your King, my spouse and my god-daughter, the Lady Allecenia, had to endure a conflict against Hedial. Hedial is known on the steppes as Jepanastor the Deceiver, the second most powerful Demon in our world. I will not reveal what happened, but suffice it to say our battle was totally successful. The Great Power granted us victory. If we had failed our world of Phentara would have been totally devastated by the forces of Evil."

"Jepanastor!" the royal guards murmured amongst themselves, for the Demon was very much feared.

"Hanshair, send a courier to Ilixiod. Ask him to inform the Deerait High Council without delay that the King of Rionder, the Lady Allecenia, Ontar and I have vanquished Hedial. The Demon will never threaten Deerait again," Admaria requested in joyful tones. She remembered for a moment how the dark brown reptilian-headed Icardo had been reduced from a mighty monster with eight eyes and two slavering mouths to a pigmy in a few brief seconds.

"At once, My Lady," the guard commander bowed, before shouting for Caejkan.

As the latter mounted up and rode for the north gate, Quinton called for some food to be brought to their tent. He asked Perlow, Felgorian and Hanshair whether they were entirely satisfied with the site selected for the grave of the fallen. The trio affirmed that it was certainly a most beautiful place, overlooking the Chofanrit Ocean. They admitted that, if they had tried, they could not have discovered a better site. The four High Courtiers and ranking officers from the castle garrison had escorted them to the ground chosen.

"The Deeraits are really trying to make amends, Sire. Oh, there's no news yet from the High Council. They may not have decided on what to do, or perhaps have done so, awaiting your return. They will be very discreet. There are a few Casmans in Hesion on trading missions," Felgorian said, wondering like the royal guard why his King and companions appeared to have grown in majesty.

"We shall just have to be patient," Quinton smiled, before sending Adrigal, who was outside the tent, to find Helijaw.

Almost immediately the Ker-Mantid returned, bring Portarid's cousin with him. The Pingalik bowed respectfully and was utterly confused when Quinton told him to be seated and have something to eat. For about forty minutes, Helijaw was permitted to call each of those present familiarly, while the latter chatted to him about Portarid and how they had respected him as a fine warrior and commander.

"I must thank you, Quinton, Admaria, Allecenia and Ontar, for the courtesy you've shown me today for my cousin. His loss is grievous but you have helped me to bear it, as the dearest of friends should. My only wish is that Portarid could have been here," the Pingalik declared when he was about to leave.

"After our battle against Hedial, Ontar and I went to realms beyond this world. Among other arcane matters we were permitted to see our valiant warriors who died yesterday. We conversed with your cousin. He is alive on the Higher Planes and sends his regards and love to you. He wishes you to tell his family and yours that there is a wonderful world beyond death. He loves you all and knows, beyond all doubt, that he will see you again," Admaria revealed to the loyal section commander.

"Thank you, My Lady. That does comfort me. It will also console our families," Helijaw said courteously, before bowing and leaving the tent.

Quinton and his foster father arose and went to visit the wounded. The latter were improving rapidly because of the excellent nursing given them. Allecenia and Admaria followed within a few moments, for Ontar's spouse wished to collect a medicinal preparation from a chest. Although the injured were very well cared for by the members of the guard trained as surgeons, the two women were welcomed for the pleasant and efficient manner in which they too tended the casualties.

Cleanliness was a paramount virtue with Ontar; this sensible attitude was reflected in the standing orders for the aftermath of a battle. Once the wounded had been brought into the hospital tents the unscathed soldiery had to clean and bathe at the first available opportunity, depending on their duties. The blood and sweat on their bodies and equipment, especially the gore picked up by their boots had to be eliminated. If this were not done, disease and sickness could spread throughout the army.

Often in past history, when one host had attained an exceptional victory over another, it had been unable to exploit its military advantage because it had found itself floundering dismally, stricken by disease and sickness through lack of basic sanitary precautions. Both Ontar and Admaria had impressed the dreadful results of this insidious peril on Quinton, Gordan and the four Polingsi. Once the two Ulgruffi had initiated the proper procedures, Casterandir especially had been instrumental in organising and supervising the medical facilities of the steppe forces.

When the Casman corps had been defeated Terfieldst and Ceanill had been astounded by the stringent regulations imposed for the disposal of the dead and the tending of the wounded. The governor of Jaddair and his general had quickly realised how this magnificent treatment assisted the maintenance of high morale. Once they had settled down in the forest, they had requested assistance from the Inner Council to learn the medical procedures as quickly and effectively as possible.

Likans and Elmendor had ensured that their respective peoples kept to the fine hygienic standards which Ontar and Admaria had demonstrated to the Polingsi and the Riondese long years before. The scouts commanded by Forsever and Mirchanrope, assisted by Ledayes, were trained to tend to one another and themselves, for they would often be on their own, away from the main body of the army during the performance of their duties.

Rahamb's younger brother and his father-in-law had been eager for their command to further their military skills and knowledge in the vast forests. The Polingsi and Riondese scouts were delighted to assist their new allies: and it was not long before the capable steppe warriors were proficiently practising their craft in their new environment. The Mescarg steppe troops were also shown which trees, plants, roots and shrubs were of medicinal value. Forsever and Mirchanrope ensured that none of their subordinates forgot this valuable information, and instituted tests, written, oral and practical, to this end.

Quinton and Ontar spent quite some time chatting to the wounded, for none of the latter was unconscious. Their physically fit constitutions fought the effects of their injuries which were beginning to heal. Four of the dozen casualties had been allowed up for an hour or two and were sitting in the sunlight. Their King and his foster father had emerged from the tent and had barely begun to converse with them when Hanshair came hurrying over.

"Governor Cottis has arrived. He is escorted by Ilixiod. They wish to speak to you, Sire," the commander of the royal guard said.

"Where are they?" Quinton asked, for he was on the far side of the encampment away from Hesion.

"Waiting in front of your new tent, Sire. Shall I fetch Lord Felgorian and Perlow?" Hanshair asked, anticipating his liege's request.

"Please do so. We'll come straight away. Admaria, Allecenia, can you come too?" the youth turned to enquire.

His foster mother and Olluinan's daughter were attending to a patient immediately inside the door of the hospital tent, the sides of which had been rolled up to admit fresh air. The beautiful Ulgruffi smiled, declaring that they had just finished. She handed her preparation to one of the orderlies, giving him precise instructions, both regarding its application and the quantity to be administered.

Ontar and Quinton preceded Admaria and Allecenia. They strode between the lines of tents and found themselves escorted by a squad of guards commanded by Quirgid. They reached the place where Cottis and Ilixiod had dismounted and were awaiting their presence. The governor of Sicruci smiled pleasantly before declaring that he was overjoyed to see them all safe and sound. He stated that the High Court would be arriving within ten minutes to inform Quinton of its decision.

"We can perhaps guess what they've decided," the King of Rionder nodded, before turning to Quirgid and commanding that refreshments be prepared for a large crowd of visitors.

"Sire, I would like to thank you for what you accomplished yesterday in the Street of Taverns. I regret that you suffered losses," Ilixiod remarked with the highest respect.

"Thank you for that. We also want to thank you most sincerely for the assistance and other invaluable aid you provided yesterday after the battle. We are most grateful,"

Quinton acknowledged.

"Thank you, Sire. Please excuse me, but I must return to my duties," the stout north gate commander stated with a slight bow before climbing into the saddle of his hecul.

"He is a fine person, your cousin," Ontar commented to Cottis, as they watched Ilixiod riding off towards the city.

"He is. You've already guessed the decision of the High Court? How?" the governor of Sicruci enquired.

"Your demeanour, my friend. Your face can hardly contain the news," the archmage responded.

"Oh! Anyway, I am really glad that you've returned safely. Hedial has been completely vanquished, I take it?"

"Yes, Hedial will not trouble Deerait. The fane of Nuoemove has been totally destroyed," the sage affirmed.

"The High Court was overjoyed when your message came that you had returned. The Courtiers and I spent most of the night in debate. I only retired to bed just before dawn. The four High Courtiers went to look at a grave site for your slain with three of your people and some garrison officers. The Elders asked me to ride on ahead of them just now. I've never known them so eager that they're actually leaving the Haromarg to meet someone," Cottis said thoughtfully, thinking how regal and majestic the King of Rionder was.

A short time later the four members of the High Council of Deerait rode into the encampment. Phorigor dismounted and waited for several moments until his associates had done likewise. He motioned to one of his escort who handed him a long object wrapped inside a beautiful white cloth of the highest quality. There was absolute silence as the Elders, dressed in resplendent brown cloaks with the insignia of their office, crossed to where Quinton, Ontar, Admaria and Allecenia stood.

Two companies of the royal guard, one commanded by Helijaw and the other by Quirgid, stood at attention with Hanshair in front, their dress and equipment immaculate. Overhead in the centre of the encampment, the magnificent banner of Rionder fluttered on its standard. The green linz on its white background rippled in the breeze, perhaps in anticipation of the important scene about to be enacted beneath it.

"Quinton, King of Rionder, we, the Supreme High Court of the Deerait people and the Deerait nation, hereby swear allegiance to you. We accept on behalf of our tribe and the Adiorenji, Vilatmori and Dariondi that you are the Supreme Overlord of Deerait. We swear this by our gods and, so that no one under the sun by day or the moons by night may doubt our intentions, we hand you this sacred gift. It is yours to use for all the days of your life and for the heirs of your body until the end of the world. Hail, Lord of Deerait!" Phorigor declared, genuflecting and offering the bundle to the youth, while those who had accompanied the High Councillor to the encampment knelt also.

Quinton opened it carefully, handing the cloth to Ontar. The wizard was surprised for he had not anticipated that such a token would be given. His foster son held a sword in its scabbard and belt, both the latter encrusted with beautiful gems, which sparkled and shone in the sunlight. The Lord of Deerait withdrew the weapon from its sheath. The sword was long with a broad blade on which were several inscriptions; the blade was highly polished while the hilt and the four guards at right angles to it were of a darker metal.

"Quinton, do you realise what this is?" Ontar spoke telepathically in Ulgruffi.

"Yes, the sword of Csiandag the Seer. He was the legendary founder of the Deerait tribe. Did you know him?"

"No. He was reputed to have lived at the Beginning of Time. With all our problems I'd forgotten about the legend. Even had I remembered I would have believed it merely a fable. This has to be the Deeraits' most sacred and secret possession. If the Elders are prepared to give it to you, then you need never fear any treachery from a single one of the Deerait tribe, once the Council reveals their decision to them," his foster father replied, adding, "but the Vilatmori, Dariondi and Adiorenji are still a problem."

"High Court of Deerait, representatives of your tribe and nation, I, Quinton of the House and Realm of Rionder, hereby swear to lead and serve you as long as I have breath in my body. This I swear on the sword of Csiandag the Seer. I ask the Great Power to witness my words, He whom I hold to be God of gods, and whom I serve," the paramount ranxem of the Mescarg steppes averred resolutely in powerful tones.

"Then, Sire, since you knew the sacred sword without our revealing it, we are your liege people to command as you will," Phorigor acknowledged.

"This sword shall be borne by me with all honour. Our land of Deerait shall be one united nation, living in harmony. Our foes will be vanquished. Rise, all of you," Quinton commanded.

"Lord of Deerait, in honour of this special occasion we have prepared a feast in the Castle. We request that you and your illustrious companions and your entire royal guard be our guests this evening," Phorigor said.

"We shall be most honoured to attend," the monarch acknowledged.

"Troops will be provided to guard your honoured dead and attend to any requirements of your wounded," the Elder affirmed.

"Thank you for your courtesy. I would like to talk with you and the other members of my Council privately in due course," the youth spoke with considerable kindness in his voice, which pleased the Courtiers not a little.

"Hanshair, please conduct my friends to the seats and tables where we have laid out the refreshments."

"At once, Sire. Gentlemen, please follow me," the tall Nai-Zind said graciously.

"I don't think Cottis expected them to go as far as this when we talked with them last night. I know I didn't. I never even knew of the existence of such a sword. I thought it merely a legend. It's unbelievable. It must be because you defeated Hedial. It may even be because of the havoc our troops wrought against such superior numbers yesterday. They probably concluded that with a quarter of a million similarly trained troops in the Rionder Valley they would be foolish to refuse our wishes," Felgorian speculated on the reasons behind the Deeraits'acceptance of his monarch as their Supreme Overlord.

"I think you should put on the sword of Csiandag. They will hope for that at least. There is more to this than our victory of yesterday, or our trained armed forces in the Rionder Valley. Felgorian was near the mark when he said it was to do with Hedial. Our victory in the Street of the Taverns by itself was insufficient to sway them to our cause," Ontar remarked, holding the Seer's sword which his foster son had passed to him.

"That did cross my mind. Remember, we arrived back here long after sunrise. Cottis said the Council had been up most of the night and they had decided by the time he went to bed.

That was before our return," Quinton pointed out, unbuckling his sword belt and handing it to Colmar. The Melcogh carried it to his liege's tent along with the beautiful cloth which had been wrapped around the ancient weapon.

"It is magnificent," Perlow complimented, at which comment his monarch smiled.

"We had better hurry. It would be most discourteous to keep our guests waiting," Admaria declared.

"I'll tell you later why they decided," Ontar smiled.

Quinton fastened on the sword belt of the Seer Csiandag and noticed that its weight was light. He mentioned this telepathically to his foster father; the latter informed him that the articles were under a spell to dispel their weight. The youth felt humble, for he now had the responsibility for another nation with millions of people. He silently thanked the Great Power for their success in achieving union with the Deerait tribe.

They spent a most pleasant interlude with Cottis and the members of the High Council, who thanked them profusely for saving their land from the curse of Hedial. In the evening a most excellent banquet was served in the great hall of the Haromarg. Quinton gave a speech, affirming his intention to serve his new subjects to the best of his ability. Ihlden replied on behalf of the Deerait dignitaries, thanking their Supreme Overlord and also averring that the preparations had been completed for the funeral service on the morrow.

After the feast the hosts entertained their honoured guests. The royal guard and Felthim were entranced by the singing and dancing provided. They marvelled at the jugglers and tumblers, who performed tricks with considerable agility. Hanshair happened to glance at his monarch, who smiled at the Nai-Zind, for both were thinking the same. The nimbleness of the entertainers had been attained after years of exercising and practising, and to their own people they would appear to be superlatively fit. Without detracting from their accomplishments, the average steppe warrior was far healthier and more athletic.

When a lull occurred, Ontar rose to his feet and asked Allecenia to sing for the company. The veiled Lady had partaken of the meal by the stratagem of pulling her hood down to conceal her face and keeping in the shadow. She left the table where she had been sitting beside Quinton and walked regally to the open space around which her audience had their places. Everyone looked at the elegant figure dressed in the brown cloak, and most naturally wondered why her features were concealed.

Allecenia lifted her right hand for silence. A hush descended. Choosing one of her godparents' favourites, she began to sing in her wondrous voice. Her beautiful tones were entrancing, the melody rising and falling rhythmically. The song had originated in Inthearna, and the words were in Ulgruffi. Although the vast majority of her listeners did not understand the language, they felt obliged to close their eyes and saw images representing the theme.

Olluinan's daughter sang part of an ancient lay, telling of the foundation of the first lands by the Great Power. This was an imaginative, fictional tale but the assembly felt that they were actually present, witnessing the creation of their world. Her voice compelled them to participate and they believed that they were walking among the hills and valleys at the dawn of Time. A wondrous languor stole into their minds, until they became completely at peace and in harmony with the Cosmic.

Quinton had been unaware that Allecenia could sing. He felt awed that a mortal voice could be so pure in every note and word of its intonation. When she finished she looked straight at him, and silently said that she loved him. He acknowledged this in the short time before her audience rose to its feet to applaud her efforts. They clapped or banged the tables for several minutes before Phorigor held up his hands for silence.

"My Lady, I have lived long years, but I say truly I have never heard anything so beautiful. Words cannot express the ecstasy and delight your song has given to us all. I sincerely believe that for all of us here your song will remain in our hearts for the length of our days. If King Quinton had allowed you to sing yesterday evening the High Court would have conceded all he desired unreservedly, without the necessity for discussion. We all thank you," the aged Deerait spoke with reverence.

"And I thank you for your most generous courtesy," Allecenia acknowledged kindly with a slight bow.

Not long afterwards the banquet ended and the royal guards conducted their King and his illustrious companions back to the encampment. After they had dismounted Ontar requested Felgorian and Hanshair to accompany them.

Chapter Nineteen
Civil War

The night was very mild and there was no chill in the air, so Admaria called for seats to be brought out and placed near one of the large fires. Once the septet had settled down comfortably Ontar expressed his personal satisfaction with the events of the day. The wizard then declared that he was going to reveal why the High Council had decided that their nation should become the subjects of the King of Rionder.

In his resonant tones Quinton's foster father said, "Long, long ago, even before the Ulgruffi had any dreams of empire, and long before the time Hedial was conjured forth in the fane of Nuoemove, there lived a Deerait by the name of Csiandag. Naturally he was not the first man to be born into the world of Phentara, for that is a poetical distortion of the truth. Nevertheless, Csiandag was the first Deerait of importance, and so is remembered to this day.

"I shall relate briefly part of 'The Lay of the Seer'. It deals with the actual sword bearing his name. The metal itself is superior to the finest steels of today. Quinton kindly allowed Admaria and me to examine it earlier before we set off for the Haromarg. Allecenia also studied it closely. She is an expert in metallurgy, and concurs that some smith fashioned it from a star, or what technically is known as a meteorite. The blade and the hilt are exceptionally strong. The inscription is in an ancient language only used now by wizards and is remarkable. On one side it states that the bearer of this sword has to vanquish demons before he can handle it. On the other it says that he has to be a more than ordinary mortal."

Hanshair and Perlow listened attentively to the words of the eminent mystic. The Nai-Zind and the Chofir noticed that their King and the veiled Lady were sitting together, holding hands. A feeling of pleasure and happiness swept over them, and the steppe warriors resolved that no one would harm a hair of her head. She was dear to their paramount ranxem, as were his foster parents, and consequently was entitled to that special protection the royal guard provided every second of the day.

"Long ago, the land of Deerait was covered in vast forests with strange exotic plants and animals. The climate was very different to our own. This region today is warm and temperate throughout the year, entirely suitable for agriculture and animal husbandry. However, in the time of Csiandag the climate was considerably hotter, in other words very tropical.

"The inhabitants of the few scattered villages were very superstitious. The story relates that one large settlement built an altar to propitiate the gods. It was evidently a simple structure which the people adorned with fresh flowers every day before making homage to the deities. For some time the gods were satisfied, but matters changed dramatically.

"There was a swamp about a hundred yards from the altar. One morning, during the sacrifice of a deer to the gods of the hunt, a fiend emerged from its depths. The demon stepped onto dry land, its body covered in dark green scales and dripping slime. It towered several feet above the villagers. Horrendous sounds came from its mouth. Its eyes were black and baleful. The entity rushed through the throng near the altar, striking powerful blows indiscriminately.

"Some of the inhabitants of the settlement were felled to the ground. Needless to say all were thoroughly terrified. The powerful fiend siezed the carcass of the deer in its long fangs, grasped the primitive altar and threw it over. With further demoniacal screeches, it hastened back to the swamp, dived beneath the murky surface and vanished, leaving a scene of havoc behind.

"The villagers tended to their fellows who had been attacked. Some of the unfortunates had been killed by the terrible buffets. They were all deeply shocked that their place of worship had been violated, and beseeched the chief priest to find a means of placating their several gods. This dignitary spent the night in prayer and emerged from his hut at dawn to reveal that he had had a vision. He gathered all the people together to tell them what he had witnessed.

"Raising his hands for silence, the priest said that the fiend had to be slain before peace and harmony could be restored. The creature would return again and again, wreaking death and devastation, unless it were stopped. However, anyone going to do battle with it in the swamp was not to bear arms. There were gasps of astonishment at this revelation, for no one believed it possible to slay the monster in any event:

without arms there was no chance of success.

"The priest called for volunteers. Only a powerful youth stepped forward. His name was Csiandag. He was afraid, but resolved to be valiant. Before his courage dwindled Csiandag rushed towards the edge of the swamp, dived from the bank and disappeared with a splash beneath the murky waters. Of course, the humble villagers and elders of the tribe did not expect to see him again. They proceeded with their daily tasks, casting many nervous backward glances at the swamp.

"Once the waters had closed over his head Csiandag felt his right leg being grasped viciously. The fiend dragged him down into the depths, while the brave youth struggled to escape. His lungs were on the point of bursting when the demon hauled him into a subterranean cave with a dank atmosphere, which the water did not enter. The youth had barely time to recover his breath before his adversary launched a smashing buffet at him.

"Csiandag evaded the blow. He even managed to seize the fiend by the arm, and swing it against the slimy walls of its dwelling place. The entity bellowed ferociously and rushed at the youth who nimbly dodged its onslaught. Although he managed to avoid the initial frantic efforts of the clumsy creature, Csiandag realised that it would eventually catch him, tear out his throat and devour him.

"He dodged behind a huge rock and was surprised to find a sword sticking out of the stone. Without hesitation he seized the hilt and drew it forth easily. The fiend advanced round to where Csiandag stood waiting for it. When the demon saw the weapon in his hand, it fell to the ground and begged for mercy. The astonished youth was taken aback, but remembered the altar and the villagers who had been killed the previous morning.

"He raised the sword to strike but the fiend produced a wondrous scabbard and belt encrusted with precious jewels. Csiandag barely glanced at them. The demon tried to placate him by declaring that he would give him the gift of prophecy. The youth paused, lowering his weapon, while his adversary grovelled on the wet floor of the cavern.

"He told the demon that he would accept the gift of prophecy. The entity whined and groaned, asking him to throw away the sword first. However, Csiandag was not so foolish as to do that, and raised the weapon once more. The fiend trembled and chanted a few phrases; these caused the young man to comprehend all things past, present and future.

"His first action was to cleave the head from the shoulders of the demon. This deed was not ingratitude. His new ability had given him the prescience to know that the fiend would slay him if he were rash enough to let it live. Csiandag cleaned the blade of the sword and fastened on the belt and scabbard. He dived out of the subterranean cave and swam to the surface where he was joyfully greeted by his friends.

"His fame spread, both as a warrior and a seer. The lay goes on to reveal that he united all the villages and settlements in his region, thus founding the Deerait tribe. Of course, fact and fiction are intertwined in the tale, but beyond doubt Csiandag was a remarkable personality. He left behind a number of predictions. I believe they were written down on scrolls and are kept by the leaders of the Deerait nation. They became the guardians of the sword, scabbard and belt which you, Quinton, received today," Ontar said with a smile.

"A very interesting story. We have a library full of them in Hesewoner. Tales from all over the world," Allecenia commented.

"There's a considerable deal of truth in most legends, if one can decipher them. Csiandag did predict the failure of the Deerait fleets to seize the Sacred Islands long ago. His words prophesied that the Wise in West would give their wisdom gladly, but that it could not be wrested from them by force. Those foolish enough to attempt such an action would suffer harshly," the archmage stated.

"He also predicted the union of the Deerait tribes into one nation against a terrible threat from the east. Death and destruction for the land, but the easterners would dread the fleets on the sea, for these would restore Deerait to its united people," Admaria said.

"Did Csiandag predict the union of his people under a Supreme Overlord?" Allecenia enquired.

"Yes, he did. He said that his sword had to be given to a youth from the North. The Deeraits would know this youth because he and his companions would leave the world of Phentara to battle against a mighty Demon. They would be successful in a time when the four tribes of Deerait were about to wage a civil war. Csiandag also stated that the chosen youth would recognise his sword without ever having seen it before,"

Ontar nodded wisely.

"So that's why," Felgorian commented.

"Yes, that's why," Admaria concurred.

"Then we have the Deeraits' help in our war against the Casman Empire, Sire. News of the King of Rionder becoming the Supreme Overlord of this nation will spread to the other parts of Phentara. We can only hope the Casmans don't learn too quickly what happened to the Jaddair corps," the Riondese ambassador remarked.

"And what will be the reaction of Baron Enmarkan and Count Tarvokel? The King of Rionder as the Supreme Overlord of Deerait is bound to cause a considerable commotion in Broechnaar, Sire," Hanshair expressed his sensible thoughts.

"I know. Hopefully, the Empire won't learn too soon about the defeat of Terfieldst's corps. Enmarkan on the Central Plains generally has his hands full at the best of times in holding down rebellions. If we make no hostile move against Broechnaar, he may believe that we are afraid of him," Quinton nodded.

"That's why you haven't attempted to retake Rionder," Perlow declared.

"Mmm. In the meantime, we shall have to spend several days in discussion with the High Council. Civil war will break out very soon. This I sense. We can only remain here about two weeks. The wounded should be able to return to their duties by the end of that time. Kinerth may soon be on his way home too. That's why I said we can only stay another fortnight in Hesion," Admaria disclosed the most recent tidings from the constant scrying.

"Two weeks. Then we leave for Estyork. We have to retain control of the capital of Sicruci at all costs. It's the key to the northwest of Deerait. I realise, if it did fall into hostile hands, we could besiege it and take it eventually. However, that would lose valuable time, not to mention many precious lives," Quinton affirmed. His intuition, heightened by the reward for his labours against Hedial, had also confirmed just after sunset that Estyork was soon to be assaulted by hostile forces.

Shortly afterwards the company rose to their feet. While Ontar, Admaria, Allecenia and Quinton walked over to check on the wounded, Hanshair, Perlow and Felgorian went to do the rounds. The young King of the House and Realm of Rionder reflected that he had gained a new title, Supreme Overlord of Deerait, which brought heavy responsibilities: it remained to be seen whether his new nation could be united and welded into one before the Casman Empire discovered that he was also the paramount ranxem of the Mescarg steppe peoples.

At dawn the following morning a contingent of the Castle garrison arrived, bringing eighteen coffins fashioned of the finest wood. The two Ulgruffi, their foster son and god-daughter were present inside the huge shamianah while the royal guards lifted the corpses of their fallen comrades into the beautiful ornate boxes. The latter were then taken and placed inside carts covered with black cloth, which were drawn by patient tall dark red rotars into the city.

The citizens of Hesion had turned out in their thousands to honour the dead of their new Overlord. Militia and soldiers from the Castle garrison lined the streets in front of the crowds. There was a most respectful silence as the funereal procession passed. In front were the rotar drawn carts, each driven by a tall stalwart steppe warrior. Immediately behind walked Quinton, Ontar, Admaria, Allecenia and Perlow, accompanied by the High Court, Felgorian, Felthim, Cottis and a complement of Zancericts led by Te-Tell-Il and Ro-Deend-Ie. The royal guard under Hanshair provided the escort, while at the rear smartly dressed militia and Haromarg officers represented their respective forces.

The city of Hesion had ceased all business activities. Every shop was shuttered: the windows of each house had its curtains drawn to show respect for the valiant dead, now being taken to their final resting place. The site chosen was on a hill, overlooking the Chofanrit Ocean and the mouth of the River Avidnive in the northern part of the city. The land belonged to Ihlden who had willingly offered it for the purpose.

A small verdant slope led down to a plateau bedecked with flowers. A fringe of tall trees formed a windbreak from the landward side. The area around was a large park, a most tranquil place for the mass grave into which the fallen were laid by their comrades. Ontar gave a short prayer before Quinton spoke the names of the dead.

Phorigor and Ihlden paid their respects on behalf of the citizens of Hesion, and beseeched their gods to bless the brave warriors in the world beyond. Hanshair did likewise, representing the royal guard, before Te-Tell-Il and Ro-Deend-Ie came forward to chant a funeral dirge in their own language. When this had ended Admaria and Allecenia stepped forward.

Both women raised their hands towards the mighty Chofanrit Ocean and sang a wondrous enchantment in Ulgruffi. Once they had finished, Ontar and Quinton walked to stand beside them, and the quartet put forth their vast power.

To the utter astonishment and wonder of all those present, the soil which had been removed to make the large grave rose and filled the hole. All traces of earth vanished, for they were buried beneath a carpet of sweetly perfumed flowers and green grass. The King of Rionder and his companions flashed light from their fingertips and a beautiful white rectangular monument, fifty feet in height and twelve feet across, appeared as the headstone.

"Phorigor, my friend, I did mention I'd require you to provide the monument and the inscriptions. Since then we decided we would like to do this instead," Quinton told the High Courtier.

"I understand, Sire. It is most impressive. Oh, the inscriptions are appearing!" the Elder exclaimed.

Writing became apparent on the monument. Golden letters etched themselves into the beautiful stone, forming the names, tribal origins and ages of the warriors. At the foot of the list of names, of which Portarid's was first, were brief details of the Cleansing of the Street of Taverns.

"Sire, we shall never neglect this hallowed spot. Every year, Hesion will commemorate the fallen until the ending of the world," Phorigor solemnly promised, thoroughly astounded by the demonstration of magic.

"Thank you," the King acknowledged with sincerity, for he felt a genuine fondness for the Courtiers, and resolved that he would assist them in their endeavours for a peaceful, united country.

For the next two weeks, Quinton, Allecenia, Ontar and Admaria spent many hours discussing future tactics. Although there were members of the Vilatmori, Dariondi and Adiorenji tribes within the city confines, no details of the many couriers sent out reached their ears. It was essential that the other peoples, who composed the maritime and agricultural nation, did not learn about the increase in military activities and preparation for mobilisation, if and when war erupted.

Although their training would not be up to the standard of the steppe army, Quinton did not think it wise to send any of his guards with the messengers to advise his new allies. Any

313

strangers performing such a mode of action would be noticed immediately, especially in the settlements bordering the hostile territories. Deerait couriers were sent to the main towns, villages and manor houses with orders to increase martial exercises surreptitiously, lest any spies ascertain the reason behind it.

In addition, secret instructions were forwarded to the provincial governors. These gave precise details of how to effect a prompt response to any request from Hesion for troops and the numbers of the latter to be on immediate stand-by. The High Court was very impressed by the efficient manner in which the new Overlord took charge of his affairs. His brilliance gave the impression that he had spent many years in military, political and ambassadorial duties. There was also the fact that he was a powerful magician with three friends of similar ability.

One very important matter, about which Quinton had often thought, was put into effect. The two Ulgruffi were also very pleased that it had now become possible to organise the production of breast plates and helmets for bodily protection. Alleecenia and Admaria were instrumental in instructing the Deeraits to whom they gave the invaluable diagrams painstakingly drawn by Ontar and Olluinan, which would not only improve their existing equipment, but also enable them to construct blast furnaces.

A large company of the royal guard proudly escorted the two Ladies to and from the ore workings which were situated a few miles beyond the city walls of South Hesion. Ontar's spouse and her god-daughter were fortunate to find that some of the city merchants, responsible for the production and sale of metallic artifacts for home and foreign markets, and a number of their employees, were capable of comprehending what was required. These Deeraits readily consented to implement the new ideas as quickly as possible.

Ontar had foreseen a major drawback, which was the difficulty of financing such operations. The problem of initial expenditure was solved when the wizard and Quinton conjured forth several valuable jewels. As his foster father said, this use of their occult power was wholly to serve their cause and not to enrich themselves, for such would have been a violation of mystical principles. The sage proposed that the merchants pay a percentage of their profits from the revolutionary process

314

to the High Court. No admonition was necessary regarding any misuse of this finance. Besides their collective motto, Honesty is the Best Policy, the merchants concerned were in awe of the youth and the mighty archmage; also, they had not forgotten the dramatic events when the Tavern area had been cleansed, and the stupendous exhibition of magic at the interment. The traders commenced the construction of the furnaces and hoped to have them in operation within a few months.

One evening almost a fortnight after the funeral service, Quinton, his foster parents and Allecenia concurred with Felgorian, Perlow and Hanshair that the time had come to depart from the capital. They would have liked to have spent more time in implementing their plans for the future, but a premonition had begun to haunt them earlier that day. The Chofir had been the first to mention it; even the Riondese ambassador and the Nai-Zind warrior had the feeling that they should depart for Estyork, although frequent scrying of the Adiorenji homelands to the west of the Sicrucian capital had shown no indication of mass hostile activity.

Two days later, they bade farewell to the High Court and the citizens of Hesion and rode swiftly off. The Deeraits watched them until the column had vanished over the brow of the hill on the commencement of the four hundred and eighty mile journey to Estyork. Phorigor, his fellow Courtiers and the inhabitants of the capital felt a loss almost as if a dear one had passed away. Nevertheless they resolved to follow the leadership and guidance of their Supreme Overlord to the best of their endeavours.

The company proceeded onwards, reaching Troldaart six days later. The towns and villages on the route turned out to greet their new ruler, for Quinton had sent messengers ahead to advise them of his coming: everyone was very impressed by his dynamic personality and he took time to talk with their leaders. Wercyn feasted them royally on each of the two nights they stayed in the capital of Chellene, during which time he advised them what his province had accomplished in preparation for the outbreak of civil war.

The first evening after their departure from Troldaart Ontar left the shamianah to inform Quinton that hostilities were obviously about to commence. During their journey from Hesion the sage had scried regularly over the Adiorenji homelands, paying particular attention to the province of Relyan on the borders of Sicruci. In the past few days since Kinerth's return home, he had noticed quite a number of riders proceeding along the dusty roads. Scanning closely, the wizard remarked the large numbers of armed men beginning to gather at many central points.

Ontar had caught sight of numerous serried companies setting out for the first time after sunset that very evening. This was an old Adiorenji strategy to prevent an enemy from discovering troop movements. Their primary objective had to be Estyork; therefore the Supreme Overlord of Deerait had to reach the city before it was surrounded. Quinton called Cottis over and told him the long expected news. The provincial governor of Sicruci was saddened; although he had known hostilities to be inevitable, he had always hoped that it might never come to pass.

"Vilatmori, Dariondi and Adiorenji!" Cottis snapped bitterly. "Just three words! The names of three tribes! Three words that mean so much! The difference between peace and internecine civil war!"

"I've been scanning the region from Estyork to the Ebrordin mountains regularly for several weeks. When I've been otherwise occupied Quinton, Allecenia or Admaria have scried. Likans, the Polingsi wizard in the Rionder Valley, will have been doing so too. Before dawn this morning I saw several large companies of riders, infantry and wagons travelling along some roads. This activity ceased with daylight. But after sunset it began again and the number of companies has vastly increased. I believe they are converging on the town of Imexcajm in Relyan province."

"How long before they all reach there?" Cottis asked anxiously.

"I estimate three days. Four at most. There could be one hundred and twenty thousand troops," Ontar replied.

"Then it is war! They'll make directly for Sicruci. It's the western border of my tribe," the governor sighed in exasperation.

"Hanshair, what do you think they'll attempt to do?" Quinton suddenly addressed his guard commander standing nearby, to Cottis' surprise.

"Well, Sire, if I were in command of the Adiorenji forces, my first move would have to be against Estyork. It's obvious.

It's the key to Sicruci province, the principal military garrison headquarters. Secure Estyork and the northwest is virtually under your control.

"Next step, gather the remainder of the Adiorenji forces. Combine them with the Vilatmori and Dariondi armies to the south. Then, in conjunction with fleets along the coast, where appropriate, to supply and transport troops, your enemies have an excellent opportunity to overrun the major portion of Deerait before effective resistance can be organised. You'll have lost your province, your country and your freedom, sir," the Nai-Zind stated frankly.

"Anything else, Hanshair?" Ontar smiled.

"Yes, Sir. The Adiorenji will have been planning their campaign for some time. We must assume that the Vilatmori and Dariondi are preparing to join them. Mind you, I'm rather surprised the Adiorenji in Relyan haven't waited for more of their own tribe or their allies. I surmise this may be because Koreorgin is desirous of revenge. His precipitate assault will not help his allies. The three tribes will be relying on the element of surprise. At this very moment they'll believe Deerait troops won't be ready to oppose their attacks for some considerable time, during which they'll have a great advantage. Now Koreorgin is about to destroy that advantage."

"Young man, you are a most excellent commander of the royal guard. I know something of your personal history. I've asked Great Ontar and your King about you. I've been very much impressed by your efficiency. Your military knowledge is exceptional. I fully concur with your appraisal of the situation. Please call me Cottis. If you should ever decide to leave the service of the Supreme Overlord there will be a high position with me, wherever I am," the commander of the Estyork garrison spoke sincerely.

"Thank you kindly. As you've already surmised, I won't leave the service of my King. Yet I shall not forget your gracious offer, Cottis," Hanshair declared courteously to the Deerait who had become his friend.

"We must alert Hesion and the High Council. We'll also have to defend Estyork. The question is how long can we hold out against such numbers? I know you agreed to use your steppe troops, Sire, but Estyork is over four weeks' journey from Rionder. Your armed forces are northwest of the city in the fastnesses of the forest. Your commanders may be

317

uncertain about what to do in your absence," Cottis declared anxiously.

Quinton smiled before replying, "Don't ever let Gordan hear you say that. You may recall during one of our conversations I mentioned how secure our chain of command was. Our supreme general will immediately execute one of our contingency plans. If he is slain we have four commanders immediately below him in rank. Each one of them is fully trained to assume the duty of chief general.

"Likans is Ontar's former pupil. He'll have monitored all movements of the Adiorenji, Vilatmori and Dariondi. Gordan will be advised and act accordingly. He'll bring eighty thousand troops to Estyork, fully armed and supplied. We also have ten thousand shock troops. They're superbly trained. They'll be on the march by midnight tonight. They are always prepared to move out swiftly if an emergency occurs.

"Our construction regiment has cleared the main trail from south of Rionder to the edge of the forests bordering Sicruci. The shock troops will take that route. The main army will follow them by early tomorrow afternoon at the latest. Gordan already has the force to relieve Estyork within easy distance of his headquarters. The rest of the army will remain to complete the Casman training. However they'll all be placed on instant readiness to come south if required."

"Estyork will be totally unaware of what's happening in Relyan. The people of Sicruci have tended not to cross the border during the past few years. We're still about nine normal days' travelling time from the town because of the Wilderness," Cottis stated grimly from where he stood near a campfire.

"I intend to reach Estyork within three days. We'll leave in two hours. It'll mean eighteen to twenty hours a day in the saddle. The trail through the Wilderness does meander to and fro and it's rough. If it were in a straight line we'd make far better progress. Hanshair, you know what to do," Quinton nodded.

"At once, Sire," the Nai-Zind guard commander acknowledged, before leaving to organise his subordinates for the arduous journey ahead.

"It will be hard," Cottis remarked thoughtfully.

"The royal guard will help your escort. We've had plenty of experience. Several weeks of it, when we traversed very many hundreds of miles across the steppes to escape the snow.

Ontar and I estimate the Adiorenji should reach Estyork in approximately eleven days. I believe a Relyanese horbspan tends to strut a bit before he sets out for battle. An old but foolish custom to demonstrate his power of life and death. Our main force will require seventeen. Don't look so surprised. They'll come from their encampments in half the normal time.

"Our shock regiments will be in Estyork before the Adiorenji arrive. We shall have eight days to warn the outlying settlements and farms in the vicinity of the town. So that's about six days of siege before Gordan arrives. We must not tell anyone in Estyork other than your officers that help is on the way. When the shock regiments arrive we'll merely say they were coming to join me. There will be spies, so we must be careful," Quinton stated decisively and Cottis marvelled again at the resolution and confidence of the youth in the face of such odds.

"Then let us hope the gods favour our enterprise. Three little words — Vilatmori, Dariondi and Adiorenji," the Deerait governor said in serious tones.

"Do not worry, my friend. We shall save your town, your province and your whole nation. It may appear that we're using your people for our own ends. There is some truth in that. But your people are now our people and they matter to us. When we've finished Deerait will be a united happy people, all four tribes," the King of Rionder affirmed.

"Sire, you are our Supreme Overlord. If you wish to use us, then it will be for our collective benefit. I know with all my heart that you and your companions, from the highest to the lowest private soldier in the guard, care. I mean, really care," Cottis declared frankly.

"Thank you very much," the youth expressed his gratitude at the governor's statement.

"And when that peace comes to Deerait you, Quinton, will not only be King of Rionder, paramount ranxem of the Mescarg steppes, Supreme Overlord of Deerait, you will also be the Emperor of Casman, Baron of Broechnaar and Emperor of Rontmethar. What happens then, we'll have to wait and see," Ontar thought silently.

"You never seem to worry," Cottis remarked in the glow of the campfire under the panoply of the myriadfold stars in the heavens awaiting the approach of the Enchantress.

"I do worry. Most definitely. But sometimes I can feel a

319

confidence rippling through my very being. It says that all will go well. It gives me the fortitude to carry on," Quinton replied, his eyes lighting up with pleasure as Olluinan's veiled daughter approached.

"We've finished our private packing. The guards are about to take down the shamianah. And your food is ready," Allecenia said, beckoning the trio to accompany her for the last hot meal they would have until they reached Estyork.

In the depths of the Rionder forests Gordan was still at work after sunset. From the efficient reports received from Likans his intuition told him that war in the south was imminent. The huge increase in military traffic on the roads of Relyan portended ominous events. The army had been on stand-by alert for four days, the shock regiments ready to ride off to Estyork at short notice. The supreme general of the army was studying detailed reports on the progress of the Casman training when the urgent sound of feet in the outer office attracted his attention. The Riondese was about to rise from his chair when Casterandir burst into the room leaving the door open. The Polingsi had ridden hard to army headquarters. Gordan knew instinctively what his friend was about to say, even before the latter spoke.

"I've a message from Likans! I just happened to be in the village when he was about to dispatch a courier to you. He's convinced the Adiorenji are preparing to march on Estyork. He's seen scores of armed companies on the move for the first time on the roads to Imexcajm. They're proceeding there under the cover of darkness. Likans reckons they should be in a position to besiege Estyork in eleven days," Casterandir spoke rapidly.

"Then it's come! I suppose you sent couriers to all the principal commanders telling them to come here?" Gordan looked at his friend with a smile.

"Everyone I could think of. I used my escort and Polingsi soldiers from the village. It's fortunate you concentrated the higher ranking officers in this vicinity. Otherwise it would take ages to gather them together. Likans estimates there must be one hundred and twenty thousand Adiorenji mobilised. He says they are all Relyanese," Casterandir stated with a quizzical expression on his dark face.

"That's the figure I wanted to hear. His reports are very good and reliable. They've been leading up to this. One hundred and twenty thousand Relyanese. Mmmm. That's odd. Very odd. I anticipated far more hostile troops. No Vilatmori or Dariondi either?" Gordan pursed his lips thoughtfully.

"No. That's odd too. What's more, Likans said there's no movement in the other Adiorenji homelands, Irewold, Tarchor and Eirstron. You'd have thought they'd all have massed instead of only a portion of one tribe from one province," the Polingsi remarked pensively.

"Then some unknown factor has caused this precipitate action," Gordan deduced.

"Just think. Quinton, Ontar and Admaria will also know what we know. Have you made your mind up? Who's going and who's staying here? How many troops are you taking?"

"I'll tell you in a moment. Excuse me. Telriche, Elcharn, the moment any of the higher commanders arrive, admit them to me straight away!" the chief general shouted.

"Yes, Sir," his two subordinates acknowledged respectfully.

"Did you send a courier to Elmendor?" Gordan asked Casterandir.

"Yes. I sent a message that supplies were to be made ready for a fast force being sent to Estyork. Elmendor will already have started to distribute them," the Polingsi replied.

"Good! I'll send a courier with precise requirements within the hour. Well, to answer your questions, I'll go. That's expected. You'll come as my second-in-command, jointly with Turubin. Sleworivan and Shlasmil will remain here to supervise the final stages of the Casman training for we won't need the Jaddair corps to relieve Estyork. If possible, and time permits, I'd like at least some of Terfieldst's troops to try the shock assault courses. But I doubt they'll have time. The Deerait campaign will really begin after Estyork's been relieved. You agree?"

"Yes, I do. Hopefully we may be able to give them the shock troop training programme before we launch the campaign against the Casman mainland. How many troops are you taking? The agreed proportion?" Casterandir asked.

"Yes. That's twenty thousand from each major command. Eighty thousand steppe troops including some Riondese and Polingsi," Gordan nodded, pleased that his comrade was thinking along the same lines as he was.

"What about Rahamb's regiments?"

"Yes. Rahamb. He and his shock troops must be away from here by midnight at the latest. I feel sorry for Larida. She'll miss him," Gordan reflected, thinking about his kindly mother-in-law.

"They all will. I know . . . ," Casterandir paused as a knock on the open door interrupted his words.

"Come in. Oh, it's you, Souriin. Leave it open," Gordan said to the young Hedunon.

"Sir, I was ordered to report here with all possible haste."

"Listen carefully. Civil war has begun in Deerait. We've to face one hundred and twenty thousand hostiles. Eighty thousand steppe troops will be leaving here for Estyork tomorrow. I shall command them. It will take us fifteen to seventeen days to get there. A maximum of seventeen days thanks to the magnificent efforts of Jamborajd and his construction regiment. When we get there the town will be beseiged by about a hundred and five thousand Adiorenji. By then Quinton and Ontar should have reduced their forces by at least fifteen thousand.

"You and Rahamb will take the two shock regiments. You must leave here by midnight at the latest! You must be inside the town of Estyork before hostile forces invest it! Quinton, Ontar and Admaria will be there before you. You'll only have eleven days at the maximum before the Adiorenji army arrives. But you must, and I repeat must, be inside the city to assist during the siege. That is vital!" Gordan stressed.

"Yes, Sir," Souriin nodded attentively.

"We cannot let Estyork fall. If we ourselves have to lay siege to it we shall lose valuable men unnecessarily. Should you be delayed due to unforeseeable circumstances, then remain in the confines of the forest until nightfall. Try to break through. Ontar will watch for you on his crystal. The north gate will be opened when you're three hundred yards distant. But I do expect you to be inside Estyork before the town's surrounded. Any questions?" Gordan asked, from where he sat behind his large desk.

"Yes, Sir. Who do you wish Rahamb and me to report to? I mean who is to be in overall command of the shock regiments?" Souriin asked, anticipating that one of the four Polingsi would be in charge.

"Rahamb is. You are henceforth appointed his second-in-command. That is official. Your reports, tests and practical expertise have merited your elevation in rank. Your potential and military skill are outstanding. This has been recognised by many officers and also by the soldiers with whom you've dealt. Quinton wished me to confirm your appointment when I thought it appropriate," the chief general declared, before rising and going round to congratulate the youth.

Souriin was overwhelmed and did not know what to say as Rahamb stepped into the room. The Nai-Zind caranxem was delighted when Gordan told him of the youth's new rank. When the captain of the royal guard informed his father-in-law that he was confirmed as overall commander of the shock regiments, the chieftain with the hooked nose was as taken aback as his junior officer.

"We're very grateful," they both managed to stammer out.

"You deserve it," Casterandir gave one of his dazzling smiles.

"Gordan, what's happening?" the Nai-Zind caranxem asked. "I came as quickly as I could."

"It's civil war in Sicruci. Souriin has your orders. Briefly, Estyork is about to be besieged. You've got to reach there to join Quinton, Ontar and Admaria before the town's surrounded. Your troops have two racing heculs each to ride in relay. I'd like you to leave as soon as possible. Midnight at the latest. Try to say goodbye to your families," his son-in-law answered seriously.

"We shall," the caranxem nodded.

"Rahamb, you take care. My children love their grandfather. So do I," Gordan embraced the chieftain most affectionately.

"Bless you, you great oaf." Rahamb hugged the handsome giant, using one of Admaria's favourite expressions when she teased the Riondese.

A few moments after the caranxem and his subordinate had left the room Terfieldst and Ceanill entered the headquarters of the army and walked into Gordan's office. The latter greeted them courteously, expressing his satisfaction at the progress of their troops in training. He then related briefly what was taking place in Relyan. The governor of Jaddair immediately volunteered to fight.

"Thank you, but not yet, my friend. There are only a hundred and twenty thousand adversaries. So I've decided that you are to remain here. It is most important that your corps continues training. They are doing very well. The reports I've received on the completion of basic training are excellent. They're now better trained than any on Rontmethar not belonging to our forces.

"Thanks to your zeal in Jaddair in maintaining a good corps, our task of bringing your regiments up to our standards has been that much easier. Your cavalry, also the infantry whom we've taught to ride, are fully conversant with manoeuvres. Within three weeks your whole corps will have completed the next stage. I also want your corps to do the shock training courses, but that will depend on time.

"We taught most of the Phlorcartids our tactics while waiting to do battle with you on the Mescarg steppes. They had a head start over you and are at battle efficiency. We shall need your Casmans in Deerait. Don't forget that. I'm taking eighty thousand men. Casterandir and Turubin are coming with me. Shlasmil and Sleworivan will be staying behind. They don't know that yet. You can imagine how delighted they'll be when I tell them. They're both due for a spell of overall command."

"Then we'll train and train. But we're here if you need us," Terfieldst spoke with determination. "Oh, there's something I've been meaning to ask you. When you defeated us, why didn't we have more casualties? With your methods we should have been slaughtered."

"Simple. We've never wished to spill blood. We hoped you might be our allies. So our troops were told to defend themselves but, if at all possible, to stun your soldiers to preserve life. Notwithstanding if our men were in mortal danger they were not to attempt it," Gordan explained.

"Then that's why so many of our men had bruises from sword hilts or shields instead of wounds," Terfieldst nodded pleasantly. "I am grateful for that," he added with a smile.

"Are you taking Elmendor?" Ceanill enquired.

"No. Though some of his companies will be coming with us. Don't try to hide your pleasure, both of you," Gordan smiled at the two Casmans.

"We must confess we do like him. Our entire army corps staff admire him immensely. The way he handles logistical problems is absolutely marvellous. Our whole commissariat worship his efficiency. I hope they'll be given more time to study him," Terfieldst declared.

"They will. As you know, once your training is complete

your regiments will be eligible for the shock assault courses. I just wanted to confirm this to you. However the drawback is the start of the Deerait civil war. It may prevent you from doing the courses for a while. But we'll put you through them at the first opportunity. Now I must ask you to go, my friends. I've a lot to do."

"Thank you, Gordan. We'll come and say farewell tomorrow. Give my regards to King Quinton, Great Ontar and Lady Admaria," Terfieldst said.

"Mine too," Ceanill smiled.

"I certainly shall. Don't forget, you are among Quinton's people. So he cares about you," Gordan responded.

"We know. We do know," the governor of Jaddair acknowledged gently.

Turubin, Shlasmil, Sleworivan and several other high ranking officers arrived not long afterwards and were admitted immediately to the chief general's office. The three Polingsi listened attentively, concurring with what the Riondese had decided. Those present quickly discussed a few pertinent points before the meeting broke up. Gordan and his four friends remained five minutes longer before embracing one another.

Sometime later the captain of the royal guard left for his home. On the way, beneath the glittering stars and the golden Enchantress, he felt the first miserable pangs of separation striking cruelly into his heart. The commander of the army was not looking forward to leaving his wife and two beautiful children but recalled what his spouse had said on the night after Quinton, Ontar and Admaria had departed to meet Felgorian.

When he reached his destination he dismounted from his linz and passed the reins of his mighty steed to one of his household escort. He was still pondering how to break the news to Sheralex. However, when he entered their comfortable quarters, his wife knew instantly from the expression on his face. She quelled the tears threatening to well in her eyes and called for the servants to prepare a bath for her husband. After refreshing himself and donning a clean uniform, Gordan went to look at his sleeping children, whom he kissed on the forehead before joining his spouse for a meal.

At precisely the same instant Gordan took his first mouthful of food, Quinton nodded to Hanshair and the Nai-Zind gave the orders for the column to set off. Half an hour earlier Colmar and Caejkan had departed swiftly for Troldaart, bearing a message from their King to Wercyn about the imminent outbreak of hostilities. The provincial governor of Chellene was instructed to pass the news on to Hesion as quickly as possible. Once they had accomplished this task the two steppe warriors were to gallop in relay to Estyork; they were certain that they would be able to reach the Sicrucian capital before the city was invested.

Throughout the cold hours of the night the company proceeded at a rapid pace which ate up the long miles. Since the air was chill everyone wore protective clothing except for the two Ulgruffi, their foster son and his beloved. The quartet had advanced so far in their mystical knowledge that they were impervious to changes in temperature.

There were only brief stops to change mounts for it had been decided to ride in relay. The fine animals seemed to anticipate their riders' sense of urgency and did not prove at all difficult to handle. The steeds commandeered from the Adiorenji were sturdy creatures and as game as their steppe cousins. The giant linz were capable of continuing relentlessly for far greater periods and appeared as fresh as ever.

When daybreak brought the first major halt Cottis and his escort felt very tired; they were extremely grateful when the steppe warriors kindly changed their saddles for them and attended to the serving of cold rations. The governor of Sicruci and his escort had always respected the physical fitness of the royal guard, their martial bearing and resolution. Nevertheless they were astonished that their new allies appeared as fresh as if they had just been out to exercise their mounts.

Quinton crossed to talk to the Deeraits who were absolutely awestricken by the handsome youth and his magnetic personality. They felt wholly convinced that their Supreme Overlord cared for their personal welfare. The King of Rionder praised them for their efforts during the night, saying that he would allow them to rest for an hour. The governor asked why the royal escort were unaffected by the enforced march.

Quinton smiled before replying, "Just training. All the guards, the royal and the household, together with the two shock regiments, have gone through intensive training which you just would not be able to imagine."

"What about the rest of your army?" Cottis wondered.

"The steppe warriors should have completed the intensive shock training courses by now. The Casmans have done basic training. They'll be working on the standard training at the moment. We defeated the Jaddair corps with Phlorcartid steppe troops who'd only just done basic training. Of course they had practised manoeuvres."

"That means the Jaddair corps is definitely at a far higher standard than anywhere else in the Empire. I recall they always were reputed to be better than any other Casman corps. Your steppe troops are far beyond them. By the gods, the Adiorenji have no idea what they've aroused! If the whole of Deerait resisted you, your troops would be able to annihilate them easily," the commander of the Estyork garrison shook his head in bewilderment.

"Exactly, my friend. Tell your escort that. It will boost their morale," Quinton smiled.

When the next dawn broke the Sicrucians were extremely tired and almost fell from their heculs. The steppe warriors did what they could for the tired aching southerners, showing a tolerance and patience which did them credit. Quinton allowed a three hour rest before giving the order to continue. Cottis and his personal bodyguard struggled into their saddles. When they had mounted they discovered that a member of Hanshair's command was positioned on either side of them. Each royal guard had been instructed to watch over the governor's personal escort carefully and prevent them tumbling to the ground should they fall asleep.

When the sun rose over the horizon on the third morning even the strong steppe warriors were beginning to show slight signs of wear, but their determination to serve their monarch would not permit them to yield to the insidious tiredness pervading their bodies and minds. Ontar, Admaria and Quinton accompanied by Allecenia exhorted the soldiers and praised their efforts, declaring that they should reach Estyork before dark: then they would be able to rest. Felgorian on his linz was equally as tired, but after months spent in the saddle that summer and autumn visiting the various centres of the four tribes, his limbs were accustomed to long treks.

They had just halted for a short rest in the late afternoon when the sound of hecul hooves caused them to look round. Cottis was about to remark that the rear scouts had not reported the presence of strangers when he saw that it was Colmar and Caejkan hastening to rejoin the column. The two messengers reported that Wercyn was following his Supreme Overlord's instructions. They had witnessed the departure of four couriers to Hesion with the news, in addition to others being sent to the population centres of Chellene, bearing orders for armed contingents to march to Troldaart, ready for war.

"Well done, Colmar! You too, Caejkan! You've made excellent time," the paramount ranxem praised his two messengers.

"Thank you, Sire," they both acknowledged in unison.

"Get some food. We should be in Estyork within two hours," their liege lord smiled.

"Only two hours," Cottis echoed from nearby.

"Yes, only two hours," Unyamed yawned tiredly. "We'll have to work fast to organise the defences of Estyork. Eight days isn't a long time to do that."

"Once we reach the garrison, you and your personal escort are to rest for two days. Then report for duty," Ontar commanded.

"What will your own men do, Sir?" Unyamed asked with the utmost deference.

"They'll rest tonight and be on duty in the morning. No disrespect to you, but they're trained to do journeys like this, both on foot and on heculs," the sage explained.

"Then they are to be congratulated, Sir," Unyamed declared with admiration in his voice.

"Column, mount up!" Hanshair called a few minutes later before climbing into his saddle and riding over to one side of the governor of Sicruci, while Adrigal assumed a similar position on the other.

The westering sun was beginning to cast long shadows when the cavalcade emerged from the Wilderness into the cultivated areas at the point where the trail from Troldaart commenced its last stage to Estyork. The vigilant guards on the east gate saw the column coming; indeed, the city had been advised in advance of its arrival. Onlestic had been sent forward to order comfortable quarters for the Deerait escort, who were thoroughly exhausted. The town was already congisant that Quinton was their Supreme Overlord for news had come by courier from Hesion and the streets of Estyork were lined with cheering throngs.

In the main square the entire garrison had turned out to salute their commander and his party. Eager hands assisted Cottis and his personal bodyguard to dismount. Quinton told the governor that he was very pleased with their determination and progress. Felgorian and the royal guard were ordered to retire and not to appear until two hours after dawn on the morrow. Hanshair did not demur but his face betrayed his thoughts.

"We shall be all right, my friend. I promise. You and your command have to rest. I need you to be as fresh as possible. We have a city to defend in eight days' time. Ontar, Admaria, Allecenia, Perlow and I shall retire within a few hours. I want to start warning the outlying villages, farms and manors this evening. You go and rest. I shall not be leaving the confines of the fortress. A bath, hot food and a good sleep will do wonders," Quinton averred, putting the Nai-Zind's mind at ease.

"Very well, Sire," Hanshair nodded, before withdrawing from the comfortable quarters which his King and distinguished companions had used during their previous sojourn in Estyork.

"They did marvellously. The shock regimental training is certainly proving to be of immense value. The stamina of our troops has increased. Look how Caejkan and Colmar caught up with us. We had to hold back because of the Deeraits," Admaria spoke thoughtfully.

"Yes, I heartily concur. We'd better have something to eat. Then we'll make a start on organising the defence of Estyork. Oh, here's Ontar," Quinton said, as his handsome foster father entered their quarters.

"Where's Allecenia?" the archmage enquired.

"She's bathing and changing," Admaria affirmed.

"I've had a quick word with Ricel. He's sending trusted riders out to warn the outlying settlements between here and the Relyan border. More couriers are going to the south and towards the Wilderness. He agreed that no one should be permitted to leave Estyork to prevent any spies from warning Koreorgin that we are expecting him to attack. I suggest we all bathe and change. It'll make us feel better. Oh, where's Perlow?" Ontar asked.

"Bathing too. He was tired, but wouldn't give in. I refreshed him," Quinton replied.

The others nodded their approval before proceeding to their private quarters. With their magical knowledge it would have been simple to cast a spell to cleanse their bodies and raiment. However, although time was precious, there was sufficient for them to tend to their physical needs without resorting to occult means. If circumstances had been far more pressing, a spell would have been used for such purposes.

When Quinton returned to the dining room, he found Perlow and Allecenia there; the latter was dressed in a long, light green dress and wearing her dark veil. He was about to speak to her when there was a knock at the door. The youth called for the person doing so to enter; a black Deerait officer came into the apartments. He bowed respectfully to his Supreme Overlord, whom he obviously held in high esteem. The Sicrucian asked permission to post sentries outside the apartments. He averred that it would be a singular distinction to command the contingent to guard the King of Rionder until his personal escort resumed their duties.

"Certainly you can. It will be an honour for me to be protected by members of the Estyork garrison. What is your name?" Quinton enquired.

"Yltormik, Sire. I am Ricel's second son," the Deerait replied courteously before withdrawing.

Admaria and Ontar came from their room a few moments later, at the same instant as the sturdy Deerait servitors in their dark brown uniforms entered and were given permission to prepare the table. Allecenia remarked how pleasant their quarters were, with the elegant furniture, the drapes over the doorway and the intricately woven carpeting. Quinton nodded his agreement and said that the interval between their first night and their second in these rooms had certainly been dramatic and fruitful.

When the servants had completed the laying of the table, Admaria told them to bring in all the courses together. The Deeraits did as requested and were commanded to retire until they were called. Once the door to the corridor had been closed,

Allecenia removed her veil and her beautiful features delighted her godparents, her beloved and Perlow, who was utterly entranced. Quinton complimented her on her pretty dress and said that she brought a wonderful aura of beauty wherever she passed. The Lady smiled tenderly at him. Then Ontar gave thanks to the Great Power for His Blessings before they commenced to eat an excellent meal.

Olluinan's daughter had shown her face to the Chofir at the first private meal after their return from Nuoemove. She had seen how sad Perlow had become when they had departed to fight the Demon and knew how highly her godparents and Quinton thought of him. Most important, he had saved her beloved's life. The consequence of her kind action, which was endorsed by the others, was that the small warrior felt very honoured.

When they had finished dining and thanked the Great Power, Allecenia refastened her veil before the servitors were asked to return and clear the table. While the Deeraits were performing this task, the quintet left the apartments for the garrison headquarters, which were situated in rooms close to the judgment hall. Their new bodyguard escorted them with a pride mingled with awe. Yltormik performed his duties with efficiency.

As they walked through the cloistered courtyard the night air was chill. Ilix cast her mellow beams into the small garden, causing the waters of the fountain to sparkle. The moon also saw the settlements and villages of the steppe and Casman forces beyond the city of Rionder. The Enchantress rippled merrily through the leaves under which Gordan marched his eighty thousand soldiers. Further south, Rahamb and Souriin had no need to exhort their shock regiments for every trooper was resolved to reach Estyork to defend his beloved King and paramount ranxem.

In response to the eminent mystic's earlier request, the senior officers and Ricel were present in the main room of the garrison headquarters. Each stood respectfully until the Lord of Deerait told the gathering to be seated. Although Ontar had already advised them of the threat from the west, the sage had not disclosed any strategy for the defence of the town for he believed that his foster son should do this.

Quinton spoke rapidly but distinctly, describing the peril which faced Estyork. He revealed that ten thousand shock

331

troops were expected to arrive in about four or five days. They would supplement the garrison; their numbers would ensure that the miles of city walls were reasonably defended. He also informed them that a major relief force would reach the town in approximately two weeks when the siege would be lifted.

Although it was more than probable that there were Adiorenji spies within the city walls, Quinton intuitively decided that it was safe to disclose such information to those present. However, the latter were strictly admonished to keep such tidings to themselves. The Supreme Overlord of Deerait dominated his large audience who did not for a second think of him as a mere youth or even the ruler of an alien kingdom, for they felt the force of his personality and sensed the power of his aura.

"Gentlemen, your first priority is to ensure that we have suffcient food within Estyork to feed everyone for three weeks. Remember, not only will there be the citizenry and the town garrison, there will also be large numbers of people from the outlying settlements and estates. Many will bring their own food. When they arrive the ten thousand shock troops will have enough left for four days. We should be capable of organising that. Water is no problem. The city is built on a reservoir of natural springs. Any questions so far?" Quinton paused.

"Sire." A stout, yellow skinned officer in garrison livery rose to his feet. "Forgive my asking. How far have the relief forces to come? Will they be fit for battle on arrival?"

"What is your name?" the King of Rionder enquired kindly.

"Sorcottis, Sire," came the reply.

"Then you must be one of Cottis' family. You are his second son. Your father talked about you and the family quite a lot on our travels. Your questions are quite sensible. Both forces are coming from beyond the city of Rionder. They'll have left there sometime within the last three days. Yes, about a thousand miles and they'll be able to fight effectively within a short time of their arrival. They've been trained to do this," Quinton answered both points.

"Thank you, Sire," Sorcottis acknowledged, before resuming his seat.

The members of the audience looked at one another, hardly able to believe what their Supreme Overlord had just said. It was unbelievable that anyone could travel such a vast distance in so short a time and still be capable of fighting a battle shortly after arrival. If anyone other than their new ruler or his renowned companions had stated these facts he or she would have been scorned. There had also been the revelation from the Hesion couriers about the Cleansing of the dreaded Street of the Taverns, and that spoke eloquently: a thousand or more ruffians had been virtually crushed by three hundred soldiers; it was believed to have taken place in the time a racing hecul could gallop from the fortress to the south gate, encircle the town thrice and return on a feast day to the gods.

The majestic youth continued to say that quarters would have to be found for his regiments, also for the huge number of refugees wishing to obtain shelter inside the walls. Although the garrison numbered about eight thousand, and the barracks could accommodate another four thousand, that still left over six thousand troops. The latter would have to be billeted in the parks with facilities provided to feed their heculs.

"We can rely on another five thousand local fighting men reaching here before the Adiorenji. These auxiliaries will have to be quartered too. So, we will be twenty three thousand against one hundred and twenty thousand. Our major advantage is the walls. But if they succeed in breaching them we are lost.

"Tomorrow morning officers from my guard will advise you on the defences I have in mind. They have been trained in the theory of strategetics. They know what to do. We have not much time. I expect you to co-operate with them all you can. If any of you have suggestions to make we shall be most pleased to listen. If they are thought suitable they will be adopted where appropriate. Remember this! If Estyork falls, then the northwestern frontier of the Deerait tribe will be under the rule of the Adiorenji. You are my people! Never forget that! Even the Adiorenji, Vilatmori and Dariondi belong with us. Civil war resembles a family breaking up. Let us endeavour to keep our family together!"

After the meeting had concluded some of the officers remained. During his earlier conversation with Ricel, Ontar had commanded that those responsible for the armoury and supplies were to give details of the weapons and food available in the town. The quintet spent quite a while listening to the reports, before commenting and advising on essential improvements. Afterwards they retired for the night for a well deserved rest, aware that the next few days would involve intense activity in preparing the defences of Estyork.

The following morning Quinton assembled the officers of his royal guard and the Estyork garrison in the main hall two hours after dawn. The steppe warriors felt much refreshed after their merited rest. The King of Rionder had had several maps of the streets and wall positions traced so that every one of his personal soldiers would have an excellent idea of the layout of the city.

"Hanshair, Adrigal, Onlestic, Colmar, Helijaw, Quirgid and Perlow, you and your subordinates have four days to prepare for a siege. The rest of the time remaining before the Adiorenji arrive will be spent in training and tactics. Everyone within the walls must know precisely what to do, both civilians and combatants. One excellent advantage we have is that the Deeraits do not like to fight at night, none of the four tribes. Rest will be assured at sunset.

"We have to hold Estyork until Gordan arrives with sufficient troops to gain victory. Your main duties are to organise the town's defences. Ontar, Admaria and I will supervise. Remember, the three of us will be available for advice at any time. Rahamb, with Souriin as his second-in-command, should be here in about four days. The two shock regiments will prove invaluable on the walls."

While Quinton spoke to his principal guards, the Deerait officers listened attentively. The Sicrucians were wholly cognisant that their knowledge of defensive tactics was inconsequential in comparison with the military capability of their Supreme Overlord and his highly trained troops.

"I suggest we make amendments to some elements of the wagon defence tactics. Use that as a basis. Improvise as we go along. I also think we should ride the city streets and boulevards this morning to familiarise ourselves with them. The guard should do this first. We senior officers may not have time, but our subordinates can be present to guide us when required," Hanshair declared, looking at the map in front of him, while the rays of the sun shone through the high windows.

"Excellent idea! Ontar and I have already anticipated that. The details are written down here," the paramount ranxem of the Mescarg steppe tribes stated, passing round a piece of hide parchment to every one of his commanders.

The meeting finished a few moments later and the guards

and Sicrucians were just leaving when Quinton called Hanshair over and said, "You did well to think of using the thoroughfares and the wagon defence."

"Thank you, Sire. What about Cottis' troops? Won't they object to our being in control?"

"I doubt it. Ontar did mention to Ricel privately that we had defeated a Casman corps. He was suitably impressed. He commanded his officers to follow your guidance. I don't think you'll have any trouble. Oh, keep an eye on Adrigal and Onlestic. I want the garrison in one piece before the siege commences."

Hanshair laughed, before bowing and following his fellows and the garrison officers. The Nai-Zind did discover that his monarch was correct; the Deeraits were only too eager to serve their new Overlord. Indeed the knowledge that their Ruler expected to be victorious combined with his dynamic personality to instil a confidence that the Relyanese, in spite of their massive numerical superiority, would be vanquished.

They quickly ascertained that the King of Rionder's guard were exceptionally efficient and knowledgeable. Very few of the garrison officers and other ranks were able to write, and were astonished by the education of their new advisers. When it came to battle tactics, the Sicrucians found themselves in the hands of master strategists; even the private steppe soldiers proved that they could formulate and implement plans.

Four days later the entire population of Estyork was astounded by the arrival of Rahamb, Souriin and the ten thousand mounted troops under their command. The previous night as Ilix set, they had encamped on the treeline which marked the borders of Sicruci. The boundaries between Deerait and Rionder had never been properly defined. The forest dwellers lived far to the north and the southerners tended to be fearful of the gods and spirits of the woodlands. Consequently, if the Kings of Rionder had decided to claim the entire sylvan region for their own, there would have been little or no opposition.

The shock regiments had mounted up just before dawn for the final stage of their immense journey. They had been abroad an hour earlier, checking their equipment and steeds. If they were lax, they would shame their beloved paramount ranxem, which they had no intention of doing. Each had his hair hanging free and wore a uniform similar in design to that of the Deerait military. However, in addition to his insignia of rank, every soldier had a white patch with a green linz sewn on the front of his tunic. This had involved many hours of hard labour for the steppe women but, when Gordan had suggested it to Larida, and his mother-in-law had circulated his idea, which was not a command, a great desire to provide the troops with such a badge had manifested itself.

The women worked so industriously that they succeeded in manufacturing sufficient numbers to supply the entire army eight days before the shock regiments rode to Estyork. When Quinton saw the badges he was most pleasantly surprised, and realised that his godfather must have been instrumental in having them made. He felt proud when he saw his troops ride into the central square where he awaited them with his foster parents, Allecenia, Cottis, garrison officers and town dignitaries, all of whom were mounted.

The citizenry watched with awe as the magnificent fighting men rode in perfect formation over the cobblestones to halt in front of their monarch. They glanced from the newcomers to the members of the royal guard astride their heculs behind Hanshair, who bore the mighty standard of Rionder. The Sicrucians fully comprehended that all these men were experienced in battle and redoubtable warriors. The presence of the latter caused the morale of the onlookers to rise and their resolution hardened against the Relyanese marching against their town.

"Greetings, Rahamb, my cousin. Your command has made an excellent turnout. Your efforts in reaching Estyork will not be forgotten. There are none who could have done better," Quinton greeted and praised the Nai-Zind caranxem.

"Thank you, Sire. And thank you for my promotion to shock regimental commander. It is good to see you again, safe and well, my cousin," the chieftain responded, his keen eyes noticing the beautiful, bejewelled belt and scabbard which Quinton wore.

"You deserved the promotion. And I am really glad to see you too. Now, I'd like to introduce you to Cottis. He is the governor of the province of Sicruci and the commander of the Estyork garrison. He wishes to address you. He is our good friend and ally, and has news for you," Quinton turned to the Deerait, who rode forward and halted beside his Ruler.

"Greetings and welcome, soldiers of the King of Rionder.

Your monarch is one with the Deerait people. The High Court in Hesion, our capital city on the eastern seaboard, decided unanimously, and swore by the sacred gods of fealty, to become the subjects of the King of Rionder. Therefore, I have the pleasure and honour to inform you that Quinton, King of Rionder, the paramount ranxem of the Mescarg steppe peoples, is now the Supreme Overlord of Deerait, its territories and entire nation. On behalf of Estyork, Sicruci and Deerait, I bid you all welcome, and thank you sincerely."

"Thank you, governor Cottis. We came here to fight for our King and paramount ranxem. Now that he is the Supreme Overlord of Deerait, we shall fight just as determinedly for you and your people as we do for our own. Since you have become the subjects of our monarch, you are now our own and we are yours." Rahamb responded with such dignity and courtesy that the garrison commander realised that here was no mere uncouth steppe savage, but a fine, highly cultured gentleman.

Quinton rode forward, accompanied by Ontar, Allecenia, Admaria, Perlow and Cottis. He guided his fine racing hecul along the lines of his soldiers, stopping frequently to chat. The two Ulgruffi did likewise and took the opportunity to introduce their god-daughter. The veiled Lady spoke in her wondrous tones, utterly captivating all those to whom she talked.

The governor of Sicruci watched with astonishment as the fierce steppe warriors became almost shy and abashed in the presence of the youth whom they so obviously adored. The Ker-Mantids and Pingaliks were especially awed in the presence of their monarch and his foster parents. The Nai-Zind caranxem was also struck by their even more dynamic and exuberant personalities and when they returned to the front of the regiments he asked the reason.

"Great Ontar, you and your Lady have changed. So has my cousin. Why, if I may ask? You're all . . .well . . . I don't quite know how to put it."

"We know what you mean. Strange events occurred in Hesion. But we are still the same towards you, even more so," the archmage answered.

"We have known you for many years, and love you and your clan. You are cousin to Quinton. He is our foster son. So, Ontar and I regard you and your family as part of our own. Remember, your grandchildren, Zolamina and Cryenig, are our godchildren," Admaria said kindly under the warm sun in the

337

square, which was the centre of Estyork, far from the rolling steppes.

"Then I must thank you sincerely," Rahamb smiled with evident pleasure and gratitude.

"And you follow Quinton. That we do not and will not forget, now and evermore, dear friend and loyal companion. We belong to many peoples. Still, there is a place in our hearts, as in Quinton's, Gordan's and the four Polingsi, which will forever be Nai-Zind," Admaria spoke in the dialect of the caranxem's tribe, which gave the chieftain much delight.

"Souriin, what have you been doing lately?" Ontar addressed the young commander who was nearby.

"Um, oh. My duty, Great Sage," the Hedunon stammered.

"Relax. You have done extremely well. Your promotion was fully deserved. You, Rahamb and your senior officers will dine with us tonight. Afterwards we'll discuss our current problems and inform the troops accordingly. First, and this is an order, you and the regiments are to rest. Your journey here was entirely praiseworthy. Bards will sing of it years hence. Especially the Deeraits who enjoy such tales," the wizard smiled kindly.

"Yes, Sir, we shall certainly all rest," the youth acknowledged.

"Souriin!" Quinton rode over to clasp his friend's hand.

"Sire, it is good to see you again. Things aren't quite the same when you are absent."

"It is good to see you too. We've come a long way together, since we fought over plaited hair, and saw the Ouselorns taken into captivity."

"Yes, Sire. Still, those days are memories to be treasured, and recalled," Souriin nodded reflectively.

"They most certainly are. Our memories of good things and friendship are ever to be treasured," Quinton concurred. "Like Hedunon day. Your people are the smallest tribe on the steppes, but their customs are not permitted to be forgotten and perish. None of our peoples, large or small, will ever be allowed to endure that indignity."

"No, Sire. We are all bound together in One. Diverse peoples and races, but still originating from and returning to the Great Power," Souriin declared to his own surprise.

"From the One to the One," Rahamb concurred. "We've been talking like this on the way here. So have quite a few of our troops. It not only helped to keep us awake and pass the hours, but it was very interesting and stimulating."

"Then you shall have to talk with Ontar, Quinton or me when we have time," Admaria spoke with hidden wisdom, for she knew that the two shock regimental officers were evincing signs of advancing on the Mystic Way.

This Path is the mysterious route each of us will travel in the course of incarnations. Sincere seekers for Truth and the Hidden Mysteries are tested, and the doors open without their being conscious of such happenings. Souriin and Rahamb had taken the first vital steps and would join with Sheralex and others in being conducted through the portals of the Sacred Order into the realms of esoteric wisdom.

During the short time remaining before the arrival of the Adiorenji horde, the shock regiments quickly grasped what was required of them. Assisted by keen Deerait officers and troops, Hanshair and his subordinates had organised matters most effectively. One of the major cornerstones of the defensive strategy was that reserve troops were to remain in the market square. When required to assist in the repulsion of the besiegers, the designated numbers were to gallop along the streets and boulevards to positions on the walls. During the remaining days after the arrival of Rahamb's command, large mounted contingents practised racing throughout the city to various places, while the citizenry and other non-combatants wisely kept off the thoroughfares.

Just before mid-morning on the eleventh day after Ontar had told Quinton and Cottis on the Hesion road of the threat from the Ebrordin mountain region, the gates of the city of Estyork were closed and barred. All those wishing to shelter within the capital of Sicruci had already entered and waited with a patient dread for the arrival of the hostile army. An hour later four steppe scouts came galloping from the east and were given immediate ingress to the town.

They rode to the garrison fortress to be met in the courtyard by Quinton and Ontar, attended by steppe and Sicrucian officers. The plainsmen informed their paramount ranxem that the Relyanese force should reach Estyork by noon. Their foes appeared eager for battle and, from what they had been able to overhear during extremely cautious nocturnal incursions into the enemy encampment, the scouts confirmed that Reorgin's father was in overall command. The latter fully anticipated that the town would fall within a day or so.

"They made no attempt to conceal their advance, Sire. They expect an easy victory," a warrior stated.

"Thank you all. Your information gives us some conception of the enemy's state of mind," Quinton praised the difficult task which had been so efficiently performed by his capable soldiers.

Just before noon a large dust cloud beyond the fields to the west of Estyork heralded the first column of Relyanese. Banners, gonfalons and a host of multi-coloured standards were held aloft by stout house carls. A few cavalry and infantry formations proceeded to within five hundred yards of each wall except the south, where the River Avidnive flowed one hundred and fifty feet beyond the city gate.

The Adiorenji did not appear distressed by the closing of Estyork against their forces. They had hardly expected that the approach of such a huge army as theirs would go unnoticed by the vigilant sentries. The only surprise which they hoped to achieve was the dramatic effect of their overwhelmingly superior numbers. This factor, so they believed, would compel Cottis to surrender the strategic capital of Sicruci into their hands without any resistance, for such would obviously be worse than futile.

To the west of Estyork, a broad flat grassy plain extended from the River Avidnive northwards to the main trail from Relyan. The larger portion of the invading army halted on that side while their principal leaders rode forward accompanied by a large contingent of house carls. The overall commander was a thickset brown skinned personage with black hair and brown eyes. He wore a green livery, yellow trousers and red boots. On his head was a black pointed helmet; in addition to a sword and dagger he bore a shield which was almost square except for the rounded base. The insignia on it was the head of a fully antlered stag with flames belching from its nostrils.

The chieftain rode forward to halt ten yards from the west gate. He shouted coarsely to the sentinels on the battlements, declaring that he wished to parley and discuss terms for the immediate surrender of Estyork. This voluntary action signified a temporary truce; a few minutes later the governor of Sicruci had the strong gateway opened and cantered out, accompanied by Quinton, Ontar, Admaria and Perlow. Their escort consisted of forty two soldiers splendidly attired, twenty steppe warriors under Hanshair's command, and twenty of

Cottis' personal guard led by Unyamed.

"Koreorgin, your unwarranted demand is refused! It is totally unjustifiable!" Cottis spoke coldly.

"Who are these strangers with you?" came the rude response.

"This is the King of Rionder and paramount ranxem of the Mescarg steppe tribes and the Phlorcartid nation. He is the overall ruler of the Polingsi people. The High Court in Hesion created him Supreme Overlord of the united and entire Deerait nation. He is your Overlord, and wears the sacred sword of Csiandag. His illustrious companions are Ontar and Admaria, of whom you may have heard," the garrison commander of Estyork calmly replied.

"Lord of Deerait? Pah! A Riondese? Pah! I have heard this nonsense already," Koreorgin sneered, his lips curling with derision.

Nevertheless, the Relyanese chieftain felt the effect of Quinton's aura, which glowed like those of the two Ulgruffi. Although a huge force of one hundred and twenty thousand men accompanied him, doubts began to invade his mind. He shook his head to banish the insidious thoughts of defeat and stared hardly at the handsome youth.

"Yes, a Riondese. You are determined to attack Estyork. Remember this! Long years ago, my ancestor, Dinmonad the Nai-Zind, wreaked havoc in the northern forests against your tribe. If you fight here, I promise you, your army will be vanquished, and your people will become my subjects!" Quinton admonished.

Koreorgin reeled back in his saddle at the power and majesty of the monarch, but managed to snarl balefully, "I am the horbspan of Relyan. I have come here to revenge the death of Reorgin, my son!"

"I regret his death. However, he was rash, cruel and dissolute. This you well know. His death was his own fault," the King of Rionder said coldly.

"Own fault? Outnumbered by ten to one is more like the truth! Hah!"

"Whoever told you that lied. We numbered three hundred. Your march riders eight hundred. We defeated them. You know I speak the truth! Kinerth lied to you!" Quinton struck home.

There was a poignant silence. The magnificent standard borne by Hanshair fluttered in the breeze and heculs moved slightly. Then Koreorgin abruptly wheeled his steed about; the ranks of his escort hastily opened to permit their overlord passage before following after him. Bugles sounded, calling the leaders of the hostile force to their chieftain's presence.

Cottis told Quinton that the Adiorenji chieftain now knew the precise truth about the death of his scion; he would rebuke Kinerth for his falsehoods, although this would not deter him from attacking the capital of Sicruci. The party returned to the city, and the west gate was closed. The defenders were ready while, outside his newly erected tent, the horbspan of their adversaries was discussing the parley.

"The King of Rionder! Paramount ranxem of the Mescarg steppes! Supreme Overlord of the Deerait nation! The High Court in Hesion aren't fools. Let no one think that! And they gave that damned youth the sacred sword of Csiandag, the treasured heirloom of the Deerait people! I did not know it really existed!" Koreorgin snapped angrily.

"Mescarg steppes paramount ranxem? What exactly does that mean?" Chsingof, an important chieftain, asked.

"Probably a term for ruler or supreme overlord. If so, that may mean more troops. The question is, how many does he have? Are they inside Estyork? Also, who are Ontar and Admaria?" Rinthalt, another leader, wondered. "The names do sound familiar," he added.

"I believe they're the names of Wizards from the Sacred Islands in the Chofanrit Ocean. Far away beyond the setting sun. They were connected with Rionder long before Broechnaar seized the city. Nothing has been heard of them since the fall of Rionder," Chsingof commented.

"Well then, if they are the same persons, and couldn't save Rionder, they will hardly be able to save Estyork. Let the sorcerers commence," Koreorgin commanded one of his subordinates.

The eight magicians of varying ability, who had been compelled to accompany the force, selected a large space in a meadow about a mile beyond the horbspan's tent to perform their arts. This sensible precaution was adopted lest their spells caused the heculs and rotars of their army to stampede in terror. They uttered mysterious incantations while inscribing occult designs on the ground and burning various herbs. The sorcerers felt that all was quite satisfactory for conditions seemed auspicious.

One of them caused a black streak of lightning to flash across

343

the meadow. Four of his confederates were responsible for the appearance of many ghostly wraiths, which flew to and fro, awaiting the instructions of those who had conjured them. The magicians next proceeded with a strong spell intended to blast open each of the four city gates. The rites, which alternated between White and Black Magic, were performed quite efficiently.

At last the wizards decided to impel the howling spectres towards Estyork. Ontar, who had been watching the proceedings in his crystal, snapped his fingers. This action caused the wraiths to vanish immediately and also resulted in the abrupt cessation of all occult activities. Try as they would, they proved unable even to recommence the simplest of their operations and ultimately were obliged to send a messenger to inform their leader.

"By Caramanj, she who has no face! Rhaitall should have been here from Castle Xzlus! He's about as much use as old Tarhalic was! Damn all priests!" Koreorgin snarled, giving vent to his frustration.

"Shall we launch an assault?" Chsingof asked when the horbspan had calmed down.

"All right. Get an assault ready for this afternoon. We'll attack the west gate in force," Koreorgin nodded.

"Only one gate?" Chsingof enquired.

"Yes. We'll probe the defences. If we are successful we can send in massive support."

In the great judgment hall of Estyork, Allecenia had been scrying the Adiorenji encampment. She saw that serfs were still busily employed in erecting tents for their masters and house carls. Nevertheless the beautiful woman did not miss the significance of the troops being gathered nearest to the town, and immediately informed her beloved.

"They're preparing to assault the west gate, Quinton," she called.

"North, south and east gates are all right at present. Companies of the enemy just watching the city," Admaria affirmed, gazing intently into her own crystal.

"Colmar, go as a courier to the square. Four thousand shock troops to man the west wall. Tell them to be ready for an assault," the monarch commanded.

"At once, Sire," the Melcogh acknowledged before racing from the hall to the courtyard, where a Deerait servitor held the reins of his hecul.

Colmar vaulted into the saddle, dug his heels into the sides of his yellow beaked steed, and galloped off under the archway into the square. He raced over to Rahamb, who listened intently to his instructions before snapping efficient orders. Within ten seconds the requisite column of steppe troopers was hurtling down the west boulevard. As it went along companies left it to proceed along streets and thoroughfares to the positions allocated to them.

They had practised such manoeuvres so diligently that they knew every single route throughout Estyork, as if they had been born and bred in the capital of Sicruci. The garrison troops and the citizenry had been astonished at the dedication to duty of their new allies. Large and small columns of mounted warriors had traversed the town from one end to the other, obeying mock orders, until they could react automatically to any command given to relieve a particular position on the high walls.

Contingents of garrison troops and auxiliaries from the countryside had been ordered to man the battlements in relay at all times during the hours of daylight. Any attacks would bring the shock regiments into action, wherever they were required. The one advantage in fighting a battle in Deerait was that none of the four tribes would continue hostilities after sunset, lest they bring the wrath of the gods down on their heads.

This belief had been a major factor in the war against the Empire centuries before. The forefathers of the Riondese had been utterly frustrated by the refusal of their southern allies to undertake night actions. However, the Deeraits had reluctantly conceded that they would march during the hours of darkness to thwart the Casmans. Ontar and Quinton had determined that Estyork was to be held until Gordan arrived with the army. Because of the ring formed by the besiegers around the town, they had decided against launching nocturnal assaults against their more numerous foes.

"You and I will have to go now," the King of Rionder smiled warmly at his foster father, moments after Colmar had departed on his vital errand.

They embraced Admaria and Allecenia and left quickly. Olluinan's daughter looked after their departing figures until they had vanished out of sight in the doorway. She glanced at her godmother for a few seconds, before voicing her thoughts.

"How can you live with the dread that they might never come back? The Cleansing of the Street of the Taverns in Hesion was over so quickly. I barely had time to be concerned in comparison with this situation. On Ordlansa it's very difficult to realise the emotions of combatants and their families.

"We watched the battles on the steppes, like a series of moving pictures. We were all confident that Quinton, Ontar and their friends would survive. We praised Perlow. I do admit I was really worried when Ontar and Quinton had to battle against Reorgin and Kinerth. Now I am very much afraid again. I don't want to lose either of them or Perlow," Allecenia expressed her feelings.

"I know. I too am worried. We must never let them know that, if at all possible. It might have an adverse effect on them. They too are afraid. The whole army is in a battle situation before the fighting begins. Nerves are very raw. Once it starts the soldiers are fully occupied. They have no time to be afraid if they are fortunate. The Adiorenji out there are afraid also. Especially those poor souls about to attack the west gate," Admaria sighed. She then added, "We have to endure this terrible waiting and fear for our loved ones. Sheralex will be worrying just the same in the forests."

"Then we have to endure! We must! They need us, and we need them. They fight in their fashion. We endure in another," Allecenia concurred from behind her dark veil at the same moment as Colmar returned to await his next instructions.

Ontar and Quinton hastened into the courtyard where two heculs awaited them. They mounted up and galloped quickly into the square before taking the western boulevard which took them to the gate about to be assailed; they were followed by Hanshair and a contingent of the royal guard. Once there, they leaped to the ground and rushed up the stone steps to the battlements, their steeds standing still beneath the overhang. The archmage had cast a spell over all the mounts to be used inside the town so that no problems would arise when the fierce animals were left unattended.

Rahamb and Souriin were busily employed on the battlements on either side of the west gate while Cottis and Ricel were checking the readiness of their platoons. The Nai-

Zind caranxem and his second-in-command surveyed the positions of their troops, their presence reassuring the Deerait garrison soldiers and the auxiliaries stationed there. Both the latter felt more confident since the extremely efficient warriors of the King of Rionder had appeared to reinforce them. Their morale was high.

"They're beginning to advance, Quinton," Perlow reported, for he had been allocated the responsibility of monitoring the tactics their foes would employ.

"How many do you reckon?" the King of Rionder asked the efficient warrior who had been observing the Relyanese for some time on the prior request of his paramount ranxem.

"Approximately fifteen thousand have been mobilised. It's not yet feasible to guess how many will be used in the first assault. Probably two thousand to attack the ramparts. Perhaps three to four thousand cavalry to keep the remainder of our forces busy along the whole wall," the Chofir replied.

"Excellent assessment, my friend," Quinton acknowledged, patting the warrior on the shoulder, which kindly action pleased his personal bodyguard.

"Pass the word along all four walls. This first attack is definitely containable by the troops on this side," Hanshair called to the defenders nearest to him a few moments later, having received this command from his monarch.

The news of the impending assault ran round the long battlements: those on the other three walls experienced a feeling of relief at not yet being involved in the fighting. However, many of the Deeraits began to think about the fact that their new allies would be facing the first onslaught; they resolved to do their duty when the time came to serve their Supreme Overlord and Estyork.

The first Relyanese to advance were light cavalry, armed with bows and large quivers filled with a considerable number of shafts. Their task was to compel the defenders to keep their heads down behind the battlements while their fellows raced forward with giant wooden scaling ladders. Simultaneously, squads of house carls and serfs were to manoeuvre a huge battering ram for the purpose of smashing through the gate. The juggernaut had been hauled by teams of rotars to a starting place just beyond bowshot of the defenders.

"Here they come!" Perlow called.

"Section commanders! Deerait officers! Prepare for action!

You know what to do! Just follow the standing orders!"
Quinton shouted.

The first ranks of hostile cavalry swept forward in a massive north to south arc. When they passed near the west wall they loosed scores of swishing shafts which flew over and through the embrasures on the ramparts. Those defenders fortunate to be behind arrow slits were the only ones to respond. They struck several of the attackers or their long yellow beaked steeds. Riders crashed violently to the ground; some had the further misfortune to be trampled underfoot by their comrades behind.

The next two lines of cavalry spread out and halted, firing rapidly at the top of the walls. They left gaps in their ranks through which the infantry came, bearing ladders, while the strongest house carls manhandled a thirty foot tree trunk on a large wheeled support towards the main gate. Riders raced back and forth, bringing supplies of shafts to the cavalry so that an incessant hail could be maintained. Koreorgin listend to the reports coming from observers. He nodded with satisfaction for the news indicated that his troops were managing excellently, and might indeed succeed in forcing entry into Estyork.

Quinton looked at Ontar and smiled grimly. His foster father crouched behind the battlements, a red, pointed, steel helmet with a nose cover on his head. The fortress supply rooms had held sufficient equipment to furnish armour for fifteen thousand men in addition to the garrison, since this was the number of trained auxiliaries Cottis could expect to raise within three hundred miles of the capital of Sicruci. None of the steppe warriors demurred when commanded to wear such corporeal protection, for they fully grasped its value.

"Wonder how near the infantry are?" Ontar spoke telepathically to his foster son.

"Admaria should tell us very soon," Quinton acknowledged.

Almost as if she had anticipated his comment, his beautiful foster mother's voice spoke in both their minds simultaneously. "They are a hundred yards from the wall. Coming quite quickly. Get ready."

"Prepare for action! Get the foot soldiers first! Then the cavalry!" Quinton shouted above the clamour from below, where the Adiorenji were yelling their savage battle cries and also pondering why the besiegers had scarcely retaliated against

348

their onslaught.

"Now! Fire!" the King of Rionder bellowed in a loud clear voice which rang from one end of the battlements to the other.

The whole line of his troops stationed on the west wall rose as one and launched deadly shafts at the infantry. In spite of the valiant endeavours of the cavalry, the lines of the latter were riddled. The accuracy of the steppe troops, supported by the Deeraits, almost annihilated the first two ranks of foot soldiers. The carls pulling and pushing the battering ram fared little better. They had a wall of shields around them but this could not prevent shafts penetrating through several gaps.

Quinton and Ontar moved to a small room at the front of the guard-house, directly above the west gate, to observe the proceedings. They managed to peer out of the window and saw the Relyanese infantry being scythed down. Several bolts from the cavalry whistled into the room, but flew over their heads to shatter against the stone wall behind. With the repulsion of the foot soldiers, the cavalry officers commanded their companies to withdraw. This caused a slackening in the volume of fire from the mounted troops. The defenders took immediate and terrible advantage of it. Almost a hundred and fifty of their foes were slain before they could ride beyond arrow range.

Perlow had noticed his liege and the archmage go into the guard-house. He decided to follow them for their vantage point would give him a central view of the conflict. The Chofir suddenly felt a nameless dread and began to run. He entered just as the final shafts were being launched by the departing Relyanese cavalry.

Quinton heard his bodyguard come in and was about to turn to see who it was. Perlow threw himself at his monarch and knocked him against the wall. A shaft swished past the latter's head to strike the small warrior in the lower part of his left arm. The Chofir emitted a groan as the arrow penetrated right through to the other side. He slumped to the floor, his face ashen with pain. His King and Ontar quickly knelt beside him. Both were cognisant that if their comrade had not acted as he did the blue feathered shaft protruding from his limb would definitely have struck the Supreme Lord of Deerait in the throat. Hanshair and Onlestic entered at the precise moment that the two mystics began to tend the wounded section commander.

"Oh no! What happened here?" the Nai-Zind spoke in anguished tones.

"Perlow threw me aside. He took the arrow. It would have killed me," the King answered.

"Hold on to my hand, Perlow. Quinton, get that arrow out!" Ontar snapped.

"Right," the youth acknowledged grimly.

While the Chofir resolutely gritted his teeth and clung to the sage, the latter's foster son grasped the arrow head and quickly snapped it off. The pain almost caused the injured guard to faint but he managed to retain consciousness even when his paramount ranxem swiftly pulled the shaft out. Arterial blood spouted in a bright crimson torrent.

Quinton glanced pointedly at his foster father who nodded. The archmage quickly traced a magical sign over the gaping hole. The violent flow ceased; the interior and exterior of the wound on both sides of Perlow's arm healed and the gash closed within a few brief seconds. The Chofir suddenly felt his pain vanish and his strength return to normal.

"Thank you, Ontar. Thank you very much indeed. I could have perished at worst, or have been crippled. It glanced off the bone. I am sincerely grateful," Perlow expressed his thanks and rose to his feet.

"It is we who should be most grateful to you, my friend. If you hadn't entered and acted when you did, Quinton would have been slain. My magic has healed you. There are only certain times when I can do this. It depends on hidden matters. Even the bloodstains on your clothes have vanished. Likewise the drops on the floor. What made you come in?" the sage asked kindly.

"I knew Quinton was in peril. I don't know how I knew. I just knew," the Chofir tried to explain.

"I thank you." Quinton embraced his guard.

"May the Great Power bless you, my friend!" Hanshair exclaimed, while Onlestic nodded his own gratitude.

"When you leave here you can tell the others of Perlow's deed. Do not mention how I healed him," Ontar cautioned.

The Chofir smiled at his comrades and moved to the window. He looked out and reported, " The enemy is retreating. They have suffered quite a rebuff. It remains to be seen if they will try again today. I believe they will. The dust makes things hard to see, but I think they only committed

350

about a third of the troops mobilised."

"I believe you're right. They will attack again this afternoon. If we can hold them back, I doubt whether they'll attempt anything else before sunset. They don't fight at night," Quinton commented.

"And tonight is one night nearer Gordan's arrival," Ontar remarked grimly.

"And that is when they'll wonder what hit them," Perlow stated shyly.

It was then that Hanshair mentioned the reason for his presence. He had received news that a city patrol had just caught another Adiorenji spy, although this still left four men from Relyan whose whereabouts remained unknown. On the morning after their arrival in Estyork contingents of the city garrison had been ordered to find all the Adiorenji, Vilatmori and Dariondi within the confines of Estyork. These people were to be treated courteously and brought to Admaria in the judgment hall.

Almost four hundred men and women were traced and escorted to the wizard's wife. Many had lived in Estyork for years, having married contentedly into the community. There were several merchants and their families from the three tribes, who had also settled down comfortably with the Sicrucians and were regarded by them as friends and neighbours. None objected to being called to the judgment hall; it was the most obvious and sensible thing to do in time of war.

Each was brought individually before Admaria and commanded to look into her wonderful gray eyes. Her magnificent beauty entranced them and, when she gazed back at them, they felt a friend talking in their minds. Ontar's spouse used her intuition, combined with a simple occult spell, to ascertain their thoughts on Estyork being attacked. The first one hundred and thirty seven men and women were appalled by the war about to break out, and sincerely wanted to do all they could to assist the town which they regarded as their home.

However, the next person was arrested for he proved to be a Vilatmori spy. Altogether eighteen more were taken into custody, both men and women. They were told that no harm would befall them and that they would be released unmolested if Estyork should surrender to the enemy. The soldiers from the garrison had scoured the town and had succeeded in finding all but five Adiorenji, the quintet having come to reside in the provincial capital during the past six months.

Further searches proved fruitless but the four town gates were closed and no one could enter or leave the city without detection. Nevertheless the quintet could perform acts of sabotage. Heralds rode around the streets and thoroughfares, proclaiming to the people to remain alert for treachery. The military personnel were also cautioned to be vigilant. Any suspicious action was to be reported immediately. Quinton also commanded that the citizens, and those sheltering inside the walls, were to treat the men and women passed by Admaria with normal consideration and courtesy. Any attempt to mistreat or harm them would incur his personal wrath.

"Where was he sheltering, Hanshair?" Ontar asked.

"The patrol doesn't know. The officer in charge sent a courier to tell you, Sir. I received the message just a few minutes ago. They were called to arrest him about twenty minutes ago when he attempted to purchase some wine. He must have gone to ground before your ordinance to close the taverns went into effect. He knocked on the door of one of the inns two streets from here. The landlord knew his face and accent and invited him inside. Once there, four of the staff seized him and held him until the patrol arrived, Great Sage," the Nai-Zind answered.

"Send someone to tell the landlord that the Lord of Deerait offers his grateful thanks," Ontar said, receiving a nod of approval from Quinton.

"Forgive me, Sire. But I took the liberty of doing so already," Hanshair said.

"Excellent. I suppose the spy has been taken to the judgment hall to Admaria in accordance with standing orders," Quinton mused, a sudden thought having entered his mind.

"Sire, I've an idea!" Hanshair exclaimed.

"So have I," called Perlow.

"Probably the same one Ontar and I are having too," the King grinned.

"Yes. Why don't we let him go and see where he runs to? He may even have been the one responsible for sending word to Koreorgin about the King of Rionder being elected to the position of Lord of Deerait," the wizard smiled.

"Hanshair, return to your post. There's going to be another attack. Leave our little scheme with us. We'll set it in motion.

And we'll certainly let you know if we have any success," Quinton declared.

"Thank you, Sire. And thank you again, Perlow," the Nai-Zind courteously bowed before withdrawing accompanied by Onlestic.

"We'll let Admaria implement it. She can use a company of garrison troops and some scouts from the reserve in the square. Better she does it later this afternoon. The spy will hardly think we'll bother about his activities when the city is under attack," Ontar conversed silently.

Quinton smiled his acquiescence, and within a minute the wizard had apprised his spouse of their stratagem. She agreed and made swift arrangements just before the Adiorenji was brought into her presence. If they were successful, the other four spies might be trapped; if they failed at least they would recapture one of them.

Half an hour passed before Perlow's keen eyes perceived that another attack was definitely about to be launched. Quinton and Ontar knew of this already but did not reveal that Allecenia had informed them telepathically. The dead and wounded from the first assault had been taken down from the wall; everyone was at his post, fully prepared for action.

In the Relyanese encampment Koreorgin and his associates still pondered the significance of the words 'paramount ranxem of the Mescarg steppe tribes.' They discussed the possibility that warriors from the high plateau beyond the mountains were serving the King of Rionder. It seemed unbelievable, but then so was the appointment of the ruler of a small kingdom as Supreme Overlord of Deerait. Chsingof and Rinthalt concluded that the title paramount ranxem was a fiction to impress them. If this Quinton possessed a host of tribesmen, then where were they? Why had they not put in an appearance? They could hardly be in Estyork, else a pitched battle would now be in progress outside the town. Koreorgin agreed, although none of them could unravel the riddle of why the youth had been created Supreme Overlord of Deerait. They turned their thoughts to the repulsion of their first attack.

"I shall send in more troops. Commit the full fifteen thousand, Rinthalt," the chieftain ordered.

"Yes, at once, horbspan," the latter acknowledged, using the title of an Adiorenji warlord.

"Ah, we'll see what they can do when they're faced with

a major onslaught," Koreorgin nodded, grimfaced.

"If it's repulsed, we'll launch assaults against two gates tomorrow. Our spies within Estyork had better try something," Chsingof commented.

"They know the contingency plan," Kinerth stated from where he stood beside his father on the edge of the encampment facing the city.

Once more the Relyanese cavalry advanced, but this time in much larger numbers. The steppe warriors on the battlements waited patiently, several of them feeling grateful for the helmets and armour they wore. Glancing blows from arrows, which would normally have slain them if they had not been wearing protection, struck them on the head and chest. Whether from Sicruci or the Mescarg steppes, each soldier waited, resolved to fight bravely for the handsome youth who was his ruler.

The tactics adopted by the besiegers were precisely the same as on the previous occasion. The main difference was the massive increase in numbers which they hoped would provide them with a quick victory. Ten thousand cavalry charged, quickly taking up positions to maintain a rapid flow of shafts at the embrasures. However the defenders were able to retaliate quite quickly, although they did not know that Admaria and Allecenia were advising Ontar and Quinton respectively.

The Ulgruffi mystic and his foster son had left the small guard-room and stood on either side of the gate. Their troops were told to remain hidden as long as possible from the hail of missiles whistling overhead and between the parapets. Ontar passed the word for the soldiers on his side to fire from their concealed positions, instructing them as to the angle at which to loose their flights. Quinton was similarly guided by Olluinan's daughter, who scried efficiently like her godmother, for both women were aware that they were saving valuable lives.

The defenders fired their shafts into the air. The projectiles cascaded down into the ranks of the cavalry. The stout Adiorenji, black, yellow, white and brown house carls, suffered a considerable number of casualties. Men and heculs crashed to the ground. Arrows penetrated throats, arms, eyes and every conceivable place not covered by heavy armour. Steeds suffered death and ghastly wounds, lying squealing and kicking futilely in the dust.

"Quinton, the infantry are nearing the walls. Some have already begun to raise their ladders. Our soldiers will have to engage the enemy directly now, instead of being guided through us," Allecenia warned her beloved.

"Ontar, the battering ram is only about sixty yards from the gate. There are hordes of infantry outside the city," Admaria informed her husband.

The archmage immediately snapped crisp commands. Men rushed to where large cauldrons of boiling water seethed over hot fires. The enemy were courageously pushing and hauling the juggernaut towards the west gate when a hail of arrows scythed into their ranks. Several fell but their places were promptly taken by others. They were partially covered by a shield wall and roof but, against the volume of shafts being fired, their shelter could not preserve all of them.

A Relyanese slipped in the blood of one of his comrades, falling below the right wheel of the battering ram support. It trundled remorselessly over his body, crushing him to an agonising death which he greeted with a dreadful scream. The carriage rolled on, leaving a gory mass of flesh, bone and brains splattered on the ground. Nevertheless his comrades continued to progress and hoped that the juggernaut would soon crash into the massive gateway.

Suddenly, all along the wall, rocks began to hail down, smashing, stunning and bruising the carls and serfs beneath the battlements; then huge deluges of scalding liquid descended on the attackers. The cruel torrent came from the cauldrons which had been tipped into wide channels. These ran downwards to spray anyone and anything within a large radius beneath the ramparts.

Adiorenji screamed in terrible pain as the liquid seared and boiled their flesh. They immediately broke ranks to flee away from the savage torment being inflicted on them. Many did not reach safety, for the archers on the embrasures momentarily appeared to impel feathered death at them. Similarly, in the area of the guard-houses, more cauldrons were being emptied onto those valiantly attempting to scale the walls.

Some had succeeded in climbing up halfway before the awful deluge cascaded over to drench them and their comrades beneath. They pitched to the ground, several sustaining broken limbs and necks to add to the intense misery which had been inflicted. The assault began to falter, and a general retreat might have resulted, had an observant cavalry officer not noticed that the volume of boiling water was beginning to trickle to a halt.

"Attack! Attack! Get those ladders into position! Move that battering ram! Shove it forward as fast as it'll go! They're out of boiling liquid!" he roared, guessing correctly.

The wavering infantry looked upwards and saw the slackening flow. They resolutely picked up their long ladders and hastened to the wall once more. This action resulted in the defenders having to expose themselves to fire at the foot soldiers. A savage conflict developed between the cavalry and those on the battlements. Casualties increased on both sides.

Sixty eight ladders were slammed into position. Relyanese warriors climbed courageously upwards, determined to fight their way into Estyork. They had been anticipating a short campaign to capture the town before reducing the rest of Sicruci. Like the majority of young men, they ignorantly believed that war was a magnificent occupation, filled with glory. The sight of their dead and dying comrades and the corpses of heculs had dampened their enthusiasm. However, they put this down to a minor initial drawback, and gamely continued.

When the first ladders appeared near his position, Souriin and four of his comrades seized a long pole with a forked end. They waited a few moments before pushing it against the top rung and heaving forwards, thrusting away from the forty foot high wall. The ladder crashed to the ground, three of the house carls on it suffering broken limbs. Elsewhere on the battlements others were performing similar actions, while the remainder of their comrades fired arrows at the attackers, or used swords and two headed axes to repel any Adiorenji attempting to climb between the embrasures.

The violent clamour of battle was heard inside the city. The non-combatants waited in their homes or places of residence, wondering how matters would turn out. In the square the remainder of the shock troops fretted at not being present to fight beside their King: but they realised that they might be called to assist on the west wall at any moment, or to ride to another position about to be assaulted. Felgorian, Sorcottis and Yltormik were stationed on the quiet east wall, and felt equally frustrated; notwithstanding, they were resolved to obey the

356

orders of the Supreme Overlord of Deerait.

Neither side desisted for an instant during the first hour of the second attack. However, the determination and moral superiority of the defenders gradually began to take effect, with the result that the Relyanese started to feel their valiant attempt was doomed to failure. The piles of dead and wounded, especially the carnage outside the gate, brought home to them the reality of war in its true, hideous shape. This was no glorious and heroic escapade, but a bloody, terrible struggle with death hovering, eager to snatch a victim at every opportunity.

While Quinton ran to and fro, encouraging and fighting wherever necessary, Ontar, assisted by Hanshair, Adrigal and Onlestic, repelled the incessant attacks on the gate. Time after time, the sturdy carls and serfs tried to haul the battering ram to a position about thirty yards distant, to give it impetus for a rush at the barrier preventing their entrance into Estyork. The sagittaries on the parapets and in the guard-room risked their lives, peering over to find targets.

The Adiorenji cavalry were thickest nearest the west entrance and suffered heavy losses. They had no means of knowing, but the position was wholly defended by the finest troops on Rontmethar, members of the shock troop regiments of the King of Rionder. Every steppe soldier was an above average archer who had spent many months on the undulating grasslands, performing the programme of martial arts developed by Gordan and the Inner Council.

The long hours of practising with a bow were now proving fruitful. Although the defenders did sustain casualties, these were slight in comparison to those which they inflicted. Their accuracy proved itself; a trooper had only to peer over for a brief instant and loose a shaft before dropping to safety behind the parapet with the knowledge that he had probably struck his mark.

Dead and dying cavalry and infantry were strewn all around the gateway. However, the Relyanese managed to haul the massive battering ram over the heaped corpses of the slain. They courageously dragged on the thick ropes, with vicious arrows cutting them down in spite of their shields and mounted support. The juggernaut trundled forward until a wheel bumped against a large rock, causing it to stop. This unfortunate accident involved more straining and pulling backwards, but they accomplished this task and withdrew ten yards, having lost twelve more comrades.

"They are brave fellows," Adrigal remarked, refilling his quiver from supplies brought by an auxiliary.

"They certainly are at the moment," Ontar agreed.

"What do you mean, Great Sage?" Onlestic asked with respect, having just fired another four shafts out of the guard-room window.

"It's their first major battle for many centuries. The young men are filled with heroic ambitions. You remember what you felt like when you were first elevated to warrior status," the mystic explained.

"Ah, I see." Adrigal launched another arrow out of the window to strike a cavalryman in the throat. "The glamour of war does not long endure the disillusionment of its reality."

"That's it, my friends. We're beating them back. The cost to them is enormous. Look at the dead out there. The reality will soon strike home, if it hasn't done so already," the wizard declared, ducking down to avoid two arrows which swished over his head to smack into the stone wall behind.

"We also have one advantage, my dear, sweet Ker-Mantid friends," Hanshair grinned from where he sat in a corner restringing his bow with the reserve twine kept in a pocket of his tunic; the cord had snapped because of the powerful strain he had used to slay a Relyanese officer who had assumed the captaincy of the battering ram party.

"What's that, you Nai-Zind numbskull?" Adrigal promptly retorted before putting his hand to his mouth when he realised what he had said in front of the Great Sage.

"That's all right, my friend. You only carry on like this to keep your and our spirits up. You did this earlier during the first attack. It cheered up the supply Deeraits. They forgot their fear to laugh at some utterly inane comment of yours. I know if Hanshair gave you an order, you wouldn't hesitate to carry it out. Hanshair, tell them the advantage. Perlow will be back in a few moments to make further observations," Ontar smiled.

"We've seen their casualties. They've seen their casualties also. And they are very heavy. What they don't know is the extent of our casualties. We will force them to withdraw, or the setting sun will. They will be demoralised, and that can only work to our advantage. May I propose that the Deeraits

358

sing one of their most cheering songs when the enemy retreats? It will really rub depression home, King's Friend," the Nai-Zind suggested.

"An excellent proposal. I'll inform Quinton. He's not far from Cottis and Ricel at the moment," the sage replied.

"How is my friend, Cottis?" Hanshair asked, fully aware that the eminent mystic would know without being near the governor of Sicruci.

"He's unharmed," Ontar reassured the commander of the royal guard.

"That's good. I do like him," Hanshair commented, completing the restringing of his bow.

Onlestic launched an arrow out of the window and ducked down to say that the Adiorenji appeared about to launch the battering ram. Ontar risked a quick glance and nodded his concurrence at the precise moment that Perlow entered to state exactly the same. The Chofir, who had grasped a feeling for the battle situation, declared that he was certain the Relyanese would withdraw should they not manage to breach the gateway.

The wizard agreed, for he entertained similar thoughts. One mighty blow from the juggernaut would not demolish the western entrance into Estyork; indeed, many would be required before it gave way. If the Adiorenji could at least crash their projectile against it a few times they would believe that their sacrifices had not been in vain. Such an action would boost their flagging morale for an assault on the morrow.

"They'll get quite a surprise if they get anywhere near here," Onlestic grinned at Hanshair, who smiled in return. The latter had been responsible for devising a defence at each of the major entrances to counteract such an eventuality. His idea had been based on a variation of the wagon defence stratagem which Gordan had demonstrated on his first day with the Nai-Zind many years before.

Ontar left the quartet in the most dangerous position on the whole wall. The sage communicated silently with Quinton regarding the suggestion put forward by the commander of the royal guard that the Deerait defenders should sing when their adversaries withdrew. His foster son concurred, shouting instructions to Ricel over the clamour of the battle.

The King of Rionder and his boyhood friend, Souriin, had been battling fiercely with swords to prevent the enemy from coming over the ramparts. Four ladders had been thrown against the wall at the same place. One was repelled by the long pole method. However, although archers and pikemen had managed to slay the Adiorenji ascending another, their foes on the remaining two had succeeded in standing on the embrasures.

Quinton and the young Hedunon had been nearest, and fought bitterly. Their task was made more difficult since the group of cavalry directly below were among the best bowmen in the Relyanese horde. The sagittaries maintained a rapid accurate fire on either side of their comrades' ladders. Two Deerait soldiers nearby were slain before Cottis managed to rally several of his personal guard with long spears. Unyamed was at the forefront. He gamely thrust his weapon into the side of his nearest opponent, who toppled backwards to the ground with a ghastly screech.

A black skinned Sicrucian soldier assisted Quinton and Souriin, while others knelt to fire shafts at any of their foes rash enough to come within their vision. Similar actions occurred along the whole wall, but the defenders could sense that the Adiorenji were less resolute. This instinct spurred them to greater efforts as the enemy launched a final attack with the battering ram against the west gate in the early evening.

The shock troops and the royal guards over the entrance fired a continuous stream of arrows at both the cavalry and the infantry involved with the large projectile. Relyanese commanders exhorted their soldiers to a supreme effort. Despite heavy casualties, they were now almost ready to launch the juggernaut. A courageous officer rallied his men and, uttering distinctive battle cries, the carls and serfs hauled on the ropes or pushed it forward.

Fortune appeared to favour them, for the battering ram trundled down the slight slope towards its objective, picking up momentum. In its wake lay an appalling trail of dead and dying; its massive wheels bloodily churned several corpses into the dust before Estyork. The attackers found that the juggernaut was now moving faster than they themselves were, so they gladly released their grip on it, elated that it was travelling in a straight line directly at the west gate.

The massive tree trunk with one end sharpened to a point rushed onwards, watched by thousands of Adiorenji eager to smash their way inside the town, if at all possible. They just wanted to see the mighty weapon crash against the gate. Even if it had to be abandoned because sunset was not far off, there were several more such lethal monsters ready for use in their encampment.

The anticipation of those watching the heavy projectile seemed to cause everyone to halt. An expectant hush fell over the battle. All activity ceased. Every eye, whether able to see the west gate or not, turned in that direction. The besiegers were convinced that it would strike home. It had to do so; there was nothing to hinder its progress. The angle and direction were perfect. Their herculean efforts had not been fruitless.

Hanshair, Adrigal, Onlestic and Perlow stood looking down from the guard-room window. Like the other combatants, they did not desire to continue fighting during this special moment. The battering ram thundered nearer. Suddenly, there was a terrible rending crash and both its wheels descended into a wide ditch. The point of the juggernaut stopped barely six feet from the bottom of the gateway.

A groan arose from the Relyanese who had laboured so valiantly. They were absolutely disgusted, and many wept while the Estyork garrison cheered. The enemy at the gate turned about, and dragged their feet towards their encampment. Several cavalry officers were about to prevent their passage, but a senior chieftain shook his head and shouted an order to four of his buglers. Moments later they sounded the signal to break off the engagement.

The defenders did not fire any arrows at their retreating foes. They did not have the heart to perform such an action. However their adversaries were further downcast when they heard the Sicrucians singing a joyful tune. Black despair burrowed its insidious path into their minds. Their desperate efforts had been for nothing and their casualties horrendous.

Suddenly, Ontar climbed onto the parapet about ten yards from the west gate. His height seemed to increase and his aura glowed. In a loud voice he called on the Adiorenji to halt, which they immediately did and turned around. Two infantry officers were nearest to his position, and the Ulgruffi mystic addressed them in his wonderful tones.

"If you wish to remove your dead and wounded, we shall give you a truce to do so. We, too, would like to gather the bodies of our comrades who fell from the battlements during the fighting."

The senior commander, who had broken off the conflict, also came forward as his juniors accepted the offer of temporary peace. He looked up at the mighty wizard and thanked him courteously. A short time later fifteen hundred Relyanese came from their encampment with a large number of wagons, their first priority being to remove the injured.

Contingents of the Estyork garrison, accompanied by squads of steppe troops from the square, had already emerged from the north and south gates and were collecting the bodies of their fallen, which were far fewer in number than those of their enemies. Quinton and Ontar accompanied their warriors, who left the Deeraits to attend to the dead. The efficient soldiers of the King of Rionder began to help the Adiorenji with their wounded, advising and tending the latter, before they were placed inside the wagons.

The men from the province of Relyan were surprised to find that they did not resent assistance from such a courteous enemy. Indeed, they saw the compassion in the eyes of the tall warriors at the slaughter of so many young men. The Adiorenji healers present listened most attentively to a youth with a dynamic personality and a handsome man with wondrous eyes, who gave them invaluable advice on the stitching of wounds and administering to the injured.

Ilix was rising in the heavens above Estyork when the last wagon departed. Once it had disappeared in the direction of the Adiorenji encampment, squads of Deerait soldiers emerged from the city to gather quickly every single good arrow they could find. They had already performed similar actions on the battlements and in the streets below. Although they had an ample quantity of shafts within Estyork, there was no point in missing an opportunity to replenish their stocks.

Admaria and Allecenia supervised the tending of the wounded by Sicrucian doctors and steppe surgeons from the shock regiments. The garrison physicians learned from their allies, and put their original instructions into practice. Cleanliness was strictly observed and the casualties received excellent attention. The two women were busily employed for some hours in their important task. It was almost midnight before they finished and were able to join Quinton, Ontar and Perlow for a meal. Rahamb, Souriin, Felgorian and Hanshair had been asked as guests.

Admaria had already informed her husband and foster son by telepathy that two more spies had been captured. She gave them further details while they were dining. When the Adiorenji seized during the battle had been brought before her, she pretended that he was innocent and commanded his release. The stout, brown skinned carl was very much relieved, and hastened quickly out of the fortress. He walked rapidly along several streets before turning along an alleyway.

Behind him several steppe warriors followed very stealthily. He did glance back occasionally, but did not see those trailing him. They used their shock training intuition and knew when to duck into doorways. Once he had entered a dwelling house about halfway along the alley, the place was quickly surrounded. When all exits had been discovered, seven tall tribesmen burst into the house and swiftly overcame the three occupants.

Their captives were brought before Admaria for questioning. Ontar's spouse learned that they had come from Imexcajm to await the commencement of civil war. When this occurred, they were to obey the instructions of the remaining two Relyanese, whose whereabouts they did not know for reasons of security. Admaria was satisfied that their explanation was true, and ordered them to be incarcerated for the present.

"We shall just have to hope the pair still missing don't cause havoc," Ontar commented, when his wife had finished relating the results of her interrogation.

"Yes. Hanshair's defensive ruse worked extremely well indeed. The planks were strong enough to support us when we rode out to parley with the Adiorenji. It was fortunate the latter didn't perceive the change in vibrations when we crossed the soil covered trench," Quinton said, picking up a piece of cheese.

"The Relyanese suffered severely today. Koreorgin will have a lot to think about," Ontar declared.

"One good thing is this heavy rain," Allecenia pointed out, listening to the sound of the wind lashing torrents of water on the roof overhead.

"Yes, it will help. If it keeps up it will cause the ground outside the town to become very muddy. I don't see them launching any attacks if they are likely to become bogged down. What do you think, Souriin?" Quinton asked.

"I fully agree with your assessment, Sire. This rain will assuredly cause delays tomorrow. And that's another day nearer Gordan and the army arriving. It's a pity it wouldn't rain all the time. That would save a lot of lives. Ours and theirs. Oh, and I am very glad that Perlow saved you again," the young Hedunon nodded with a smile.

"They fought courageously. Especially the brave fellows employed in manhandling the battering ram. I felt proud of them, and sorry when it crashed into the ditch," Hanshair spoke reflectively.

"Yes. I know," Ontar declared, "but your strategy will have helped to shatter their morale."

"And they're in the dilemma of not knowing whether there are hidden trenches outside the other gateways," Allecenia said in her wonderful, enchanting voice, from where she was sitting in a corner with her hood drawn over her face.

"The first day is over. Gordan is a day nearer. I think we should all turn in. We have to be abroad early. My thanks for the meal, Sire. My thanks to you too, Perlow." Rahamb smiled at the Chofir, who nodded shyly in response.

"Yes, I agree. Little boys like Quinton and Souriin should be in their beds by this time," Admaria laughed merrily, being joined by the others in her mirth.

364

"You know, Souriin, if the rain weren't so heavy, you and I should just go and join the Adiorenji," Quinton grinned.

"You can go. I'm staying. They don't plait their hair either, Sire," the Hedunon responded warmly.

"Here I am surrounded by friends! Huh! Koreorgin get a tent ready for me!" the King of Rionder declared in tones of mock despair.

When their guests had departed, Allecenia removed her cloak and hood and took off her veil. She walked over to Perlow who was about to leave for his bedchamber. To the Chofir's utter embarrassment, she embraced him and kissed him on the cheek.

"Thank you, my dear, dear friend. Thank you for Quinton," Olluinan's daughter said in her wondrous voice.

"Yes, thank you," Admaria concurred, kissing him in turn.

"It was my duty. I just knew. Somehow I just knew Quinton was in danger," the Chofir tried to explain.

"I'm glad. I'm so very glad. The guard and the shock regiments were overjoyed. So were Cottis and the Sicrucians," Ontar stated, his arm on Perlow's shoulder, while his foster son voiced his own gratitude.

"You were willing to sacrifice yourself to save me. I shall never forget that. Your valour is beyond that normally expected. What reward do you think, my friend?"

"None. I'm only too happy to be of service. And you, Ontar and Admaria have taken me to live with you. And I've seen Allecenia's face. The first outworlder other than you, Quinton. That is sufficient for me."

"Then, my unselfish friend, we thank you. Ontar, Admaria, I respectfully believe we should teach Perlow magic and mysticism," the King of Rionder spoke the last sentence in Ulgruffi. He did not address the archmages as his foster parents, but as the Heads of the Sacred Order of Light.

"I agree," the wizard said to a nod of acquiescence from his wife. "We'll start with a little magic and elementary mysticism when the siege is over and time permits," Ontar smiled, little realising, even with his prescience, how vital this beginning would prove for their small friend after the end of the present conflict.

Perlow was informed of the decision of the two Ulgruffi. He looked at everyone in wonderment, and expressed his gratitude, before commenting, "I hope there is an easier way for others to find the gateway to esoteric wisdom."

His remark caused considerable amusement, and Ontar was still chuckling when he and Admaria entered their bedroom.

"I'm glad Quinton made the suggestion. I still wonder when he'll meet his goddess," the beautiful Ulgruffi remarked, as she finished disrobing.

"I've received no inkling. Nothing since the revelation on the steppes. We'll just have to wait and see," the archmage responded.

"We still have no idea of his origins either," Admaria said softly, as they climbed into bed.

"Another mystery," her husband murmured, extinguishing the candle on the table beside him.

The Relyanese horbspan and his fellow commanders watched in grim silence while the wagons returned with the dead and wounded. The besiegers had suffered casualties amounting to almost fifteen hundred men; they had no means of knowing what their adversaries had sustained, but believed with certainty that their losses would be far less than their own; in fact, they actually amounted to just over three hundred.

Strange reports were brought by serfs from the field surgeons. The latter revealed that their opponents had given them revolutionary but simple instructions on how to treat their injured. There was also the inexplicable circumstance that every single one of those scalded by boiling water was not suffering pain. Each said that his agony had suddenly vanished within a few seconds, although he still felt very weak. Again, their skins showed no trace of the terrible damage expected, and their temperature was normal.

Koreorgin attempted to put this down to a sign of favour from the gods, declaring that Caramanj was with them. However, although none dared contradict his leader, many held an unshakeable belief that the Supreme Overlord, Ontar and Admaria were somehow responsible for the incredible partial cure. They were not altogether wrong in their conjecture; Quinton and his foster father had decided that any victims of scalding should be assisted and their suffering ameliorated; consequently, Allecenia and Admaria had put forth their power once they had seen the cauldrons deluging the besiegers.

Nevertheless, Koreorgin did have private doubts that his gods were responsible, for his forces had sustained a defeat. The very inclement weather during the night did not encourage him either. The horbspan was resolutely determined to launch simultaneous assaults against two walls, provided conditions proved suitable in the morning: he also hoped that his spies within the city would be able to provide him with an advantage.

When dawn broke the rain was still teeming and continued thus until almost midday. The Relyanese sorcerers chanted spells without success, for Allecenia and Admaria promptly nullified their occult operations. Koreorgin and his troops were thoroughly miserable in the chill, dank atmosphere. Their spirits did recover somewhat when the sun finally broke through the blanket of gray clouds to bring a welcome warmth.

However, this change in the weather occurred too late for any fighting to be commenced that day. The heat of the sun did dry the muddy ground, but it was far into the afternoon before the areas in front of the battlements had firmed sufficiently for large numbers of cavalry to traverse them without transforming the soil into quagmires. The Adiorenji sent patrols out from time to time to check on conditions, but apart from that made no hostile overtures.

Every moment which passed brought the eighty thousand relief troops nearer. Gordan and his two Polingsi friends had little need to exhort their command to increase its effort, for each warrior was only too eager to reach Estyork and serve his King and paramount ranxem. Fortunately, the heavy rain further south did not reach them; the clouds were blown westwards, with the result that the massive column of men, heculs, wagons and rotars did not have to slacken its pace.

One junior commander had asked Gordan why they did not leave the wagons behind with an escort and push on more quickly. The chief general praised this thought, before explaining there was the possibility that more Adiorenji troops might arrive before they did. If this did occur, they could be heavily outnumbered. It was essential that their enemy did not attempt at some stage to by-pass them, strike into the forests and come between them and their valuable supply train.

Long before dawn the next morning the shock regiments, the garrison soldiers and the auxiliaries had breakfasted. Ahead of them lay a very arduous day, during which each expected to find himself engaged in fighting on the ramparts. Runners darted to and fro, carrying orders from officers to various positions on the walls to which the troops were filing up the stone steps in the gloomy twilight before daybreak.

On the west side of Estyork those on the battlements could see the Adiorenji campfires and hear the sounds of activity as their adversaries prepared for the conflict. Even now, large contingents were departing and riding towards the city. Allecenia and Admaria had resumed their positions in the judgment hall, where they were watched closely by Colmar and several Deeraits detailed to act as couriers under his command. The Melcogh thought about his comrades in the guards manning the defences and wished he were with them. Yet, his beloved King had selected him especially to work with Ontar's spouse and the mysterious veiled Lady, so he shrugged his shoulders and waited patiently.

Perlow strode into the hall and came over to Allecenia who had sent for him. He listened attentively, but with delight to the musical tones of her voice. Since the Chofir was not required to begin his observational duties until daylight, she told him to investigate a certain area on the battlements. Both her crystal and that of her godmother revealed masses of cavalry on the move. The two women guessed that their foes would attack the north and east walls, for already columns were beginning to encircle the city, making for these positions.

"I want you to ride to the southwestern corner, Perlow. There is a lot of enemy activity in that sector. Large numbers have gone directly to the north wall. Yet some are moving past the south, ostensibly going to the east wall. That's odd, because it's unnecessarily dangerous," Allecenia pointed out.

"I agree. It is odd. Anything special you wish me to look for?" the Chofir asked courteously.

"Yes. Some cavalry troops appear to have halted about fifty yards along the south wall from the west. They're not making any hostile movements at the moment. But our men may not be able to see what they're doing in the gloom this morning. Too many clouds at the moment. Just check into it and report back," she said.

"At once, Allecenia," the guard declared and hastened from the hall, while Olluinan's daughter began to scry the Relyanese encampment once more.

Emerging from the main building, Perlow ran down the steps

and vaulted into the saddle of his hecul. The reins of his steed were held by an elderly Deerait servitor, who passed him his shield. The light skinned Chofir smiled kindly at the white attendant before digging in his heels and galloping off into the square. He passed the shock troops, who were checking their equipment, and acknowledged the greeting from some of his acquaintances.

Perlow went by the quickest route, which was down the southern boulevard, and then along the street beneath the walls. He could have taken a diagonal course, but the meandering streets of Estyork would have involved several detours. He was galloping the last few hundred yards when he reined back, startled to discover that a contingent of three hundred auxiliaries was marching towards him. These soldiers were part of the southwestern defences and should have remained in position.

"Where are you going?" he demanded.

"To the east gate, sir. We've just received an order to proceed there immediately. The Supreme Overlord commanded us to do this with all haste. He's expecting an attack shortly," the captain leading the infantry column replied.

"Who gave you the order?" Perlow snapped.

"One of the garrison officers. I don't know his name, but he had another with him. They said a small holding force was on the way to replace us," the Deerait explained.

"Right. Carry on. I'll check this out," the Chofir called, wheeling his hecul around.

Within minutes his steed had galloped the distance to the garrison fortress. Perlow raced under the archway and across the courtyard. He reined up fiercely, leaped from his mount, and ran like the wind up the stairs, along the passage and into the judgment hall. His liege was standing with Ontar in conversation with Cottis and Ricel, beside the table where Allecenia sat.

The Chofir rushed over to his monarch and said, "Quinton, the Deerait auxiliaries in the southwestern corner have left their positions. They were ordered to the east gate by two garrison officers, using your authority. Forgive my discourtesy, but did you give this order? Have you sent a relief force? The Adiorenji could come over the wall."

"No, Perlow! Well done! Spies! They'll bring men over the parapets! Ontar! Hanshair! Come quickly!" Quinton snapped,

369

running towards the doorway.

Within twelve seconds they were mounted and in the square beneath the last few twinkling night stars. The King reined up briefly in front of the shock troops. Rahamb and Souriin were nearby and hurried across to hear their sovereign's terse commands. Almost immediately they too were in the saddle, followed by four hundred steppe warriors.

The leaden sky overhead was lightening slightly, a reflection of the first fingers of dawn which were probing across the horizon. Distant shouts and the clamour of battle indicated that assaults were being launched against the north and east walls. Behind in the square, Colmar was already forwarding Admaria's orders to the shock troops. A thousand left for each of the battlements being assailed. Those riding to the southwestern corner fully realised that these attacks were feints to draw attention away from where the spies had successfully duped the Sicrucians into abandoning their posts.

Even as Quinton's force turned along the street parallel to the south wall, soldiers from the Ebrordin region were climbing up ladders and reaching the parapets where they were met by the two spies. Behind those ascending, queues on the ground expectantly waited to follow their comrades. This was the opportunity for them to capture Estyork. The early morning twilight still concealed their activities and a slight haze from the river also helped to hide them from view of the defenders further along the south and west battlements.

Suddenly the Adiorenji spies, who had cunningly manufactured false regulation garrison uniforms, and those fanning out from the parapets heard the thunder of hecul hooves. To their utter horror and chagrin, tall resolute troopers appeared. Since these were not Deeraits, they had to be the subjects of the King of Rionder. The newcomers, bearing shields and drawn swords, leaped from their steeds and ran to the broad steps.

Rahamb, Souriin and Hanshair raced to one side, while Quinton, Ontar and Perlow headed the rush to another. A hundred and fifty of the enemy were already on the battlements. Many charged down to keep their adversaries at bay, until more of their comrades could ascend to give them assistance. Contingents of shock troops ran quickly towards nearby stairways, their intention being to enclose the Relyanese and thus prevent them from wreaking havoc further along the ramparts. Some of the enemy recalled the tales of Dinmonad, Quinton's renowned ancestor, and quickly found themselves in a bitter and costly re-enactment of times long ago.

If the enemy were to succeed in obtaining a bridgehead, they could prove very difficult to dislodge. The Lord of Deerait realised this as he, his foster father and personal bodyguard clashed swords with their foes and fought their way upwards. The shock troops down below did not dare risk archery in the gloom, because the combat had to be at close quarters. They shouted their war cry, "Quinton! Quinton! Ontar! Ontar!" while they surged forward, eager to battle beside their beloved monarch and the eminent mystic whom they adored.

A black Adiorenji slashed downwards at the King of Rionder. Quinton automatically warded off the blow with his shield and smashed the boss into the face of his adversary. The latter staggered. Perlow on the left struck him with the pommel of his sword and down he went. Another lunged at the paramount ranxem, but the youth had received his training from masters. He parried brilliantly before thrusting his weapon into the throat of his opponent.

Perlow became the source of wonderment. The Chofir was known to be an excellent swordsman, especially after his courageous performance during the battle against the Jaddair corps. He cut, thrust and parried with a skill which was more than extraordinary. The enemy fell before his sword, five toppling to crash onto the cobblestones. Four more perished and slipped in their blood on the broad steps, while the small warrior battled upwards like a whirlwind, and finally reached the parapet.

Beside his foster son, Ontar proved that he was a more than capable fighter. Quinton silently thanked Gordan for the long hours the giant warrior had spent training him. The youth found that the beautiful sword of Csiandag felt light yet strong, and seemed to assist his every movement. He was smaller than the Adiorenji, but the latter quickly found themselves facing an adversary almost as capable as the handsome dark haired man with the aura of eternal youth.

Dawn was breaking when they reached the top of the steps behind Perlow. They heard shouts from both left and right, which indicated that several of the shock troops had also ascended to the same level.

The sun forced its way through the clouds. With its emergence, the rooftops of Estyork began to sparkle and glisten. Its rays shone on the north and east walls, where the besiegers had launched massive assaults of twenty thousand warriors against each side. This was to further Koreorgin's attempt to draw attention away from the southwestern corner of the provincial capital of Sicruci.

Swords clashed. The enemy began to fall back rapidly before the shock troops and their courageous leaders. The Relyanese realised they had lost their gamble to capture Estyork by such an artifice. Their opponents were the warriors of the House of Rionder, not members of the Estyork garrison. Those on the ramparts unselfishly shouted a warning to their comrades scaling the ladders that all was lost; the latter heeded their advice and descended to the ground.

Hanshair, Rahamb and Souriin were in the van of one flanking party which had managed to fight its way up to the same level as their monarch. The two Nai-Zind and the Hedunon parried, hacked and slew, forcing their foes to withdraw until they were able to retreat no longer. There was no opportunity to execute the finer points of the art of swordsmanship; only Perlow, Quinton and Ontar had the ability for that. Quite a number of the invaders began to surrender, captivity being preferable to certain death, should they continue to resist.

Adrigal and Onlestic headed platoons of the shock troops, who had outflanked and contained the enemy on the other side. After extremely fierce fighting the superior training of the Lord of Deerait's troops caused their opponents to think of submission. Among the foes who yielded to the Ker-Mantids and their companions were the two remaining spies. One had sustained a slight wound in his side: but both, when questioned by Admaria later, affirmed that they were the last of the group within Estyork sent by Koreorgin to disrupt the city when war broke out.

In the final conflict for the central position, Quinton, Ontar and Perlow fought savagely. No adversary dared remain long before their flashing blades. If any were rash enough to try he was quickly slain or received a blow from a shield or sword pommel. Both the latter actions resulted in an opponent falling, if he were fortunate, to the cold stone at his feet or, adversely, toppling over to crash down onto the cobblestones many feet below.

When they realised that there was no hope of success, the remaining Adiorenji threw down their weapons and surrendered. The King of Rionder ordered them to be escorted to the fortress for incarceration. All ladders remaining against the outer walls were quickly pushed over to the ground. Two squads of shock troops were commanded to hold the position until they could be replaced by Deerait auxiliaries. In order to facilitate this Ontar communicated telepathically with his spouse; it was not long before the relief companies arrived: the Sicrucians, who had left on the orders of the spies, were now engaged in the conflict on the east wall.

"That was close. Too close almost. Well done, Perlow! But for your alertness, thousands of Relyanese could be pouring over the wall here," Ontar praised the Chofir.

"It was Allecenia who sent me here," the royal guard modestly stated.

"We know. But she left matters in your capable hands. You raised the alarm and saved Estyork," Quinton lauded, as they began to ride back to the main square.

"Our paramount ranxem is right, my friend. If they'd managed to get sufficiently large numbers over the wall, there might have been little chance for the garrison and ourselves to eject them. They'd have opened the south gate. There are about a hundred and twenty thousand Adiorenji outside. We could have been overwhelmed. That's a certainty," Hanshair praised his subordinate.

"Thank you all very much," Perlow acknowledged. "Thank goodness, they didn't use their bows," he added.

"No time. And not much time for manoeuvre with their comrades coming up quickly after them. They collectively panicked. Our men would have dealt with that too," Ontar declared.

"Souriin, you fought bravely. You too, Hanshair," Quinton complimented.

"Thank you, Sire," the two commanders acknowledged in unison.

"Rahamb, you did very well also. Thank you, cousin," the King of Rionder spoke with sincerity to the caranxem riding on his right.

The chieftain smiled his pleasure, saying, "It doesn't seem so long ago since Great Ontar and the Lady Admaria brought you to the steppes as a babe. You were a child of Destiny. I thank the Great Power that I am a part of it."

"And I am glad you are too. The years are filled with memories. You three Nai-Zind, Perlow, and you two Ker-Mantids, and all of you, take care of yourselves. I have no wish to lose a single one of you," Quinton declared in a loud voice, showing how much he loved and appreciated the efforts of his adherents.

"Sire, without any intention of presumption, you were right in the thick of the fighting with Great Ontar. We would not like to lose either of you," Souriin spoke with sincerity.

"Sire, you would be all right. You have Perlow. But, if Great Ontar were separated from you and Perlow, and slain, that would be disastrous. We survivors would have to tell Lady Admaria. It would break her heart, as it would ours. I'd hate to be the one to bear such grievous tidings," Adrigal declared with concern and solemnity. "I respectfully submit that we guards act as guards. None of us could bear to lose either of you."

"Thank you very much, my friend," Quinton smiled kindly as he turned to look at the fierce Ker-Mantid.

"I tell you what. Your King and I will endeavour to take good care of ourselves. Besides, there is Perlow," Ontar spoke with gratitude.

On their return to the main square, they discovered that six thousand shock troops together with two regiments of garrison soldiers had been sent to reinforce the north and east walls. The defenders on the west and south stood on the alert, ready for prompt action should they be assailed. However, quite a number were destined to assume the role of spectators all that day and watch the columns of cavalry and infantry encircle the town on their way to the assault points.

Although it was anticipated that at some time an attack would be made against the southern ramparts, the drawback facing the Relyanese was that there was insufficient room for their cavalry to manoeuvre to protect their infantry if the latter were employed against the wall and the gate. Quinton and Ontar were not unaware of the possibility that their adversaries might use barges to replace the mounts of the cavalry. Such a tactic would compel the defenders to commit valuable forces which might be required desperately elsewhere.

Perlow immediately rode off to the north gate to observe and gather information for his reports. Simultaneously

Allecenia and Admaria were wholly occupied in monitoring the tense situation. Ontar joined them, using his crystal to assist in the vital surveillance. He realised how dangerous the situation was becoming. Koreorgin had transmitted orders for another ten thousand troops to be sent into the fray.

"We'd better send another thousand shock troops to each wall," the sage said to his foster son.

"Colmar, see to that. When you've done it, tell Caejkan to divide the guard and send half of them to each wall. Cottis, my friend, I need your help," Quinton called to the governor who was about to depart for the north gate.

"Yes, Sire," the Deerait acknowledged, hastening over to his Supreme Overlord.

"Send couriers to the south and west walls. Tell them to send half their defenders equally to the north and east walls. At the same time organise the dummy replacements. I believe Sorcottis and your eldest son Mejchaert know what to do about that. They're on stand-by with the auxiliary reserves," Quinton stated.

"At once, Sire. Excellent idea Hanshair had," the commander of the Estyork garrison complimented, before hastening off in obedience to his Supreme Overlord's requests.

The relief shock troops and guards spread themselves along both walls under attack. They quickly found themselves involved in a very bitter struggle. Thousands of yelling, screaming Adiorenji were hauling ladders towards the walls, while their cavalry loosed a virtual rain of shafts at the ramparts. Many a defender thanked his gods for the helmet and armour covering his body. Arrows swished from every direction and matters began to look very serious indeed for the besieged.

Hanshair had suggested that straw dummies be made, dressed like garrison soldiers. His idea was that these could be used to fool their enemies into believing that a wall was fully manned, when a large proportion of its defenders were elsewhere. Those remaining had to move the dummies from time to time, lest the watching Relyanese realised that they were inanimate.

During one of the meetings with Cottis and his garrison officers on the third day after their arrival in Estyork, Quinton and Ontar had discussed the manning of the walls. The population of the town furnished the majority of the troops for its defence, and on them and the shock regiments would rest the major burden for the survival of the provincial capital. The auxiliaries were also involved, but their general training was not up to the standard of the average soldier in the city.

The total number of defenders was twenty three thousand. These men were required to protect six miles of battlements; theoretically, this approximated to two to every yard. However, when massive attacks were involved against one wall, reserve forces had to be made available, hence the vitally important tactic of the shock regiments being on the alert in the square throughout the day. Contingents of garrison and auxiliary troops also joined their steppe colleagues there, retiring to their quarters after sunset. The auxiliaries were spread evenly among their fellow Deerait combatants, although a number were used for the transport of food, drink and military equipment to the fighting men. They were also responsible for the removal of the dead, wounded and any enemy prisoners taken on the battlements.

Quinton told Cottis and his subordinates that the shock troops would be on active duty every minute throughout the entire siege. The fighting against such terrible odds would be extremely harsh. The ordinary garrison troops and the auxiliaries might not be relieved as often as they should during the day but, if at all possible, this would be done. Ontar pointed out that they had to husband their forces. Koreorgin could easily afford losses of ten to fifteen thousand, but similar losses among the defenders would spell disaster.

No one throughout Estyork, whether a city dweller or an outsider, thought for a moment of unconditional surrender. Long ago, the Adiorenji had been renowned for their cruelty in capturing a town, even when little or no resistance was offered. It was possible that their ruthlessness might have changed, but most doubted it. The citizens recollected the arrogance of Reorgin, Kinerth and other similar visitors. No one was prepared to risk the town being sacked, men murdered, women violated and children butchered, as had happened centuries before.

There were three principal factors responsible for this determination. The first was that the insidious threat of civil war had now erupted into reality. Relief was felt that hostilities had broken out, not because any of the Deeraits desired the conflict, but it brought a definite direction to pursue. The second and most important was the appearance of their dynamic, youthful Supreme Overlord. His personality, combined with obvious considerable intelligence, thrilled them whenever they saw him. They resolved to follow his leadership; also there was the aura of his three closest companions, especially those of Ontar and his spouse.

Thirdly, Quinton wore the beautiful belt and scabbard, containing the sword of the legendary Csiandag. Hesion might be far distant, but the capital of their people and united nation was the seat of the High Council. The notables selected for such important posts were only chosen from the finest leaders. Cottis, their provincial governor, possessed such qualities. Everyone in Sicruci was aware that he would have been elected to the High Court if he had not been so concerned about the defence of the region under his rule. It was rumoured abroad that he had been present when the decision was made to give the King of Rionder the sacred symbol of the Deerait tribe, which meant that the youth must have fulfilled some ancient requirement or prophecy in the scrolls.

"Can you manage here?" Quinton asked Ontar.

"Yes," the sage nodded. "You go. Take care, My Son."

"You know I shall," the youth replied, picking up his round red helmet, which covered the back of his neck, had openings for the ears and a metal covering for the nose.

Quinton bent to kiss his foster father on the cheek before going to do the same to Admaria. Allecenia adjusted her hood slightly so that he could kiss her forehead. She watched him stride confidently down the hall, greeting and encouraging everyone he passed. Olluinan's daughter held her fears down, and continued her scrying, while her beloved left with Adrigal, Onlestic and Helijaw.

Quinton and his three guards mounted up, and galloped directly to the north gate. The sound of hooves behind caused them to look around and see Cottis and ten of his personal guard racing after them. The governor had found both his scions, to whom he had transmitted the orders of the Supreme Overlord. His principal duty was to fight and exhort those manning the most dangerous defensive positions, unless his liege gave him other instructions.

Koreorgin was personally directing the assault against the north gate. The horbspan was dressed in a bright purple cloak, green tunic and yellow trousers, and sat astride a sturdy hecul

377

adorned with the finest accoutrements. Nearby, his son was mounted on an equally magnificent animal. His left leg still ached slightly from the wound he had received in the Wilderness.

The two were resolved to capture Estyork that day, if such could possibly be accomplished. Although Kinerth was impetuous, his father was more realistic, and nurtured the uncomfortable feeling that they might have to settle down and starve the inhabitants of the town into surrender. Assistance would appear in a few weeks time, when a large force from their allies was due to appear.

Koreorgin had launched his own troops precipitately to avenge the death of Reorgin. If the latter had not been slain, the Relyanese would have waited, as the chieftain had promised, for an army of Vilatmori and Dariondi, combined with Adiorenji from the other homelands. This would have demonstrated to the Deerait race that the three tribes appeared united in their resolve to enslave the most sensible section of their nation.

Quinton and Cottis reached the north gate and climbed the steps to the ramparts where they were greeted by Perlow. The Chofir quickly gave his assessment of the situation. He anticipated that their adversaries would follow a similar course of action to what had been attempted on the first afternoon. The enemy were pinning their hopes of victory on the massive forces to be employed in the assault on Estyork. When he had completed his report the royal guard departed for the east wall.

Arrows swished through the air overhead in a deadly black hail to rain down on the battlements and the street behind. The furious fire was returned by the defenders as best they could. Koreorgin raised his left hand, and fifty house carls began to manhandle a battering ram down the slight incline towards the massive gate. They shouted and yelled their battle cries, valiantly attempting the most perilous task of the attack.

Quinton risked a swift glance from the side and silently praised their courage. The carls bore shields, but the latter provided small protection against the accurate flow of shafts directed at them from the windows of the guard house. They were cut down. Their numbers dwindled alarmingly to such an extent that the horbspan was compelled to signal for more warriors to assist the survivors. The majority of these newcomers too were scythed down, but did succeed in

378

impelling the juggernaut towards the beckoning gateway before dying.

Their warlord, who had just received the news that his subterfuge in the southwestern corner of the town had failed, was further dismayed when the battering ram crashed into a trench, exactly like the one outside the west gate late on the first day. Koreorgin cursed, before sending a courier to the east side to inform those assailing that quarter not to use their juggernaut, for they had been awaiting the result of this attempt.

In his chagrin, the horbspan snapped a command to his son, which caused Kinerth to gallop off, accompanied by an escort of twenty house carls. He rode hard for the vast encampment. Once he reached it, he slowed down his hecul to a trot before guiding it between the long lines of tents. After a few minutes he reined up outside the dwelling of the principal sorcerer, who was awaiting his approach.

"Lepwhiros, you are to summon the Demon Hedial. Invoke his power to destroy the four gates into Estyork, and vanquish our enemies. My father desires this to be done quickly. How long will it take?" Kinerth demanded arrogantly, still wrathful that Ontar had put him under a spell. The enchantment had lasted until the precise instant his father had demanded the whereabouts of Reorgin.

"It will take several days. The rituals are complicated. Hedial is no minor demon, but one of awesome power. We have to be sure we keep control of him. If we are neglectful, Hedial will turn on us. We will be driven mad and our souls will be dragged screaming down to Hell. Make no mistake," the magician answered in apprehensive tones.

"Very well then. Get a move on," Kinerth snapped viciously.

Admaria had been scrying the enemy encampment to ascertain whether their foes were intending to employ some other equipment. She had noticed Koreorgin's scion hastening to the sorcerer's tent. The beautiful Ulgruffi communicated to her husband, Allecenia and Quinton what her intuition had revealed, regarding the occult operation to be undertaken. After scanning further afield, Ontar's spouse discovered Relyanese carpenters busily engaged in building wooden towers; she realised the purpose for which these constructions would be used, although they would not be ready that day.

"We have an excellent reserve of arrows, Sire," Cottis commented to his Supreme Overlord, as they crouched behind the ramparts.

"So have they, but the question is, when will they realise that their expenditure is greater than their replacement, even if they have wagons filled with shafts? They have only a certain number of fletchers. These craftsmen can only manufacture a certain number of shafts. Someone is bound to realise this," the King of Rionder responded, simultaneously mentioning this fact to his foster mother.

Admaria's voice broke silently into his mind to say, "Yes, you're absolutely right. I've been watching their archers. The rate of fire per person this morning is definitely a little slower than two days ago. You might not notice it from where you are. That's because of the greater numbers of bowmen. I anticipate really bitter attacks for the remainder of the morning. More this afternoon, but the later attacks will probably show a reduction in arrows. They just can't keep up that rate of fire, unless they intend to have a day or the greater part of a day without any assaults."

"I think they're going to make a major effort this morning. Hence the excessive use of shafts. I'm convinced they'll strike all four walls simultaneously, even the southern one, but not today. Besides, they don't have any idea how long this siege will last," Quinton commented thoughtfully.

"This is the usual Adiorenji attitude in such a situation. They like to have everything finished quickly. When things go against them, they become dull and just plod stolidly along," Admaria said.

"It was stupid of Koreorgin not to send in a troop of cavalry to check whether we had a trap before the north gate. He wouldn't have lost so many men."

"Felgorian did say the other day that Koreorgin tends to be dull witted, and often won't listen to his subordinates."

"I'll have to go. They're throwing ladders up again," her foster son said, breaking off the conversation.

Cottis followed in the wake of the youth, as Quinton sprinted past several archers to assist some auxiliaries. The latter had suffered casualties, and were frightened by the noise and clamour of the conflict. The sight of comrades being slain and toppling over the battlements, or backwards into the street, sickened them. Each wished that he was back on the estate of his lord of the manor, tending the fields or the livestock.

However, none thought of deserting his post. Their Supreme Overlord was willing to lay down his life for them, and he possessed a magnetic personality filled with love and resolution. They could not fail him. Suddenly, he was beside them, and a further surprise was the presence of the provincial governor in his fine armour and helmet, with the two crossed arrows insignia of Estyork on both.

Quinton and Cottis assisted two of the auxiliaries to manoeuvre a giant pole into position, before shoving powerfully to thrust a ladder away from the wall. Hanshair and his Ker-Mantid friends ducked under the pole, dodged a shower of arrows and used their long swords to fight three Adiorenji who had appeared between the embrasures. The royal guards paid no heed to the deadly shafts whizzing around them. Indeed, one bounced off Hanshair's breastplate without harming the Nai-Zind.

The steppe warriors crossed swords with their foes, and cut and thrust until the Relyanese were slain. Those at the base of the ladders saw their three comrades' corpses hurtling to the ground and felt very much dismayed. However, the carls and villeins knew better than to disobey the commands of their horbspan, for Koreorgin had the tendency to punish severely anyone who thwarted him. The infantry shrugged their shoulders and began to climb, praying to their deities for protection.

All along the battlements similar scenes were being enacted. Screaming, yelling Relyanese attempted to force their way onto the ramparts, only to be repelled by very determined men. The casualties mounted on both sides, but the besiegers were more than holding their own. Koreorgin's forces could make no headway in spite of their overwhelming superiority. The Adiorenji leader could have brought in more men, but did not do so yet.

The main source of trouble to the defenders was not the battering ram, or even the hostile enemy repeatedly attacking the walls; it was the incessant hail of shafts from the cavalry. They even welcomed the thuds which indicated that ladders had been raised near their positions. This meant hand to hand combat, for their own archers hardly dared risk looking over now to select a target. However, the vast numbers of mounted enemy did not loose their shafts once one of their own side had climbed to the top of his ladder lest they slay him by mistake.

During the assault on the west wall on the first afternoon the cavalry sagittaries had been containable. However, this morning on each battle front, they numbered eighteen thousand. Even if they had all been poor archers, the awesome volume of shafts the Relyanese loosed upwards was bound to cause increasing casualties. While he fought, Quinton tried to ponder this question. Something had to be done about the mounted troops.

Perlow, too, recognised the problem for he had the advantage of perceiving the situation on both fronts. His observational duties took a considerable time before he was able to report back to his paramount ranxem. The small warrior descended the east wall, going down one of the series of steps. At the bottom he ran and vaulted into the saddle of his steed which he had left in a stable nearby. The Chofir galloped at full speed until he reached the north gate. Hastily dismounting, he threw the reins to an auxiliary and raced up the stairs. Reaching the top he found himself roughly dragged into the guard-house by Adrigal.

"Hey, Perlow, don't go along there. There's arrows like hornets on the rampage. Everyone's under cover beneath the ramparts. Only time we move in is when the lull signifies a ladder. 'Sides which, Hanshair would only get mad if you got killed," the Ker-Mantid grinned.

"You great moron, you nearly choked me when you pulled me in here. Say, you can hardly see. It's really dark," the Chofir retorted.

"Course it is. They were even trying to get in the window a short time ago. We held them back while the auxiliaries brought a table from a house or shop in the street. How's things on the east wall?" Adrigal asked, becoming serious again.

"Just as bad as here. Still, as long as we keep our heads down, we should be alright. Where's Quinton?"

"With governor Cottis. About a third of the way along to the left when you leave here?"

"Why are you on your own?" Perlow asked, listening to the ominous thud of bolts against the table jammed into the window opening.

"Orders from the King a couple of minutes ago. If they try to get in, I'll be reinforced. I've four quivers of shafts to fire through the arrow slits at the cavalry. Just collected them when I saw you coming up the steps," Adrigal explained.

"The cavalry's the trouble. Get rid of them, or cause havoc in their ranks, then we can retaliate, instead of cowering here all day long. I've an idea. Look, take care of yourself," Perlow grinned with affection.

"You too, my friend. Wish Gordan was here. Just think how he and the army'll sort those Adiorenji out. Keep your head down," the Ker-Mantid cautioned kindly.

The observer crept out and crawled to the left past several corpses from which arrows protruded. He had no time to examine them, for he saw Quinton moving towards him, bent double. The youth smiled at the Chofir, who promptly made his report. The Lord of Deerait concurred that the Relyanese cavalry represented the main difficulty. Perlow paused for a moment before taking a deep breath and revealing his strategy for dealing with the hordes of hecul riders.

"That's a ghastly idea. But it's definitely worth a try. It'll take some time to collect the material. I'll organise it. If it works, and I believe it will, the cavalry will find themselves in dire straits," Quinton praised the Chofir, before asking the latter the whereabouts of the nearest company of auxiliaries.

"There's quite a number of them, about a hundred. They're sheltering in reserve in the stables below with the heculs. I saw them when I dismounted."

"Good. They'll do excellently. I want them to fetch water when they can," the monarch nodded, before telling Perlow to accompany him, for his normal escort was scattered all along the battlements, exhorting and encouraging the defenders.

While they proceeded to find the auxiliaries, the King of Rionder contacted his foster father in the judgment hall by telepathy, and disclosed the observer's stratagem. Ontar expressed his agreement that the plan be adopted. It was a harsh measure, which would not only save the lives of their fighting men, but might also deal a devastating and demoralising blow to the Adiorenji. If it were successful the attackers would have to employ another device to protect their infantry, provided they could think of one.

Beckoning Colmar, the eminent sage gave him concise orders to which the Melcogh listened intently. The royal guard then called a garrison officer, requesting the latter to obtain transport, materials and assistance. The Deerait promised there would be the minimum of delay in accomplishing what was required.

Meanwhile on the walls, massive assaults were being launched with increased frequency. The defenders had barely time to repulse one attack before another followed. Hand to hand combat occurred all along the battlements, for the large number of Relyanese involved were beginning to obtain footholds on the ramparts themselves. The boiling water, with its accompanying misery, had been used up very early and the fate of Estyork depended on the courage of the fighting men on the north and east walls.

The only slight relief in the midst of the continuous activity was when the cavalry had to slacken their rate of fire to avoid striking their own comrades high over their heads. Although this meant intense fighting at close quarters, Quinton and his troops found that they had two slim advantages. The first was, of course, the lower volume of shafts from the masses of mounted men below; the second was that they were able to use their own bows with considerable accuracy.

Many Adiorenji perished for the instant they attempted to clamber over the parapets into Estyork arrows were directed in their direction. A shaft in the face, chest or shoulder sufficed to cause the victim to release his grip on the stone battlement or ladder and topple with a scream to crash onto the ground. Those who succeeded in gaining a foothold on the battlements quickly discovered that tall dark haired soldiers with a more than ordinary grasp of swordsmanship awaited them.

The steppe warriors displayed a skill born of long practice

in archery and swordplay. They fought savagely, hacking and cutting their foes down. Any of the latter who asked for quarter or who sustained wounds were conducted or helped away by the auxiliaries. Although the fighting was intense, the defenders lost very few men in close combat for the royal guard of Rionder and the shock troops bore the brunt of the conflict. The intensive training which they had all undergone in the distant forests proved its immense value. They were superbly fit and strong and their reactions were very swift, as any Relyanese encountering them found out to his cost.

In the guardhouse Adrigal used his arrows with great accuracy. From the safety of an arrow slit to the right of the window, he struck down sixty four enemy cavalry from his position without being detected. However, when more extensive attacks were launched against the north wall the Ker-Mantid heard the sound of four ladders thudding against the table barrier. He drew his sword and waited for them to break into his sanctuary.

When Quinton was advised by his foster mother that heavier assaults were about to be launched, his immediate reaction was to defend the gate. If any of the enemy succeeded in capturing it, they could quickly provide access for the hordes outside. Admaria told him that she had already sent couriers to inform Rahamb, Souriin and the other commanders on the east wall of the imminent onslaught. Ontar's spouse had been scrying behind the cavalry lines and had noticed infantry platoons picking up the enormous number of ladders placed there earlier. She affirmed that similar activity was occurring on the eastern side of Estyork.

The intense hail of arrows was suddenly reduced after bugle calls. Hordes of foot-soldiers shrieked their battle cries and raced forward to the high walls. The defenders promptly loosed flights of shafts high into the air, which rained down into their packed ranks. The Relyanese suffered wounds or death; hands clawed at arrows which sprouted from their bodies, while their comrades behind ran forward into a second volley. More fell but large numbers remained who finally managed to throw their ladders into position.

Rocks cascaded down to stun or crush those ascending. Poles thrust back ladders as quickly as men were capable of performing the action, but many of the enemy were destined to reach the battlements. On both fronts the commanders realised that the issue would have to be settled on the ramparts themselves, and prepared their soldiers accordingly. Koreorgin sat astride his hecul, watching the dramatic unfolding of events; he believed that victory just might be in his grasp.

Quinton snapped crisp efficient orders. His steppe warriors adopted appropriate stations to face the massive onslaught. Cottis and his garrison officers had taken considerable heart from the bearing of their Supreme Overlord and his elite troops. The Sicrucian commanders knew that they were facing tremendous odds, but their morale was high and they encouraged their subordinates. The result was that no sooner had one of the Relyanese clambered onto the battlements than he and his comrades encountered stiff resistance.

"Hanshair! Onlestic! Helijaw! Follow me! Adrigal's on his own in the guard-house. They're bound to attack it. The outside should be alright. Our shock troops are there. The window is the weakest point. They'll attempt to come through that way. Let's go!" Quinton exhorted his royal guards.

With his trio of loyal soldiers at his heels, the King of Rionder hurried towards the gate about fifty yards distant. Between them and their objective scores of defenders were engaged in mortal combat. A white Adiorenji jumped down from the battlements. Quinton promptly fended off his sword thrust, before kicking him in the stomach and striking him full in the face with the boss of his shield.

"We'll take care of him, Sire!" Unyamed shouted, beckoning to two auxiliaries to remove the unconscious soldier.

The monarch nodded his gratitude, before he ran on and finally reached the guard-house. He and his three companions entered the small room quickly. Adrigal smiled with pleasure at seeing his beloved liege. He put a finger to his lips to signify silence, for the Relyanese outside were battering the table top to force it inwards. Their strenuous efforts were not far from success, for dust and daylight were beginning to appear on the right side of the opening.

There was a swish, followed by a strangled cry. An arrow fired from the wall had struck one of the attackers. He slumped sideways and pitched to the right, before falling headlong to break his neck on the dusty ground below. There were several of his comrades still on the ladder. They felt fear gnawing in the pits of their stomachs, and their mouths were dry. Terror clutched insidiously at their hearts, chilling their minds. The ghastly sight of their companion tumbling past caused them to gape with horror, for each thought how easily it could have been himself.

They held their shields up pathetically, while their thoughts of a glorious victory were completely banished. It was a pity that Koreorgin was not with them. It might make their precious horbspan think again. One of them clambered to take his dead comrade's place and began to push with all the strength he could muster against the top of the wooden table. There were four Adiorenji employed in this labour, and two more were slain by deadly arrows before it was suddenly dragged back into the guardroom. The unfortunate attackers had little time to defend themselves before tall fierce warriors bellowed, "Quinton for Rionder! Quinton for Estyork!" and slashed at them with long sharp swords.

The enemy on the top of the ladders were slain almost immediately. All four were decapitated. They toppled backwards, lifeless, arterial blood spouting in crimson fountains. In their fall the cadavers caused another six to lose their grip and crash to the ground. Five of those dislodged perished from broken necks, the sixth being fortunate to land heavily on a pile of corpses, sustaining no more than a broken arm.

An officer below bellowed orders for those on the ladders to proceed. The serfs and house carls felt almost naked, perched forty feet above their superior, whom they silently cursed. Nevertheless, they reluctantly advanced. Two of them reached the guardroom window and managed to put their hands on the sill. One brandished his sword, which was immediately smashed back by Adrigal's weapon. The force of the blow caused him to drop his blade which hurtled, point downwards, to strike the officer in the left eye, continuing through to emerge bloodily from the back of his head.

The Relyanese closed his eyes, expecting to receive a death thrust. However, his companion had hastily descended several rungs. When the Ker-Mantid saw this, he dropped his sword and leaned out to grasp the enemy soldier by the throat. The latter was too astonished to attempt resistance, even when the strong warrior dragged him inside.

"Now, you just sit over there. Be good," Helijaw admonished their captive in the Common Speech.

"Yes, Sir," the Relyanese gulped, scuttling to the corner

indicated.

"Well done, Adrigal," Quinton said, patting the guard on the shoulder, which pleased the latter considerably.

"You, Adiorenji! You, on the ladders! It's death if you try to fight your way in here. If you stay out there, our archers will kill you eventually. If you retreat, your officers will punish you severely. So, come in here peacefully, and be our prisoners," Helijaw shouted through the open window.

"This is crazy," Onlestic grinned.

There was a moment's pause before two more heads appeared cautiously over the sill. The Relyanese held their swords high so that those in the guardroom could see their intentions. They then tossed them inside with their shields, before clambering into the room to surrender. Altogether fifty five of the enemy yielded and were taken away into captivity. When their superiors realised what was happening they screeched at their subordinates to return to the ground. The guard-room window was immediately resealed with the table, after the ladders had been tossed aside.

"That was simple," Adrigal commented with satisfaction.

"That was entirely due to you," Quinton smiled.

"Somehow I hated to think of slaying them piecemeal. They had no chance. I was going to offer them the opportunity to surrender, but Helijaw felt the same," the Ker-Mantid explained.

"I know. We've had a rough time with all those arrows they've been firing. Those men climbing the ladders into such a confined space as that window would have been slaughtered. I'm glad they yielded. Most praiseworthy, Helijaw. Oh, Perlow, how's the fighting going?" Quinton asked as the Chofir entered. The latter had resumed his observational duties after escorting his liege to the auxiliaries.

"We're doing fairly well. The Adiorenji are less resolute. All positions on both walls are secure."

"Good. How are our losses? Any idea?"

"Not too many. We've suffered some casualties of course. Mainly Deeraits and auxiliaries. Steppe and royal guards, very few. There's a lull at present. I think they are about to pull back temporarily," Perlow replied.

"I hope the materials for your scheme arrive soon. Then we'll take care of the cavalry," Quinton stated.

"We heard of your plan. You sadistic little Chofir," Hanshair praised, patting his comrade on the back. "The Relyanese won't like it at all."

At that moment, Allecenia spoke to Quinton, saying, "The enemy are falling back to reform for another assault. Ontar, Admaria and I saw what happened in the guard-room. Believe it or not, My Dearest, Souriin and Rahamb were in the guard-room above the east gate. They did precisely the same. They captured thirty four before the enemy commanders discovered what was happening."

"Excellent. How long do you estimate before the next major assault?"

"We three believe intuitively about an hour at the least. If you go outside, you'll find the arrows have just about ceased. The last hail of shafts was to cover the withdrawal of the ladder parties. They've had enough for the moment."

"And it's almost midday. The auxiliaries are starting to distribute hot food and water for everyone on the battlements," Allecenia's beautiful melodic voice said.

"Fine. I'll organise matters here," Quinton acknowledged.

During the interval before the battle recommenced, the dead and wounded were removed; reserves replaced the casualties; the auxiliary troops brought nourishment to the fighting men. The latter were pleased to receive sustenance and to be able to stand erect without the deadly rain of shafts to which they unfortunately had become accustomed. Most important of all, the materials to implement Perlow's plan were being brought and apportioned along the walls.

After he had eaten, Quinton decided to tour the troops on both ramparts. He descended the stairs, mounted his hecul and crossed to the southeastern corner. Hanshair, the two Ker-Mantids, Perlow and Helijaw proudly escorted their paramount ranxem. Rahamb, Souriin and those on the east wall were heartened by his brief visit. The Estyork garrison soldiers and the auxiliaries were especially pleased to see their Supreme Overlord, whose presence cheered them immensely.

Quinton's clothing was stained with the blood of those whom he had slain in the frantic skirmishes earlier. He contrasted dramatically with Koreorgin, who was as elegant as when he had left his tent that morning. On the other hand, Kinerth had ridden to join the cavalry on his return from the Adiorenji encampment. After he had spent some time in directing their action, he had dismounted and advanced with the infantry.

Whatever might be said about Kinerth's personal attitude, he was no coward. Although his mobility was severely hampered because of his stiff leg, the son of the Relyanese leader realised the awful peril and dread which the foot soldiers faced on the way to the battlements. He urged them forward, saying that the outcome of the siege depended on their valiant efforts. Even though he was generally disliked because of his arrogance, the horbspan's scion was sincerely believed when he declared that he would have led the assault if he had been fit.

Rahamb and Souriin were especially delighted to see Quinton, and receive his praise for their courageous actions. Once the King of Rionder had completed his tour of the battlements and returned to his position above the north gate, his forces felt their strength renewed. They believed more than ever that somehow they would emerge victorious against such vastly superior numbers.

In the meantime, the materials essential for Perlow's plan had been distributed to all the steppe troops scattered along both the north and east battlements. Their Deerait comrades felt no rancour at this, for they had quickly realised that their allies were far more proficient archers than they themselves were. It only remained for the Adiorenji to recommence their assault. Then the effectiveness of the Chofir's stratagem would become apparent.

Quinton ascended the pointed roof of the guard-house, and looked around. The sun was shining brilliantly from an azure sky in which only a few fleecy clouds were moving slowly westwards, blown by the gentle breeze. For a few moments, he looked north to the dark distant line marking the beginning of the vast forests of the Rionder Valley. It hardly seemed that several weeks had passed since he had ridden from there into Estyork.

He smiled reflectively, and briefly glanced at the myriad of rooftops behind. The fate of the inhabitants of the capital of Sicruci had become intertwined with his destiny; the youth had no wish to fail them since the Relyanese would exact a harsh retribution for the suffering they had sustained during the siege. The four Deerait tribes would become his subjects, which Quinton realised, another vital stage on the long, arduous road to world empire.

The monarch momentarily smiled to himself, recollecting how Allecenia and he had been puzzled by the strange fact that

Ontar had stated that crystals were not to be taken to the Occult Dimension. When he had asked his foster father the reason, the archmage had replied that Hedial could have used the vibrations from scrying as a channel for assault. There was a very strong possibility that the Lord of Iniquities would have caused the wondrous globes to explode in the faces of his adversaries, blinding if not actually killing them. Such was one of the differences between the Occult Dimension and their own physical plane.

Quinton turned back to the north once again, this time looking towards the Adiorenji lines. Although the ground below was littered with the corpses of the slain, the wounded men had been removed when the attack was broken off. Hanshair climbed up the outside ladder to stand beside his monarch, and likewise gazed at the grim scene below.

"What do you think will happen now, Sire?" the Nai-Zind asked respectfully.

"Oh, they'll attack once more. They may have sent for more cavalry from their encampment. Koreorgin will be exasperated at our stubbornness. If Perlow's plan succeeds, and I'm certain it will, I think the attack will be broken off for today. They'll ask for a truce to remove the wounded and the dead," Quinton replied. He looked over towards the River Avidnive glittering far away beyond the trees where the sun had caused its water to sparkle and attract his attention.

"They're about to start another assault. We believe they'll attempt to ignite the north and east gates. They've been preparing portable braziers. With enough fire arrows, it's just conceivable the gates could begin to smoulder. Colmar's sent a courier to advise Rahamb. Make certain you've enough water on hand to douse the gates," Ontar said telepathically.

"Thanks. I will. We did anticipate such a move. Gordan's idea one night last winter, if I recollect rightly," Quinton responded.

"Yes, it was. Once the fighting recommences, more cavalry regiments will be coming from the enemy camp," his foster father stated, before adding, "but I know we shall succeed. Look, I'm going to the east gate. I'll check on the water situation there. Admaria and Allecenia will control things from here. I've a feeling that this attack won't last too long."

"Yes, I do believe you're right," his foster son agreed, breaking off their silent conversation.

The King of Rionder gave quick instructions to Hanshair, which the latter left to carry out. Quinton remained where he was, looking again towards the vast northern forests. Somewhere beyond the trees his godfather, Gordan, was approaching with eighty thousand highly trained troops and should relieve Estyork within three days. Then the tide of conflict would flow against the besiegers, for it was improbable that they would be capable of making a stand against the powerful, resolute, disciplined steppe warriors.

Several minutes passed during which Quinton took the opportunity to talk to Allecenia. She was very pleased to learn that her beloved had not sustained the slightest injury and boosted his morale by saying that she was absolutely convinced that the inhabitants of Estyork were fully behind him. Olluinan's daughter reported that Admaria was maintaining a regular surveillance on the area beyond the Adiorenji encampment where carpenters were fully employed in the construction of the tall towers.

Suddenly bugle calls resounded from the ranks of their foes on the north and east sides of Estyork. Quinton bade farewell to Allecenia before hastening back down to the battlements. Hanshair met his monarch at the foot of the ladder. The commander of the royal guard informed his Overlord that sufficient water was available to douse the gate in the event of fiery arrows being used. The builders of Estyork had had the foresight to provide channels above all four entrances to the town, down which quantities of liquid could be poured to extinguish any fires from without or within which might endanger the strong gates.

Once more the Adiorenji cavalry galloped to battle outside the high walls of Estyork. They were resolved in their endeavour to finish the siege that afternoon. To this end ten thousand extra horsemen and eight thousand more infantry were just leaving the camp for each of the two walls being assailed. With these fresh troops to supplement the soldiers already involved, Koreorgin hoped that sunset would see his forces ransacking the provincial capital. When that occurred the Vilatmori and Dariondi would scarcely dare complain at his premature launching of the civil war against the Deeraits in Sicruci.

The hostile cavalry swiftly charged into position, and the defenders were once again compelled to cower against the stone of the battlements. However, this time they were awaiting the signal to retaliate, hopeful that the massed mounted columns would receive a drastic lesson. Quinton realised this from where he stood inside the guard-house, listening to Admaria's concise details on the positions of the approaching infantry.

The Relyanese trotted towards their designated objectives. Although the majority bore the customary long ladders, quite a number hastened directly towards the north and east gates. Except for a few who carried charcoal braziers on metal poles like stretchers, everyone bore a bow, a quiver of arrows and several strips of cloth soaked in oil. Their intention was obvious to those scrying from within the town.

Under cover of the immense volume of missiles directed at the battlements, the infantry sagittaries tied pieces of rag to their shafts. They dipped the arrows into the hot brazier, which action resulted in igniting the cloth, before firing their shafts at the gate on their side of Estyork. Scores of burning arrows arched through the air to strike the obstructions thwarting their access into the city.

The significance of the thuds was not lost on the defenders immediately above the entrances. Allecenia and Admaria each scried a gateway, advising Quinton and Ontar respectively about the effectiveness of the burning shafts. Eventually the Supreme Overlord of Deerait and his foster father nodded to the soldiers on both sides of the guard-houses. The latter immediately manoeuvred the huge cauldrons until large quantities of water cascaded into specific gullies cut into the stone. The liquid splashed downwards and emerged to spray the gates copiously. The Adiorenji were very much dismayed when they saw their arrows being extinguished and the wooden entrances being thoroughly soaked.

The defenders hastily refilled the cauldrons from barrels nearby and awaited the next move. However, their adversaries did not have time to think of any counter measures, for Perlow's plan was put into immediate effect. All along the battlements, the command had been passed to act on the signal which the King of Rionder would give. Every Mescarg steppe soldier waited patiently, eager to attempt the stratagem which might break the dominance of the Relyanese massed cavalry in the siege.

Suddenly three mighty rotar horn blasts resounded over the

roofs of Estyork and the violent battlefield before the north and east walls. In response to the call given by his paramount ranxem, each warrior performed a similar action to the one which the hostile infantry had accomplished against the city gates. They ignited the oil-soaked rags fastened to their shafts, notched their arrows to their bows, and drew the cords back. After swift glances between the embrasures to select suitable targets, dependent on the volume of hostile fire, the bolts were released on the way to their marks.

To the astonishment of Koreorgin hundreds of fiery arrows arched through the air. The Adiorenji leader was very surprised for several moments for he could not think what the defenders' intentions were. He soon learned and with this knowledge came the destruction of his cavalry as a protective screen for the infantry. New tactics would have to be instituted; perhaps the towers being built by his carpenters might give the advantage.

Perlow had conceived a very simple but drastic plan. Shafts fired into the thick of the horsemen would slay some of the enemy but the majority would still remain to fight. Mounts would be killed or wounded; again the cavalry would continue to fight. However, fiery shafts shot into the rumps of the heculs would panic the animals, and that was precisely what occurred. Havoc resulted beyond the walls.

The effect of an arrow in the side or rump was bad enough. A burning shaft, which penetrated to the blazing rag, was devastating. The searing of its flesh, combined with the pain from the missile protruding from its body, was too much for any hecul. Every animal not fatally struck bucked and reared in its torment, kicking and lashing out at its fellows. It proved entirely unmanageable, for the creature threw its head round repeatedly in vain attempts to use its tied yellow beak to remove the source of its terrible irritation.

Scores of burning heculs stampeded to and fro. Others raced round in circles, desperately attempting to eliminate their agony. Many riders, unable to keep their saddles, were tossed to the ground. A large number were trampled to death or injured in the chaos which reigned. The majority of the cavalry were still mounted on uninjured steeds, but the stench of singeing hide and the terrible panicking of their fellow wounded creatures caused their mounts to react in a similar fashion. In less than a minute the flow of arrows from the

Relyanese riders had completely ceased.

The defenders immediately took full advantage of their enemies' distress and misfortune. While half of the steppe warriors continued to fire burning missiles into the heculs below, the remainder, aided by the Estyork garrison troops and auxiliaries present, loosed ordinary arrows directly at the cavalry and the infantry as fast as they possibly could. The Relyanese foot soldiers on the ladders were scythed down while their comrades on the ground, who had either been attacking the two gates, or who had been preparing to assault the ramparts, found themselves in very dire straits.

They were slaughtered by well aimed arrows from above, for their customary avenues of escape through the cavalry were blocked by demented heculs. Very few attempted to run the gauntlet for they dreaded being trampled underfoot by the panic-stricken animals; also their eyes could not penetrate the thick, grimy, dust clouds being created. Instead they huddled against the base of the city walls, holding their shields to protect themselves from the devastatingly accurate bowmen above, and praying that no steeds would blunder into them.

Koreorgin could scarcely believe his eyes. His fairly disciplined force had crumbled into absolute chaos. He quickly ordered his buglers to sound the retreat. As Perlow had anticipated, this action was futile. Everything depended on the cavalry and the latter were in total disarray and despair. However, the unfortunate beasts suddenly took it into their pointed heads to race off into the distance, believing that such a course would restore their normal equilibrium.

The delighted defenders witnessed most of the Relyanese cavalry employed against them disappearing in all directions. The horbspan cursed and ranted but there was nothing he could do. Many of the riders on the east side clung to the backs of their mounts, for the creatures refused to acknowledge the pulling on their reins. They held on, even when the animals galloped headlong across the wharves and tumbled into the River Avidnive.

The soldiery on the southeastern ramparts obtained an excellent view of this circumstance, and were highly amused by the whole proceedings. Their loud laughter annoyed the Adiorenji but the latter could do nothing about it; they were too busy trying to save themselves from drowning in the water churned up by their terrified chargers. Scores of men and heculs indeed perished in the river but the majority of the cavalry managed to remove their feet from the stirrups and swim or wade to safety while their steeds continued to the far bank.

The latter herd of heculs found a depression up which they climbed to the fresh countryside beyond. Much later in the afternoon riders were sent from the Relyanese encampment to round up any stray mounts they could find. Parties rode for miles; although they did find most of their animals, a considerable number had departed for areas unknown. When the siege ended, many of the agricultural workers and their overlords found the heculs wandering on their lands and promptly became their new owners, cleansing any wounds the creatures had sustained.

Koreorgin had the unpleasant problem of moving hastily from the path of a large bunch of stampeding animals. One of their riders was Kinerth, and his father gaped as his son disappeared in the direction of the orchards on the Hesion road. His scion and those accompanying him in his pell-mell dash did not return to the camp until sunset for their mounts proved to be wholly unrestrainable for several hours.

Once the cavalry had departed, the infantry began to creep away from the walls. They anticipated further hails of arrows, but their fears were groundless. Buglers on the ramparts blew the ceasefire. From their respective positions Quinton and Rahamb called down that they would be unharmed and that they were to tend their wounded. The Adiorenji were extremely grateful, even in their moment of deepest depression. The Lord of Deerait also commanded some of the cavalry, who had successfully controlled their uninjured steeds, to hasten back to their encampment and return with physicians and wagons. Koreorgin, although still wrathful, grudgingly consented to a truce.

This gracious action caused much comment in the ranks of the enemy, as it had done two nights before. The north and east gates opened; wains were driven out to bring back the slain who had tumbled from the battlements during the conflict. Once more, assistance was given by the tall, dark warriors from the Mescarg steppes to the Adiorenji on the battlefield.

The south gate also opened, because many Relyanese cavalry lay stunned along the wall there too. Those defenders who had been highly amused by the stampede into the River Avidnive were, nevertheless, extremely active in bringing out boats to save as many men as possible from drowning. Some of those rescued tried to resist at first but when they were informed that a truce had been arranged they gladly accepted the helping hands proffered.

By late afternoon the enemy dead and wounded had been removed to the camp on the western side of Estyork and the gates were closed once more. Cottis and Ricel took the first opportunity to converse with their Supreme Overlord, to thank him personally for implementing the plan which had so totally devastated the Adiorenji cavalry. Quinton acknowledged their courtesy and called Perlow forward. He explained that it was the Chofir who had proposed the shattering stratagem as well as giving the alarm before dawn which had foiled the spies' plans.

"Then I thank you on behalf of my town and my province, Perlow. The results this afternoon were magnificent, beyond all our expectations," the governor of Sicruci spoke sincerely in his judgment hall.

"I thank you kindly," the steppe warrior inclined his head graciously.

"You must be rewarded. What do you say, Hanshair, my friend?" the commander of the Estyork garrison asked the royal guard, who was standing behind his King.

"I wholeheartedly agree. The Lord of Deerait and I have already discussed this. Also, several of my command and some of your own officers have expressed a similar sentiment. They reckon anyone clever enough to devise a plan to deal with those hails of arrows should be rewarded," the Nai-Zind smiled his answer.

"Perlow, I have decided you shall be promoted from section commander to second-in-command of the royal guard under Hanshair. You have the ability for this. It means you are now the third most important officer in the guard after Hanshair and Gordan, who is its captain as he was under my father, King Quintar. I would also like you to have the belt, sword and scabbard I wore before the High Court gave me those of Csiandag," Quinton said kindly.

"I endorse that. They belonged to a Ker-Mantid slain in the battle when Admaria and I first took Quinton to stay with the Nai-Zind." The archmage squeezed the Chofir's shoulder very fondly.

"Thank you. But I only wanted to help. It's enough that it

worked. It helped to save lives on our side."

"We know. We also realise that now we can fight back more effectively the next time they attack. And so do they. We are all proud of you. Deeraits, steppe warriors, Ontar, Allecenia, Quinton and I. And you saved Quinton's life two days ago," Admaria smiled charmingly.

"I shall be most pleased to wear these accoutrements," the Chofir acknowledged shyly, embarrassed that such eminent personages wished to honour him.

"And Ricel and I shall give you a special gift," Cottis praised.

"You have also given us another pleasant surprise, Perlow," the hooded Lady declared in her wonderful tones as she came across to stand beside the King of Rionder.

"What is that, Allecenia?" the Chofir enquired, puzzled by her statement.

"I'm certain Ontar will confirm this. There will be no fighting whatsoever tomorrow. The Relyanese will require time to reorganise their forces and also to plan," Olluinan's daughter replied, holding Quinton's right hand.

"Yes. My intuition tells me the same. Still, we'll post adequate patrols on the battlements. It will help keep our troops alert," the wizard nodded.

"And that means Perlow has not only given us the greater part of the afternoon free from attack, he has also given us the whole of tomorrow, Sire. A lot of lives will be saved," Hanshair stated solemnly with pride in his comrade.

"And that makes his efforts more than worthwhile," Quinton concurred.

In the Adiorenji encampment, Koreorgin, Rinthalt, Chsingof and the other chieftains still alive began to reorganise their demoralised forces. The casualties were heavy, far more than had been expected. Now that their principal cavalry tactic had failed a different strategy would have to be devised. Future assaults on the walls would involve higher fatalities. The leaders had to decide whether to proceed with an active campaign, or to settle down to a long siege and starve the town into surrender.

Parties were sent abroad to search for and bring back the scattered heculs which had dislodged their riders. The physicians were fully occupied in tending the wounded troops; quite a number of them put into practice some of the novel treatments which the strange soldiers of the King of Rionder had demonstrated. They were kept busy administering to those unfortunates who had sustained broken limbs from the violent reactions of the heculs to the flaming arrows.

When night came, several blustery showers added to the melancholy within the encampment. Privately, Chsingof and Rinthalt regretted the impetuosity of Koreorgin in commencing hostilities against the Deeraits. If he had only kept to the secret arrangements and waited for the forces being raised by the Vilatmori, the Dariondi, and the other Adiorenji, Estyork might have proved easier to capture.

Although they had sufficient fresh troops to commence another assault against the battlements standing between them and their objective, Koreorgin and his subordinates agreed that there should be no fighting on the following day. The morning afterwards would be time enough; every man capable of bearing arms would be rested and also the towers would be ready for use. If they were not, the carpenters had been promised an excruciating form of torture, which threat their horbspan would not be tardy in carrying out.

Gordan, Casterandir and Turubin halted their army an hour after sunset that same day. Fires were built, food was cooked and the vast force settled down for six hours rest. The Riondese general had decided that a longer break than his force had had since the commencement of their arduous journey was due. The troops would gladly have continued their long march. However much Gordan wished to press forward, common-sense dictated that this halt was essential. At the end of their trek, they would have to fight a pitched battle.

The Riondese and his two Polingsi friends slept in their cots in the same tent. Before closing his eyes, the supreme general of Quinton's army thought back to the last time he had seen his wife. It had been just before dawn on the morning after the shock troops had departed. He had kissed his children fondly before embracing her. The beautiful Nai-Zind held her husband close for a long moment.

"The time for farewell is here again," she murmured softly, with a brave smile.

"I know. Larida will come and visit from time to time, when she's not with Enmaxine. You like Elestia, don't you?" Gordan said tenderly.

"Yes. I most certainly do. She and I are firm friends. I got to know her when you were fighting the Casmans on the steppes. Why?"

"I'm going south like Felgorian. How would you like her to come and stay with you? Her children are grown up. She has two sons leaving with the army. I arranged this some weeks ago. She agreed, but it's up to you."

"Oh, that would be marvellous! I really would enjoy having her here. She adores the children. They like her too. When will she be coming?"

"Actually, I sent a courier to her last night. I asked her to come about now," Gordan replied.

"Good. That was kind of you. I know I shouldn't ask this." Sheralex paused.

"I don't know either. But as soon as it's thought safe you and the children, Elestia, and the Polingsi families will be brought south to Deerait."

"I shall be patient. You take care of yourself."

"I will. I've you to come back to. You know I don't seem to remember a time when you weren't part of my life," Gordan murmured, before kissing her tenderly.

A few moments later, there was a sound of a wagon approaching and a sentinel knocked on the door. When he was told to enter, the household guard said that the Lady Elestia had arrived and he would be pleased to assist her with her belongings. Gordan consented to this courteous offer before he and his wife went outside to greet Felgorian's spouse. She was a very handsome woman and was renowned for her valiant actions during the fall of Rionder.

Elestia smiled kindly at the couple and remembered briefly the days when Gordan had been a mere youth. Now he was the principal commander of the King of Rionder's forces, which numbered almost a quarter of a million men under arms. The giant nine foot tall warrior kissed her on the cheek, as did Sheralex. Felgorian's wife nodded to Gordan who embraced his spouse before bidding them farewell. He mounted his linz and gave a wave of his right hand before galloping off into the trees accompanied by his loyal escort.

"We'll see them again," Elestia murmured softly, her thoughts with her husband far to the south.

"Yes, we shall. Have you had some breakfast?" Sheralex asked, glad that she would have company during the long days

400

and nights of waiting.

As Gordan drifted off to sleep, his final thoughts returned to Estyork and the civil war in the south. Although he was naturally concerned about Quinton, Ontar and Admaria, he used the mystical techniques taught by the two Ulgruffi, and learned intuitively that all was going remarkably well in the beleaguered city. During the morning Casterandir and Turubin had concurred with his belief that the defenders were extremely hard pressed. Consequently they had increased their rate of progress. However, by early afternoon the trio suddenly sensed that the tide had turned and the attackers were being routed.

The fourth day was a most welcome interlude for the inhabitants of Estyork and the troops defending the town. In the morning, orders were transmitted from the judgment hall that all weapons and equipment were to be cleaned and checked. Officers from the different regiments supervised their commands, and reported back that morale was very high indeed. The certain knowledge that the massed Relyanese cavalry had lost its domination of the fighting had given the Sicrucians new courage and resolution.

Quinton, Ontar, Cottis and Ricel planned their strategy for the following day, conscious that Estyork would be relieved the morning after. However, they did not permit themselves to become complacent since that was the start of the slippery path to error and ruination. When they had discussed and agreed on all points, the high ranking commanders were called in to be briefed and to comment on what they were required to accomplish.

Admaria and Allecenia maintained a continuous scrying of the Adiorenji encampment. From what they had been able to perceive, they reckoned that two towers would be completed by mid-afternoon. Consequently, the defenders could expect major assaults on two walls, probably the west and north since those were the nearest points of access for the enemy. Quinton and his foster father were also convinced that a feint attack would be made against the east wall.

"How long before more towers are ready for use, Sire?" Yltormik asked.

"Two days. Then Koreorgin will most likely launch an all out assault on all four walls. We should be able to repel the towers tomorrow. Koreorgin has tried attacks against one wall, then two walls. Tomorrow three walls. So, the day after, weather conditions permitting, we believe he will try all four walls simultaneously," the King of Rionder answered.

"And that's the day Estyork will be relieved," Sorcottis nodded.

"Anyone want to make a comment?" Ontar asked, looking

keenly at the officers in their various uniforms.

"Yes, Sir," Souriin said respectfully, evincing the military instinct which one day would make him a brilliant general in the service of his Emperor and earn him the soubriquet 'The Bold'.

"Quinton thought you would. Go ahead," the archmage smiled kindly.

"When the Relyanese attack all four walls, this naturally includes the south. If they pass beneath its battlements they'll have very little room to manoeuvre. Since they know we'll use fire arrows to stampede their cavalry, they are not going to squander men and heculs in a situation where they would have no hope. It's pointless. But they'll wish to keep valuable defenders busy." Souriin paused, looking round at the other officers, who were taller than he was.

"Pray continue," Cottis said in attentive tones.

"Well, sir, they'll keep our troops pinned down there. To do this, they'll have to use barges and any kind of boats suitable for the purpose of firing arrows over the wharves. The enemy will have protection. That's all they'll want to do. There's no point in using burning arrows to repel them. All they'll do is douse everything with water from the River Avidnive. So, they'll be gathering boats upstream," the young Hedunon explained.

"And that's precisely what they have been doing. They're getting a fleet of barges ready. As you are aware, Admaria and Allecenia have been scrying the enemy camp. I, too, have been using my crystal, but further afield. Just after dawn this morning I caught sight of a fleet of barges being floated downstream. The boats are about twenty five miles distant. Their intention is obvious. Very good, Souriin," Ontar praised the second-in-command of the shock regiments.

"So what do we do?" Ricel wondered.

"Nothing at all. Just let them get on with it," Quinton stated to looks of surprise on many faces around the table in the great judgment hall, on which maps and diagrams were laid.

"I understand. The more the Adiorenji are dispersed, the simpler will be the task of your army, Sire!" Ricel exclaimed.

"Correct. I shall ponder some more about the south wall. But remember this. It is our army," the King of Rionder stressed.

The next morning dawned, with dull leaden clouds

effectively concealing the sun. However, this was not uncommon for the season. Koreorgin's sorcerers, who were still engaged in the complex rituals for summoning Hedial, informed their leader that the sky would clear by noon and that there would be no rainfall during the day. Satisfied with this prognosis, the Relyanese chieftain prepared to launch another assault against the capital of Sicruci.

About three hours after daybreak, the enemy started to move towards Estyork. The two towers were pulled forward by teams of giant red rotars. The beasts of burden toiled placidly and without complaint until their masters had the enormous structures in position opposite the west and north walls. The rotars were then unharnessed before being driven back to the encampment, for they did not possess the temperament necessary for battle. If they had been used the large animals would have become terrified by the noise of the conflict.

Companies of villeins greased the eight huge, metal rimmed, wooden wheels which were twelve feet in diameter; the protective screens were checked, and all was ready for the monstrosities to be manhandled into place against the walls. The interiors had securely fastened ladders running from each floor to the platform at the top. When each tower had been pushed so that it overlooked the battlements, the soldiers were to emerge from within and throw planks across between the embrasures, before rushing to attack the ramparts, supported by comrades on the stairway.

However, before such an eventuality could occur, the Adiorenji had first to reach the walls. Koreorgin sat astride his hecul on the west side of Estyork, and raised his hand. In compliance with their horbspan's signal, the buglers blew a call, and both towers were trundled towards their objectives. House carls and serfs pulled long ropes at the front, while others pushed from behind. Chsingof, on foot, urged them onwards; the chieftain hoped that this time they would gain access to the town of Estyork, and secure the northwest for themselves and their Vilatmori and Dariondi allies.

On the east wall, Felgorian and Ricel found themselves facing archery assaults from enemy infantry. Most of the latter were cavalry who had dismounted to play their part in the attack. As Ontar and Quinton had conjectured, the hostile troops on the Hesion side of Estyork were just a feint, but one which could not be ignored. Since ladders were not in evidence, it was blatantly obvious that no attempts to secure the battlements would occur.

The Riondese ambassador and the deputy commander of the town garrison found that their soldiers were engaged in what amounted to an exchange of arrows with the enemy. The defenders were much relieved to discover that the volume of shafts from their foes was slight in comparison to what the Relyanese cavalry had accomplished before the implementation of Perlow's strategy.

The Adiorenji advanced cautiously. Their first rank bore shields behind which protection the second fired blue feathered shafts. Once the arrows had whistled overhead, through the embrasures or smacked against the thick walls, the defenders retaliated swiftly, launching their own bolts. Since a contingent of one thousand shock troops was interspersed with the Deerait soldiery, the enemy began to suffer far more casualties than their adversaries.

While Felgorian and Ricel capably managed on the east wall, Quinton was in charge of the west, supported by Rahamb and Souriin. Ontar, Hanshair, other officers and men from the royal guard were with Cottis on the northern sector of Estyork, watching the massed infantry columns manoeuvre into position prior to launching their attack. Every soldier on the ramparts had a plentiful supply of arrows and morale was high.

Indeed, had the Relyanese but realised it, their encampment and martial activities were being watched by strange eyes. Forsever, Mirchanrope and a contingent of thirty steppe scouts had galloped ahead of the army and reached the battle area. They saw the horde of Adiorenji moving into positions beneath the city walls and, from their place of concealment about a quarter of a mile from the north gate, several of them were elated to catch glimpses of the archmage marshalling and encouraging his troops.

"No sign of your cousin yet, Forsever," Mirchanrope spoke softly.

"If Great Ontar's on that wall, then King Quinton will be on the west wall. Those are the two main areas of assault. The east wall is only a feint. Wonder if Lady Admaria knows we're here," the Nai-Zind sub-caranxem said to his father-in-law.

"How will she know that? Oh, a crystal, like all wizards have. I hope she does see us. It will cheer them up. Gordan and the army will soon sort this lot out," Mirchanrope stated with grim confidence.

"Pity we can't send scouts round the east side or further than the encampment. I'd like to know what's going on over on the south side too," Rahamb's younger brother said.

"So would I. But there's too much activity on the roads from Relyan. Supply wagons. Replacement heculs. Even last night the roads were busy. Adiorenji patrols have the whole area under surveillance," Mirchanrope pointed out.

"True. Under ordinary circumstances I'd certainly have tried it tonight. Anyway, Gordan's orders were specific. Observe Estyork and the Relyanese encampment, but make no attempt to enter either or go round to the south side of the city."

"He's right. Ledayes and our patrol should be back within an hour. Then we'll sneak out of here and walk back to the treeline for our heculs," the Ouselorn ranxem nodded.

Admaria had indeed glimpsed the scouts, which was heartening news. She relayed the tidings to Quinton and Ontar, and both were extremely delighted. Although they did not reveal this information to anyone else, their pleasure and satisfaction at the telepathic communication bubbled over, and the soldiers all along the lines of defence became infected with their exuberance.

The infantry regiments to the north and west, which had marched from the Adiorenji camp to Estyork, were deployed in long lines. They stood motionless and were able to hear the clamour of battle from the east side of the town. They knew that their dubious opportunity would not be long in arriving; there was not one who did not pray to his gods for his personal survival. The setbacks suffered had totally destroyed any remaining illusions of glory and magnificent victories. However, they suppressed their fears and attended the signal to commence the attack.

Quinton and Ontar took advantage of the interval before the fighting started on their respective positions to study the towers looming ominously in front of them. Koreorgin had had the structures halted just over a hundred yards distant so that, even at this late juncture, serfs could smear more grease on the axles of the huge wheels. The monstrosities were fashioned of exceptionally strong timber. Every beam and part, whether large or small, had been cut and measured several weeks before using old diagrams. The chieftain had prepared for his war in the manner he thought best, as had his Vilatmori, Dariondi and Adiorenji allies.

The horbspan raised his right hand once more to signal his buglers. He had the considerable satisfaction of having just received the welcome tidings from his sorcerers that, by the following morning at the latest, Hedial would be summoned. The Demon would be directed against Estyork, to destroy the city completely, and slay every living human and animal. News of such an awesome massacre would spread throughout the lands of the Deeraits, and the latter would yield without further resistance; this was what Kinerth's father believed. Nevertheless, lest his magicians prove unsuccessful, he was still resolved to capture the town by force of arms, if such could be accomplished in the meantime.

Naturally, Allecenia, Quinton, Ontar and Admaria were cognisant of the intention behind the occult operations being conducted in the Relyanese encampment. The warlocks were following the directions in an ancient tome; the instructions did not require the obscene rituals and blasphemies performed by the Dannimite sorcerers at Nuoemove long ago, since they were not planning to give Hedial a gateway to Phentara. When asked by their foster son and god-daughter what should be done to counteract the magic of their enemies, the archmages smiled and told them not to worry in the slightest.

The Relyanese infantry advanced against the north and west of Estyork, while the strongest house carls and serfs pushed and pulled the towers towards the battlements. Once the first rank had reached the distance of a bowshot from their objective, they knelt holding their shields in front. The second row bent over them, placing their targes on top of those held by their comrades, so that a small wall was formed. The archers in the third rank knelt behind this barrier and commenced to loose their shafts at the ramparts.

Gaps had been left so that those bearing long ladders would not be impeded. Similarly, sufficient room had been allocated for the slower passage of the towers. The hail of arrows, directed against the principal sides to be assailed, was noticeably far less than when the cavalry had been employed. Two thirds of the soldiers were engaged in forming the shield walls, of which there were four large formations on each side of the town, while the remainder functioned as sagittaries.

Inside the city, one thousand shock troops remained in the square as a reserve, while the other nine thousand were on the battlements. Of the latter, four thousand had been allocated to the north, another four thousand to the west, and the remaining one thousand soldiers were assisting in the defence of the east wall. They returned the fire with accuracy, requiring only a brief glimpse at a possible target before releasing their deadly missiles. Many an Adiorenji soldier discovered the harsh reality which occurred when he unwittingly allowed any part of his body to become visible through a gap in the shield wall.

Dead and wounded men began to litter the ground before Estyork in ever increasing numbers. When the conflict ended that day, Koreorgin was to be apprised that his total casualties since the commencement of hostilities amounted to just under fifteen and a half thousand: this was more than twelve times those within the beleaguered city. A high proportion of these losses came from the forlorn hopes who bore the ladders.

The stout carls and villeins, dressed in a variety of coloured tunics which denoted the houses of their respective masters, hurried forward to be met by showers of arrows, rocks and cauldrons of boiling water. The unfortunates who were scalded experienced the wonder of their terrible pain suddenly vanishing, although they remained weak. Admaria and Allecenia had continued with this humanitarian duty.

Quinton, Souriin and Rahamb peered cautiously through a wide embrasure, watching while the huge vehicle was dragged ever nearer. Those pushing it were reasonably protected from direct arrow fire, unlike their comrades pulling at the front. The latter suffered terrible losses, arrows slaying them indiscriminately. A hapless Relyanese fell with a shaft in his shoulder into the path of the tower. He had no time to crawl out of the way before the enormous metal rimmed wheels crushed his head to a yellow bloody mush.

One of his comrades, shoving energetically from behind, felt his left foot tread in something soft. He glanced down to see the gruesome remains of a shattered skull and brains adhering to his sandal. The effect was too much for him. The shocked villein screeched, vomited and ran to the side to be slain by an arrow; the missile struck him in the middle of his forehead, the point boring its deadly path until it emerged gorily from the back of his neck. Scenes like this were repeated all over the dreadful battleground, ramming home the horror of warfare and the consequences of irresponsibily indulging in it.

"How are you doing, Quinton?" Ontar spoke telepathically.

"Our tower's just over twenty yards distant. Where's yours?" the youth replied.

"About the same. We've a lot of ladder attacks. They keep coming, but not so eagerly as they used to the other days, even though they have more regiments attacking at the moment," the sage stated.

"That's what we're finding. When they first began this morning, they seemed quite keen, but their casualties are mounting. They must miss the effectiveness of the cavalry. Still, not far off thirty thousand troopers to face on each wall is quite a number. Must go. We've got some opponents on top of the battlements," Quinton said.

"So have we. Hanshair's gone for four of them," Ontar declared, hastening to help the Nai-Zind.

The commander of the royal guard had just slain a carl when the archmage reached him. Adrigal and Onlestic were at his heels. The remaining three Adiorenji froze at the sight of the grim faced, battle hardened warriors rushing towards them. The one slain had been the principal overseer on the estate where they laboured and were treated like slaves. They were mere youths, and Hanshair took pity on them.

"Toss your swords away! Surrender! No harm will come to you! I promise!" the Nai-Zind shouted.

"Alright, sir!" the nearest one cried.

He threw down his blade an instant before his companions did likewise. Ontar beckoned to two auxiliaries nearby who were giving assistance to a concussed shock trooper. The latter was able to stand shakily, even though he had slipped in some blood and had struck his head violently.

"Take these young men to join the other prisoners. Fetch sand or ashes to absorb any liquid on the stone. I'll look after Xenggarrot," the wizard commanded.

"At once, Great Sage," one of the auxiliaries nodded with the highest respect before he and his comrade left to comply with the archmage's requests.

Ontar and his companions moved back to stand behind the protection of the guard-house. The Ulgruffi mystic placed his right hand against Xenggarrot's forehead; the warrior felt his concussion and nausea vanish, to be replaced by strength and vitality. He smiled shyly at his benefactor, before thanking him for his kindness.

"Not at all, my friend," Ontar acknowledged.

"How do you know my name, Sir? I've never had the chance to speak to you, Lady Admaria or King Quinton. General Gordan has not conversed with me either, nor our Polingsi commanders. Oh, except one time in the forest. That was when Commander Casterandir asked me to hold the reins of his linz," the shock trooper recollected.

"You are one of Quinton's people. Difficult as this may seem to believe, he, Admaria and I know all of you by name, every single man, woman and child. Even every Casman soldier. If we have not spoken to you, that's because of time, but we do care. You are a Querdot," the handsome sage smiled benignly.

"I am, Great Ontar. And I know you all care, all of you in the Inner Council," the young warrior responded.

Hanshair looked at the wizard from behind the latter's back, and mouthed a suggestion, to which the archmage nodded with pleasure, before saying, "Xenggarrot, when the fighting is over today, you will come and dine at the King's table this evening. Now you had better return to your duties."

"Thank you, King's Friend. I shall be most honoured," the Querdot bowed graciously, before hastening back to his allotted position further down the wall.

"I hope I wasn't too presumptious, My Lord," Hanshair said apologetically.

Ontar put his hand on the Nai-Zind's arm, and smiled, before replying, "Certainly not. It was a most sensible idea. You've started something, my friend. You and the guard, when time permits of course, quietly chat to the troops. When you find any like young Xenggarrot who has never spoken with Quinton, Admaria or me, you let us know. Thank you sincerely, Hanshair. Let's see how the tower is progressing."

In spite of the intense fire directed at them, the sturdy house carls and serfs had succeeded in bringing the towers to within approximately fifteen yards from the ramparts. Scores of those assigned to manoeuvre the monstrosities into position lay dead or dying; the line of bodies revealed the extent of the bow range of the defenders. Koreorgin had watched the progress of the tower on the north wall, and prayed to his gods for victory.

The principal deity in the Adiorenji pantheon was Caramanj. The goddess was the most powerful. Her wrath was feared by those who worshipped her. Caramanj was also commonly called "She who has no face". All statues and totems of the deity had blank features. The legend behind this strange belief stated that, if anyone were ever to behold her countenance, he or she would know her immediately and suffer the consequences of the action which had caused her visage to be revealed.

There were temples and shrines dedicated to her in all the Adiorenji homelands. The most important one was Castle Xzlus on the Keollin escarpment about eighty miles from Estyork. Two years previously, the old and revered High Priest, Tarhalic, had died in mysterious circumstances. His position had been taken over by a friend of Koreorgin called Rhaitall. Unlike his predecessor, the latter supported the horbspan in his desire to conquer Deerait. Although the warlord had launched his war precipitately and had not informed Rhaitall, Koreorgin had expected that the High Priest would have joined him, for the priesthood employed sorcery and should be aware of his actions.

The towers slowly trundled ever nearer, while the defenders deluged the ladder parties with boiling water or launched rocks and shafts. Corpses were callously dragged aside. The wheels crept forward until an officer shouted a command to halt. The soldiers on the ramparts immediately above ceased fighting and waited for the Relyanese to make the first move. The launching of fire arrows would have proved ineffective because the structures had been thoroughly saturated with water throughout the night.

Four floors had been constructed on each tower. Admittance to a higher level was by a securely fastened ladder in one corner. Protection was given by stout wooden walls to which thick layers of hide had been nailed securely. The intention was that no shafts, rocks or other objects hurled against the vehicles would damage them or penetrate to harm the men within. The latter were to leave by a door leading to a broad platform on the top floor.

The first troops to emerge from the protection of the tower were to throw strong broad planks of wood between the embrasures, before rushing across to jump down onto the battlements. Since the constructions were sufficiently large, five such bridges had been manufactured. Lest the defenders seize the planks and pull them from the platform, holes had been gouged out near one end. These fitted over the ends of round poles, the bases of which were nailed to the wood covering the bottom of the second floor, thus giving them extra strength.

411

Each pole emerged two feet above the roof of the third floor and the interval between it and its neighbour was calculated so that a plank would go across at right angles through an embrasure. The King of Rionder and his foster father admired the precision with which the two towers had been manouevred so that none of the twelve feet long planks would strike the battlements instead of an opening.

"Quinton, what's happening?" Ontar spoke urgently to his foster son from the north wall.

"Our tower's just stopped in front of us. They'll be coming any second," his ward replied.

"We're at the same stage here. It would have been touch and go if the Sicrucians alone were defending the walls against such devices. This is what our shock troops are intended to face. Oh, by the way, I've invited Xenggarrot to dinner," the sage smiled as he silently mentioned this to Quinton.

"Excellent! He's that good looking young Querdot. He has two brothers. One's a scout with Mirchanrope and Forsever. The other's with one of the medical companies. I'll have to go. You take care."

"You too. Marvellous news about the scouts being out there. We'll see Gordan tomorrow," Ontar declared.

Although the fighting was very fierce along all three walls, the King of Rionder had no intention of withdrawing men from any position to contest the towers. When the giant constructions were about forty yards from their objectives, Admaria had commanded Colmar to send two companies of one hundred shock troops from the square to support her spouse and foster son. On receipt of this instruction the steppe warriors mounted their fine heculs and galloped swiftly off, one contingent heading along the western boulevard, while the other took the northern.

These squadrons of the best trained troops on Phentara were met by an officer of the royal guard. He told them which steps they were to use to climb to the ramparts and the number of men for each party. These particular shock soldiers had spent an hour the previous afternoon with their King and the Great Sage in the judgment hall, when they had been fully briefed on what they were expected to accomplish once the towers were brought into the conflict.

Similarly, the troopers already on the battlements had received instructions on what was to be done should they find themselves in close proximity to a tower. Every small detail had been anticipated; it simply remained for the Relyanese to begin their assault. Indeed, Koreorgin and Kinerth hoped that this move would bring about the downfall of Estyork. Then the King of Rionder would pay dearly for the death of Reorgin.

"Quinton, Ontar, enemy columns running towards the towers!" Allecenia advised her beloved and her godfather what she was seeing in her crystal.

"Thank you," both acknowledged simultaneously for their telepathic power permitted any of the four of them to converse with the other three at the same time.

The west wall was the first to be attacked from a tower, two minutes before a similar action began against the north where Cottis had taken control of the battlements; in this authoritative position he was assisted by two steppe officers. The governor of Sicruci found that he had very little to do since the majority of the defenders were shock troops, whose reactions were very fast. Consequently the Relyanese, even though they lacked cavalry support and were more numerous than before, both down on the ground and on the scaling ladders, found themselves being far more pressed than on any of the previous days when they had attacked the provincial capital.

Quinton, Souriin and Rahamb peered cautiously between the embrasures at the door on the tower opposite them. Close by, a number of shock troops knelt, holding arrows notched to their bowstrings. Further along on both sides, their comrades and the Deeraits were battling ferociously with the hostile ladder assaults. The house carls who had clambered over the ramparts were swiftly repulsed, leaving scores of their fellows lying in pools of blood to be removed by the auxiliaries.

The corpses of their adversaries could easily have been tossed through the embrasures or down to the streets, but Quinton had commanded that such an action was not to be performed. During the last truce several wagons had been handed over to the Adiorenji: these transports were found to contain the bodies of the slain, which had been carefully placed in the interior of each vehicle. The enemy had returned the wains to Estyork once they had been emptied. Rinthalt and Chsingof sent a message of thanks for such courtesy: this consideration for the fallen had impressed Koreorgin, although he would never have admitted it.

The Sicrucian auxiliaries were kept fully occupied. They worked industriously to remove the dead and wounded of both sides as quickly as possible. Men with severe injuries were tended in houses and buildings close to the battlements where field stations had been prepared to receive them. Those who had sustained lesser hurts were transported to hospitals further away. The fallen were taken to the fortress barracks for identification before being buried in mass graves in one of the parks.

"Quinton!" Perlow called, weaving and ducking along the battlements to reach his paramount ranxem.

"Yes?" the King of Rionder asked his observer and close friend.

"Those are fresh troops going into the tower. They're wearing flat square black helmets with a crimson skull insignia at the front. Their livery is dark blue. I've not seen them before in any of the previous attacks. They look more dangerous than the other Adiorenji. There's something eerie about them. Something very sinister. I don't know what. And I don't like it," the Chofir replied seriously.

"Thanks. Stay down. You can stop what you're doing for the present. You'll be needed here. Ontar will know about these troops too," the youth declared, telepathically informing his foster father.

Just after he had done so Admaria spoke to both of them. She had been scrying the entrance at the rear of the tower on the north wall, and had taken the opportunity to scrutinise the newcomers closely. Ontar's spouse had scanned the faces of several men and quickly realised that the latter were either under an enchantment or had taken some powerful opiate. The troops were already climbing up the inside of the structure on the Lord of Deerait's side, and would soon emerge onto the platform to throw the planks across.

"My intuition tells me it isn't a spell. They've been given the drug ublisstan, Quinton. It comes from a yellow and green broad leafed plant of the same name. It gives a person the sensation of being all powerful and impervious to pain. If someone takes too much, he or she goes berserk. It's an hallucinogen. Those Relyanese won't have consumed enough to cause them to hallucinate. If they had, they'd have turned against their own people. You've a vicious fight on your hands. Warn our troops to be especially alert," Admaria cautioned.

414

Ontar and Quinton immediately did as she requested. The wizard averred that the garrison troops would not have been capable of withstanding such an onslaught. He asked his spouse to cast a spell to destroy the potency of all supplies of ublisstan in the Adiorenji encampment. Koreorgin must be feeling desperate to employ such methods; that was obvious, but his use of the drug was reprehensible. The beautiful Ulgruffi quickly did what her husband requested. She had barely finished her enchantment when the door opened opposite her foster son's position.

"Here they come. Remember, they are especially dangerous. They've been drugged," Quinton spoke tersely to the warriors beside him.

Ten Adiorenji with glazed expressions on their countenances emerged, and hurried to lift the five planks which were to be used to bridge the gap from the platform to the battlements. The boards had been bound securely by ropes to the walls of the structure. The cords went through holes to the inner room and had been slackened before the Relyanese soldiery appeared.

The moment he saw the enemy, Quinton nodded. Immediately arrows hissed across the gap and the ten were struck. Six tottered backwards, finally slumping against the wall. The other four lurched, clawing at the shafts in their chests. They staggered, before crashing against the protective rail on the left side and falling over to the ground. The defenders were assisted by the strange fact that the drug had caused the Relyanese to believe that they would be immune to any weapon used against them, for the latter had not brought shields with them.

When this attempt was seen to fail, thirty of the enemy poured onto the platform. Half of them carried bows and tried to launch shafts at the deadly archers behind the battlements. The latter promptly released a continuous stream of bolts, causing havoc among their foes. The platform was quickly littered with corpses, but these were callously tossed to the ground by the apparently endless flow of troops who wore the skull helmets.

Eighty four perished before two of the planks had been inserted onto the poles and dropped to span the gap to the battlements. Although the defenders had sustained some casualties, they did not flinch under the fire from their opponents. Nearby, the ladder assaults had increased on the orders of Rinthalt down below while Chsingof exhorted similar squads on the north wall.

The skull troopers did not attempt to rush the battlements immediately, but continued with their frantic endeavours until they had succeeded in completing all five bridges to their objective. The steppe warriors loosed scores of shafts at the platform, and were utterly sickened by the wholesale carnage. The horrified Adiorenji on the ground watched, while those on the platform kicked or tossed the dead and wounded over the sides. They felt anger at Koreorgin that such callousness was permitted, and there were murmurings against his use of ublisstan.

Ontar, Hanshair and the two Ker-Mantids felt equally disgusted, but did not dare let their compassion allow these particular foes into Estyork. The sage and Quinton had revealed that the skull soldiery would indiscriminately slaughter every man, woman and child in the town for the drug would cause them to act in such a devilish manner. It was absolutely essential that none of them was allowed access into the city.

The attacks on the east wall were being pushed home with less enthusiasm. Felgorian and Ricel kept their command alert and did not let their efforts slacken in the least. Koreorgin was to find that his feint had cost him a far greater number of casualties than he had foreseen. However, the chieftain was observing the attack on the west wall. He was delighted by the report that all five planks, fashioned from an extremely hard wood, spanned the distance from the tower to the embrasures.

On the north side, Kinerth felt an evil glee when he saw a similar sight. Reorgin would be avenged very soon. The King of Rionder and his troops would be put to death in a hideous fashion. Such callous thoughts ran through his mind as he anticipated what he intended to do. They were his last. He had ridden just a shade too close to the city. Behind an arrow slit in the wall, a garrison soldier took careful aim at the cruel Adiorenji. His shaft missed the chest above the armour but penetrated his victim's head below the helmet.

Kinerth did not know what had occurred for death was instantaneous. He fell from the saddle and crashed to the ground. Blood oozed from his mouth and down both cheeks, for the arrow head had emerged covered in gore from the other side of his neck. Those who saw him perish did not have any regrets. However, they moved away, pretending that they had not witnessed the incident, for Koreorgin was liable to slay the person rash enough to inform him of his scion's demise.

Finally, the drugged Relyanese, whose eyes shone most peculiarly, started across the planks to the battlements. The defenders maintained a rapid fire which under normal circumstances would have caused such an attack to be broken off. Large numbers of their foes were struck by deadly bolts and uttered dreadful screams before they toppled to the ground far below. Nevertheless, they had picked up shields before venturing forth, which helped protect them against their adversaries.

Several did succeed in reaching the ramparts, only to be met at each embrasure by stiff resistance. On the west wall Quinton, Perlow, Rahamb, Souriin and Helijaw met their charge. Ontar, Hanshair, Adrigal, Onlestic and Quirgid leaped into the openings to repel the Adiorenji on the other front. Shock troops further along on both sides of the tower maintained an accurate fire at the Relyanese bowmen on the platform.

Although they did not wish their King to imperil himself, the sight of Quinton in his helmet and armour fighting fiercely uplifted the already high spirits of his soldiers. The ladder assaults had increased but the resistance of the defenders overwhelmed every onslaught. The attackers were hewn down or captured on the battlements while their comrades on the ladders, which had not been thrust backwards by the long poles, found the greatest difficulty in climbing over the ramparts without being struck by accurate shafts.

The sagittaries on the ground attempted to relieve the pressure on those going forward but found that their adversaries were causing an increasing number of fatalities in their ranks. Felgorian and Ricel commanded their contingents so efficiently that their opponents began to believe that they had been engaged in a major assault rather than a feint attack. Indeed, when Rinthalt was informed how bad the situation was, he sent couriers to command the Relyanese to withdraw beyond the range of the deadly archers.

On the north and west sides of the city the ladder squads became most reluctant to press home their assaults. Their officers had the greatest difficulty in compelling them to advance. Although still ignorant of his son's death Koreorgin, too, was beginning to harbour some doubts on the advisability of continuing the attack. The estimates of the casualties for that day were appalling. Even he could see that his drugged skull regiment was not succeeding as quickly as had been anticipated; its losses were daunting.

The drugged Adiorenji screeched their terrible battle-cries but the sounds made no impression on the two tall warriors, the two youths and the small Chofir defending the western ramparts. The quintet possessed a skill beyond their assailants. Even with the effects of the ublisstan causing them to feel invincible, they could make no headway. Quinton and his comrades fought silently with a grimness which was terrifying to watch.

Their superb fitness, from months of training on the steppes and the honing of their fighting instincts to perfection on the first shock troop circuit, combined with intensive weapon practice to make them appear insuperable. They stood, perfectly poised on the end of the planks jammed into the embrasures, and were undeterred by the drop to the ground below. A similar scene was being enacted on the north wall. The tower strategy, which Koreorgin had hoped would bring him victory, began to flounder.

Quinton kept his position resolutely. He met every attack on his person in a manner which would have gladdened the hearts of Gordan and the four Polingsi. The handsome youth held his shield in his left hand fending off vicious blows. The wondrous sword of Csiandag cut, hacked and thrust to slay his adversaries. Between them the King of Rionder and his companions had already slain fifteen opponents. Some sustained violent blows which decapitated them; their torsos, spouting fountains of blood from severed arteries, would lurch forward drunkenly, their hands still pathetically holding weapons and targes until they either fell or were thrust aside by their antagonists to tumble after their heads.

The Supreme Lord of Deerait fought bravely. One enemy slashed at the monarch. Quinton ducked beneath the powerful swipe which just missed his helmet. A thrust penetrated the stomach of the white Adiorenji beneath his armour; the latter screamed, dropped his shield and sword to clutch at the painfilled region. His hands tried to hold back his entrails but the gap was too wide. He was still trying to replace his intestines, when his glazing eyes finally dulled and he lost his footing on the plank.

Souriin had no opportunity to glance around to see how his comrades were faring. The Hedunon deflected a blow, before swiftly retaliating. He swung his long sword and its keen blade severed the wrist of his brown opponent. The latter gaped in horror as his hand, still holding its weapon, fell to the ground. He staggered, grasping his injured arm. A piteous moan came from his lips, the terrible pain beginning to sear through to his mind. He tried to turn to escape but slipped in a pool of blood from an unfortunate predecessor. Since the soldier had only one good hand he could not maintain his grasp on the plank and tumbled to his death.

The tall, handsome Nai-Zind caranxem with the hooked nose stood on the embrasure next to his cousin. Rahamb fought like the veteran he was. Not for a moment did he let his thoughts become emotional, for that could invoke fatal error. Clash, deflect with shield, thrust, slash, parry, his actions were automatic. The Relyanese fell before his sword.

Perlow defended the other side of his monarch. The Chofir demonstrated that he was the finest swordsman in the conflict. Some Deeraits watching nearby were awed at his prowess. Helijaw battled beside him with grim determination. Daily exercise combined with interesting, intelligent education to produce sharp minds and reflexes. Not one of the enemy passed the defenders; those unfortunate reckless Adiorenji under the influence of ublisstan foundered and fell against the quintet on the western wall.

Ontar and his four companions fought fiercely. Around and behind them, a squad of archers fired shafts into the masses of the enemy when they emerged from the door onto the platform. The slaughter there and on the planks next to the embrasures was appalling. Hanshair, like his tribal chieftain, did not permit his thoughts to wander, but reacted to every personal attack quickly and effectively. Quirgid, Adrigal and Onlestic contested in a similarly efficient manner.

The wizard defended his position with a cold calculated ruthlessness, for he and Admaria had witnessed the effects of the drug ublisstan long ago. It had occurred on an occasion when they had been using the Master Crystals on Ordlansa. The two Ulgruffi wished to survey a bitter conflict between the Vilatmori and Dariondi, a few years before Deerait became embroiled in war with the young vigorous Casman Empire.

They saw the inhabitants and livestock of a peaceful village butchered by a contingent of Dariondi under the influence of the opiate.

The sage closed his mind to the carnage. He fought on with superb skill, which was much appreciated by the archers behind. Time dragged slowly past but the skull troopers still rallied, impervious to their frightening losses. Their casualties had not gone unnoticed by their fellows on the battlefield who were engaged in attacking the walls. Indeed, the impetus of the besiegers had slowed down, for all eyes below and above kept turning repeatedly to the horrendous slaughter taking place on the towers.

Adrigal had just dispatched another foe to his doom when his right foot suddenly slipped in a pool of blood. His next opponent rushed eagerly towards the Ker-Mantid with sword raised and madness in his eyes. It seemed that the royal guard must perish for he was in the middle embrasure. The archers behind were reluctant to fire over his head lest he regain his feet too quickly. Nevertheless help was at hand.

Hanshair had slain a powerful adversary, the latter having fallen to sprawl backwards and straddle the plank. The Nai-Zind glimpsed what had happened to his friend. Without a moment's hesitation, he sprang onto the makeshift wooden bridge in front of his comrade, and smashed his shield into the face of the astounded soldier from the skull regiment. The force of this unexpected blow caused its recipient to fall sideways to his death. Hanshair quickly leaped back to assume his former position and deal with the next attack for his new assailant had just kicked the corpse out of his way.

Adrigal swiftly regained his feet, thanking the Great Power for his deliverance. He did not even glance at his guard-commander or attempt to shout his gratitude; there would be time to express that later. The Ker-Mantid already had another opponent coming towards him and continued to fight resolutely. Ontar had glimpsed the dramatic occurrence and smiled grimly to himself in approval. The sage also sensed that the resistance of the Adiorenji was beginning to slacken almost imperceptibly.

"Admaria, how long have we been fighting?" the wizard asked his beautiful spouse.

"Almost two hours. The drug is beginning to wear off. Another fifteen minutes and they'll realise their dreadful situation only too clearly," his wife replied.

"Good. If they'd been given a slightly larger dose they'd have attacked their own side in frustration at not being able to pass us up here. Probably even attacked them before they entered the towers," the archmage averred, blocking a sword slash with his shield, before thrusting his own weapon into the thigh of an adversary.

A few minutes before Admaria was proved right in her assessment, an epic occurrence took place involving the small Chofir. Perlow fought with a brilliance beyond compare. His skill was almost unbelievable and he won undying fame for the most valiant stand in the siege of Estyork. The royal guard was absolutely sickened by the slaughter. His wrath suddenly erupted. Before Quinton could stop him, he began to advance across his plank. His flashing blade slashed and slew his foes. Seven died before he reached the other side. Facing him on the large platform were twenty Relyanese who promptly turned their attention on him.

The enemy bowmen had no opportunity to fire at him. Caejkan, in charge of the steppe squad on the battlements, had his men direct accurate fire at their foes before any could unleash a shaft at the Chofir. The latter was not dismayed by the archers, nor by the other opposition. In a superlative display of swordsmanship, his blade flickered like four weapons. His reflexes were such that eight of his assailants died in a few seconds. Although still under the drug, the remainder became afraid. They retreated to the doorway, shouting to their comrades below to withdraw. At the same time Quinton, Helijaw, Rahamb and Souriin battled to come to their comrade's assistance.

"Surrender or die!" Perlow shouted with rage, slaying another two with quick thrusts.

"He's invincible! By Caramanj, he's a god!" a skull trooper yelled, and threw down his sword, followed by those of his confederates still on the platform.

A moment later the effects of the ublisstan suddenly drained away. The elite Relyanese soldiery shook their heads as if they were awakening from a trance. Those on the platforms and the planks had the full force of their perilous situation brought home to them with dramatic shocking suddenness. Outside the top doorway of each tower, especially the one on which Perlow stood, blood stained the woodwork and grotesque corpses were strewn around.

Some glanced downwards. They saw the bodies of hundreds of their comrades who had been living, breathing beings only that morning. Those who had been queueing on the ground and the stairways inside the towers felt the precariousness of their position. Chsingof had dreaded the moment when the effects of the ublisstan would wear off. Both he and Rinthalt had protested against its use but Koreorgin was adamant and would not be thwarted.

Once the opiate no longer worked on the system, the taker suffered from fear, terrible hallucinations and depression for about an hour before returning to normal. The ten valiant defenders of Estyork had won, for, on both fronts, their adversaries had thrown their weapons down and were weeping like frightened children. The steppe archers immediately ceased firing at the enemy bowmen on the platforms, for they realised that something was drastically wrong.

Quinton, Ontar and their valiant companions sheathed their swords. They tossed their shields to their allies on the battlements before going forward and assisting the terrified skull troopers. The Adiorenji were led back to the ramparts where their foes helped them down gently. The auxiliaries were called and led them off to captivity. Perlow's wrath evaporated and he helped his opponents who were in absolute terror of him.

While this was happening, the Relyanese on the stairs were descending to the safety of the ground as quickly as possible. Those who had been queueing outside had cast their weapons down and were wailing in great mental distress. Cottis immediately had the ceasefire blown while buglers on the north wall did the same following the command which Ontar shouted to them.

Despite what the horbspan might desire, the assault had ground to an ignominious halt. His commanders all along the battlefield had had enough for that day. The sound of the cease-fire from the battlements caused their senior officers to order their buglers to signal likewise. The time was very early in the afternoon and the conflict could have continued much longer. Rinthalt, Chsingof and other chieftains galloped to find their leader.

Koreorgin had ridden to the north side of Estyork and had just discovered the body of his son lying in the dust. His subordinates found him; their warlord was cradling the dead Kinerth in his arms singing a death chant. The horbspan was absolutely grief-stricken, temporarily deranged, unable to make any coherent decisions. Rinthalt sent for a wagon, into which the corpse was placed. The suzerain of the Adiorenji in the province of Relyan climbed in beside his son. Chsingof signalled to the driver who cracked his whip and headed for the encampment.

Ontar stepped once more onto the plank where he had fought so courageously. The archmage crossed over to the tower and stood thoughtfully on the platform, while down below the Relyanese were either departing or tending their wounded. Even as he pondered on what to do about the giant structure, a truce was arranged for the remainder of the afternoon. Quinton and he had originally expected that the embrasures would have to be defended until sunset.

The wizard and his foster son had decided that once the Adiorenji had withdrawn for the night, huge quantities of extremely combustible materials were to be carried out under the cover of darkness, and placed inside each of the massive creations. Fires would be lit, and hopefully the towers would be reduced to smouldering piles of wood and ash by morning. It was very unlikely that the Adiorenji would reappear that afternoon to rescue their juggernauts, for they were thoroughly disillusioned. However, the eminent mystic was not going to permit them the opportunity.

After a short telepathic conversation with Quinton, Ontar returned from the deserted monstrosity to the battlements. Down below, steppe warriors and Deerait soldiers marched out from the city to bring in their dead and assist their enemies. The latter were very listless, the sense of defeat falling like a dead weight on their shoulders. It took approximately two hours for their wagons to be loaded with first the wounded and then the slain, which included those on the platforms high above.

When the last of the huge wains had left for the encampment, the defending soldiers returned to Estyork, and the gates were closed once more. When this occurred, the sentinels on the north and west battlements were astounded to see the towers suddenly collapse and fall to the ground with a thunderous crash. Pieces of wood and torn hides were strewn for some considerable distance. The observers were not only elated by this demonstration of the Ulgruffi wizard's magic but also by the satisfactory outcome of events.

The remainder of the day was spent evaluating the strategy for the morrow. Allecenia had seen Kinerth die: the council of officers concurred that once Koreorgin had recovered sufficiently from the shock of his scion's death he would launch simultaneous assaults against all four walls in an overwhelming desire for revenge. At present no one in Estyork, other than the steppe warriors and high ranking Deerait military personnel, was aware that the provincial capital would be relieved on the morrow.

The main topic of conversation throughout the city that night was the fantastic efforts of the ten defenders, especially Perlow, who had battled against the elite skull troops of Koreorgin's personal regiment. The height and the fearsome attacks by the drugged Adiorenji could not have been withstood for long by Cottis' troops, which the latter were the first to admit. The admiration for Quinton, Ontar and Perlow, too, increased considerably. If their youthful Supreme Overlord could fight like a veteran warrior in defence of his Deerait subjects, then they would follow him unreservedly.

Before they went to the judgment hall the King, his foster father and their eight valiant comrades bathed and changed their bloodstained clothes. Unknown to Hanshair, Rahamb and the others, the wizard made several magical passes with his hands. These caused the elimination of the psychological effects of having slain so many foes in such a bloody contest. It simultaneously quelled the subconscious reaction to having stood so long over such a fearsome drop.

The Ulgruffi mystic and his foster son, together with the others in the Inner Council, fully recognised the terrible stresses which battle could inflict on the mind. There was a limit to the courage of an individual, no matter how brave he or she might be. It was like a vessel with a spigot; drain it, quickly or slowly without replenishment, and its contents diminished to the point where nothing was left. The troops in the armed forces had to be watched vigilantly for battle fatigue. Adequate rest with interesting recreation had to be ensured for both their mental and physical welfare.

After they had bathed in the warm waters of the garrison pool, the heroes dried themselves thoroughly with soft cloths, before dressing in clean raiment. Their soiled garments and other accoutrements were taken away for cleaning. Elderly Deerait servitors were appointed for this task and felt especially honoured. One of them had the task of polishing the magnificent armour and helmet which Ricel and Cottis had given Perlow that morning in appreciation of his efforts on behalf of Estyork. The Sicrucian was very proud to spend some time in the performance of this duty.

When they had finished dressing, Adrigal turned to Hanshair and smiled his thanks. The two warriors embraced and Onlestic crossed over to put his arms around both his comrades. None of the trio spoke a single word; they were friends and loved one another as dearly as they did Quinton, Ontar and Admaria. No cheeky quips were uttered by either Ker-Mantid on this occasion; each realised that both of the other two would lay down his life for him.

A few moments later Quinton invited them all to dine with him that night before lauding their valiant actions. He especially praised Perlow for his courage. The others saluted their small comrade. Their paramount ranxem told them that he was very proud of them and would never forget their mighty deeds that day. Ontar declared that Hanshair's bravery in leaping across the eight foot gap between the planks to save Adrigal was one of the most unselfish and courageous acts he had ever seen and he would be honoured to embrace the Nai-Zind.

The commander of the royal guard felt shy when both the wizard and his King clasped him. Admaria too embraced him and kissed him on the cheek before dinner that evening. Beyond all doubt those whom he and his comrades served cared for them. Both he and Xenggarrot sat on either side of Quinton, addressing their monarch familiarly. The young Querdot found his awkwardness vanishing as those of whom he was in awe drew him out.

When their meal was over, the governor of Sicruci chatted privately with his Supreme Overlord and mentioned something which had been causing him slight concern. Quinton listened closely before concurring with the Deerait's analysis of the situation. He said that he would take steps to deal with it. The youth himself had given considerable thought to the problem in question since the discussion with the officers the previous day. He now determined that something must be done, and decided to talk it over with his foster parents later that night.

"Cottis is right. Gordan has to be informed of the assault against the south wall. Koreorgin will send in his entire army. We can reckon he must have approximately a hundred and five thousand fit troops. That's roughly twenty six thousand for each side. It will stretch us to the limit to defend the whole perimeter simultaneously," Ontar nodded thoughtfully, looking at the others who were seated with him in their apartments.

"I agree. Even before Cottis mentioned it, I've been wondering since last night what would happen if one wall were captured tomorrow. Fighting in the streets. Innocent people being killed. We will win in the end, but it would take a while to disarm several thousand Adiorenji rampaging inside Estyork, even with Gordan and the army here. I'll go to the forest," the King declared resolutely.

"No. I'll go," the small Chofir volunteered shyly.

"You both can't. Quinton, you're needed here. You are the fulcrum as far as the Deeraits are concerned. Perlow, after your deeds this afternoon, your presence will hearten everyone. Ontar must remain too. Allecenia and I shall go. Two are better than one. We'll get through the enemy cordon and reach Gordan," Admaria stated emphatically.

There was a poignant silence. Quinton was about to forbid it, when Allecenia touched his arm and shook her head. He looked at his foster father, who nodded. The youth shrugged his shoulders and smiled, saying, "Alright. The city gates are being watched. How do you intend to get through unnoticed?"

"The Adiorenji are working enchantments to summon Hedial. They're using magic. I think it's only fair we do the same. It will save lives on our side. Theirs too," the beautiful Ulgruffi replied.

"I believe that is fair. As we have agreed many times in the past, our people must fight for their freedom. We could use magic to repel the enemy tomorrow, if they do get inside the town. Still, I wish to adhere to our agreement that all our peoples stand against tyranny without occult dependence. If there's any scrying needed in the morning, well, Quinton, you or I can do it," his foster father remarked.

"When do you intend to go?" Allecenia asked.

"Now. Fetch your cloak and fasten your veil, My Dear," Admaria ordered.

When Olluinan's daughter had done as instructed, the quintet left their apartments. The royal guard outside the door escorted them to the courtyard where Deerait soldiers hastened to saddle heculs under the mellow beams of the golden Enchantress. Hanshair and several of his command were summoned to accompany their monarch and his four companions. The steppe warriors had no idea of what was taking place, but were quite prepared to charge through the Relyanese cordon around Estyork if such were required of them.

Once the party reached the north gate and had identified themselves to the vigilant Sicrucian sentinels, Admaria and Allecenia turned their steeds a few yards away from their companions and began to chant softly in Ulgruffi. The two women continued thus for several minutes, during which time Ontar and Quinton joined in at appropriate places. Then, to the utter astonishment of the guards, both Ladies rode straight at the stout gate and passed through with no difficulty whatsoever.

The very instant that they emerged on the other side, they and their steeds became invisible and vanished from sight of the astounded sentries on the battlements. With this occult advantage effectively concealing their presence and the sound of their passage, they galloped their heculs past the mounted Relyanese contingents watching the city. Admaria and Allecenia continued swiftly on their way to the forests, the latter looking forward with the greatest pleasure to meeting Gordan, Casterandir and Turubin for the first time.

Two hours after midnight, Gordan passed the order for the army to halt. An air of expectancy ran through the entire force, partly because of the battle on the morrow, but the principal reason was that they would see their youthful paramount ranxem again. Each warrior resolved to perform his duty to the best of his ability. The giant Riondese realised this, as he dismounted from his linz.

He was gratified by the efficient manner in which his subordinates proceeded with their tasks. It spoke extremely well for a fully equipped army, which had travelled so far in such a short time. Sentinels were patrolling, fully alert; fires were being lit; soon each warrior would receive hot food before snatching a brief rest.

Gordan was expecting a routine report from the scouts, when the sound of hecul hooves caused him to turn round. To his surprise and delight, he saw Forsever approaching, accompanied by Admaria and a hooded woman, the latter wearing a dark veil which covered her features. They dismounted and he hastened over to greet them, while overhead the Panther shone brightly, casting soft mysterious purple shadows through the canopy of myriadfold branches.

"Gordan, dearest of friends," the beautiful Ulgruffi said, kissing him on the cheek. They held each other close for a long moment, happy to be together again. "It is really good to see you. Oh, let me introduce Allecenia. She's one of our people from Ordlansa."

"Greetings to you, Gordan. I am sincerely pleased to meet you at long last. Quinton is always talking about you, and Sheralex and the children," the wondrous voice spoke. Its marvellous mellifluous tones caused the troops at campfires nearby to pause and listen, for they had never conceived that such beautiful utterances were extant.

"Greetings to you, Allecenia," the handsome giant smiled in wonder. "Would you both like some food and drink? Say, why are you here? How did you manage to get through the Adiorenji cordon around Estyork?"

"A little food and water will suffice. We got through by making ourselves and our heculs invisible and silent. We returned to normal just before we met Forsever and four of his scouts at the edge of the forest. As to why we came, first send for your commanders. We have a problem. What do you know about Estyork?" Admaria asked.

The general nodded to one of his equerries before saying, "Just what Forsever, Mirchanrope and Ledayes have managed to report. What's the latest?" he asked the Nai-Zind scout officer.

"Much the same as before. We estimate the enemy will assault all four walls tomorrow with every available trooper. That's only a guess. Large contingents are moving westwards in the dark away from their encampment. They're heading towards the Ebrordin mountains. If they keep in a straight line, they'll reach the river. We concluded, Mirchanrope, Ledayes and I, that they're not returning home. Since the Avidnive loops beyond their camp, a boat attack on the south wall is the most likely assumption. We didn't dare probe further because of orders, and in case we were discovered," the Nai-Zind sub-caranxem said succinctly.

"I agree with that assessment. Casterandir and Turubin do too," Gordan stated seriously.

"That's why we're here. You're absolutely correct. We didn't know if your scouts had been able to learn any of this. Quinton wanted to be sure you knew about the boats. No disrespect intended, Forsever," Admaria smiled kindly.

"None taken, My Lady. Ledayes and eight scouts tried for two days to find out for certain but were unable to do more than speculate. The Adiorenji were everywhere in large numbers."

"Your men did well to guess that from what they were able to perceive. Please tell them I honour their bravery and intelligence in an exceptionally difficult situation," the beautiful Ulgruffi declared sincerely.

"Thank you, My Lady," the Nai-Zind sub-caranxem bowed graciously to acknowledge her compliment.

"Then tomorrow we go. I'm glad you confirmed the boat assault against the south wall. Your confirmation helps the battle plan. We've eighty thousand soldiers. The Relyanese should have about one hundred and five thousand able bodied troops left. If they've more, Ontar and Quinton are slipping. Ah, here's the food," Gordan indicated, as his equerry returned with several warriors. Some carried chairs and a table, while the rest bore platters of food and beakers of water.

When they had seated themselves, the handsome Riondese politely enquired if Allecenia would remove her veil, to which the Lady replied, "Yes, but I'll pull my hood forward to conceal my face. I'll eat in the shadows on this side of the table. My face must remain hidden. That is very important."

"As you wish," Gordan replied in Ulgruffi, which was the language Olluinan's daughter had used, before asking Admaria for particulars about the siege.

Ontar's spouse gave him concise details of the events at Estyork during the last few days. She also revealed the decision of the High Council in Hesion to elect Quinton their Supreme Overlord. The general was elated by this news; he listened intently while Admaria told him about the presentation of the sacred sword of Csiandag the Seer. She concluded by stating that morale was high within the capital of Sicruci, especially when Ontar, Quinton and Perlow appeared.

"That Chofir save Quinton again! Oh, thank the Great Power! And the siege will be lifted tomorrow. We'll be in battle positions in five hours. Sufficient companies will remain half a mile inside the forest to guard the supply wagons and reserve herds. It's my intention to cast a spell to bring a mist down from the edge of the forest to within three hundred yards of Estyork. It's the only way the army's advance will remain undetected. We'll try to avoid damaging any crops in the fields," Gordan explained.

"Excellent! All the farmers in the near area have brought their families into Estyork for safety. Thus far, the Relyanese have not burned or destroyed any homesteads. We did wonder how you were going to cross undetected from the forest's edge," Admaria praised.

"We'll commence hostilities exactly thirty minutes after the Adiorenji launch their attack. Here's Casterandir!" the captain of the royal guard exclaimed. He had just glimpsed his friend dismounting a short distance off among the trees.

The Polingsi had received the news of Admaria's arrival from one of the runners sent by Gordan's equerry. He was warmly greeted and embraced by the archmage before she introduced him to Allecenia. Turubin appeared shortly afterwards, accompanied by the leading army commanders. The chief general called his scribes, who brought detailed maps of Estyork and its vicinity. The Riondese, advised by the beautiful Ulgruffi, ran through precise details of the military operations each had already been delegated to supervise.

The officers listened closely, asking pertinent questions,

before being dismissed. They left hastily to brief their subordinates. Every single soldier in the force possessed a surprising alertness and lack of fatigue, which was remarkable after the very long days and nights with little rest. All of them had attempted the shock courses, with a large proportion successfully discovering the vital instinct on the first circuit. When the commanders had left the meeting, Allecenia complimented the Riondese general by saying that she comprehended more clearly how the Casman corps had been defeated.

The army rested for two hours before rousing itself to continue its epic southward march. Although they proceeded at a fairly brisk trot, Admaria managed to let Allecenia go ahead. She took the opportunity to tell Gordan, Casterandir and Turubin the reason why the veil was worn. Ontar's spouse also revealed the love which Olluinan's daughter had for Quinton, and his reciprocative tender feelings. The quartet conducted their conversation in Ulgruffi lest any of the troops nearby understood its theme.

"You three are among our dearest friends. Allecenia is mine and Ontar's god-daughter. She keeps her face hidden because she is modest and exceptionally beautiful. She also loves Quinton, and he loves her in return."

"You know, that is wonderful. Your god-daughter is surely a match for him." Gordan smiled with pleasure, for he desired the happiness of his young King.

"Does she always wear a veil? I mean you don't, and you come from the Sacred Islands too," Casterandir observed.

"Yes, she does. Except of course, in private or on Ordlansa. How can I explain it to you? Mmmmm. Allecenia is more beautiful than the stars shining in all their resplendent glory, carpeting the heavens high above the Chofanrit on a mellow summer's night."

"Even more beautiful than you? That is impossible!" Gordan exclaimed with astonishment.

"Yes, far more than I. I could be termed very ugly by comparison. Allecenia would put the very angels of the Great Power to shame. She is Beauty Incarnate come from on High to this mortal plane. There has never been her like before, or will ever be again, so Ontar and I believe. She is beyond what any Phentaran race thinks as exquisite," Admaria tried to express her thoughts.

431

"Then she is a wonder," Turubin said softly with awe.

"Say, you are different. There's a more powerful aura and a hidden majesty about you. Allecenia is the same too. I noticed it when you arrived tonight. Am I right?" Gordan asked.

"Yes. Quinton, Ontar, Allecenia and I had to battle with the Demon Hedial in a dimension beyond this world. The Great Power rewarded us for our efforts in defeating the Fiend," the archmage answered.

"Hedial is reputedly as evil as Lubeln. How bad was it?" Casterandir enquired with concern.

"Very bad. Ontar and I were taken to the centre of Hell to the Innermost Circles."

"By Ilix and Selix, you were actually there and you returned! Tell us what happened!" Gordan ejaculated, while overhead the Panther in all his magnificence contrasted strangely with the topic of their conversation.

"Not now. When the battle is over. Sometime soon. How were the families when you left?" she asked, eager for news, as Allecenia waited for them to catch up to her.

The trio affirmed that everyone was in good health. Gordan disclosed what his wife had remarked about Quinton being destined to rule Phentara. Admaria looked at the Riondese in considerable surprise, before nodding, "We should have guessed. The signs were there. Your wife has the beginnings of esoteric wisdom. Sheralex is wise. Her foresight indicates she is more than ready to enter the portals of the Sacred Order of Light."

"I would be honoured if she were to be conducted through," Gordan spoke with humility.

"I shall be delighted to take her through the initiation ritual. I would like that very much. Sheralex is your wife. You are Quinton's friend. It will be my privilege," Allecenia said kindly.

"There will be others. Felgorian and Elestia. Hanshair, Adrigal, Onlestic. Also Rahamb and Souriin. Terfieldst and Ceanill. Their auras show they are ready. Perlow too. We're going to teach him some magic when the siege is over," Admaria smiled.

"He deserves it. We'd have lost Quinton without him," Turubin stated.

"Fancy those two Ker-Mantid rascals. I'm pleased for all of them. They're going to proceed on the Mystic Way. Just think, everyone on Phentara will do that eventually. Perhaps not for many incarnations until the Light dawns, but the wonder is that everyone will. I do believe there are other worlds, where men and women have their problems to face. I feel there are Mystical Orders on their planets waiting to instruct them," Gordan said thoughtfully.

"Those are inspired comments," Allecenia praised.

"Thank you. Also for wishing to assist my wife through the portals of the Order. I am grateful. You know, except for Ontar and Admaria, you're the first person from Ordlansa we've ever met," the supreme general remarked from the height of his massive dark green linz.

"And you, Casterandir and Turubin, and Shlasmil and Sleworivan, all of you in the Inner Council, who support the future Emperor of Phentara, are highly respected on the Islands. I once said to Quinton that we on the Islands work at our researches. We do what we know best. But you are the ones who are engaged in the fighting, and that entails death and suffering. And we do not ever forget that," the veiled Lady spoke most emphatically.

At last the long night ended. Dawn broke, with the early morning sun walking across the firmament to strike the southern Rionder forests and the town of Estyork. The Adiorenji encampment had been astir for quite some considerable time before daybreak. Chieftains and officers shouted orders; carls and serfs checked weapons and snatched some mouthfuls of food, each wondering if he would survive to see evening fall.

The sorcerers continued with their rites and incantations, cognisant that their occult operations would finish shortly. Koreorgin determined to use the Demon to destroy Estyork absolutely. His sorrow at the death of Kinerth had turned to black hatred for the King of Rionder and the beleaguered city. He vowed that not one stone would remain on top of another and that every man, woman, child and animal would be annihilated by Hedial. Rinthalt and Chsingof were appalled by the intentions of their horbspan, but were terrified of what he would do to them should they be rash enough to oppose his wishes.

Nevertheless, the two Relyanese complied with his orders to assault all four walls of the town. Couriers maintained contact with the fleet of barges sailing down the Avidnive, so that a simultaneous attack could be launched. No one paid any heed to the mist rolling down from the forest, for such was thought to be a natural phenomenon. Perhaps, if the wizards had not been fully occupied in their large tent, one of their number might have realised that it was the result of magic.

None of the Relyanese thought for a moment about the peculiar circumstance that no mist was emanating from the river itself, since the Avidnive was the first place it should have appeared. Gordan had cast the spell under Admaria's supervision. The Riondese demonstrated that he was developing into quite a competent wizard.

In the great judgment hall of Estyork, the King of Rionder used his foster mother's crystal to scan the area around. While he did this, he conversed silently with the Ulgruffi mystic scrying beside him. Both were very pleased to see that the steppe army was advancing through the mist. Every soldier had fastened pieces of bison hide to the hooves of his steed in an effort to make the approach to the provincial capital as quiet as conceivably possible. There was the additional advantage that the enemy would be shouting battle cries and moving noisily to and fro.

Felgorian and Ricel were in command of the east wall, Cottis and Hanshair on the south, Rahamb and Souriin on the north, while Ontar and Quinton would depart for the west side once the fighting commenced. Estyork awaited the mightiest onslaught yet, for Koreorgin had ordered every able bodied man to take part. His sorcerers had informed him that it would not be long before Hedial appeared. However, they were unable to predict the precise time and the horbspan was resolved that the town would be attacked until the moment came; then his army would be withdrawn to watch the Demon wreaking destruction on his hated adversaries.

Bugles were blown, and the columns of Relyanese infantry advanced to form shield walls, or to commence the futile ladder assaults. The defenders on the southern ramparts saw the large flotilla of barges floating downstream to moor beside the quay, and the first contingents of enemy archers creeping carefully forward to fire at the ramparts. Behind them, other barges were being fastened to those already tied up. More house carls and serfs clambered across to dry land.

Those on the battlements reacted with the deadly resolution which they had displayed throughout the siege. The entire shock troop force had been distributed equally along the four walls. Colmar was delighted to find himself beside his paramount ranxem, the sage and Perlow. The Melcogh felt that he was personally justifying his presence in Estyork, although he fully realised that his task of organising the couriers during the previous days had been essential.

The Adiorenji began to sustain casualties from the accurate steppe marksmen on the battlements. The ground between the river and the south wall was quickly littered with dead and wounded. Cottis and Hanshair realised that their position would be the most vulnerable that morning. It would be the last to be relieved by Gordan; the two friends, the Deerait governor and the Nai-Zind, were resolved that their Supreme Overlord would not be shamed by their conduct.

Under cover of the mist conjured forth by Gordan, the long columns of the army advanced towards Estyork. The soldiers were bewildered at first when they discovered that their eyes easily penetrated the gloom. They were amazed that they were able to perceive clearly the features of the landscape and the north wall of the town some distance off. However, if one of their enemies happened to glance in their direction, he was unable to discern anything at all.

The ladder parties, who had struggled to the embrasures, encountered such resistance that they began to surrender in quite large numbers. The ground troops were found to be most reluctant to remain within bowshot of the ramparts, demonstrating how far the morale of the besiegers had fallen. Even the relatively fresh contingents engaged for the first time soon began to sense the futility of their efforts.

Koreorgin remained in camp to supervise his sorcerers. Although four more towers had been completed, he had decided not to use them that morning. Rinthalt and Chsingof had informed him that his use of the drug ubblisstan, even though it had only been consumed by his personal skull regiment, had caused much resentment and muttering in the ranks of his army. Indeed, the soldiery were becoming firmly convinced that Estyork could not be taken.

Gordan's command deployed quickly and efficiently, for each platoon knew precisely what was required. Shortly before the handsome giant Riondese gave the signal which would launch his force against the Relyanese, the horbspan's sorcerers completed the final rites within the confines of their large tent. They waited with trepidation in the innermost circle of their protective configuration for the hellish Fiend to make his appearance.

However, instead of the Lord of Iniquities, a radiant angelic figure, surrounded by a brilliant golden light, descended through the roof, and spoke in cold, crystal tones, "Foul magicians, know this! The Demon Hedial and his Master Lubeln have been vanquished by the Ulgruffi archmages, Ontar and Admaria. Their beings are precious and beloved by the Great Power. The King of Rionder and the Lady Allecenia assisted in this valiant endeavour. You performed wicked rituals for immoral purposes. You will take the consequences!"

The holy entity vanished, leaving the sorcerers blinded and crippled. Koreorgin, who was standing a short distance away outside the tent, suffered the same fate to the horror and astonishment of those nearby. The chieftain and his magicians writhed in unbelievable agony for almost ten minutes, sweat pouring from every pore.

Then the angelic voice spoke once more, "You will now be released from your punishment. Never again will you attempt or even contemplate the use of magic for evil reasons. Use your knowledge only for Good. Be warned!"

The sorcerers and their horbspan felt their pain vanish, from where they lay on the ground. Each felt grateful that his sight had returned, and his distorted limbs had been restored to normal. Koreorgin lurched to his feet and managed to stagger to his hecul. Once he had mounted, he kicked his heels into the sides of the animal and galloped from the encampment towards Estyork. To his surprise, the mist on the left had disappeared and large numbers of strange riders were visible.

Gordan's strategy to lift the siege was simple. Massive cavalry columns were to be used. Casterandir and Turubin were to take fifty thousand men and relieve the north and east walls. Three thousand under Forsever and Ledayes were to ride directly for the Adiorenji encampment and secure it, for it was only occupied by the wounded and physicians. Gordan and Mirchanrope, with the remaining twenty six thousand soldiers, were to fight their way around the west side and join up with Turubin and Casterandir beside the Avidnive. The final stage would be to ford the shallow river and, in conjunction with regiments on the town side, hem in and capture the barges still coming downstream.

"Charge!" the supreme general of Quinton's army bellowed, and the disciplined battalions galloped forward.

For a brief moment, Gordan recollected something the popular Terfieldst had said, the last time he had conversed with the governor of Jaddair, on the morning of his departure to Estyork. The Casman commander and Ceanill had come to bid him farewell, after chatting privately to Casterandir and Turubin. The warlord had smiled, and said that a pleasant surprise awaited the Riondese when the fighting commenced outside the town. Ceanill had also been highly amused, but did not betray his superior.

Gordan's linz leaped to battle. Admaria and Allecenia rode beside him, while a bodyguard of the finest fighting men on Phentara surrounded the trio in an impenetrable square. The army charged to rescue their liege, which task they were wholly resolved to accomplish effectively in the shortest time possible. Suddenly they emitted a new battle cry.

"Quinton! Quinton! Ontar! Ontar! Gordan! Gordan!" to the surprise of their modest commander.

"Terfieldst, I'll skin you," he thought with a broad grin.

The Relyanese outside the north wall heard the mighty shouts which heralded new adversaries. They turned to see phalanxes of grim faced warriors bearing down on them. These were strangers to them: they could not decipher the tribal identity of the steppe warriors, even though the latter had not assumed Deerait dress or hairstyle. However, the besiegers quickly caught sight of the linz badges worn by these new foes and realised that the end had come. Melcoghs, Ker-Mantids, Pingaliks, Ouselorns and members from every single clan on the western Mescarg plains rode with Phlorcartids, Riondese and Polingsi to battle with the foes of their beloved King and paramount ranxem. Quinton was in peril; that was sufficient for them.

The Adiorenji cavalry had continued in the role of infantry, and, apart from supervising officers, relatively few were mounted. The enemy bowmen, stationed all along the outside of the north wall, found themselves in a dilemma for, if they attempted to fire at this new enemy, the defenders would loose a hail of shafts into their exposed rear. Their dithering proved fatal. They did not have time to resist the newcomers before

437

they found themselves assailed by hostile sagittaries, lancers and swordsmen.

Many Relyanese tried to withstand the onslaught but deadly accurate archery swept through their ranks. Casterandir and Turubin led their command in a devastating charge which swept all before it. The steppe contingents rode in perfect formation. All resistance was swiftly crushed; the defenders of Estyork assisted by loosing shafts into the ranks of their foes to wreak further havoc.

When the newcomers shouted to them in the Common Speech to surrender, the Adiorenji quickly threw down their weapons and were rounded up. Similar scenes occurred along the length of the east wall. The broad wave of superb cavalry broke through everything before it. In accordance with their orders, regiments deployed from the main body to eliminate all opposition effectively. The Relyanese were absolutely terrified by the mighty warriors on heculs who had appeared from nowhere.

The sight of Turubin, Casterandir and squads of Riondese on huge linz caused consternation, for such creatures were believed to be forest demons. The two Polingsi found themselves totally protected. From their high saddles they obtained an excellent view of their surroundings and the conduct of their cavalry. As the friends remarked later, the whole action was just like being on very realistic manoeuvres.

Forsever and Ledayes led their three thousand troops towards the enemy encampment at the same time as Koreorgin was riding towards Estyork. The Adiorenji chieftain tried to turn his hecul away from the long ranks of the approaching strangers. He wrenched savagely at his reins with a strength born of desperation. This unexpected violence from its rider caused the hecul to lose its balance. The yellow beaked animal fell on its left side, smashing its rider's leg beneath its weight.

As the frantic mount scrambled to its feet, its forehooves stamped viciously down on Koreorgin's face, crushing his skull like an overripe fruit. Two steppe warriors came galloping from the flank of the charging column to see if they could proffer any assistance, but a quick glance revealed that the victim of the accident was dead. They raced to rejoin their comrades and helped secure their objective without any trouble.

Allecenia and Admaria rode swiftly and capably, surrounded by tall steppe warriors led by Mirchanrope. Gordan smiled grimly as his column smashed its way along the west wall. He saw the Lady's hood fly back because of the wind blowing from the south and the rate of their progress. However, he was totally unprepared for what happened next. The breeze whipped the veil covering her face, and the ties snapped.

For the first time in the outworld, other than in private, Allecenia's divine face was exposed to view. Her lovely visage caused amazement among the steppe warriors, and Gordan caught his breath in wonder and admiration. The effect on the Adiorenji, through whose scattered ranks they were passing, proved very dramatic. When they saw her radiant loveliness coming towards them in the midst of a terrifying enemy they threw down their weapons and prostrated themselves in abject fear.

"Woe is upon us! Caramanj! Oh, Caramanj! She who has no face! She is with our foes! We are doomed!"

By the time the steppe column had reached a point two thirds of the length along the western wall, the Relyanese were surrendering in their thousands. The sudden revelation of such ethereal pulchritude in mortal form was too much for them. Gordan led the mad dash to meet up with Turubin and Casterandir beside the River Avidnive. Everywhere Allecenia passed, hostilities ceased: she made no attempt to cover her face, realising that lives were being saved.

Within a very short period of time, the entire enemy army had submitted. The inimical forces arrayed against the south wall did not try to escape across the River Avidnive. The sight of Olluinan's daughter caused them to yield instantly, lest Caramanj send them to the plane of oblivion. Turubin and Casterandir gazed reverentially at the beautiful woman, while Gordan told Admaria that her description of Allecenia's divine beauty had been totally inadequate.

"I know. It is like trying to describe Cosmic Consciousness in words," the Ulgruffi archmage nodded, while they watched the last of their foes on the barges throwing down their weapons.

"That's true. It saved us valuable lives. The Adiorenji too. And since they believe her to be the incarnation of Caramanj, it will help us enormously," the Riondese said reflectively.

Once the enemy had been completely disarmed, the steppe troops began to organise them with their customary efficiency. All wounded were examined, the more serious cases being given prompt temporary treatment before removal to field stations. Steppe casualties had been very light, and the few injured were immediately removed with honour into Estyork. The Relyanese collected the dead of both sides. The fallen were interred by late afternoon with all due ceremony and respect.

Couriers were sent to the forest to inform the one thousand troops guarding the wagons and reserve herds that they were to proceed to Estyork. When they reached the city, squads of steppe warriors went to work erecting tents, lighting fires of dried hecul chips, and preparing food. The Deerait sentinels on the west wall gaped in astonishment at the quick, competent manner in which a vast encampment was pitched down below.

When the last Relyanese had surrendered, the troops all along the miles of battlements were commanded to stand down. Ontar contacted Quinton telepathically, and they left matters in the hands of their able lieutenants. The King of Rionder, the archmage and Perlow descended from the west wall to street level and mounted their heculs. Several of the royal guard accompanied them on their journey across Estyork to the south gate.

While they rode, Quinton and Ontar conversed silently about the fact that Allecenia's face had been revealed. Since the Adiorenji believed her to be Caramanj, this could be used to advantage in quelling any further rebellion from that particular people. Both were very pleased by the performance of the army in vanquishing their foes. They were also happy to be meeting Gordan, Casterandir and Turubin after long weeks of separation.

When their Supreme Overlord signified that he wished the south gate to be opened, the Sicrucians on duty were only too delighted to obey him. The siege had been lifted, and the vastly superior enemy overcome, all because of the handsome youth and his armed forces. They felt awed when he and the mystic with their magnificent auras rode beneath the archway and trotted out to join the supreme general and the two Polingsi. The trio were easily distinguishable because of the size of their gigantic steeds.

"Greetings, all of you, dearest of friends," Quinton called when he, Ontar and the Chofir dismounted.

The captain of the royal guard and his two companions jumped from their linz, and went to embrace their ward. All smiled with pleasure at being together again.

"You did well to hold Estyork. Both of you," Gordan praised with delight. "I had the impression that the Adiorenji were really depressed."

"You could say that. Look, you did well too, my godfather," Quinton smiled. "Oh, yes. Felgorian told me. Why didn't you? I would have loved to have known."

"Ontar and Admaria were taking good care of you. And I was always there, like I promised your parents. Say, you're different. So's Ontar. Just like Admaria," Gordan declared, while the efficient troops of his command began to organise the defeated Relyanese.

"Don't change the subject. Certainly, you were always there, all the days of my childhood and beyond. You were like a father and much older brother in one. Even Sheralex was like a mother. You and she used to take me for picnics beside the Dentworl. Without you, I would not be alive," the King of Rionder spoke gently, looking up into the handsome face of his captain of the royal guard.

"Thank you. But you are different! More majestic. Your aura's increased. Was it to do with Hedial? Admaria mentioned a little about your battle with the Demon," the general spoke in Ulgruffi, so that the guard enclosing them in the large square would not comprehend their conversation.

"Yes. Ontar, Allecenia, Admaria and I had to battle against the Demon on the Occult Dimension. Our majesty and aura and other knowledge were given to us as a reward."

"I'm glad you survived and are safe. And you're the Supreme Overlord of Deerait," Gordan nodded with satisfaction.

"Only the rest of the Adiorenji added to the Vilatmori and the Dariondi to deal with. Let's not forget the Empire or Broechnaar," Casterandir grinned broadly, looking at Quinton with affection in his dark eyes.

"Still, we've defeated this bunch. We should easily gain control of the province of Relyan and the northwest. We may have pockets of resistance, but it's an excellent beginning," Turubin declared, squeezing the youth's arm contentedly, for he had sincerely missed him.

Ontar also embraced the three warriors, before walking over to greet Admaria; his spouse and her god-daughter had considerately decided to allow the men some privacy. He now returned with the two lovely women. When Allecenia reached

Quinton the couple held hands, as if it were the most natural thing in the world for them to do, their action considerably delighting the others. The steppe warriors, who formed the protective screen, were utterly captivated by the very beautiful woman. They kept glancing at her face, but did not permit its ethereal attractiveness to impede their vigilance.

The Adiorenji, being rounded up nearby, caught glimpses of Olluinan's daughter through small gaps in the escort, and the terror in their eyes was wholly apparent. The sound of hecul hooves from the south gate indicated the approach of Hanshair, Caejkan, Colmar, Adrigal and Onlestic. Behind them rode Cottis, Ricel and Felgorian, accompanied by Rahamb and Souriin.

Gordan nodded, and the new arrivals were permitted to enter the large square which closed securely behind them. After he had been introduced to the governor of Sicruci and his deputy, the Riondese general smiled, watching the reaction of the newcomers to Allecenia. They gazed in a reverential wonderment, and Cottis murmured that he now understood the reason for Ontar and Quinton standing bravely against Reorgin and Kinerth on their first day in Estyork.

"Dear Lady, you, whose beauty is divine, it is a high honour for us to see such a vision. To you and to Quinton, whom you and we love, all of us here pledge our loyalty and devotion. None shall harm a strand of your lovely hair, or lay hands upon you, while we draw breath," the Riondese general declared gallantly, to solemn nods of acquiescence from his companions.

Allecenia smiled tenderly, before acknowledging in her wondrous voice, "I thank you all sincerely. Especially you, Gordan, captain of the royal guard and supreme general of the army."

"Hanshair, as my deputy, you will assume full responsibility for this Lady when I am absent, for she is more special than words can express," Gordan said to the Nai-Zind, his remarks reflecting what Ontar and Admaria had always believed about their god-daughter.

"Yes, Sir. King Quinton has promoted Perlow my second-in-command for his services in the defence of Estyork. It will be a high honour for both of us and every royal guard. Fair are you, My Lady, beyond the measure of mortals," Hanshair bowed with courtesy.

"Thank you, all of you," Allecenia smiled radiantly.

"Oh, Perlow, Perlow. Come here, most valiant of warriors! You saved Quinton again and almost died. Admaria told us too, how you fought on the ramparts, and about the bravery of the others there," Gordan said.

The giant embraced the small Chofir to applause from the guard. Casterandir and Turubin did likewise, for they were proud and fond of him.

"I thank you all for your kindness," Perlow acknowledged in his shy manner.

"If anyone ever insults our little Chofir, I'll...," Onlestic murmured to Adrigal and Hanshair, who nodded their concurrence.

"Let's mount up. We'll survey the battlefield. Then we must see to the wounded," Quinton commanded, replacing his helmet which he had removed to greet his friends.

They began to encircle the city. The King of Rionder was satisfied with the actions of his troops. Uppetshar and the steppe surgeons were already busy tending the casualties. The Ker-Mantid magician greeted his paramount ranxem with awe mingled with pleasure at seeing him once more. He confirmed that the few steppe wounded were receiving treatment from the shock troop physicians in Estyork, and that the Adiorenji healers had been summoned to assist with their own people. Quinton nodded his approval, and declared that he, his foster parents and Allecenia would assist in the treatment of the vanquished soldiery.

A few moments later, Unyamed came riding over from the direction of the enemy encampment, for he had been commanded by Cottis to arrest all the Relyanese chieftains; the latter were to be brought before their Supreme Overlord for judgment later that day. The efficient Sicrucian had left his subordinates to proceed with the designated task, since he had some very important tidings. He informed the company that Koreorgin had perished, and that his body was being prepared for burial by his personal house carls.

"Thank you, Unyamed. You have done well, ever since I've known you. Carry on," Quinton acknowledged.

"Thank you, Sire," the Estyork garrison officer replied, before wheeling his hecul about and riding off.

"That takes care of that, Sire," Felgorian commented.

"It does. All this slaughter for revenge," his liege sighed with regret.

"Say, what shall we do about the prisoners?" Casterandir suddenly grinned, mischief twinkling in his eyes.

"You know very well what we'll do," Ontar retorted in the same vein. "We'll let Gordan do some work."

"Who? Me? What about Quinton?" the giant Riondese promptly complained.

"Never mind me. Lazy Turubin will do fine," the King of Rionder wagged a finger at the Polingsi.

"Won't! Perlow can do the work," came the swift reply to the amusement of Cottis and everyone else within earshot.

"Who? Me? That's right! Pick on the smallest," the Chofir retorted with a broad grin to considerable laughter.

"I wonder how you lot ever managed this far. Inner Council! Total idiots!" Allecenia averred solemnly.

"You're a member too. I need support with all these men," Admaria nodded, her beautiful face filled with merriment.

"Oh, no! Two women!" Turubin groaned in mock despair.

"You forget, Sir. I am a goddess to the Adiorenji," Allecenia declared pertly.

"There'll be no living with her now, Quinton," Gordan laughed.

"We know," the youth and Ontar chorused.

"And to think I left Ordlansa to meet you and your friends," Allecenia said gravely, to smiles from her companions.

She fully realised and united with the bonds of love, understanding and loyalty which permanently encircled all of them. The future would be arduous, yet, in their strong attachment to one another, there was a safe haven in the anarchic world of Phentara.

On completion of their ride around Estyork, and after praising the steppe forces wherever they encountered them, they rode to assist with the wounded Adiorenji. The latter were astounded by the efficiency and care shown to them by the victors. The slain Relyanese were being collected for burial in mass graves beside the River Avidnive close to their own encampment. By mid-afternoon, all weapons and other signs of conflict had been cleared from the battleground. Auxiliaries removed the two battering rams and quickly filled in the trenches outside the wide city gates.

Food supplies from both sides were used to provide meals for the huge numbers of fighting men. No trouble was expected from the vanquished regiments, for Allecenia had sent a message to the Adiorenji to say that she would address them on the following morning. Caramanj would be extremely angry if any one of them caused the least disturbance.

The two Ulgruffi, their god-daughter and foster son knew intuitively that the casualties both from the army and the shock regiments were receiving excellent attention inside Estyork. Accordingly, their efforts were concentrated on the hospital tents and field stations being erected outside the west wall. Throughout the day, apart from attending the funeral services for the fallen, they supervised Uppetshar and the other steppe healers, as well as washing, stitching, bandaging, and setting broken limbs. Hypnosis, herbs and evryl juice were frequently used in their operations, and occasionally a simple spell was also cast to relieve constant pain.

The dullness of early morning yielded to the warmth of midday, and the flaps of the tents were kept open to provide fresh air. The Relyanese treated by Allecenia were absolutely terrified by her marvellous beauty. However, she spoke soothingly to them in the Common Speech to alleviate their fear. They were told that, because of their suffering, she forgave them for fighting against their lawful ruler. Her divine loveliness was overwhelming, while the touch of her fingers and the tones of her wondrous voice calmed them. One remarked later that it seemed as if he had been permitted a brief access to the realms of the gods where Caramanj reigned supreme.

At precisely the same moment as the last casualty finished receiving attention, the sun set in the western sky. Quinton, Allecenia, Ontar and Admaria returned to their apartments where they bathed before having a welcome meal with Gordan, Perlow and the two Polingsi. Once they had eaten they all proceeded to the judgment hall, where the Relyanese leaders waited to learn their fate.

When Olluinan's daughter entered, they fell to their knees, for she was still unveiled. Quinton strode to the dais and sat down in Cottis' seat while the remainder of his party stood around him. The governor of Sicruci approached his Supreme Overlord and signalled for the chieftains to be brought. Stout Deerait guards hoisted the prisoners to their feet and pushed them forward.

When they were all standing before him with dejected

countenances, the King of Rionder demanded to know the reason for the siege of Estyork. Rinthalt shuffled nervously before confirming that Koreorgin had been responsible for the hostilities to avenge the death of Reorgin. On being pressed further, the Relyanese admitted that the dead horbspan had acquiesced to a major campaign, in conjunction with the Dariondi and the Vilatmori, to seize control of Sicruci and the northwest.

"Your sorcerers summoned Hedial. He did not appear. Allecenia — she whom you call Caramanj — Ontar, Admaria and I have the Power to overcome such Black Magic. None of your spells worked against us. Regarding battle tactics, your vastly superior forces were repelled by military means. We did not need to launch our occult knowledge directly against your forces. We did use it to destroy all the ublisstan in your encampment," the King of Rionder stated coldly.

"Sire, the drug was Koreorgin's idea. This I swear by Caramanj," the brown skinned Chsingof nodded. His use of the title was immediately remarked, especially by Cottis, who felt satisfaction.

"Koreorgin began a civil war precipitately to avenge the death of his son. Revenge I can understand, although I do not necessarily concur with it. Civil war is another matter. It sets a nation against itself. Justification for such an action involves far better reasons than you can possibly give. This is not Broechnaar!" the Lord of Deerait snapped.

Ontar and Admaria did not evince any emotion, but felt pride in the dynamic youth, their beloved foster son. Quinton was behaving like a veteran statesman, and the Adiorenji realised this. Allecenia stood on the right hand of his seat, her exquisite features very beautiful and implacable against the surviving leaders of the force which had rashly commenced hostilities against the capital of Sicruci only a few days before.

"We wished to be rid of the Deerait yoke and their laws," Rinthalt said falteringly, knowing even as he spoke that his excuse was inadequate.

"The Deerait laws are just and fair. They sufficed for your forefathers for many centuries after the end of the Casman war. You, the Dariondi and the Vilatmori have always had very fair representation in the High Court at Hesion. Moreover, several of your highest horbspans were full members of that illustrious body until a few months ago. The Deerait people have more

446

knowledge of reading, writing and education than you. Is it not folly to refuse such knowledge with all its advantages, especially when freely given?" the Overlord of their entire nation asked.

"We've had enough of written things and the like. What good are they?" Chsingof cried pathetically.

"The troops who came from the north this morning, and the others under my command, can read and write, every single one of them. Their families and children have similar knowledge. The majority are Mescarg steppe tribesmen. Yes, Mescarg steppe tribesmen!" Quinton repeated with pride.

"Oh," Rinthalt spoke involuntarily.

"You would call them brigands, savages and barbarians. Yet even their children are better educated than you. Education is essential for the advancement of civilisation. The Phlorcartid nation are receiving such invaluable instruction together with others of our allies.

"The differing laws of each clan have been thoroughly examined. After discussions with representatives of each tribe, no matter how small, a code was agreed for the benefit of all. We do such things democratically. You should have acted in a similar fashion. Your forefathers did so. They co-operated fully with the Deeraits as equals. The Deeraits are not perfect. They do make mistakes. So do you! But, whatever their faults, the High Council in Hesion has always tried to be just, and move forward.

"They acknowledged me as Supreme Overlord. To seal their loyalty, they gave me the sacred sword of the Seer Csiandag. They accepted me on behalf of the entire nation. The Dariondi, Vilatmori and yourselves are included in this. It is well known that quite a proportion of your peoples support the unity of your whole country, but are afraid to speak out against their leaders," Quinton stated, nodding to Felgorian, for this was one of the invaluable items of information the ambassador had gleaned during his travels.

"What are you going to do with us, Sire?" Rinthalt asked falteringly, his red tunic stained with sweat and dirt.

The term of address to the Supreme Overlord signified acceptance of the King of Rionder as their ruler. The latter waited for a few moments before replying, "You will leave here and comfort your wounded. Tomorrow, Caramanj will address your forces. Let no one try to escape, lest her wrath descends

447

on you. She shall tell you your fate in the morning. Yltormik, kindly conduct these gentlemen to the hospital tents. There will be no necessity for further supervision."

When the Adiorenji had been led away, Gordan and Ontar expressed their approval of the proceedings. Quinton beckoned the garrison commander of Estyork to his side, and confirmed privately that a campaign would be commenced to subdue the rebellious tribes. However, such an enterprise would take several weeks to organise, since the three peoples could field large armies. The remainder of the troops still in the forests of the Rionder Valley would be summoned to assist in this endeavour; the armed forces from every Deerait province and units from the battle fleet would also be involved.

"Cottis, my friend, I know you wish to assume a seat at the High Court in Hesion. It is my pleasure to appoint you to such an honoured position. However, I shall need your help in the forthcoming conflict," the King of Rionder said, having risen to his feet.

Quinton put his arm affectionately on the governor's shoulder, which gesture pleased the latter immensely, as he replied, "Sire, when your war with the Empire is over, and Broechnaar has been liberated and peace has returned, then I shall take up my position in Hesion. Until then, well, how could I not follow you?"

"Thank you very much indeed. Your loyalty and devotion are things I will always treasure. Hearken everyone! Let us go and take some refreshment with Cottis. It's time we all met his wives and family. I believe you would like Hanshair to come too," Quinton declared, signalling to the Nai-Zind.

"It will be an honour, Sire," the governor bowed, before leading the illustrious party from the judgment hall.

The King of Rionder permitted the Deerait to go on ahead, and waited for Gordan, Casterandir, Turubin, Admaria, Ontar, Allecenia, Felgorian and Perlow. They paused for a brief moment, looking at one another. Each knew that the past few days augured many difficult ones to come, but with love and fortitude they would continue to forge Quinton's destiny. This was a turning point, like the time when the mighty steppe army and its Casman allies had finally reached the haven in the vast immensity of the forests.

The youth held Allecenia's hand, and felt content. Ontar smiled thoughtfully, hearing his spouse informing him telepathically that the Casman Empire might be vast and outnumber them, but the Emperor Heolanwertin possessed no subject such as their foster son. In the end, Casman would be conquered, and Broechnaar liberated. When this finally occurred, Quinton would be Emperor of Rontmethar. How his authority would stretch forth to the other continents of Phentara was unknown, but without doubt he would succeed. The future always provided opportunity.

Ontar, Admaria and Perlow were the last of the party to leave the hall. The Chofir looked perplexed, and the beautiful Ulgruffi asked him the reason.

"I don't know. It's this talk of Caramanj. Ever since I first heard it, I cannot get the name out of my thoughts. I don't know why."

"Just one of those things," Admaria commented, putting her hand on his left shoulder, while her spouse did likewise on the other side. The royal guards behind them smiled with much pleasure at this honour to the Chofir, for he certainly merited it.

"Just one of those things? Perhaps. But Caramanj could be his goddess," Ontar speculated telepathically to his wife.

"Who knows? If Caramanj is his goddess, then I do hope she is worthy of him," Admaria replied silently.

"We'll have to wait and see," the archmage averred.

In the next Volume, Quinton and his friends have to free the sacred temple of the Adiorenji, Castle Xzlus on the Keollin escarpment. Allecenia and Admaria liberate the mighty goddess, Caramanj, from entrapment on the Celestial Plane of Immortals. Quinton, Ontar, their shock regiments and the Cosmic Masters have to fight on the Celestial Plane against evil deities to assist the goddess to prevent her Universe from being ruled by Evil . . .